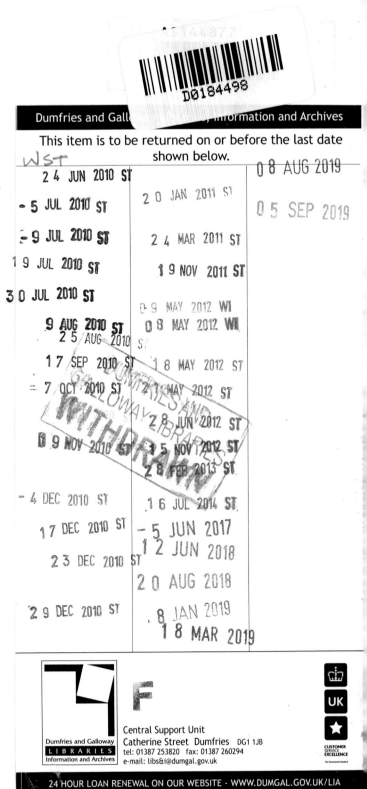

Strip

THOMAS PERRY

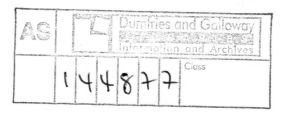
Quercus

First published in Great Britain in 2010 by

Quercus
21 Bloomsbury Square
London
WC1A 2NS

Copyright © 2010 by Thomas Perry

Published by arrangement with Harcourt, Inc

A CIP catalogue record for this book is available
from the British Library

ISBN 978 1 84916 167 1 (HB)
ISBN 978 1 84916 168 8 (TPB)

Printed and bound in Great Britain by Clays Ltd, St Ives plc

10 9 8 7 6 5 4 3 2 1

*In grateful memory
of my parents,
Richard and Elizabeth Perry*

STRIP

1

THE TIMES CAME OFTEN when Joe Carver felt like retreating from Los Angeles into the hinterland, maybe the sparsely populated northern plains. But the frequency of these urges meant little. They were weaker and less insistent every time, and by now they were only uneasy instants, like skipped heartbeats. He had chosen to come to Los Angeles, and some choices could be permanent. He couldn't go back now to some place where just being alive was work. It was as though when he had crossed the California line, he had stepped off a cliff. There was no way back up.

Carver had always been smart enough to know that when he did anything he was choosing to let a thousand other things remain undone, dooming them to nonexistence. But he was also wise enough not to allow himself to waste much time thinking about all of those unborn futures.

Carver raised his head slowly and carefully and peered downward from the cab of the tower crane at the world two hundred and fifty feet below him. The construction of the big ugly office building was going very well. The steel I-beams were being assembled in a rigid Tinkertoy framework very efficiently, and he could see piles of lumber in the yard below him that indicated the next step would be to add to the flooring that had already been laid on the lowest levels.

Carver could evaluate this building's progress with something of an expert eye, because he had been sleeping here each night for weeks. Large commercial projects like this were the best protected from thieves and vandals, and they were the most comfortable because there were pieces of heavy equipment with cabs for shelter and seat cushions he could use for a bed.

He didn't like the look of the site tonight. The crews had been accelerating for weeks. Soon he would have to stop sleeping in the cab of the big crane, and that disappointed him. There were other places for him, but they were all inferior to the tower crane. On this site there were high fences with coiled razor wire to keep intruders out, and even if thieves cut their way in looking for tools or building materials, they weren't about to climb two hundred and fifty feet to find Carver asleep in the cab.

He judged that he would have to find his next place within a week. Once the steel frame of the first few stories was in, there would be an army of carpenters laying down rough plywood floors. He could see they'd already been installing temporary stairs on the nearest corner of the building. Very soon his crane cab was going to lose its remoteness and privacy. He would have to search for houses with FOR SALE signs and empty stores with FOR LEASE signs on them. Before he had found the crane, he had slept in the back seats of new cars on dealers' lots.

From up here, Carver could see the beauty of the city, the long, straight thoroughfares lined with brightly colored signs, the dark shoulders of the Hollywood Hills just above. In the distance he could see the cluster of tall buildings at the city center. He always looked for the tallest, the cylindrical office building he thought of as the Nose-Hair Building, because it looked like a device he'd seen advertised on television late at night for shaving the nostrils. He looked out his window at the streets just below him. Running east-west was Bronson, and north-south was La Brea. From here, up above the lights, he could see every car crawling along below him.

He knew he should sleep now, because he could be here for only a few hours. The construction crew began work at 6:00 each morning, but the crane operator always arrived around 5:15 and spent some time walking around with a cup of coffee and talking to people. Carver supposed he talked while he could because he was alone all day, sitting up here. Carver approved of the operator's thinking, and he liked him. The operator had photographs taped in his cab, some of them signed to "Mitch," so Carver thought of him as Mitch too. One of the pictures was of a blond woman, presumably Mitch's wife, and four blond kids who looked a bit like her. There were a few shots of the same kids, one at a time, playing baseball or riding a horse, swimming in a pool behind a suburban house. There were also home-printed digital snapshots of the wife wearing nothing — one on a bed, one sitting on the thick arm of an overstuffed couch, one in a shower — but always she was looking right at Mitch's camera and smiling. Nobody but Mitch ever came up all two hundred and fifty feet to go into the cab, so Mitch must have thought his cab was as private as the inside of his skull.

Carver brought nothing up the ladders each evening but a snack and some water, so he'd had nothing to read but Mitch's manuals. He'd acquired a fairly clear notion of what Mitch did for a living and had learned how to raise and lower the hook, turn the crane's boom, and a few other operations. He had originally planned that on his last night here he would move the crane into some odd position and leave it that way, but since he'd started to think of Mitch as a real person, he had become reluctant to give him the creeps.

The construction crew always started to pack up at 3:30 in the afternoon, locking up tools and shutting down equipment, and then left at 4:00. Any time after that, Carver could show up, pick the lock on the heavy chain at the front gate, then the other lock that secured the door to the ladder that led up the mast of the tower to the cab. When Carver was two hundred and fifty feet up in Mitch's tower crane, he considered himself the safest man in Los Angeles.

The crane was more important to him tonight than before. Today Carver had seen some of the men who were hunting for him. They were the ones who nurtured the growing fortune and nasty reputation of Manco Kapak. Carver had been eating lunch at Farmers' Market when he had seen five of them, moving along a narrow aisle single file like a trade delegation from the Republic of Hell. They moved stiffly, because the guns they carried under their sport coats or in the waistbands of their pants were uncomfortable and made it hard for them to bend.

There they were, stiff-walking through Farmers' Market between the juice bar and the toffee place. They moved up the aisle in a slow, deliberate side-to-side gait, and Carver stayed at his table near the doughnut counter, watching. The front man, one of the redheaded Gaffney brothers, would mutter "Excuse me" or "Behind you" to the people ahead of them in the aisle. Whenever he did it, the person would turn to glance and see the five of them coming on. The bystander would be visibly startled, then compress his body against the side of the aisle as though it were a herd of bulls moving past him.

Carver knew they were searching for him, and that someone must have seen him at Farmers' Market and rushed to call them. But he was sure now that none of them knew him by sight. They were just relying on tips and descriptions from informers. Carver turned away, got up, and moved up the long, narrow aisle between bins of fruit and shops full of jars of hot sauce or cheap luggage. He turned between the L.A.–Beverly Hills–Hollywood souvenir shop and the chocolate shop to get to the aisle beside the open area where the stalls sold pizza and Chinese pork buns and Mexican tortas, and finally made it to the Cajun gumbo stand, then made a left turn into the corridor that emptied into the parking lot. He made his way quickly onto Fairfax, where people moved in and out of shops that sold Russian souvenirs while cars blocked the street waiting for parking spaces.

He walked a few blocks north, then went in the front door of Canter's Delicatessen and out the back door to the alley and on to the next street. Carver backtracked a few blocks south to Wilshire Boulevard, then down Wilshire to the La Brea Tar Pits. The park was pretty, it was full of people who didn't want to hurt anybody, and it was pleasant as long as he watched his step and avoided the new places where tar was seeping up through the lawn. He kept going and went into the Los Angeles County Museum of Art.

Carver spent his first moments in the museum thinking about his predicament and sitting on a series of smooth wooden benches placed in the centers of rooms full of paintings. But after only a few minutes, what Carver was watching was the array of women who had come to see the paintings—long-limbed and blond, or short with hair black as shoe polish. When he had arrived in California, he had noticed immediately that the most beautiful women in the world—the best of every race and country—were roaming the malls, beaches, and clubs of Los Angeles, more common than sparrows. He had known instantly that to be anywhere else was to be in exile. Learning this truth had been the start of his trouble. He had gone to too many nightclubs, bought too many bottles of overpriced champagne, made himself and his cash too visible.

He had become a fugitive, a man who slept on a construction site, because of a simple misunderstanding. One night a month ago, Manco Kapak had been robbed of a considerable amount of cash. This had not been a robbery of one of his businesses—the dance club on Hollywood Boulevard he owned, or the strip clubs in the Valley, or any of the shady enterprises the cash from those places made possible. The victim was Manco himself. He had been carrying a canvas bag with Friday night's receipts to put in his bank's night deposit drop and been held up by a lone man.

Manco Kapak had sent men to ask the people who made a habit of trafficking in information whether they'd noticed a lone man, newly arrived in town, who seemed to be spending an unusual amount of cash. These people in turn put out the description of what was wanted to their networks of spies and tattlers. Apparently, what had come back through the middlemen was the name Joe Carver. After that, Carver had begun to hear that somebody had been asking for him. After about the third time, he'd also heard who it was and why.

He knew how it had happened. People must have interpreted his generosity as a natural overflow of sudden, unearned wealth. The truth was that Joe Carver had never robbed anyone in his life. He had simply done what anyone might have done when he had come to any new city. He had gone to clubs to meet women, and he had spent freely.

When Carver looked out the window of the crane, everything below was beautiful, even the endless streams of headlights and taillights on the freeway, the white coming toward him and the red flowing away. There were colored neon splashes and swirls on the fronts of businesses and soft yellow-pink pools of light marking the grid of streets. He could see police helicopters circling a distant patch of dark green trees. Now and then a cone of light would shine down from a helicopter's belly and illuminate a little circle of green.

He was sitting in the crane operator's seat, watching the lights of a fire truck weaving up Beverly Boulevard, when he saw two big SUVs arrive at the gate of his construction site. They were both Hummers, both black. From above they looked like two small, shiny black boxes, all squared corners. He couldn't see the passengers because the windows were tinted, but they couldn't be anyone he wanted to meet. The Hummers were stopped at the curb right outside the gate. They had an intention, and he sensed it had to do with his construction site. While the crane was a wonderful hiding place, it was not a good place to be cornered. He stood, opened the door, and stepped onto the platform.

Carver began the long climb down. The tall mast of the crane was divided into a series of gratelike floors connected by ladders. Each ladder led to a platform below, and then another ladder to the platform below that. Up above two hundred feet the world was dimly lit. There were few bright lights higher than the streetlamps, and even those were aimed downward at the ground. Until he reached that level, Carver would be difficult to see. He descended ten, twenty, thirty, forty feet, still hidden by darkness. He prepared himself for the run into the shadows. He lowered his right foot to the bottom step on the sixth platform and looked down at the two black Hummers, trying to see who got out of them.

The doors didn't open. The first Hummer swung wide into the left lane, and then hooked right so it was going head-on when it rammed the gate on its right side, where the chain and padlock held it. Even from up in the air, Carver could see the chain snap and fly wide as the gate swung open.

The second Hummer followed the first through the open gateway and onto the construction site. The vehicle stopped and two big men got out and pushed the gate shut again. One of them tipped a hundred-gallon drum onto its rim and rolled it against the gate to keep it shut while the two Hummers turned around to face the street.

Carver was shocked. He had been trying to descend and slip off into the darkness, but there were already two of Kapak's men with their shoes on the ground inside the gate. In a moment there were five. Carver had underestimated these people. They shouldn't even know which side of town he was on tonight, but here they were.

The five men began to fan out across the lot, keeping forty or fifty feet of open space between them. They advanced in a line, scanning for him and keeping straight so nobody got more than a step ahead into the line of fire. Their pace made it look to Carver as though they might arrive at the base of the tower crane just about when he did.

Carver stopped and lay on the platform to peer down through the steel grating. He could see the men as they approached, stepping into the overlapping pools of light near the main steel structure and the tool sheds and the high stacks of wood and steel. He recognized the same five men he had seen at Farmers' Market: the Gaffney brothers, easy to spot because of their red hair and paper-white skin; Voinovich the Russian, because he was taller than the others; and Corona and Guzman, because they had brown skin and shiny shaved heads and necks that were tattooed with filigree script.

Carver was glad he hadn't descended any farther. He saw the Gaffney brothers reach the base of the crane, where the huge steel structure was bolted to its concrete slab. Carver waited until he could see they had stopped and were walking away. Then he moved to the ladder to climb back toward the cab. His foot slipped off the first rung and made a clang on the iron grate floor that resonated in the quiet night air.

A shot whistled through the floor grating he was standing on, and then three more shots. Carver held himself flat against the nearest strut. There were more shots—two, then four in a rapid volley. Some bullets hammered solid pieces of steel in the frame of the crane, and others pinged as they grazed the steel grating and whistled off into the dark sky.

Carver climbed steadily, and the next few shots were less accurate, but they came from four or five directions. All the men seemed to be shooting at him now. He climbed faster so there wouldn't be time for a well-aimed shot. Carter kept looking upward to verify that the triangular pattern of struts going by were really registering movement, and at last he reached the top and scuttled into the crane's cab.

He sat in the operator's seat for a few seconds, simply holding himself still and feeling grateful for the steel seat beneath the leather padding, waiting for more gunshots. When he didn't hear any, he looked out the window of the cab to see where the men were. They were still down on the site, but they had stopped to confer. It occurred to him that the reason none of them was shooting might be that they hadn't seen him get into the cab. They must believe he'd been hit and was lying on one of the lower platforms dead or dying.

Carver waited. Maybe they'd declare victory and go away. He stayed low but moved his head close to the window and looked down. He could see the five men were moving again. This time they were walking toward the steel frame of the building, preparing to climb the temporary staircase that had been erected along the near side. If they got up to the top floor, they'd be almost beside him and could fire at him through the cab windows.

He was trapped. He had no more than a minute or two to do something to preserve his life. He stared straight ahead, through the windshield of the cab. From where he sat, his eyes were aimed out along the seventy-five-yard horizontal arm of the crane. Along its underside, he could see the trolley on rails that held the cable and the hook, a piece of steel the size of a man.

He glanced out the side window at the five men moving toward the stairway that led up onto the skeletal building, and then he looked straight ahead again at the arm of the crane. Right before him was the control console of the crane, a black, sloping surface full of switches and dials and levers and knobs. His hours reading the manual and comparing the pictures with the controls had made them familiar. His hand reached out for the toggle switch that said "master power," and he flipped it.

Lights glowed on the console. He tentatively moved the control stick to swing the crane's long, horizontal arm—called the "jib" in the manual, as though this huge machine were a sailing ship—slowly to the left, then stopped. The cab moved with the arm, so the movement made him dizzy. He reached out for the winch control and lowered the cable with the hook on the end. As he lowered it, he pushed forward on the control to send the trolley out on the horizontal arm.

The hook descended to the heavily trodden lot and landed in a small explosion of dust. He pulled back on the control and raised it a bit, so it dangled from its cable about a foot off the ground. He reached for the lateral control, and the long, horizontal arm of the crane began to move again. He pushed it farther, his cab turning faster with the arm.

The heavy steel hook on the end of the long cable stayed a bit behind the moving arm. When he stopped the dizzying lateral movement, the cable swung toward the men and the heavy hook swept into their midst. The five scattered, and the hook swung past them and clanged against a horizontal steel girder of the building a story above their heads. As the hook swung back, Carver turned the arm back a little to guide the hook into the gang of men a second time. It narrowly missed Voinovich, who flung himself to the side on the dirt and gravel.

Carver felt the vibrations as bullets banged on the bottom of the steel cab. He could see the five men dancing from one side to another, trying to get a better shot at the glass windows.

Carver glanced beyond them at the streets. By now, cops should be surrounding this area. He could see for many blocks, but there was not a single flashing light coming from any direction. Was everybody around here deaf? The past few minutes had sounded like a war. But this was a commercial neighborhood, and everyone nearby had probably gone home hours ago. Whatever Carver was going to do, he would have to do it alone.

He looked below for the men, but they had scattered. His gaze settled on the two Hummers. He moved the trolley that held the hoist farther out on the crane's arm, almost the full seventy-five yards, and turned the crane at the same time, so the hook on the end of the cable was in motion again. The men below seemed to understand the meaning of his movement immediately. They abandoned their hiding places, desperate to kill him before he could carry out his intention. They fired rapidly, and he could feel the vibration each time a bullet hit the cab's steel shell. One shot hit a side window, and glass exploded into the cab.

Carver brushed the glass off his lap, and then swung the big hook again. To his disappointment, it missed the back of the closest Hummer entirely. But before he could readjust the angle, the hook swung back, directly into the windshield of the Hummer parked in front of it. He could hear the bang of the impact and the crash of breaking glass as the hook burst through the windshield and buckled the roof. Carver swung the arm back and saw that the hook was caught on the vehicle. His movement dragged the front Hummer into the back Hummer, crumpling its hood and grille. He activated the winch and raised the front Hummer forty feet into the air, and then lowered it as quickly as he could onto the back Hummer. The hook came free, and the front Hummer rolled off onto its side.

Two men ran toward the gate, sprinting as hard as they could while he moved the horizontal arm backward. As he prepared to swing the hook again, they toppled the barrel and rolled it away, shouldered open the gate, and ran outside and across the street to disappear between two buildings. A moment later, the other three made a dash for the wide-open gate. He tried to move the arm to swing the hook toward them, but by the time he got it moving, they were already across the street. He watched them from his height for a few seconds until they disappeared beyond a building.

He knew a couple of them would be lying in wait for him across the street. The others would make their way around the block to surround the construction site. As soon as he came down from his crane, they'd kill him or try to take him alive and make him give up the money he didn't have. They knew he couldn't be armed if he was reduced to defending himself by swinging cars at them with a crane.

Carver sat still in his crane, trying to spot the men moving to positions where they could fire through the chain-link fence into the lot. Then his eye caught a new brightness. From this height he recognized the blue and red flashing lights long before he could hear the sirens. There were two, four, six police cars now, coming fast along Beverly Boulevard. He saw two more appear on Bronson, trying to cut off an escape. He looked for the five men again. This time when he spotted them, they were blocks away, running hard.

He opened the cab of the crane to step onto the first ladder. He looked back once, noticed the three nude pictures of Mitch's wife taped to the inside of the cab, and hesitated. Tomorrow morning there would be people all over this cab—probably cops, supervisors, all kinds of people. He tore the photographs down, bent them into a little tent shape, set them on the floor, lit each of them with his lighter, and let them burn. Mitch would see the ashes and know what had happened to them. Then he hurried down the ladders to reach the ground before the cops arrived.

He ran to the contractor's trailer at the edge of the lot farthest from the gate. He picked up a plank and propped one end on the roof of the trailer and the other on the top of the chain-link fence, compressing the coiled razor wire. He climbed to the roof of the trailer, walked the length of the plank, and jumped to the sidewalk outside. In a few moments, he had dissolved into the night.

2

MANCO KAPAK AWOKE to the sound of the master bedroom door swinging inward. He tugged the sleeping mask up onto his forehead with his left hand, reached under his pillow with the right, grasped the .45 pistol, and held it under the covers, squinting against the morning sunlight as he prepared to fire through the blankets. He had been jumpy since the night a month ago when a man in a ski mask had stuck a gun in his face and robbed him.

"It's me, Mr. Kapak. It's only me." The male voice was soft and calm.

It was Spence, Kapak's driver and bodyguard. Kapak brought the pistol up and put it into the top drawer of the nightstand. "What do you want?"

"It's the police on the phone. They say they need to talk to you right now."

"Shit." Kapak sat up and yawned, then rose to his feet. He caught sight of himself in the mirror and once again felt the shock of seeing his naked body. His shoulders and upper arms were still hard and muscled, his forearms and thighs still had sinews like cables under the leathery skin, but over the years his torso had grown thick and soft, the belly rounded now like a pear, and the pectoral muscles loose like little breasts. His skin was gray-white like a dead man's, except in the places where it was blotched and reddish from sleep.

Spence held the phone out and Kapak took it, then looked over his shoulder at the small shape under the covers on the other side of the bed. He saw long blond hair on the pillow, but her name didn't come to mind. He stepped into the living room and closed the door to let her sleep.

"This is Mr. Kapak."

"Good morning, sir. This is Lieutenant Nicholas Slosser, Los Angeles Police Department. We would like you to come in this morning to talk to us."

"Where is 'in,' and what do we have to talk about?"

"'In' is Parker Center, Room Five Thirty-two. We're investigating an incident that took place last night on a construction site in Hollywood. Two vehicles registered to the Kapak Corporation were found wrecked there."

"Wrecked? Are you sure?"

"We'll talk about it. It's seven now. Can you be here by nine? Or I can send a unit to pick you up."

"I can get there myself."

"See you then."

Kapak pressed the button to end the call, then punched in the cell phone number of Gerald Ospinsky. After a couple of seconds he said, "Gerald."

"Yes?"

"It's me. I just got a call from a Lieutenant Slosser at Parker Center. They want me to go in there at nine."

"What's it about?"

"It's about a police lieutenant rousting me out of bed to go down and talk to him. It would seem to me that my lawyer would want to be there."

"Of course I do. I just meant . . . it doesn't matter what I meant. I'll be there."

"Thank you."

Kapak switched off the call and tossed the phone across the living room to Spence. "Did any of the guys call me before that cop?"

"No."

"Idiots," he said. "It's stupid not to call me." There was a mixture of resentment and amazement in his expression.

Spence was aware that no answer was expected of him. He stood with the telephone in his hand and waited while Manco Kapak stepped to the large sliding-glass window that overlooked the sandstone path between Australian black gum trees and sago palms and through a jungle of tropical plants.

Kapak absently scratched his bulbous belly in front of the window. "I'll get a shower in the guesthouse. Take the girl home, wherever that may be. Then come back and drive me downtown to Parker Center."

"Got it."

Kapak opened the door, then walked naked down the path toward the guesthouse.

As Spence went back into the bedroom, he glanced at his watch. It was already a minute or two after 7:00, and he would have to get the woman moving if he wanted to get Kapak to the police headquarters on time. He closed the bedroom door behind him and assessed the physical evidence to decide how to proceed. The girl's clothes were draped with a reasonable attempt at keeping them unwrinkled on the couch at the foot of the bed, so he was fairly certain she had not been drunk. She had worn a nice summer dress and a pair of relatively tasteful strapped heels—nothing that would make her look like a weakened nocturnal creature trapped in the daylight. The bra and panties were of good quality, a matching set of Easter egg purple with a bit of lace.

Spence cleared his throat and watched the woman stir, pulling the blanket up near her ears to preserve her unconsciousness. Spence walked to the bathroom, brought back a clean white Turkish bathrobe, and placed it at the foot of the bed where she would feel the weight of it on her feet. Then he walked along the wall beyond the foot of the bed, opening the curtains of the tall windows, pair by pair.

He heard her groan.

"Good morning, miss," he said in a cheerful voice. "Good morning."

She began to sit up, revealing for a moment a pair of breasts that seemed to be unaugmented but above criticism to Spence's eye, then realized she was not alone and pulled the covers to her neck.

Spence said, "I'm afraid Mr. Kapak has been called away unexpectedly on important business. He asked me to give you his regrets and to take you home myself. There's a robe at the foot of the bed, and the master bath is just behind you and to your right. When you're ready, I'll be in the kitchen at the far end of the house. Would you like coffee or tea this morning?"

The girl took a moment to look around her in the glare of reflected sunlight as though she had no idea where she was, so Spence began to fear this might be some kind of ugly surprise, but she said, "Coffee, please" in clear, unaccented English. Spence was relieved. If she hadn't spoken English, the rest of this would have been very difficult.

Spence pivoted in place, went out, and closed the door. He walked the length of the house to the kitchen, and then entered the small office off the pantry and watched the row of high-definition color security monitors.

When the young woman got out of the bed and put on the bathrobe, he could see she had a very fine body—cream with a blush here and there. She cinched the robe around her waist and explored the master suite a bit, opening dresser drawers and cabinets, not methodically like a burglar, but randomly, like a snooping child. Spence didn't blame her. She was a pretty woman in her

16

twenties who had just spent the night with a sixty-four-year-old gangster who was a fearsome sight naked—an old boar. She was probably searching for something—a bit of compensation, maybe even a souvenir to prove the story was true if she chose to tell it. Let her.

He moved his attention to the cameras around the guesthouse. He could see a light on behind the smoked glass window of the bathroom, so Kapak must be in the shower out there.

In a few minutes the girl appeared in the kitchen. Spence treated her like a starlet dropping in for an appearance at a charity event. "What would you like in your coffee, miss?"

When he had given her the coffee and settled her on a seat at the granite counter to drink it, he said, "It's already getting hot this morning. I'll go bring the car around under the awning and get the air conditioning circulating."

He went out. The biggest step was already over—getting her up, showered, and from the bedroom to the kitchen with all her clothes properly on her and secured without incident. Getting her from the kitchen to the car would also be a big step, though. This one was sober, well-behaved, and apparently sane, so he sincerely felt kindly impulses toward her. She wasn't trying to keep from leaving. She knew it was time, and that there was no sense in her teasing and wheedling anybody but the man who had brought her here.

Spence returned with the car and made her take a second cup of coffee with her in a thermos mug. He sat her in the back seat and put the mug in the cup holder on the console so she could reach it. As he backed out of the long driveway, he said, "Now, miss. What's your address?"

"I'm Kira," she said. "I live on Coldwater."

"North or south of the 101 freeway?"

"Practically on it, but a little bit north. It's a big apartment building."

"Okay," said Spence. He pulled out of the driveway and headed for the freeway. It wouldn't be too hard, he decided. He might be able to do it in twenty minutes if the traffic let him. Nothing about this one was hard. A certain percentage of Kapak's women visitors were terrible. A lot of them had been nasty and crazy. Some had been drunk in that odd, unfortunate way that some women got drunk—they shouldn't have been able to walk and talk, but they did.

Others that Kapak had brought home with him had been hoping for some kind of bonanza and seemed to feel that leaving his house in the morning would be relinquishing their claim to the reward. When Spence had become insistent, a couple of them had even started hinting at the possibility of making claims that they had been raped. Spence had no illusions about Manco Kapak's ethics, but he knew that Kapak was prone to erectile dysfunction, and that Kapak's appetites didn't include anything as strenuous as overpowering anybody. Each time the blackmail strategy came up, Spence had said, "Think about him. Do you really want to be the person he sees as capable of sending him to prison for the rest of his life?"

He glanced at the girl in the rearview mirror. "Are you comfortable back there, miss?"

"Kira. My name is Kira. I'm fine. Have you worked for him long?"

"Nearly six years."

"Is being a gangster exciting?"

"Not for me."

"You're too tough for that?"

Spence chuckled. "I'm not tough at all. I'm not a gangster. I drive his car. I answer the phone. I make sure there are enough fresh vegetables and the garbage is taken out to the curb on Tuesday night."

"You don't get to go to the clubs or anything?"

"He doesn't spend a lot of time in the clubs. They're an investment. When he goes in, I usually stay with the car."

"Aren't you interested in women?"

"Sure. But there aren't many women in a strip club, and the ones who are there are working."

"If there's nothing fun about it, why do you work for him?"

"Because he pays me a salary and health insurance and contributions to my 403b."

"I heard he got robbed."

"I heard that too. I wasn't there."

"Doesn't it scare you?"

"You're in a car with a man you never saw before, and it's going over a mile a minute. Doesn't that scare you?"

"Not really."

"Then you understand. Anybody can get in an accident any time. Anybody can get robbed. Changing jobs doesn't do anything."

"He's different. He's a rich old criminal. He's a big target."

"Then why did you sleep with him?"

"I was at Wash. It was kind of a slow night and I was just dancing with my friends. In comes Manco Kapak, and everybody in the place starts staring at him and telling each other who that is. He's the guy who owns Wash and about three other clubs, and he's this big, powerful guy with all these connections. After a few minutes he practically bumped into me in the crowd and asked me to sit with him and have a drink. It made my friends get all agitated and warn me not to go, and so I couldn't resist."

"But later on, you were disappointed?"

"Well, you know. He's got money and power and all that, but those things don't come to bed with him. What's there is a sixty-five-year-old fat guy with a hairy back and trouble getting hard. So I guess that's what I get out of the experience. I learned that."

"I suppose that's worth something," Spence said.

"Yeah. I suppose."

Manco Kapak stood in the shower in the guesthouse, feeling the jets of warm water scouring his body, then running down in soothing streams to his toes. He had mixed feelings about this shower. It was perfect in every way. It was much better than the ones in the various bathrooms in the main house, because he had decreed it. He had not merely bought this one when he bought the property. He had talked with the architect and the contractor during the building of the guesthouse and made sure they understood what he wanted. He had also made sure they understood that Kapak wanted what he wanted, not something they thought was similar to what he wanted. The more he enjoyed the beauty, tastefulness, strength, and even warmth of the shower, the more resentful he became that it was so much better than the ones he usually used. Was he supposed to walk all the way out here to the end of the path every time he took a shower, or stay in the main house and use inferior facilities? The whole idea made him furious. He was going to have to remodel the main house.

His train of thought brought him to how much money it would cost, and how much money he had been losing lately. His mind struggled with the thought. He was beginning to feel the unfamiliar sensation that he wanted to go see the police as quickly as possible. They seemed to know what had happened last night, and he certainly didn't. This morning he could hardly call any of the five men he had sent after Joe Carver. That police lieutenant might very well have forgotten to mention that his five men had found Carver and killed him or something.

But Kapak knew his luck wasn't that good. This guy Carver was an unknown. The man had simply appeared beside Kapak one night wearing a ski mask, stuck a gun against his head, and said he would pull the trigger if Kapak didn't drop the bank deposit pouch and stand with his hands on the wall of the bank for five minutes while he disappeared. At first Kapak had almost laughed. He had considered saying it out loud: "You really don't want the one you rob to be me."

But small-time characters were the most likely to panic and shoot somebody. There was no point in incurring that risk. For five minutes Kapak could be silent and stand there. After that it would be different. It would be his turn. It still seemed perfectly fair to Kapak. He had been robbed of cash receipts, so he had asked around about new people with a lot of cash and come up with the name Joe Carver. Kapak had never seen or heard of the robber before, and he had never seen or heard of Joe Carver, so it seemed like a match. It had to be somebody new if he didn't know who Kapak was.

He had to admit to himself in the solitude of his guesthouse shower that he had probably been overconfident in being satisfied with Joe Carver as the robber. The truth was that he had not really considered it absolutely essential that he catch and punish the right man. It was essential that he find and punish *some* man and get his money back, if only so that everybody knew he had done it. If he had the wrong man, it wasn't the end of the world. These things had happened to people before. Carver could either put up with the loss or go find the real thief and get the money back from him.

Kapak dried off and walked naked back up the path toward the big house. He was sure the girl would be gone by now, and he could get dressed for the police interview in peace. The tedium of these interviews was their most striking quality, and this made it difficult to maintain the level of concentration he would need to avoid their purpose, which was entrapment. The cops obviously knew something was up, and the two cars registered to his company proved he was somehow connected with whatever had happened, and they needed to wear him down so they could fool him into incriminating himself. Actually, the process was more like being nagged than fooled.

Kapak came into the house through the sliding door into the living room and padded along barefoot on the polished hardwood floor for five paces before his eye caught the unfamiliar shape and identified it as a man.

The man was about forty, with a short beard that looked as though he hadn't had a chance to shave. He wore a pair of black jeans and a T-shirt with a long-sleeved cotton shirt open over it like a jacket. He was standing absolutely still near the fireplace.

Kapak was naked and unarmed, and there was no way to retreat unnoticed, so he resorted to bluster. "Who the hell are you?"

"I'm Joe Carver."

"You're . . ."

"Yes. I came this morning because I wanted you to get a chance to look at me. Now you know that I'm somebody you never saw before. I never held you up."

Manco Kapak's mind was stalled, caught up in the contemplation of details. It was absolutely undeniable that this Joe Carver did not seem to be the man who had stuck a gun against his head a month ago. He hadn't seen the man's face, but the voice seemed different, and the shape of the body. But had Carver forgotten he'd been wearing a ski mask? Kapak tried to follow these thoughts to some kind of conclusion but was distracted by the feeling that he was exceptionally vulnerable.

At the same time, he couldn't help thinking that this situation was likely to change radically within ten or twenty minutes. Spence would return, perceive instantly that there was an intruder in the house, and probably shoot him. Or a couple of survivors of last night's debacle would show up to tell Kapak all about it, recognize Joe Carver, and take revenge for whatever he'd done last night. And, if nothing else happened, the police lieutenant would probably send a patrol car out at 9:01 to drag Kapak to headquarters. They'd bang on the door, get no answer, and then kick it in. Not only would Kapak's immediate problem be solved, but so would the larger question of what to do about Joe Carver. The courts would put him away for a home invasion and for the sheer weirdness of keeping a naked man prisoner. Kapak had to stall until one of these things came to pass.

"Look," he said. "I can see you're a sensible, reasonable man. You didn't come in here talking nasty and waving metal around. I'd love to talk to you about this and come up with some sort of mutually satisfactory arrangement."

"That's exactly what I want."

"Good, good," Kapak said, nodding his head. "Since we're both civilized and neither of us is crazy, I'd like to get dressed before we do that. I feel at a loss here, standing around like this. It's hard to concentrate."

"That's okay," Carver said. "This doesn't need to take a lot of your time. Now that you know I'm not the one you've been look-ing for, I'll just go. You and I don't have a problem." He turned and moved toward the back door.

That wasn't satisfactory. It would allow Carver to slip out into the yard and probably through the tall grove of bamboo on that side of the yard and over the fence. It wouldn't bring him into a collision with Spence or the Gaffney brothers or the police.

"Wait," said Kapak.

Carver stopped and turned to face Kapak. For a moment Ka-pak endured Carver's stare and tried to hold his eyes on Carver's. The expression on Carver's face changed to disappointment — not, Kapak reflected, anger or fright. "Sorry. Got to go."

Kapak persisted. "It's all well and good that you didn't take my money. But what if you did something to my guys, or my cars? Is everything supposed to be even because you didn't do one thing, but did five worse things?"

"If I could do five worse, I could do ten worse. It's best to be forgiving."

"But is that fair to me?"

Carver slid the window open on the other side of the room and sat on the sill. He swung one leg out. "Be satisfied with peace. I could have hurt you today."

"I'm just saying . . ."

But Carver's other leg swung over the sill and he slid off. Kapak heard him drop to the grass below, then heard him begin to run. Kapak had already begun moving, sidestepping closer to the mas-ter bedroom suite. Now he ran toward it. His bare feet gave him good traction on the slippery floors, and he made it to his bed-room quickly.

Spence or the girl had opened the curtains, so he could see Carver trotting toward the tall, graceful bamboo stalks that swayed in the breeze another hundred feet ahead of him.

Kapak dived onto the bed and rolled to his side to tug open the drawer of his nightstand. He grasped his pistol, nudged the safety off with his right thumb, then did two rolls in the other direction so he would arrive at the window-side of the bed. He swung his legs to get his feet on the floor. Carver was still visible through the nearest of the twelve-foot double-pane windows, and still in possible range. Kapak sprang to his feet and reached for the window latch, but was overcome by a wave of dizziness from all the rolling. He leaned against the wall to steady himself. He knew there wasn't enough time left to get the big window open, so he took aim at Carver's back through the glass and fired as Carver disappeared among the twenty-foot bamboo stalks.

Kapak watched as the hole he had blown through his bedroom window seemed to move. His vision wavered a little as cracks shot upward to the top of the window frame and big shards of glass dropped toward the floor.

Kapak stepped back just before the first shards hit the sill and the floor and shattered into a large number of sharp splinters and fragments. Tiny bits of glass flew, spinning in the morning sunlight to flash rainbows and explosions of reflected brightness as their sharp edges stung his face, neck, chest, belly, penis, testicles, thighs. A few little daggers of glass arced upward off the sill, turning to slash at his shins on the way to the tops of his feet.

"Holy shit," he muttered.

He heard a noise and painfully half-turned to see Spence shoulder the door inward and drop to his knees beyond the bed, sighting down the barrel of a gun at the tortured flesh of Kapak's glittering chest.

Kapak dropped his gun on the bed and stood still.

"What the fuck?" Spence seemed to intend it as a question.

Kapak looked in the full-length mirror near the head of the

bed. His fat, bulbous body was pocked with single droplets of bright red blood. In the sunlight, he could see his skin was powdered with tiny bits of glass from scalp to toenails. "Look what that son of a bitch did."

Spence stood up, put his gun in his belt, and approached cautiously. "We'd better get you cleaned up. You've got to be at that cop's office in, like, thirty-five minutes." He plucked a few shards out of Kapak's bushy eyebrows. "Maybe you can go into the shower again and try to spray the little bits of glass off you with the heavy jets."

"Good idea. While I'm in there lay out some clothes for me. But keep your eye on that bamboo grove. I don't want the bastard coming back just because he heard a gun go off." He waddled carefully toward the master bath. "That's the way he thinks—like everything's got to be even." He went inside, closed the door, and locked it.

Spence looked out at the bamboo grove and saw nothing, then hurried to the closet and collected some clothes for Kapak. On the way back he noticed that there was a trail of small blood spots on the carpet. Kapak must have stepped on a sharp piece of glass and not noticed it yet. He set the clothes on the other side of the bed and went to find the first-aid kit.

3

LIEUTENANT SLOSSER WAS IMPATIENT. Ever since his phone call to Manco Kapak, he'd had a peculiar feeling about this. He was almost sure that he was the first person to mention to Kapak that whoever had been driving his two Hummers last night had gotten into trouble in a construction site downtown. It had been the silences, the first indrawn breath, and then the pauses while the man tried to figure out what to say.

Slosser was not sure whether he had made a mistake in telling Kapak so much. Maybe he should have told Kapak to come to the station for a conversation, and then let the news explode in Kapak's face so he could watch the reaction. It was Slosser's job to find out all he could about what was going on in the city, and any insight about something as odd as the ruined Hummers might be a big break.

There was nothing Slosser could do about surprising Kapak now, so he concentrated on what he should do next. He had already awakened Kapak, and Kapak was on his way. Slosser had to keep him off-balance. If he wasn't here by 9:15, Slosser would dispatch three cars to pick him up. No, make that two. Part of the problem with many of the small-time crime bosses in this city was that they began to think they were important. Make that one car to pick him up, and one to wait a block away unseen, not to move in unless there was resistance.

Slosser was surprised that that the Hummers belonged to Kapak. He had always assumed that Kapak was a crook, but not the ugly, violent kind. He had seemed to be the sort who skimmed cash and understated his income. He seemed like someone who would someday find himself owning a club that wasn't profitable anymore and would set fire to it for the insurance. He didn't seem to be the sort who would send people to a construction site after midnight. The only two reasons that seemed to make sense were large-scale theft and extortion, and both seemed to be somewhere outside Kapak's universe — too gritty and risky for a strip club owner. Slosser had never seen evidence that there was any enmity between Kapak's company and Veruda Construction. It didn't seem likely. The Coventry Towers project was a billion-dollar development, and it was only one of about five projects that Veruda had going. They were a herd of elephants, and Kapak was a gnat.

Slosser looked at his watch and felt frustration. It was 8:50, only five minutes since the last time he had looked. He had hoped Kapak would get here early so he could make him wait.

Slosser kept himself from looking at his watch again, and in a few minutes he heard footsteps outside his office door. Owens, his assistant, slapped his palm against the doorjamb once in a military knock and then opened the door. "Lieutenant, Mr. Kapak is here." He added, "He brought his attorney."

Slosser kept himself from swearing, but he was aware after a second that his jaw was working, and he was grinding his teeth again. He stood and watched the two men step into his office. The first, he knew, was Kapak. He was a big man in his sixties, with broad shoulders, the thick neck of a fighter, but a paunch that hung over his thin black belt. His hair was still a coal black that made Slosser suspect it was dyed. He had a sour, almost pained look on his face. The second was the attorney, a slight man in his forties with a sallow complexion, pale eyes, and thin, spidery hands that kept fiddling with his Blackberry as he stepped in with his briefcase on his wrist.

"Gentlemen. Right on time." Slosser turned to Owens. "We'll use Room Six." To the others he said, "Follow me." He set off down the hall, threading his way past the people in the hallway. He got to Room Six and opened the door to let the others in. He was mildly surprised that Kapak had brought his lawyer. In one way it was a gift. It meant he was scared of Slosser, and that meant he was guilty of something.

There was a quiet understanding in the world of police and criminals. When you first pulled them in, you would have a conversation. The suspect would use the time to rat out his enemies, try to strike a bargain, and listen for clues as to how much the police knew. The cop would use the time to try various stratagems— say somebody else had named them as the perpetrator already, or that cops had found the gun, or tested their DNA, or some other lie. Lying was a privilege that had been upheld a hundred times in a hundred court cases. When the suspect got tired of the discussion, he would ask for an attorney. That was the signal he was done talking, and it was time to end the interrogation. Cops seldom asked a question after the subject of attorneys came up, and the suspect tended not to answer any. Slosser looked at the attorney.

"I'm Lieutenant Nicholas Slosser. And you are . . . ?"

"I'm Gerald Ospinsky, Mr. Kapak's attorney."

"Oh, yes. I remember the name from Mr. Kapak's files."

"Ahh. What files would those be?"

"As you know, Mr. Kapak has a couple of business licenses and liquor licenses, and you filed the papers for him. He's also been cited for several violations of zoning, parking, nuisance, and noise codes. You responded to several of the complaints. Any other questions before we begin?"

"No."

"Mr. Kapak, could you state your full name, please?"

"Claudiu Vidor Kapak."

"Manco Kapak is a nickname, right?"

"Of course. The first king of the Incas. And the last was named that too." Kapak shifted in his seat. He looked sick. He seemed to have some kind of skin rash. There were tiny red spots on his cheeks and forehead. He began to lean forward and put his elbows on the table, but stopped himself abruptly as though he had set off a pain. "What did you want to talk about?"

"You have two sport utility vehicles registered as property of Kapak Enterprises, correct? Two Hummers?"

"Yes. My staff use them to transport people and supplies."

"What people and supplies?"

"All kinds."

"Can you give me one example?"

"Some of the time, one will be used to pick up a visiting artist at her hotel and bring her to one of the clubs for a show."

"You're talking about your strip clubs, so it's strippers?"

"Gentlemen's clubs. The entertainers are exotic dancers, yes."

"Got it. Why Hummers?"

"They're big, they're high, and they attract the attention of potential customers. They look as though you're delivering something valuable. It's like having an armored car pull up at the front door. People look to see what comes out."

"Why do your vehicles have armor?"

As Kapak paused for a moment, Ospinsky interrupted. "Who said they had armor?"

"They both have steel plates welded to the insides of the doors. They have bulletproof glass on the side windows. Why do they?"

"It's not illegal," Ospinsky said to Kapak. "You don't have to answer."

29

"It's all right, Jerry." Kapak said to Slosser, "Do you know I got robbed just about a month ago right outside the Bank of America? I was there with the night deposit. It was probably because I drove there alone in my Mercedes."

"I read the police report."

"Then you can see the kind of things a businessman has to worry about. I would have been better off driving to the bank in a bulletproof Hummer with a couple of bodyguards."

"Who did the robbery?"

"If I knew, I'd have told you already."

"I understand the North Hollywood division is investigating. Maybe they'll be able to tell us both soon. But I was going to ask about the Hummers. Do you know where they are now?"

"Since you say it like that, I guess you have them."

"You're right. They're in our impound lot. Here are some photographs of them I got this morning." He set them on the table in a row in front of Kapak.

He stared down at them for a few seconds. It was hard to imagine what had happened to his two vehicles to make them look that way. They appeared to have been pounded on all sides by a giant hammer. He became aware of Ospinsky leaning against his shoulder so he could get the best view of the pictures without craning his neck too much. His breath was horrible, a noxious vapor being rhythmically pumped into Kapak's face. He shrugged Ospinsky off, then looked up at Slosser.

Slosser said, "What happened to your cars?"

"You tell me."

"I think a few of your guys drove your Hummers to the Coventry Towers building site, trying to cause some trouble. The chain that secured the gate had been broken, so they weren't invited."

"Who are you accusing?"

"The crime scene people are running the fingerprints now, so we should know before long who was in the vehicles."

"What if somebody stole both Hummers and drove them to the building?"

"What were your men doing at the building? Did you have some business with the Veruda Construction Company? Did your men have orders from you, or did they just go there on their own?"

"That's all ridiculous," Ospinsky snapped. "Don't answer any of these questions."

"Then was it a burglary? Were your men there to fill the two Hummers with tools and equipment?"

Ospinsky was incensed. "Another ridiculous accusation. Mr. Kapak is a businessman with no record that would suggest anything of the sort. He had two vehicles stolen from his company and then, apparently, utterly destroyed."

"Stolen? We don't have a theft complaint."

"You will immediately after we're free to file one. Mr. Kapak works in an industry that requires him to be at work late at night. His first notification that the vehicles weren't parked at one of his clubs came from you—a police officer—at seven this morning, two hours ago, and six hours before he would usually be awake. The fact that he hasn't reported the theft yet doesn't prove it's not a theft."

"And it doesn't prove it was, either." He studied Kapak. "I don't know you at all, but I had assumed you were a semilegitimate businessman."

Ospinsky was getting angry. "What exactly does that mean?"

Slosser kept his eyes on Kapak, as though he had spoken. "You're in a business that's perfectly legal most of the time, but not very nice. You're selling people things that aren't good for them. And you keep bouncers and backup men on the payroll, but not to protect your customers. It's the way the business works. I haven't seen anything in your files that makes you stand out or worries me. Until now."

Kapak held his hand up so Ospinsky wouldn't go into an oration. "What do you see now?"

"I've got to be honest with you. Coming in here with your lawyer all paranoid and you sitting there stone-faced and sullen just to tell me why your two cars turned up on a deserted construction site this morning, well, it doesn't make me feel good about you. It's the way a small-time guy running a criminal enterprise acts. And I'm not just guessing. I've spent a lot of time with people like that. Maybe after I've got my pension vested next year, I'll quit and go to law school and make some real money. I know exactly what I'll tell my clients. 'Don't act like you're guilty.' Simple."

"Are you advising my client to waive his right to legal counsel?"

"I'm just saying it might be a good strategy to behave differently. If you come in and act like you're preparing a legal defense when all you're doing is reporting that you're a victim of a crime, a cop gets suspicious. He wonders what you're hiding."

Manco Kapak said, "You're right." He looked at Ospinsky for a moment. "Gerry, maybe you ought to be getting to your office. Thanks for coming."

Ospinsky said, "Do you think this man is trying to help you?"

"I'll be fine. I'll call you later."

Ospinsky shrugged. "Suit yourself." He stood, stuffed his yellow notepad into his briefcase, and assumed an unnaturally straight posture to salvage his dignity, then left the room without looking back.

"I didn't mean to offend him," Slosser lied. "I was just making conversation. When you go into a police station, you generally have some specific business in mind. In this case maybe you want to report a car theft. You'll be sent to talk to an auto theft officer. This may be the first time you've had a car stolen, but it isn't his first. On average he's seen maybe a thousand grand theft autos a year since the day he started. He knows exactly what you're going to say and how you're going to act. If you do or say something he doesn't expect, he wonders why. He won't stop until he knows the answer."

Kapak said, "I hope you understand that for an ordinary man, it's hard to know how to react to an early morning summons from the police."

"You put on your shoes and come down and have a chat. Unless you've got something to worry about."

"Like what?"

"Oh, I don't know. Like maybe there are drugs in the Hummers. Or blood. Or maybe you think I'm going to find out that there's a child in Intensive Care at Cedars with Hummer tracks across his back."

"None of that is true, I can tell you. I don't get involved with anything that's illegal. I run two gentlemen's clubs, a dance club, a gym, and a couple of other businesses. Some years have been good, and some bad, but I never have time for things like drugs or whatever."

"Is this a good year or a bad year?"

"A bad year. Did I tell you I got robbed?"

"Yes."

"And besides that, my health isn't too good."

"What's wrong with you?"

"I'm tired all the time. You can't put your finger on when it happened, but you know you're not the man you were. That's old age. And it seems like I'm getting robbed all the time. First it's a guy with a gun to my head, and now two expensive vehicles turned into junk." Kapak could feel each of the hundreds of tiny scratches and punctures from the broken glass on his skin. Every time he shifted in his chair, he felt his shirt or his pants moving some tiny, unnoticed sliver of surgically sharp glass against the skin of his belly or genitals. He was being goaded toward madness like a bull in the ring, but he pretended to be a harmless, aging man. He used his torments to build an impression of candor.

"Maybe we can do something about the robberies, at least. Your lawyer wasn't letting me ask you any questions. Is there anything that happened before last night that you haven't thought to mention?"

"You're my only source of information. I don't think anybody who works for me knows the damned things are gone yet. They're worth, like, fifty grand each. Were worth, I mean. You said they were impounded?"

"Yes. They were put on flatbeds with a crane and driven to impound."

"Can my insurance company go look at them? I'd like to get a claim started. From the looks of those pictures, it could take a while."

"Sure. Have them call me." Slosser handed Kapak a business card from his coat pocket. "I'd guess there's not much question they're totaled. They looked like they were pushed from the fifth floor of the building."

"Jesus. It sounds like a nasty prank or something. Do you think it was kids?"

"No. Adults."

"What adult does this? If they took a car and drove it across the border to sell it, or to a garage to chop it for parts, I could agree, it's adults. But if you wreck it completely, you can't be making any money on that. Who does that but kids?"

"Both vehicles had their keys in them."

"They did?"

"Yeah. That means your guys drove them there. So who was driving when it happened?"

"None of my people would do that. Somebody must have left the keys in them. Or maybe a burglar broke into the office and took the keys off the board on the wall."

"Who could that be?"

"I couldn't even give you a guess."

"I suppose not," Slosser said. He stood up. "Well, thanks for coming in."

"No, thank you, Lieutenant." Kapak still had the mad bull's determination. He stood up too, trying to make his painful movements seem only careful, the movements of an old man.

They parted in the hallway, and each went in a different direction. As Slosser walked back to his office, he smiled. He had managed to talk Kapak into getting rid of his lawyer for an interrogation, a feat for the record books, and one that would pay off later, because client and lawyer had lost confidence in each other. He still didn't know exactly what was going on, but he could tell Kapak knew, and that it was something that would get him into serious trouble. That was plenty to accomplish before 10:00 in the morning.

Kapak walked toward the portico where he had entered the building, and he was satisfied. He had planted enough in Lieutenant Slosser's mind to keep him busy for a while. Instead of hiding his surprise and being ashamed of it, he had used it to persuade Slosser that he was a victim of the theft and destruction of two expensive vehicles. He had planted some facts that might make Slosser draw the wrong conclusions. Since there was no hope of gain from wrecking a car, this could only be an attack on Kapak and his businesses. Slosser would try to find out who Kapak's enemy was, and that would give Kapak a bit of room to work.

4

SPENCE WAS OUTSIDE the police station when Kapak emerged from the front entrance, walking with a strange stiffness, as though his knees had locked. Spence knew that it was the terrible discomfort of having glass fragments in his pants, so he took pity on Kapak, got out, opened the door of the Town Car, and stood at something like attention while Kapak eased himself onto the passenger seat. "Thanks," said Kapak. "I feel like my dick is being sawed off."

"Better try sitting in a bath or something, until you get all the glass off."

Spence got in and drove. He knew Kapak's main concern for the moment was to get away from the toxic atmosphere of police headquarters and begin the important work of forgetting he had ever been there. Spence drove with some urgency, moving in and out of lanes to work his way among the slow stream of cars through the city.

He was up the freeway ramp and on his way out of the downtown section, where tall buildings shouldered up to the streets on both sides and made them seem narrow and dark. Kapak sat in the passenger seat, staring out the window at the glimpses of sunny hillsides far off beyond the buildings.

At last he seemed to catch his breath. "That was something. I've got a fucking police lieutenant showing me pictures of the two Hummers, which looked as though they'd been dropped from an airplane. There was no sign of any of the guys in them. Meanwhile, not one of our guys has seen fit to call me and tell me what's up. Did Joe Carver kill them all and drag their bodies to a pit to be covered by cement? Did he scare them off? Buy them off?"

"Leave them alone and they'll come home. If there were bodies, the cop would have said something."

"What if he killed them quietly and took the bodies with him?"

"Can you imagine killing the Gaffney brothers without noise and blood?"

"No. You're right. But the whole thing worries me. What is this Carver guy? He could be the wrong man. What if he's just some pissed off little guy who got surprised by a case of mistaken identity? What if he's not? He could be anything, even the advance man for some big players."

"You met him and talked to him. What did he say he wanted?"

"'Nothing,' is what he said. He told me he just wanted me to leave him alone. He didn't do the robbery, so he should be allowed to do whatever he wanted."

"Then what were you shooting at him for?"

"You don't think I was going to let him go just because he said that? Maybe he didn't do the robbery. Whoever put the gun to my head got twenty-three thousand bucks. Joe Carver wrecked a hundred thousand dollars' worth of cars, did God knows what to five of my employees, and brought me face to face with the kind of police lieutenant who isn't going to leave me alone until one of us dies. He also broke into my house and sprayed my nuts with pulverized glass."

"He did that? It looked like you shot the window out."

"It's like capital murder. If a thief forces the cops to shoot at him and one of them hits the other, he's the one they charge with murder, not the cop. This is just like that."

"I see," said Spence.

"You should."

Kapak's cell phone rang. He put it to his ear. "Yeah?" He listened for a few seconds. "Is anybody dead?" He listened again. "Let me tell you something. I got dragged out of bed, practically at dawn, to go down to police headquarters to explain why two Hummers of mine were in a construction site, wrecked, with the keys in them. And did any one of you think to call me and say, 'Hey, Joe Carver is alive, and he's probably on his way to your house to kill you.' Yeah, that happened. He didn't kill me, but that's no thanks to you. Where are you? We'll be there in a minute." Kapak hung up.

Spence drove the last few blocks, and then pulled into the driveway. "There's somebody in the house. I saw the front curtain move."

"Yeah, it's the fucking geniuses." As the car moved up the driveway toward the house, the Gaffney brothers, the big Russian, Corona, and Guzman all stepped out of the front door to stand on the front steps and wait. Their suits looked dusty, and one of the Gaffneys had a long rip at his knee so the paper-white skin showed. "Look at them," Kapak said. "Jesus, I'm actually paying these people."

"You need me for anything?"

Kapak leaned in to say, "No. I won't need you until midnight. Go ahead."

"Thanks."

Kapak shut the car door and walked stiffly toward the front of the house. Spence backed out of the driveway, turned, and drove to the freeway entrance, merged with the traffic, and pulled into the left lane. The freeway was still clear and fast moving into the Valley. He switched to the Ventura Freeway, got off at Coldwater, and found the apartment building where he had left the girl two hours ago. He parked the Town Car, walked to the entrance, and looked at the names beside the buzzers at the door. When he saw "K. Noonan" he decided that it must be the right one. It was the only *K*, and she was the one who had volunteered her name, so maybe she hadn't lied. He pressed the button, heard a click and a sudden sense of space like the other end of a telephone call, then her voice. "Who is it?"

"Spence, the guy who drove you home this morning."

"Well, don't advertise to the neighbors that I came home in the morning. When I buzz you in, come to the second floor landing. I'll meet you."

He heard the buzz and the click, and he tugged the door open and went up the stairs to find her barefooted and leaning against the wall wearing a T-shirt and sweatpants. Her arms were folded across her chest, and she had a puzzled smile. Her long hair was wet from a shower, hanging in loose strings that dampened her T-shirt.

"Hi, Kira."

"Forget something?"

"I tried, but I couldn't."

"What?"

"You."

She put her hand over her mouth to stifle her laugh. "Oh my God. That is so cheesy. How can you say something like that?" She stopped, shook her head in disbelief, then laughed again. She turned and walked down the second-floor hall, and Spence followed her. He noticed how much shorter she was now that she was barefoot. She stopped in front of a door that was open six inches.

He pushed the door open for her and she looked up at him. "Did I say that was my apartment?" She walked on along the hall while Spence quickly reached for the door and pulled it back the way he'd found it. But as he turned to follow her, she doubled back, slipped inside the door, and closed it.

When Spence knocked lightly, she opened the door and pulled him inside. Her apartment was decorated with framed photographs of Kira and a changing group of men and women about her age in various places, always outdoors. They were on a mountain just at the tree line near some wind-tortured pines, in the stands at a baseball stadium, on a big sailboat ducking low to avoid the boom. She stood three feet from him while he glanced around him. She folded her arms and said, "Please don't tell me that your boss wants to see me again."

"No. He's busy right now. He's got his mind on other things."

"Good, because I won't."

"Good." He stood there, making no move to leave.

"Then what do you have on your mind?"

He took one step and gathered her into his arms. He kissed her with a certainty that overwhelmed her tentative first attempt at resistance. She was already off-balance, clinging to him to keep from falling backward. "I thought you weren't interested in your boss's leftovers."

"You're not a leftover." His hands moved down her back to the bottom seam of her T-shirt and abruptly lifted it so the T-shirt came off and left her arms in the air above her head. "You mentioned he had trouble getting hard. He sure didn't tell you about it. He couldn't get it up last night, so all either of you got was a good night's sleep. I'm here to make it up to you." He hugged her to his chest.

"What if I don't want to do this?" She caught herself enjoying the way the soft fabric of his shirt felt against her bare chest.

"I hope you do. You like me."

"Oh?" She had tried to make it sound at least argumentative, but she had a chill at that moment and shivered, so it only sounded breathy.

He plucked the bow in the drawstring of her sweatpants. She grabbed for the waistband, but they were so loose that they fell to mid-thigh before she could, leaving her in only a pair of white panties. She had to step back and tug the sweatpants up with both hands, leaving her breasts exposed. "There are laws against this."

"I'm an outlaw. A gangster. You said it before."

She was holding her sweatpants with one hand and trying to ruin his view of her breasts with the other. "So you admit it."

"Sure." He gathered her in his arms again and began kissing her neck, her eyes, her lips.

"You're making this very hard. But then I suppose I brought this on by what I left in the car, right?"

"What did you leave in the car?"

"I left my name and phone number on a piece of paper in the back seat. You could have called ahead and asked me to go out with you tonight. I would have said yes, and I could have worn something pretty, and we could have had a beautiful date."

"I didn't see your piece of paper. Will you go out with me now?"

"I just got out of the shower and my hair is stringy, and you've really gotten a bit ahead of yourself. I mean, really."

"I apologize. I thought you liked bad guys."

"Well, I do, but . . ." She kept trying to move, to turn away from him, to hold him off, but he held her as though he were unaware that she was struggling. Finally she said, "Oh, what the hell," put her arms around his neck, and kissed him.

Spence gave her a long, gentle kiss. When they backed apart, she kicked the sweatpants away from her ankles. He began to remove his own clothes and step away from them toward her. She backed into her bedroom as he advanced. The bed had not been slept in, so when they reached it they moved to opposite sides and tore the covers open together. Kira hurriedly yanked open the top drawer of the nightstand, tore a wrapped condom off a long strip, and put it in Spence's hand. She had the air of a woman committing one last act before being swept away in a flood.

They met in the center of the bed, eager and uninhibited, always in motion. After a time they ended breathlessly and lay together for a few minutes, letting their hearts slow to a normal rhythm. Then he got up, stepped to her dresser, and tore the next condom off the strip before they came together again in the center of the bed, almost like opponents in a fierce contest.

After two hours they lay on their backs staring up at the ceiling, touching only slightly at the hip and the side of the foot. She said, "Can I ask you something?"

"Anything."

"Do you do this kind of thing often?"

"Never. But suddenly this morning I felt like my life was changing—that big things were happening that I couldn't control, so I had to go along. I took a guess that it was you."

She snuggled close and put her arm across his chest. "That's so . . ."

"True?"

"No, false. But this has been so, I don't know, primal. When I think about it now I feel as if I'm going to faint." She brought her leg across his thigh, straddled him, and stared down into his eyes.

"You don't seem faint," he said.

"The good kind of faint. It brings its own revival. I'm beginning to revive."

"So am I."

"How long can you stay?"

"I don't have to be at work until midnight."

"Oh," she said, then closed her eyes. "Oh."

5

JOE CARVER STOOD in the Citibank branch in Studio City and watched the pretty teller count out the hundred-dollar bills. They were the cash advance on the business credit card he had stolen from Manco Kapak's wallet while he was waiting for Kapak to return from the shower.

It was taking a long time for the teller to count out four hundred bills, and the wig, mustache, false eyebrows, and dark makeup were all hot and itchy. Carver didn't worry that the long wait might be dangerous, because the unseen people who had verified the card and approved the transaction wouldn't blink at a charge of forty thousand dollars from Kapak's company. That was probably about the size of his company's weekly liquor bill. And Carver wasn't trying to hide the charge forever, just until he got outside. After that he wanted Kapak to see it and howl.

He was confident that Kapak would be occupied with the fate of his Hummers until at least lunchtime. After that he would be trying to make decisions about how to do Carver permanent harm. He wasn't going to walk into a random branch of a random bank and see Carver using his business credit card.

Carver was taking the money only out of annoyance anyway. When he was making his way into the bamboo forest behind Kapak's house, he had heard a shot, looked back, and seen Kapak standing by one of the tall, narrow bedroom windows, still naked, with a gun in his hand. His eyes were not on Carver, they were turned up to watch big sheets of glass falling.

Carver had gone through the grove of tall bamboo, over the back wall, and out to the next street. But he had been brooding over the sight since he had seen it. Stealing the business credit card from Kapak's wallet had been a small precaution. He had not formed a genuine intention to actually use it, only had a vague idea that if he had to pay Kapak off, he might use the card and pay him with his own money. But as soon as he'd heard the shot, he had changed his mind. The card was going to help him send Kapak the message that attacking Joe Carver was a bad idea.

The little teller behind the bulletproof glass counted out the last ten bills and looked pleased with herself. She put the first two stacks in the tray under her window and waited while he picked them up and put them into his canvas bag. Then she put the last two stacks into the tray. As he put away the rest of his money, he said, "Thank you."

"You're welcome, Mr. Kapak." That was what he liked the best.

Carver knew he had very little time, and that he needed to be moving. He walked out of the bank into the warm sunshine along Ventura Boulevard. At the first corner, he crossed to the south side, and then went over to Cantura Street. It was much quieter as he walked along in the shade of the overarching branches of the sycamore trees. Carver made his way east to the end of Cantura, then turned onto Ventura again, and walked the last three long blocks to the zone where the used-car lots began. He stepped inside the gate of the first one, because he saw just the car.

After a test drive, he made an offer for a year-old Toyota Camry. He liked the car because it was black and nondescript. It was the kind of car that could get left in a parking lot and found only after every other car in the lot was driven off. He paid some of Kapak's cash for it.

All Joe Carver had wanted was to stay safe so he could start a new life here in Los Angeles. He had owned a restaurant and bar in Chicago for years, and now he wanted to start a similar business here. He could hardly expect to do that if a powerful man kept sending thugs out to find him. He had done his best to make the problem go away. He had simply evaded them, stayed out of sight, and waited for the threat to pass. He had thought that maybe Kapak would run into the real thief, or the source that had made Joe Carver the suspect would lose its credibility. Kapak himself could get into trouble of some other kind and get arrested or killed. Not only could anything happen, but if a man waited long enough, it usually did. Carver had waited a month, but nothing had happened.

He had done his best. He had taken a big risk to go to Kapak unarmed and show him his face, so Kapak would know that Carver wasn't the man who had robbed him. He had politely asked Kapak to start leaving him alone.

Within minutes Kapak had shot at him from behind. There was no way to make a simple truce with Manco Kapak. The man didn't care that Carver had done him no harm. Now he was going to have to learn how expensive it was to persist in a wrong decision.

Carver drove to a Big Five sporting goods store and picked out a Remington Model 870 twelve-gauge shotgun with a short barrel and a magazine tube that held eight shells. He couldn't imagine Kapak sending fewer than eight people next time if he sent any. Carver drove to Griffith Park to find a lonely parking lot beside a small picnic grove so he could take it out of its box and load it with double-ought buckshot. He laid it in the trunk under a mat and put the rest of the box of twenty-five shells in the plastic bag, then flattened the boxes and burned them in one of the picnic grills.

He drove to Sherman Oaks, parked in the lot of a grocery store, and walked to a Wells Fargo Bank branch. He opened a checking account for an entity called the Fortuna Company, deposited five thousand dollars, and received a sheaf of temporary checks.

His next stop was the Westfield Mall. He used Kapak's card to pay for a hundred American Express gift cards at two hundred dollars each, then bought a new wardrobe of suits, shoes, and informal clothes, the most expensive he could find.

The next series of purchases were simply an effort to drain as much money out of the card as possible before the account was shut down. He bought diamond jewelry and high-end wristwatches for men and women from two different stores. He was aware that there was a federal law that would prevent Kapak from losing much money through a stolen credit card, but he also knew that the charges would horrify and enrage Kapak. Carver took everything he had bought out of the bags, hid the large items in the car trunk, and stashed the rest under the front seats.

Carver had bought enough so he felt he had to move to another shopping center. He had estimated that he could keep charging until late afternoon, so when he got to the Glendale Galleria, he decided it was time to run a check. He went to the food court and ordered a dozen cookies, and handed Kapak's card to the teenager at the counter. The boy ran the card, waited for the approval, and then handed it back to Carver with an apologetic expression. "Sorry, man. This isn't any good. Would you like to cancel the order?"

"That's okay," Carver said, and handed him the cash for the cookies and a tip. He decided the boy looked too embarrassed for a simple declining of credit. Some other message must have come up on his machine like "Confiscate card" or "Call the police." Carver hurried away and slipped out of the Galleria through the big Nordstrom store that opened into the parking garage. He looked at his watch. It was just 4:00. He'd had a pretty good day. He had a gently used car for free, still had thirty thousand cash and twenty thousand in American Express cards, some very nice clothes, about sixty thousand dollars in jewelry, and a loaded shotgun.

As soon as he was two miles from the Galleria, he took off the uncomfortable fake hair, eyebrows, and mustache, and then used hand wipes to rub off the dark makeup from his face, neck, and hands as he drove. He stopped at a grocery store and used cash to pay for a roll of duct tape, a box of kitchen matches, two hundred feet of clothesline, and a can of charcoal starter.

When he reached the neighborhood where Kapak lived, he began to drive up and down the streets. The next step was going to take some thought and study. If only he knew who had really robbed Kapak, none of this would be necessary.

6

Jefferson Davis Falkins lay on the spine-snapped couch under the big window in Lila's apartment, feeling the faint motion of air across his bare chest and bare feet and bare legs up to the place where his baggy khaki shorts began.

The couch smelled like dog, and because he had been sleeping on it, he supposed he did too. He sat up. The sun must be very low now, because to the east he could see the hint of the deep indigo rising from somewhere beyond the curve of the earth.

Eldon the dog raised his head and turned to Jeff, knowing that in a minute Jeff would probably insist on getting up and spoiling the community and comfort of the couch. Eldon sniffed the air, learning things from it that he kept to himself. All Jeff could tell was that he had not sniffed anything that worried him, like the approach of hostile strangers. Jeff shifted his leg and the heavy dog stood up on all fours, stepped down from the couch to the filthy yellow shag rug, and trotted off. A few seconds later the *scrit-scrat* sound of his toenails announced he had arrived in the kitchen. Falkins could hear Eldon's long tongue lapping the water in his dish.

Jeff didn't hear Lila say anything to Eldon, so he called out. "Lila?" There was no response, so he said it louder. "Lila!" He stood up, rubbed his stubbly chin, and joined Eldon in the kitchen. The note was on the kitchen table. *To Mr. Jefferson Davis Falkins. Went to Work. You should try it sometime.* That was perfect Lila. She had such a superstitious reverence for work that she capitalized it. Her respect for it transcended even her attachment to arithmetic. She worked the evening shift at the Siren Club from 4:00 until midnight five nights a week and made so little that she couldn't have afforded to eat at that club without tips. She was slim and pretty and naturally blond, so she at least got good tips, but that was beside the point.

Jeff went into Lila's tiny bedroom, opened the small closet that she let him share, and began to move aside the pile of shoes on the floor. He found the white laundry bag he'd left there, carried it to her bed, and poured out the bills. Most of them were small now — ones, fives, tens. That was chump money, not the kind of money you could flash. If he wanted to show off and buy a bottle of Cristal at a club, he would have to count out around fifty five-dollar bills, even more at some places. It completely defeated the purpose of buying the Cristal at all. Over the past month, he had spent hundreds of dollars every night buying dinners, champagne, the occasional hotel room for a few hours.

He plucked the twenties and the two fifties out of the pile and stuck them in his wallet, then dutifully gathered the smaller bills and made them into a four-inch stack. He went to Lila's dresser, found a black elastic hair band, slipped it over the stack, and tossed it on the bed. He began to open drawers, found a pair of black stockings still in a package. He opened it, lay the stockings out on the bed, put a pair of high heels where the feet would be, put a black bra up above, and put a big pair of sunglasses above that to indicate the eyes. He took her nail scissors and cut the cardboard backing from the package into the shape of a heart, wrote "I love you" on it in lipstick, and placed it in a strategic zone above the stockings. In the lowest drawer of her dresser, he found her leather gloves, put them on either side of the effigy, and put the stack of bills in the right glove.

Two last items had fallen from the laundry bag—his Browning .45 Hi-Power pistol and the spare magazine. He checked to be sure the gun and the extra magazine were both loaded, the way he had left them. If Lila had found them sometime while he was out, it would be just like her to unload them and think she was making him safe. No, she hadn't found the gun. He clicked the safety off and on again, put it into the inner pocket of the leather jacket hanging in the closet, put on a pair of jeans, a blue shirt, and a pair of running shoes.

He took the jacket and turned off the lamp by the bed so when Lila came in she would turn on the light and see what he had left for her. He stepped out to the kitchen feeling good. He had been feeling bad—uncomfortable, at least—about letting her pay for everything when he had a bag full of money, and this was the last chance to throw some her way. As of now, there was no bag of money.

That meant today was the day to go out and get something to fill the bag again. He went to the door, picked up his keys from the sideboard, and pulled his gloves and ski mask out from under the couch.

Eldon walked to the door, stood still, and stared at him patiently.

"Yeah, what the hell. I'll take you out for a few minutes before I go." He took the leash off the hook behind the door and snapped it onto Eldon's collar, then pulled some plastic bags off the stack Lila kept by the door for walks.

Eldon went out ahead of him, and his step seemed livelier and more youthful than it had before. Eldon was no puppy, but walking seemed to make him happy. Jeff followed the dog. He went down the sidewalk to the curb, then across the street with a slight diagonal to the left, and Jeff decided he understood. To the left were the little women's stores that Lila liked, and the coffee shops. The dog apparently didn't realize there was anyplace to go to the right. Jeff tugged his collar in that direction once, and the dog turned and eagerly headed to the right.

Eldon stopped now and then to sniff each object along the way and then to work up some urine to mark his trail, but otherwise he was all for the road ahead. Eldon was Lila's dog, but since Jeff and Eldon had both been living in Lila's apartment at her discretion, they shared a certain feeling of fellowship. Lila had that strange female mixture of emotions about taking in useless creatures and raging fits of hormone-fueled ferocity that made her shout and throw things and slam doors.

Eldon and Jeff liked peace. One of Lila's sudden rages a month ago had caused Jeff to stumble on his new profession, robbing people who did their banking at night. Jeff had weathered her anger that day until she slammed the door shut on her way to work. He had contemplated the situation and begun to wonder if she was simply trying to drive him off so she didn't have to throw him out. Then he wondered if her nasty mood was because she had another man she wanted to move in to take his place.

Later that evening he turned off the television and drove to the club where Lila worked. She was a waitress at Siren, one of Manco Kapak's clubs. Since it was a strip club, he had assumed that the atmosphere would be charged with pheromones and that a beautiful girl like Lila would be mired in temptation—the attraction of a really pretty girl who worked in a place that sold at least the idea of sex, and at times, pretty much the actual commodity, must be overpowering, he thought. Men must be hitting on her at a frightening rate. All of these dumb, half-drunk guys probably thought that the waitresses were strippers-in-training, at the very least.

Jeff went in, pretended to watch the show from a dark, remote table in the bar area, but actually watched Lila. He couldn't spot any boyfriends hanging around waiting for her to get off work. She didn't treat any customers as if she had ever seen them before. She was a waitress in a place where men got drunk and loud and gave big tips, but she was still a waitress. Early in the evening, she had to serve actual meals. Later on she had to concentrate mainly on carrying a tray through a tight, clumsy crowd without spilling the drinks — mainly heavy beer glasses — then making change and noticing the next customer who wanted a fresh drink. And being in a strip club, where other women were all over the place uncovering their particulars, didn't appear to make her feel especially romantic. In fact, it seemed to have the opposite effect. After Jeff had completed an hour and a half of surveillance on her, he got distracted by one of the acts for a minute, and Lila caught him.

She told him that if he thought she was going to work her ass off so he could sit in the bar wasting money paying other women to show him theirs, he was out of his mind. She was pretty mean about it. She followed him all the way to the front door, yapping at him like a little dog until he escaped.

Afterward, while he was walking across the parking lot to the back, where he had hidden his Trans Am, he happened to see a man he figured was Lila's boss, Mr. Kapak. He was coming out the kitchen door at the back of the building carrying a maroon canvas bag with a zipper on it. It was the kind of bag he'd seen store owners holding in the business teller's line at the bank. The man got into a Mercedes and drove off.

Jeff started his car and followed him. It was a dark, quiet summer night, and he drove with his window open, listening to the silence. He realized he knew exactly what to do. He parked his car on a residential street that was out of range of the cameras mounted on the bank. He took his gun from under the seat, pocketed the ski mask he'd used to rob a liquor store in Arizona, and ran up the alley between the commercial buildings along Ventura Boulevard and the Los Angeles River's concrete channel. All he did was come up behind the older man beside the bank's night deposit, stick the gun in his face, and take the bag away from him. He stepped back into the alley behind the building, ran for the car a street away, and drove back to Lila's apartment.

She came in an hour later, reminded him that he was stupid, went into her bedroom, and locked the door. He hid the money in his car and slept on the couch. When he had time to look at his money, he discovered that he had a lot. He didn't count it, any more than he would have stopped to count the potato chips in a bag. The meaningful measures were a lot, a little, and none. He put the money and the gun in the laundry bag in Lila's closet and spent the money happily over a period of about a month.

During the month he took Lila to restaurants and clubs, and on a couple of shopping trips. Her mood improved and she let him leave the couch to Eldon and join her in the bedroom. But Lila worked nights, so he could hardly be blamed if he went out by himself while she was gone. He had discovered that one of the best things about having money was not having to count. Every night he would reach into the money bag, take out bills, and make a roll of hundreds and fifties of a size that felt good in his hand. The next night most of it would be gone and he would make another. It was a life without worries—almost without thought.

Eldon and Jeff went around the block and returned to Lila's apartment just as the twilight reached its best moment, with the last rays of the sun tinting the clouds above the western horizon bright orange, leaving the sky in the east a deep, luminous purple about to turn to black. Jeff took Eldon inside, refilled his water dish, and poured some more kibble into his bowl. "There, dude," he said. "That should hold you until she gets back. Got to go."

He went out, got into his old Trans Am, fired it up, and listened to its low, throaty growl. He had bought a new muffler while he still had money, and new tires, and had the oil changed. After nine years he could tell from the sound that the engine was okay. He had driven it here from Arizona only a couple of months ago, and he had decided the night when he had begun his new career that a new muffler was a good idea. He drove out to the Valley, stopped at a Mobil station to fill up his tank, and paid in cash. When he went into the little store to pay, he was at the end of a line of four men, all about twenty to thirty, all six feet to six-two and thin, all wearing denim and dark-colored T-shirts. He was sure that five minutes from now nobody would remember him, because in five minutes he would be replaced ten times by the next guys who looked just like him. One of the things he loved about L.A. was that there were a million of everything.

Jeff drove to the Siren Club and checked the parking lot for Lila's shiny little red Honda. It was there, right where she liked to park it, under the bright lights mounted along the edge of the roof. Jeff turned south and west and drove to the diner he liked best because hardly anybody else did. He wanted a chance to be by himself and think through the acts he was going to have to perform later.

In the only stint he had ever done in prison, he had met a man named Girard. He preferred to be from France, but when he spoke French it didn't sound like the French that Jeff's teachers spoke. He was about sixty years old, but he could still do all sorts of gymnastics. During exercise periods he would do flips and cartwheels, and when he was in his cell he would walk around on his hands. He told Jeff that walking upside-down on his hands was the secret of his strength. It was true that he had very muscular arms and shoulders. He also told Jeff that his way to do anything difficult was to visualize it first, step by step in proper order. The method didn't work very well for Jeff, because he usually did things on impulse and was very easily distracted. But he was determined to try again tonight.

He went into the diner and sat down facing away from the door. When the waitress came, he ordered a turkey dinner with gravy and potatoes and green beans, looked up at the mirror that ran the length of the back wall of the restaurant, and watched her walk away to hand in his order. Then he began the work of visualizing. He would arrive near the bank at 1:30 A.M. and spend some time studying the area to be sure there were no cops watching the building. He would then place himself in the parking garage near the back of the bank.

He looked straight ahead and saw the reflection of two young women walking in the front door. They were both about twenty-two or twenty-three, and they wore tight, low-cut, straight-leg jeans, and tops that had a little lace along the edge and straps like camisoles. They both had long brown hair with highlights streaked in to look like the effects of the sun, and skin that probably hadn't been exposed to direct sunlight since they were nine. They saw the sign that said PLEASE SEAT YOURSELF, walked deeper into the restaurant, and stopped at the table right behind him. They both looked into the mirror briefly—first at themselves, then at him. His eyes met theirs and they looked away, kept smiling at each other and talking, and sat at that table anyway.

Jeff's consciousness opened and filled itself with the two women until there was room for nothing else. His mind was captive. He listened only to them. The waitress brought his turkey dinner, and he was glad because it drew the attention of the two women, whose eyes followed it to his table. He cut his food into half-inch bits so he could eat slowly, letting his eyes move upward to the mirror at varying intervals to stray across the women. The one in the lime-green camisole had no trouble catching him at it every time. The first couple of times she pretended to give him a reprieve, looking away as though she thought he might actually have met her eyes accidentally. The third time she looked directly at him, gave him a quick smile, and raised her eyebrows in a question.

The woman seated with her back to Jeff glanced at her companion, half-turned to verify that the one she was silently communicating with was Jeff, then leaned forward to whisper to her. She set her napkin by her place, stood up, and walked past Jeff to the stairway that led to the restrooms. Jeff was aware that every-thing was some kind of test, so he willed himself not to watch her.

"I'm sorry if she looked at you in a weird way." It was the girl in the lime green, who was still at her table behind him.

He looked into the mirror at her. "No, please. Don't feel that way. I was trying to think of a way to talk to you anyway."

Her smile came back. "What did you want to say?"

"That I wanted to talk to you."

"So *now* what do you want to say?"

He shrugged. "That you're beautiful. I suppose everybody who talks to you says that."

"Pretty much. Men say that to every girl the first time they talk, no matter what she looks like. After that, most of them seem to think of something smarter to say."

"I'm not very smart. Did your friend get mad because you were looking at me?"

"Not really. She went to the ladies' room to give us a chance to see if we had anything."

"What would we have?"

"Potential."

"I think we do. Would your friend mind if you and I went somewhere for an after-dinner drink?"

"She's my sister—a year older. Please don't say you thought so. It's like saying you had the right answer on the tip of your tongue. You didn't."

"No, I didn't."

"So you've decided to be honest."

"Yeah. To tell you the truth I never really looked at her. From the first second, it was you all the way. She was just the person who came in with you."

She laughed. "You're such a liar. You have that plain, innocent face, and you never go out of character. Are you an actor?"

"Maybe I'm telling the truth. I'm a simple guy."

"I saw you look at both of us the second we came in the door. When my sister turned around to sit down, you were staring at her ass. I saw you."

"The mirror distorts things. I was probably looking at my shirt to see if I got gravy on it."

"What's your name?"

"Jeff."

"Show me your license."

He took out his wallet and handed her his driver's license.

"Arizona? You live in Arizona?" She seemed disappointed.

"No. I moved here a couple of months ago."

She handed it back to him. "It says Jefferson Davis Falkins, all right. It's also expired. You might want to do something about that before you get arrested."

"I will. At least before I get executed. What's your name?"

"Carrie."

"I won't ask for your license. But will you give me your phone number?"

"I haven't decided yet. What do you do?"

"I haven't decided yet."

"Then no."

"I'm an entrepreneur. I invest in good ideas, turn them into businesses, run them for a while to prove they work, and then sell them." He had heard someone say that on television and it had sounded good to him. "That's why I don't know yet what business I'm going to be in."

"Is that true?"

He rolled his eyes. "I've never lied to you before, have I?"

"No, never in all these years." Her eyes focused on something beyond his head, and she quickly took a business card out of her purse and handed it to him, then withdrew her hand.

He could tell it must be her sister coming back, so he palmed the card and said, "When can we go for a drink? Are you free later?"

"After we pay our check, give me an hour to get back here."

He nodded, pocketed the card, and then Carrie's sister reappeared. As she prepared to resume her place at the table, Jeff stood and held out his hand. "Hi," he said. "My name is Jeff. I thought I should introduce myself."

The sister looked down at his hand with distaste. "Why?"

He let his hand drop and she turned to Carrie. "Are you two friends now?"

"We've just been talking for a minute."

Jeff said, "Is it okay to say I can see the resemblance now?"

"Resemblance to what?" The sister seemed suspicious, hostile.

"Each other. You're sisters."

The woman glared at Carrie. "We are not sisters."

Carrie shrugged and smiled at Jeff. "We're such close friends that it feels like sisters sometimes. This is Laura."

Laura looked at Jeff with undisguised contempt as she picked up the check from their table. "Come on. I'm not feeling this. Let's go."

"All right," said Carrie, and stood up. When she saw Laura start out for the door, she gave her three seconds, then said, "Remember. An hour," turned, and hurried after her.

Jeff considered. He had to kill time until around 2:00 A.M., and Carrie was cute. No, she was actually beautiful, but she was also young and playful. He was aware that the number of men who had waited in some public place for some girl they didn't know and got stood up was in the billions. He decided not to mind. It gave him something to think about while he waited for closing time. But he knew that most of the women who stood men up were playful and cute in exactly the same way Carrie was, and she had already lied to him once about her friend.

He stayed where he was and ordered a piece of pie and coffee. As he sat at his table drinking coffee, he wondered about women. There were girls who seemed to be completely sane. They wanted things a man could understand—maybe a good time she couldn't afford but the man could, or sex. Actually, the sex they wanted was not so much sex in itself, but a nice friendship that might include sex at a future time. Or they just had an honest wish to kill a long night without being alone in a crummy apartment in a city they weren't born in. But then there were these strange, incomprehensible women who wanted to play tricks and humiliate men they didn't even know, who had done nothing but show interest in them. If Jeff had met a girl he wasn't interested in, he wouldn't have said he was giving her his number and really given her the number of the police or the YMCA or something. It was a mystery.

After he'd had two cups of coffee, he was nearly ready to leave. He went upstairs to the men's room, came back down the stairs, and found Carrie sitting in the seat across from his.

"I was afraid you stood me up," she said. "But you didn't."

"Never crossed my mind." He took out a fifty-dollar bill, tossed it on the table by his check, and took her arm to guide her up. "Come along."

She came. "Where are we going?"

"I think we said 'out for a drink.' But since you had practically nothing but coffee for dinner, we might want to go someplace that sells food."

They went outside and he walked her to his Trans Am and opened the passenger door for her.

"What's this car?"

"What do you mean—model? It's a Pontiac Trans Am. It doesn't look hip, but it's got an engine and transmission and stuff in it that cost me more than most cars. It's pretty fast."

She looked at him in wonder. "My God. You're a throwback, aren't you?" She cocked her head and squinted at him. "Are you a good kisser?"

He shook his head. "Not as good as you deserve."

"Amazing," she muttered, and put her hand on his chest to make him hold still while she kissed him softly on the lips.

Jeff put his arms around her, pulled her to him, and extended the kiss a few more seconds.

She pulled back to end it, her hands pushing off against his chest. "Oh my God."

"What?"

"I felt the gun under your jacket, asshole. What did you have in mind? Were you going to bury me in the desert or the mountains?"

"That's crazy. I would have told you about having it, but I never expected you to kiss me like that. I have to carry it as part of my job."

"I thought you were a big-shot investor or something."

"Not a big shot. But sometimes I have to carry money or negotiable securities. And sometimes kidnapping is a concern. That's why the police gave me a permit."

"Come on. The police never issue permits to anybody here. Try again."

He sighed and shook his head in frustration. "You win. I'm a crazed pervert who finds pretty women and shoots them. Let's leave it at that." He shut the passenger door and walked around the back of his car to the driver's side.

But she followed him, not satisfied. "Well, what are you, then? I never believed that entrepreneur shit. You can barely say the word, and this car . . . It's all just ludicrous. Are you a robber?"

He was not sure why he was saying it, but he said, "Yes, I am. I was in the restaurant by myself because I like to get focused before I go pick up some money."

He watched her face go through a series of expressions, one following rapidly on the other. First was fear, but fear had a way, once the person noticed it, to change to anger. Or maybe her expression was a simple fight-or-flight response, her body reacting with a huge release of adrenaline, and her face showing only that.

Her next expression was a widening of the eyes as she stared at him. The slight curvature of the upper lip that he had thought was going to be a snarl stretched into a grin. She laughed. "I knew it. I could tell you were, like, this outlaw. That is so cool. You're a bandito. Armed and dangerous."

"I am."

She gripped his arm and pulled her body as close as she could to his. "You've got to take me with you."

As he got into his car and started it, she rushed to get into the passenger seat and slam the door. In the second or two he was allowed to think, he supposed that her reaction to his real profession could only be to say "You're scum" or "You're hot." He was amazed that she had chosen the second. It was even more amazing that it didn't feel like good news.

"It's not a good idea. People don't want to get robbed. They just don't like it. You'd think the sight of a gun would make them go all weak in the knees, and it usually does. I've robbed a few stores where the clerks were so scared they wet their pants. But that's not always."

"God, I'd love to see that."

He wondered about her, but only for an instant, because he needed to win this argument quickly before her heart was set on it. "But not always," he repeated. "Sometimes the sight of a gun makes them so mad they look like they'll explode, and then they sort of do. They try to kill you first. It's not a rational thing, because even if they can see there's no chance that they'll succeed, they come right after you."

"Then you have to kill them, right? Just open up."

He wondered about her again, this time more seriously. Her face was so close to his that he couldn't really see it all at once, so he wasn't sure if she was just being ironic. Her eyes seemed huge, and he could feel her breath on his cheek. "Well, sometimes. I mean you have to be prepared for something ugly to happen. But you don't actually want to shoot anybody. If you get caught they put you away forever, and there's nothing in killing for you. It's the robbing part that gets you the money."

"Just let me go," she whispered into his cheek. "I want to. I'll do whatever you tell me. I won't ruin it, I promise."

She was so insistent, and she kept pressing herself closer, across the front console and in his face. It was flattering and erotic and confusing. He couldn't think of a way to resist, and he wasn't sure he even wanted to. "Let's get out of this parking lot," he said. "It's a long time before I have to make a decision. I'm not pulling this until two A.M."

"I understand," she said in a small, earnest voice. "I really do." She released his arm, sat back in her seat, and let him drive ahead out of the parking space and off the lot. He turned east on Ventura because it was a right turn and a left was more work.

He drove along past Colfax, then Tujunga, before he felt a sensation that was familiar, yet unexpected. He looked down to confirm that it was her hand on him, and then his eyes moved rapidly up her arm to her shoulder to her face.

"I don't want to just drive around," she explained.

"You're killing me."

"There are two nice hotels right up the hill at Universal Studios."

"Hotels aren't a great idea if you're pulling something."

Her beautiful smile returned. "No?"

"A crime. You give them your name and your credit card number and they get a video record of you and your car. If anything goes wrong, there you are."

"We can spend some time at my house, then," she said. "It's just up in the hills."

"Where?"

"Make a right at Vineland and go straight up."

He made the turn at Vineland, then let the upward slope slow his car down. "Do you have roommates or family? A real sister or somebody?"

She looked at him but didn't move her hand away from his lap. "I have a boyfriend."

"A boyfriend?" He veered to the right and stopped by the curb.

"But he's away. For, like, the last two weeks and the next three weeks. It's a work thing."

Jeff drove on up the hill, stopping to look both ways at each intersecting street. Everything seemed unnaturally quiet. He saw only a couple of cars in motion on the cross streets. The curbs were lined on both sides with cars parked so close they almost touched.

She guided him up into the neighborhood. "Turn left here, then a quick right. Now left up here. See the house with the brick front and the big garage?"

He turned into the driveway, and she stopped him. "Stay here but keep your motor running. I'm going in to open the garage."

7

IT WAS NIGHT NOW. Since his visit to Kapak's house, Joe
Carver had been taking a more aggressive attitude toward Manco
Kapak. He had come back early in the morning, driven past Kapak's house, and looked at the signs on his front lawn. They all
said PROTECTED BY DEDICATED SECURITY, and under that,
ARMED RESPONSE. He drove to the Sherman Oaks public library and signed up for half an hour of computer use.

He wrote Dedicated Security an angry letter from Kapak. He
demanded a full refund of the cost of the monitoring service for
the past six-month billing period, because the alarm system had
not detected a break-in or summoned the armed response. He
said he also intended to sue the company for the cost of the alarm
equipment in his home. He demanded that his security service be
terminated immediately and warned the company not to bother
him with other offers, but to simply send the refund check or suf-
fer consequences he did not name. Then he printed out the letter
and drove it to the post office to send it by certified mail.

Since his recent infusion of money from Kapak's credit card, Carver was able to pay in cash to sleep in hotels around the city under false names, but he only did it once. He found that day that the new clothes he had bought with Kapak's credit card helped to make him more acceptable to hotel staff and guests. Women seemed to be the ones most aware of the quality of his costume. His uncle Joe had told him when he was young that if he wanted to get people to take him at his word, he should spend the most he could on his shoes, watch, and haircut.

Early in the morning, Carver had gone to the Department of Building and Safety in the governmental complex at 6262 Van Nuys Boulevard and found the records counter on the second floor. The woman at the counter eyed his suit as she asked him, "What can I do for you, sir?"

"I wondered if I could see the blueprints for my house."

"You'll need written authorization from the licensed architect of record, and the owner, and a copy of the grant deed."

"Gee, I'm the owner, but it's an old house. I don't even know the name of the original architect."

She leaned forward and said in a conspiratorial tone, "You know, this office also has copies of all permits, with the approved building plans. Those are public and they might tell you what you want to know. If not, at least you'll have the name of the architect."

"That would be great."

"Address?"

He handed her a piece of paper with the address written on it and signed the name "M. Kapak."

"And you're the owner?"

"Yes."

"This could take a few minutes."

"Thank you."

She disappeared through an open door and returned fifteen minutes later with a file. "This is all permits, certificates of occupancy, plot plans, electrical, plumbing, mechanical. If you need the geology reports, I know where they are."

65

He smiled. "No, thank you. I just wanted the plans."

Joe Carver paid to have the papers copied and walked off with the records of Kapak's house. When he was in his car in the municipal parking structure, he examined what she had given him. The drawings submitted for approval by the inspectors were extensive and detailed. The only reasons they weren't blueprints were that they weren't blue and they were on letter-size paper.

The house was built in 1956 by an architect named Paul Bruning for a client named Ralph Thompkins, was sold to Myrna Sorley, whom Carver recognized as the actress who played Mrs. Cole in the old television show *Raising Danny Cole*. It was bought again in 1985 by Claudiu V. Kapak and his wife, Marija. Whoever Marija had been, she certainly wasn't around now. In fact, it was difficult for Carver to even imagine Kapak married, and even more difficult to imagine a woman who would have married him, even if he assumed that Kapak at that time might have weighed forty pounds less and not yet have bushy eyebrows. Carver was fairly sure he had stumbled on a first and only wife, a woman Kapak had brought with him from whatever backward country he had come from.

Carver found another permit issued shortly after Kapak bought the property. With it were plans to build a large guesthouse behind the main building. That could have been the place where Kapak had been coming from on the day Carver had visited him.

Carver put on his wig and mustache to drive to Kapak's neighborhood. He drove up and down the surrounding blocks studying every car, every house. In his left hand he held the new digital camera he had bought, steadying it on the door of the car and taking pictures without appearing to as he drove up and down the streets. He did the same for the two clubs, Siren and Temptress. Then he drove to a Long's Drugstore and used the photo machine to print the pictures, walked up Ventura Boulevard to the FedEx-Kinko's, found Kapak's block on Google Earth, and printed the best satellite picture he could get.

66

Minute by minute, Carver worked on Manco Kapak. He held the man in his mind and turned him around like a mysterious object. Carver had avoided him, but it had not worked. He had humiliated Kapak's men at the construction site, but it had no effect. He had visited Kapak and shown him that he meant no harm, but that had not worked either. Since then Carver had pulled a few tricks on him. The intended effect had been to make Kapak ask himself whether he really wanted to waste so much time and money to hunt down a man who had done him no real harm. Now it was time to take a closer look.

It was already evening, and he had made his rounds twice. Tonight all the cars parked near Kapak's house were ones he had photographed the first day. There seemed to be nobody patrolling the property, and no activity in the house. The big black Town Car with the chauffeur was not in its space in the garage.

Carver selected a parking space along the curb one street away from the back of Kapak's house. It was near enough to the apartment building on the main cross street to belong to a tenant, so nobody would be curious about it. He was more cautious now than he had been before he'd met Kapak. When he walked away from the car, he had a knife strapped to his ankle and carried his shotgun in a laundry bag. He made his way to the back of Kapak's yard, went over the wall and into the bamboo grove.

Carver found a path through the bamboo that led downward and away from the main house. It was a smaller path, not one that had been expensively laid out by the landscapers. It was more like a shortcut that animals or children used to get from the wall into the yard. He followed it down the incline all the way to the guesthouse. The guesthouse was at the center of the property, far back from the main house, which had been built as a wide obstacle that ran nearly from one side of the lot to the other, only about fifty feet from the street.

Carver made his way to the guesthouse, walked to the back of the low building so he wouldn't be seen from the main house, and began to try the doors and windows. The first few were tight and unmoving, as though they had been nailed shut. But when he reached the north side, he found a louvered window beside a sun window that jutted out from the kitchen. He touched a couple of the glass strips and found that he could rattle them. He slid his knife between one of the louvers and the aluminum frame that held it, bent it slightly, pulled out the rectangle of glass, and set it on the ground. He repeated the process with all of the louvers below it, then crawled in through the window onto the kitchen counter. He slid off the counter and went deeper into the guesthouse to be sure it was empty, then opened the kitchen door and brought his shotgun inside with him. A shotgun was reassuring. If he made a mistake, he could erase it.

In Woodland Hills, Lieutenant Nick Slosser turned the corner at his street and then turned again into his driveway. He stopped in front of the three-car garage. Mary's Volvo and the Audi that Nick Junior and Sally shared were already parked there, so he pulled into the third space. He got out of the car, walked around to the trunk, and picked up his two cases. One was the locked aluminum briefcase that held his extra pistol and magazines and some police department paperwork he had brought home. The second was his suitcase, after three days mostly filled with dirty clothes.

He stepped to his front door, used his key to open it, and went inside. He smiled, happy to catch a glimpse of his wife just cleaning up in the kitchen. Tonight and for the next three nights, the wife he would come home to would be Mary.

Slosser set his two cases down just inside the dining room, walked into the kitchen, and looked at her. She looked up and came to kiss him. "Nick. Right on time. The kids had to eat early because they're both going out. If you're ready, I'll heat ours up in the microwave."

"Sounds fine to me." He stood by while she put the first of the plates into the machine, closed the door and punched the buttons, then loaded the second plate with roast beef and spinach and potato. They took their plates into the dining room and sat next to each other on the long side of the table.

"Well?" she said. "You look pretty good. You having an okay week?"

"Not bad," he answered. "I'm managing to keep busy and healthy. I got a thing this morning that looks kind of interesting. I missed you, of course."

"There. That's what I was waiting to hear," she said. "I'm doing pretty well too. I think I managed to sell the place on Longridge. Our counteroffer is in, and the buyer's realtor didn't flinch. It could go through tomorrow."

"Wonderful. Congratulations, baby."

"No congratulations yet. You'll jinx it. Just so far, so good."

"Right. How about the kids?"

"They're on a roll too. Sally got a ninety-eight on a Chem test today, and the teacher read Nick's essay on Thoreau out loud."

"We should have them bronzed just as they are," he said.

The Slossers were talkative, and it would have struck only the most observant of eavesdroppers that Nick Slosser never said anything specific about his work. Slosser believed in self-discipline the way some people believed in God or the scientific method. It was a way of seeing. The problem with all of the petty criminals he ran into was that they had no sense of how to govern themselves. They were thirty-five- or forty-year-old men who lived the lives of teenagers, following every impulse without any acknowledgment of responsibility to the greater society, to their families, or even to themselves.

Slosser's own life had begun to thrive only after he'd learned the benefits of self-discipline. He had come home from the army and married Mary, the girlfriend he had met in college. They had bought this house in Woodland Hills that she had spotted as a bargain as soon as it had come on the market. They'd had Nick Junior and Sally within two and a half years, and Mary had kept working in real estate even after they'd come along. Nick had been so happy with his wife and family that he had married again right away.

He met Christa when he was at a police training conference in Phoenix. He was a young detective at the time, and he had found that the convention atmosphere that prevailed after hours didn't make him happy. He didn't drink. He was used to getting up early and lifting weights, and then going out for a run before the weather got too hot.

Christa happened to be staying at the same Phoenix hotel. She sold pharmaceuticals for a big drug company and had a route that took her from city to city over much of Arizona, New Mexico, a sliver of California, and Nevada, excluding Las Vegas. She was a lot like Mary, he thought. They didn't look alike. Mary was short, with curly chestnut hair, big breasts, and wide hips. Christa was tall and thin with straight blond hair that she felt was her worst feature. She would say, "Give me a minute to brush my string," or call it "this limp spaghetti." But otherwise, Christa was a lot like Mary. He loved her almost immediately. In the first hours of joyful recognition, he had an impulse to call Mary at home and tell her, "I just met this great girl." He didn't do it, because he'd lost his heart, not his brain.

His infatuation caused anxiety. His train of thought on the first day went "What a terrific woman. If I tell her I'm married, she'll lose all interest in me and go away." So he didn't tell her. That first night they met for a drink, and both ordered iced tea. Later they shared a large bottle of mineral water in his room. The second day of the conference, he skipped the meetings to go for a run among the desert rocks with her. During the walking breaks she told him all about herself—her family in Nantucket, her intense love of children. She said she wasn't a frivolous person. If he wasn't at least open to the idea of marriage and children, then they would have to end it after one night.

He was overjoyed. He loved marriage, and he knew he could

be a good husband and father, because he already was a great husband and father. They never parted during the weeklong conference. She had to make a week of sales calls by phone while lying in his bed, and he pretended to be too sick to go to any seminars.

Then the week was up. Dating required planning and care. It had to occur without disrupting Christa's regular round of sales visits. A young detective like Slosser had little control over his schedule. They managed to see one another, sometimes only for a daylight tryst in hotels along her route in Victorville, California, or Elko, Nevada. The following spring he took two weeks off, told Mary he had to give expert testimony in a trial in Massachusetts, and got married at Christa's family's church in Nantucket.

Christa's family were exactly as he'd imagined them: tall, fair New Englanders with the same long, sinewy limbs Christa had, with high cheekbones, blue eyes, and faces reddened by the sun. They were great people.

Now, as he ate his dinner, he turned to glance at Mary Slosser. He had been married to her for twenty-two years. This house was the same one she'd picked out as a young realtor. Nick junior was now eighteen, and Sally sixteen. He and Christa Slosser had been married for nineteen years. Their children, Martha, Ross, and Catherine, were eighteen, sixteen, and fourteen. He lived with them in a house in Burbank. He slept three nights a week in each house and took a night shift on the seventh night.

His life required that he be a paragon of self-discipline and consistency. His families could count on him. He had not always been present for every piano recital or championship game, but few parents were, and he always made an effort to spend time with the child whose event he'd missed, and listen to the story or see the videotape or hear the piece replayed for him alone.

He even took both families on vacations. He had a police career punctuated by long, unexplained undercover missions, and while he was undercover he couldn't be reached by phone. Now and then he would be sent on training assignments run by the FBI or the Department of Homeland Security. There were even a couple of Western Hemisphere Anti-Narcotics conferences at Cancun and Puerto Vallarta.

Slosser had been disciplined. He was always aware that he could be unmasked and destroyed if he got careless. Even a single word in the wrong place could do it. He allowed himself no vices or even luxuries, so he could support both households. He grossly understated his salary to both wives to make it easier, and he encouraged them to invest most of their own income, just in case he was caught and they had to live on their own after that. The system had worked because he had willed it to work. The well-being of the women he loved and his five perfect children depended on it.

The disaster that had been creeping toward him since the beginning was drawing very close now. He had begun trying to avoid it more than ten years ago, but he had been unable to do it. His two eldest children, Nick of the Woodland Hills family and Martha of the Burbank family, were high school seniors, and both had been accepted to expensive, competitive colleges for next fall. Nick had decided to go to the University of Pennsylvania, and Martha to Stanford. Slosser had managed to avoid their going to the same college, but only narrowly, by telling Nick that a Western student needed to broaden his background by going East, and Martha that Silicon Valley was where the future would be designed and built. Tuition, room, and board at each of these institutions was over fifty thousand dollars a year. That meant he would need to come up with a hundred thousand dollars a year, while he still had three more children to educate.

There was financial aid available, but between the federal forms and the ones supplied by the College Board, there was no way he could apply without committing perjury and unmasking himself. The forms required an incredible amount of personal and financial information, starting with the parents' Social Security numbers. False Social Security numbers, in his experience, never happened without a crime being committed, and so if the feds caught it, they would not shrug it off as a typographical error. They would begin to dig. His fraud trial would lead smoothly into his bigamy trial, which would invalidate his marriage to Christa, and then to the proceeding when Mary divorced him. Then there would be prison.

He had saved money, but if all five children went to private colleges, the tuition costs would be over a million dollars. Even if he managed to borrow that kind of money, through mortgages and the police credit union, it would only stave off the disaster for a time. And then retirement was looming ahead. When he was no longer working as a detective lieutenant, his income would shrink dramatically. But even worse, he would no longer have a plausible reason to give his wives for spending three or four nights a week away from home.

Time was tightening its grip on him. Tuition would be due at the end of the summer. The normal retirement age at the LAPD was fifty-five, and he was fifty-two. There had to be more lies, and that meant more chances to be caught. His five kids were all getting older, smarter, and more worldly. At first all he had to worry about were the two women watching him and comparing his words with what they observed. Now it was seven people.

He had been thinking about this impending disaster for years. It hadn't taken very long to realize that the only way to avoid the conflagration that would destroy him was to get more money. He had tried to save enough, tried to work extra hours and temporary part-time jobs, and invested the money he made. It was never enough, and could never be enough.

His wives and children were his share of the best the world had to offer. His job was the best he could do for the world. He was about to lose it all. And as far as he could tell, the only choice he had was to keep his family happy as long as he could. When the secret was revealed, all he could do would be to stand up straight and try to protect them as his life disintegrated around him.

8

MANCO KAPAK LISTENED to the music, always heavy on the bass and terribly loud so the girls wouldn't lose the beat in the noise of the club. Whenever they lost the rhythm, their bodies stopped moving, and they looked like marionettes—not still, but sort of hanging from invisible threads until they caught the beat again and let it animate them.

Usually he fled the music and kept his eyes off the girls after their first day on the job. The girls were only his way of ensuring that customers came. The men paid the cover charge that didn't even guarantee them a seat, let alone a table, and they were still forced to buy the minimum two watery drinks. They didn't have to tip the dancers and the waitresses, but nearly every one did, because denying a partially clothed woman anything was beyond most men's power of self-control.

There really was no need for Kapak to personally screen every dancer who worked for him. There were more beautiful young women in Los Angeles than there were in heaven. They came from everywhere in the world looking for something to do that would put them in front of people's eyes. Siren and Temptress had hundreds of applicants a year. Any of the managers could have chosen well enough.

And Kapak wasn't so much interested in operating that part of the business as he was in keeping it credible. A reasonably intelligent observer had to be able to believe that the dance club in Hollywood and the two strip clubs were the main source of his income. That was all he really needed them to accomplish.

What he was doing was taking the money he made from other enterprises and combining it with the nightly receipts from the clubs. Each night at 2:00 A.M., when the state required him to close, he and his people would go to the clubs, count the night's receipts, and prepare a bank deposit slip for the money. Added to the money that had come in from each club would be a few dollars that had come in from his short-term loan business. But the rest of the money was cash he was laundering for Manny Rogoso's drug business.

He'd had a call from Rogoso on his home phone today while he was out, and it was making him a bit uncomfortable. Rogoso had never called him there before, and it showed a new kind of recklessness. Drug dealers were a volatile, unstable bunch, and Manny Rogoso was worse than most. It seemed to Kapak that he had become more violent and crazy in the past couple of years. Kapak didn't get involved in any direct way with the world of drugs, but anybody who could read a newspaper knew that the big gangs of drug suppliers just over the border in Tijuana had been fighting among themselves and against the authorities for years. There were assassinations and kidnappings, and big gun battles every week involving dozens of men on a side. Army troops were stationed on the streets to keep order. Rogoso seemed to be taking on the mannerisms and attitudes of the big *narcotraficantes* he dealt with. Kapak liked to keep things quiet and peaceful, and, when possible, legal.

A long time ago Kapak had learned an expensive lesson. The

way the government got people they couldn't catch in the act was catching them with money they couldn't explain. When he was young he had left Romania for Hungary, and then gotten to Czechoslovakia with his wife, Marija, early in the brief summer of 1968 that ended when the Russian tanks rolled in to remove the liberal government. It had taken them until 1979 to make it to the United States. Then he had gone to work with a group who smuggled stolen cars from the upper Midwest into Mexico to sell them to Central and South Americans. The buyers were supplied with papers saying they had driven into Mexico and were simply returning home with their cars.

Kapak had started out as a driver for the car thieves, then realized that the Mexican distributor who sold the cars southward was the only irreplaceable person, and made a separate deal with him. Kapak built a second healthy business of his own based on the observation that the one car bringing his four drivers back to the United States was otherwise empty of cargo.

He never got caught for smuggling or car theft or anything else he'd done. He got caught in a tax audit. One day there was a letter from the government telling him to come to a meeting, and a few weeks later there were treasury agents with guns strapped to them tearing his house apart looking for money and evidence of secret bank accounts. He lost everything to them.

To this day, he was sure that some of the cash he had hidden in his house had probably ended up in the pockets of treasury agents. Why should government agents suddenly behave differently than they had for five thousand years just because they were in a new country? He had never counted all the money he had been stuffing behind the insulation in the attic. The agents had taken it to their office to count it and had given him a receipt to sign with a number on it. Of course he had signed. Government agents were all the same, no matter where they lived. If you didn't sign, more of them came the next time.

So he had lost all his money, his house, his cars. Going to jail for thirteen months had also lost him Marija and the children, John and Sara. Marija had used the time while he was in prison to take up with their neighbor the periodontist, and to write letters to everyone back in Hungary and Romania to tell them he was a criminal and in jail. It was accurate enough and had not startled anybody on his side of the family, but a cousin of hers had written to him to say it had been a shock to some of the people who didn't know him well.

He had been in love with Marija, a beautiful woman who had put up with quite a bit in private, but who could not stand public embarrassment. He was lucky that he wasn't deported to Hungary, or Spain, his last stop before America, or even all the way back to his birthplace, Bucharest. He probably would have been, except that the hard-line Communists in charge in those days would have made some kind of political point about the people who left home being degenerates. The American authorities didn't want that.

Since then he had paid his taxes, tried to comply with all of the small laws, and reserved his risks for the big, profitable infractions. It had worked for a long time, and he didn't miss the money he had paid for taxes, permits, licenses, and assessments. A government that left people alone most of the time was worth a lot of money.

His cell phone vibrated in his pocket, and he stepped into the back hallway outside the office to answer it. "Yes?"

"Mr. Kapak?" It was the voice of Morgan, the manager at Siren. "I thought I should let you know that one of Mr. Rogoso's people called a minute ago. They said he's coming here."

"To Siren?"

"That's what the guy said. He was conveying the message that Rogoso was on the way."

"Thanks, Morgan. He probably just wants somebody to know he's coming so they'll pay attention to him. I'll drive over and meet him."

"Should I get one of the girls to keep him distracted until you're here? Maybe give him a lap dance and so on?"

"No. Give him what he pays for and nothing else. Which of my guys is there right now?"

"Jerry Gaffney. Guzman and Corona."

"Good. Can you reach any of them?"

"Jerry's right in the office."

"Put him on."

After a bit of shuffling, Kapak heard Jerry Gaffney come on. "Mr. Kapak."

"Jerry, I want you to handle Rogoso until I get there. He's apparently coming to deliver the cash himself."

"What should I do?"

"Keep a gun on you, and maybe a second one he won't see. Meet him outside the door. Smile and be friendly, and take him right into the back office. Make him feel important, but get him out of sight so we don't have him drinking and scaring people and attracting attention."

"I'll take care of it."

"I hear Guzman and Corona are there."

"They're out in the club."

"Tell them to stick close to you. Rogoso hardly ever goes anywhere without Alvin and Chuy, and they talk to each other in Spanish. Corona and Guzman will pick it up first if what they're saying isn't good. Rogoso will give you some cash. He'll tell you how much it is, but count it. Then get him out of the club. Be friendly, but don't show any weakness. He's always looking for it."

"Are you coming?"

"I'm leaving Temptress now. I should be there in fifteen or twenty minutes. You'd better get ready for him."

"Right. See you."

Manuel Rogoso arrived at the door of Siren a few minutes later in a black four-door Maserati. The driver sat in front of the entrance for a few seconds, goading the engine into a grumble a couple of times while the three men in the car studied the building and the parking lot. Then the car glided forward and made a wide turn into a space in the middle of the lot. Two men got out of the front seat and stepped to the right rear door. They were both big men who had obviously lifted a great deal of iron to get that way. Both wore lightly tinted glasses, leather jackets, boots, and black jeans. One of them opened the door and Manuel Rogoso swung his legs out and stood.

Rogoso was only five feet seven, but he too was a body builder. The impression he gave was not of a small man: with his wide shoulders and thick limbs he seemed to be a creature designed for fighting. As the three men walked away from the car, they moved stiffly, listing a bit from side to side.

Jerry Gaffney was leaning against the front of the building smoking a cigarette a few feet from the door. As Rogoso and his men approached the door, he pushed off the wall and stepped in front of them as he flicked his cigarette away. He held out his hand, smiled, and said, "Mr. Rogoso. I'm Jerry Gaffney. Mr. Kapak asked me to welcome you to Siren."

Rogoso's eyebrows pinched together in a scowl. "Where is he?"

"He'll be here in a few minutes. He was over at Temptress when he got the call that you were coming here. Come with me, and we'll go inside where we'll be comfortable."

Jerry Gaffney stepped in and nodded to the bouncer, who stepped back to let the four men pass him. Gaffney led them along the front of the bar past the gaggle of customers three-deep waiting for drinks.

Rogoso stopped for a second. "How about getting us a drink?"

"I'll have drinks sent in, so we can hear ourselves talk."

Rogoso didn't look happy. He glanced up at the face of his driver and bodyguard, Alvin, then at Chuy and conveyed irritation, but he went with Jerry Gaffney to the hallway that led to the back room.

Gaffney stopped, reached out to detain a passing waitress, and said, "Honey, we'd like some drinks in the office, please. Gentlemen, what would you like?"

"Three zombies," Rogoso said. "With 151 rum."

"Got it," the woman said, and walked off toward the bar.

Gaffney opened the office door and the three men entered. Sitting in chairs on either side of the door were Guzman and Corona. It was not lost on Rogoso that there were now three men from each side in this one relatively small room, all of them armed.

Rogoso spoke to Guzman and Corona in Spanish. "I remember you two. If you want to make some real money you can come work for me."

Guzman said, "No, thanks. I don't want to be a drug dealer."

"Oh, I wasn't offering anything like that. You'd need some balls to deal. I just figured two matching Honduran boys could shine both my shoes alike."

Alvin and Chuy and Rogoso laughed, but Guzman and Corona stared at them, their faces unreadable. Gaffney said, "What's that all about?"

"Nothing," said Corona. "He's just telling jokes."

Rogoso seemed frustrated. "How long is this going to take?"

"I don't know," said Gaffney. "Mr. Kapak said he would be around twenty minutes."

Rogoso took off his raincoat and set it on the table along the wall. He unzipped the lining and revealed a row of pockets full of money, and began taking the stacks of cash out of it and tossing them on the table with an audible flap. When he was finished, he said, "This is eighteen thousand five hundred dollars. I don't have time for him to drive over here at ten miles an hour like an old lady."

Gaffney took the money and began counting rapidly, laying each thousand to the side as he finished counting. Alvin and Chuy, Guzman and Corona stared into each other's eyes and occasionally touched the pocket of a coat or behind their backs, the places where they had hidden their weapons.

There was a knock on the door, and Guzman backed to the door and opened it. The waitress tried to come in, but Corona stood and said, "I'll take the tray."

She looked unwilling, because she could probably see at least some of the money, and she wanted her tip. She caught sight of Rogoso and his men, and seemed to reconsider. "All right."

"Bring her in," Rogoso said.

"No, that's okay," she said, and started down the hall.

Alvin and Chuy brushed past Guzman, ran three steps, and caught up with her. They seemed to lift her by her elbows, then turned around, walked back with her, and shut the door.

Rogoso came close, smiling. "Are the zombies any good?"

"Sure. But I just deliver them. I don't make them."

He took one from the tray and held it up to her lips. "Taste it for me."

"I'm not supposed to drink when I'm working."

"Sip it or I'll think you put something in it." He pushed it against her mouth and began to pour.

The waitress looked at Gaffney for help, but he was still counting rapidly, unaware of her, so she took some in and gulped. She started to cough, and Rogoso put his hand on her back and patted it, hard. "Here. You'd better finish it and bring me another one."

Gaffney said, "You made a mistake. It's not eighteen five. It's only seventeen thousand."

Rogoso put the glass down and glared at Gaffney. "I think you're wrong."

"No, I'm not. I put each thousand in a stack on the table as I went along. You can count it for yourself. Did you forget some, leave it in the car by mistake?"

Rogoso looked at Alvin and Chuy, then saw they were staring at Guzman and Corona. While he was teasing the waitress, Guzman and Corona's guns had somehow found their way into their hands. The two men still sat where they'd been, but each of them had a gun resting on his lap.

The stillness lasted for a few seconds without anyone lowering his eyes or moving. Then Rogoso said, "I'll take a look." He released the waitress, who hurried out the door to return to the club.

He went to the table, picked up a thousand-dollar stack, riffled through it, and set it aside, then another. Next he counted the stacks. "I guess you were right. I counted wrong. Only seventeen thousand here." He shrugged. "I probably left the rest on my desk." He glanced at his watch. "Now we've got to move on. Tell Kapak I'm sorry I missed him."

"Sure," said Gaffney. "Want me to ask him to call you?"

"No," said Rogoso. "This eighteen thousand was the only business we had with him tonight."

"Seventeen thousand."

"Right." He smiled. "See you around." The three men went out the door toward the club. Gaffney and Guzman and Corona followed them to the parking lot, and then watched them drive away.

Later, when closing time had come, Manco Kapak looked at the ranks of tall stacks of bills on the counting table in the back office at Siren. He was momentarily tempted to do some skimming—just fold a few hundreds into his pocket. It would be stealing from nobody. But by now his attitude toward the Internal Revenue Service had become a superstitious dread. He put both of his hands in his pockets and watched his three men putting the money into the maroon canvas deposit bag.

When they were finished he knelt by the wall and opened the locked desk drawer where Gaffney had stored the seventeen thousand dollars in cash that had come from Rogoso's drug business. He added it to the twenty-one thousand that had come from the food, liquor, and cover charges, and the house's rental fees for private lap-dancing rooms.

Kapak put the money together, wrote in the total on the deposit slip, and handed the canvas bag to Jerry Gaffney. Corona and Guzman slowly tugged on their sport coats over their thick arms.

Tonight Kapak wanted to maintain the impression of trust. He had been around long enough to know that some people could be trusted. But he did have a precise sense of what each of his associates could understand, remember, and do. He had an approximate sense of what their financial thresholds were and tried hard not to exceed them. He could be confident that Corona and Guzman would guard his thirty-eight thousand dollars, transport it, and get it into the night deposit of the Bank of America branch, even if St. Michael and all the angels stood in the center of Ventura Boulevard swinging fiery swords to stop them. But he would never have asked Corona and Guzman to deposit five or six hundred thousand. He would not have asked Jerry Gaffney to deposit any money with his brother, Jimmy. They could never be counted on to watch each other. They were a conspiracy from birth.

He walked out with the three men and stood by the doorway to watch them get into Jerry Gaffney's car and drive off. He could see that the majority of cars still in the lot belonged to his employees. The rest belonged to young men who didn't see any need to hurry home. He could remember being young and feeling that way. Even boys who were good at arithmetic couldn't quite get themselves to believe that there would be thousands of other nights just like this one, so they could afford to stop and let the girls go home.

It didn't seem necessary to stay around here while the bouncers herded the last few customers out and the rest of the staff finished cleaning the place up. They knew enough to lock the doors. Kapak got into his black Mercedes and started the engine. As he pulled away from Siren, he saw the front door open again and the last group of customers file out. The big lighted sign high on the pole above the flat-roofed brick building went out and the door closed, but the floodlights on the parking lot would stay on until dawn. At 6:00, Harkness the day manager would be in opening things up and preparing the building for the morning deliveries: liquor, soft drinks, linens, bar napkins, food. By 9:00, they'd have the place restocked, and the cooks would start preparing for the lunch crowd. The first of the dancers would arrive around 11:00

to limber up and put on their costumes. Most of the early shift had kids they took to school in the morning. They arrived with no makeup and hair either in ponytails or under scarves, carrying cups of coffee. They left in the early afternoon, out the back door to the lot to pick up the kids. Then the sequence of evening shifts would begin again.

He drove along Vanowen Street at forty, not taking a chance that a cop would pull him over, search the trunk, find the money he was going to add to the take at Siren, and think it was his lucky day. When Kapak drove late at night, he always saw cars driven by people who appeared to be drunk, nearly all of them young men. He supposed he deserved the risk because he was one of the bar owners who made them that way.

The drinkers in their twenties who were his main customers didn't bother him. The generation now in their thirties and forties were different. They were the first Americans he hadn't liked. They drove around in their ridiculous fat SUVs with phones clapped to their ears talking about things that couldn't possibly amount to anything, and they didn't care if driving a vehicle they couldn't even steer with one hand made them kill you. When they were on foot they demanded to be first in line, to get theirs first. They sincerely believed in their own importance. The men were loud-mouthed and pushy, trying to be intimidating when they didn't get what they wanted, but most of them had never felt a serious punch or heard a shot fired. The women were self-obsessed and lazy. They were greedy for money and wanted to dress like movie stars. They neglected their children, hired immigrant women to raise them, but wanted other adults to refer to them as "moms." Seeing them grow up had been like watching a disease arrive and take over a herd of cattle. All he could do was hope that they died off before the disease spread further.

Kapak liked the young ones best — the teenagers and the ones in their twenties. For some undetectable reason, most of them were good, steady, serious people. Maybe it was because life had steadily gotten harder as they had grown up. It wasn't just the girls, either. It was inevitable in his business that the dancers were young. But he found the boys to be hard workers too. He hired young people for nearly every job that became vacant.

He drove toward Temptress. It was exactly 3.3 miles along Nordhoff Street. He loved the broad, straight boulevards of the San Fernando Valley. They were relics of the period when he had arrived in Los Angeles over thirty years ago, when people were still optimistic about the place they were building and believed it had to be planned on a grand scale. After closing time, these streets were nearly empty. If he picked the middle lane, he could sometimes drive the whole way without deviating an inch, timing the lights all the way so his foot barely touched the brake. It was what he imagined driving a train would be like.

He thought about Marija and the kids for the second time in an hour. Marija could easily have died by now. She had been only two years younger than Kapak, and he was sixty-four. The women in her family were pretty but delicate, and didn't live long. John would be thirty-eight by now, and Sara, thirty-six. It seemed impossible, but those were the numbers. Whatever they were going to be, they were by now. He hoped — but it didn't matter what he hoped. It was done. She had given herself to another man, and he had not gone to claim his children. His life had gone another way. There had been many nights when he lay in bed in his big, expensive house and wished that she could somehow have seen him — what he had accomplished, what he had. Every time he had thought about that scene, he had tried to picture her repentant and regretful, but the vision was cloudy and insubstantial. If she had really been there, she would have been bitter and contemptuous. After ten years or so, he had stopped thinking about her very often. She wasn't even a person anymore, just a word and a faint, faded picture in his memory.

He drove into the parking lot at Temptress and surveyed the cars in the lot. They were all ones he had seen here many times:

the manager Dave Skelley's green Chevy Malibu, the head bouncer Floyd Harris's blue Kia, the white Volvo that Sherri Wynn had bought a couple of years ago. Kapak felt affection for that car. Sherri needed to keep up the payments, so she'd had to become the best waitress in the place to get enough tips. He could tell there were nights when she was considering selling it so she could get the pleasure of being moody and hostile, but she hadn't yet.

He parked close to the building under the lights, took the briefcase from his trunk, and walked to the front door. He knocked, and Floyd Harris opened the door and stuck his head out to be sure there wasn't anyone lurking behind Kapak outside the range of the security camera. Floyd's face was set in the expression that kept order, but it changed as he pulled the door open and held it. "Hi, Mr. K."

"Hello, Floyd." As Kapak entered, he held his head high and his chest out and looked around him with a hawklike glare, his eyes going everywhere, as though there were things that someone was scurrying to hide from him. He strode into the bar area looking at the two bartenders cleaning up, and then into the main room, and stopped. The three busboys looked up from wiping off tables and mopping, so he nodded his head once and smiled at each of them and turned on his heel to enter the kitchen. The big industrial dishwasher was humming as it sterilized the racks of glasses. The kitchen floor man had emptied the garbage cans, steamed them, and replaced the plastic liners, and was just completing his last floor-mopping of the night.

Kapak said, "Everything looks good, guys. But take a close look before you go, because the inspectors would love to find something wrong." He always said that.

Kapak moved on. He had planned to catch a few of his employees sitting down somewhere instead of working, but he had seen nothing of the kind. He had only one more stop. He walked across the bar area between the rows of small, heavy steel tables with their chairs upside down on them and into the manager's office.

86

Dave Skelley was standing at his big, empty desk finishing the evening's count with Sherri Wynn. Skelley had opened the top of his white shirt and tossed his black uniform jacket on the couch, but Sherri's waitress uniform was cooler—a satin vest, black briefs and tights, and high-heeled shoes. Skelley looked up. "Hi, boss."

"Hi, Dave. Sherri. What sort of business did we do?"

"Nineteen thousand six hundred forty-two dollars. No fights, no breakage to speak of, no wear and tear on anybody tonight."

Sherri smiled in a way that could only be called professional. "And how are you tonight, Mr. Kapak?"

He suspected she was hoping to get something—a small raise, a bonus, a present that would take the pressure off her to come up with the car payments for a while. She would always remind him that she was there and smile a little when she talked.

Kapak said, "Who's going to make the deposit tonight?"

"Harris and I and the Russian," said Skelley.

"Is he around? I didn't see him."

"He called a few minutes ago. By now he's waiting in the lot."

"Three guys. Good," said Kapak. "And this goes to the Wells Fargo branch in Simi Valley. I'll make out the deposit slip." He set his briefcase on the desk, took out a deposit slip, read the total again from Skelley's tally sheet, added twelve thousand dollars to it, and then took the twelve thousand dollars of Rogoso's drug profits from his briefcase and added the stacks of bills to the ones on Skelley's desk. He took his briefcase and stood up to watch Skelley putting the money into the canvas deposit bag.

Kapak walked out with Skelley and watched him get into the Russian's big Toyota Sequoia with Harris the bouncer, then watched the car go out to the street. He considered getting into his own car and driving off, but instead turned around and went back to Skelley's office. Sherri was still there in her waitress costume, sitting on the desk and swinging her feet. When she saw him she slid off, looking a bit embarrassed.

"Still here, eh?" he said.

"Yeah. I didn't know if you needed anything else, so I thought I'd stay and see."

"You've been doing a good job, Sherri," he said. "The reason I came back is that I've been meaning to give you a little bonus." He reached into the bulging pocket of his sport coat and pulled out a stack of bills marked "One thousand." He had been planning to include it in the bank deposit, but for some reason he had changed his mind. He handed her the money.

"Wow, thank you," she said. She looked at the money, then at him. She cocked her head. "What do I have to do for this?"

"Nothing. At least nothing you haven't already been doing. It's been nice to have somebody around who smiles." He stepped backward, toward the door.

"I can do that," she said. She took a quick step toward him and placed a kiss on his cheek before he opened the door and went out to his car.

He sat in the car, started the engine, drove out to the edge of the parking lot where there was a little dip to the street, and stopped. He stared into the darkest spaces he could see — the shadowy alley between a warehouse and the little factory where they customized car parts, the narrow strip of weedy land where the disused railway tracks disappeared at the back of a strip of stores. Joe Carver could be out there right now, watching for his chance.

9

JEFF TURNED THE BLACK Trans Am off Ventura Boulevard into the huge lot that ran from the Vons grocery store, past the CVS pharmacy, the Gap store, and past a dozen other stores and restaurants all the way to the chain-link fence that separated it from the two-story strip mall. Even though it was late at night, there were plenty of lights. The pharmacy and the grocery store were open twenty-four hours, so there were a few other cars on that end of the lot, and Jeff pulled to a stop among them.

He got out of the car and so did Carrie. She started walking toward the lighted glass wall of the pharmacy. "Not that way." He pointed in the opposite direction. "The bank is back that way."

"I want to go through the drugstore," Carrie said. "I need a couple of things."

"Not now."

She stopped walking. "I won't be able to stop on the way back, will I?"

"Well, no, but—"

"One of the things is condoms." She stared into his eyes, watching his resolve weaken. "Maybe you've had enough pussy for one day. It's okay with me." She took a step in the direction of the bank.

He reached out and held her arm. "Maybe we could go without protection one time."

She frowned. "Just because we've done it a couple of times tonight doesn't mean I want your baby, much less anything you caught last week and don't know about yet."

"There's nothing like that. I'm monog—" He tried to gulp the last two words back in, but she raised an eyebrow.

"Sure you are. Do you even know what 'monogamous' means?"

He was desperate to save himself. "Sure. I just meant I don't sleep around. I saw you and you're just so beautiful that I couldn't resist. It was like you're the girl I was always supposed to meet but didn't until now."

She smiled and patted his cheek. "You're right. I always needed a really hot, stupid guy, but never knew it until tonight."

"Go ahead," he said. "You can go in and get what you need."

She stepped off toward the pharmacy and said, "I'm not buying condoms. If you want them, you get them."

"I thought you said—"

"I changed my mind. Now it's up to you."

Jeff followed her in the door, but she pretended to be shopping alone. He went to the aisle near the pharmacy counter at the back of the store and picked up two boxes of condoms. He couldn't go home to Lila with an opened box.

He walked up to the cash register at the front of the store. He had to wait in line behind a man paying for a prescription, then watched Carrie pay for nail polish, an emery board, and hand lotion. She walked off, still pretending she didn't know him. When he went outside, he found her waiting at the car. The man with the prescription drove away, and the lot was deserted. Jeff unlocked the trunk and they placed their purchases inside, then walked together down to the end of the parking lot, onto the strip mall where there was a pedestrian-size opening in the fence, and then to the rear of the parking structure behind the Bank of America.

They sat down to wait on the low concrete wall that enclosed the parking structure. Jeff glanced at his watch. It was 2:40. If Siren and Temptress closed at 2:00 and cleared people out on time, then it would take until around 2:45 or 3:00 to count all the money and get it ready to transport to the bank.

"It should take another fifteen, twenty minutes."

Carrie opened her purse, took out a cigarette, and lit it.

"If you see anybody, hide behind this wall and don't leave the butt here either. I saw a show on TV where they got somebody's DNA from the filter."

"There's an ashtray right there with, like, fifty or sixty butts in it. Are they going to test all of them?"

"You think Bank of America doesn't have the money?"

After an interval that indicated she was ignoring him, she put out the cigarette, then wrapped the butt in a tissue and put the tissue in her purse. That action seemed to remind her that she had a gun in there. She lifted the gun, looked down the barrel, removed the full magazine, and slid it back in. Then she handed the gun to Jeff. "Pull back that slide thing for me, will you? I don't want to break a nail, and I need to crank a bullet into the chamber or it won't work."

"You don't need a round in the chamber. We're not shooting anybody."

"Just do it, will you?" She held it out by the barrel.

He took it, chambered a round, and handed it back gingerly. "Just keep the safety on and be sure it doesn't go off."

"Thank you." She put it back in her purse, took out another cigarette, and then pushed it back into the pack. She slid off the wall, moved quietly to the side of the bank building, and flattened herself against the wall. Jeff didn't know whether she had seen someone or was just too excited to keep still.

A car pulled up and stopped by a parking space in front of the bank. Three large men got out of the car. They all wore dark suits, the kind that security people or pit bosses in casinos wore — work clothes for these men, tight-fitting and all the same. Two of the men were stocky Hispanics in their late twenties, with shaved heads and mustaches. The other was taller and less muscular, with red hair. He carried a maroon canvas bag like the one Jeff had taken from the older man a month ago, but this one was bulging as though it held more money than the last one. That was probably why there were three of them. His heartbeat began to speed up.

The two stocky, bald men turned toward the boulevard and scanned the sidewalks. When they did, Jeff could see that the backs of their necks were tattooed with some curly, unreadable writing. They backed up to flank the red-haired man as he approached the front of the bank building.

Jeff whispered in Carrie's ear, "Stay here. I'm going around to the other side." She nodded and whispered something back, so he set off around the building. He was already ten steps away from her before he realized what she'd said. It was "I'll cover you," just like in the movies. What did that even mean? He wasn't sure, and he didn't have time to guess. He had to be around the building before the three men put the canvas bag in the steel door contraption built into the wall of the bank.

Jeff reached the front corner of the building, tugged the ski mask over his head, then peeked around the building. The tall man had his arm extended, reaching for the handle of the night deposit door.

"Hold it," he called. It was just the right sound level, because they all turned their heads toward him in a single motion. They saw he had his gun in his hand aimed in their general direction.

The red-haired man stared at him with a fierce watchfulness but lowered his hand away from the night deposit. He shifted the canvas bag from his right hand to his left, to free his gun hand.

"Drop your guns and the bag and step away from them," Jeff said.

"You got to be kidding," said the red-haired man. "There are three of us and one of you."

Behind the man, Carrie's head and right arm appeared at the corner of the building. Jeff was relieved.

"Look behind you," he said.

The three men all half-turned to look, and Jeff sensed he should have said "slowly." To Carrie it must have seemed that they were going to rush her or pull all three guns at once. She fired, the men jumped, and the noise made Jeff want to clap his hands to his ears.

Carrie seemed to enjoy the shooting. She was the first to recover her composure, so she pulled the trigger three times more. The first round hit the sidewalk and ricocheted up into the shin of one of the two short, bald men and dropped him to the pavement. Her second went wide and hit the brick façade of the bank. Chips flew near the night-deposit door. The redheaded man dropped the money bag and crouched, either to pick it up or to pull out a gun, as the third shot made the other short, bald man fall down. The redheaded man, seeing that his advantage had vanished, remained still. Carrie fired two more shots, one that hit the sidewalk in front of the redhead and stung him with tiny concrete fragments, and one that bounced off the brick wall of the coffee shop on the strip mall.

When she stopped firing, Jeff ventured out from behind the bank building. "Time's up. What's it going to be?" He felt that his voice had lost some of its authority and gone up an octave, but it seemed to be audible.

The red-haired man threw the canvas bag toward him and raised both hands. The other two men lay on the ground, blood pooling between them. Jeff kept his gun on the men, picked up the canvas bag, and retreated around the corner of the bank. He ran toward the parking structure but heard running feet ahead of him. He stopped and aimed at the sound, but the shape that dashed across his vision was small and female, so he followed her.

Carrie was surprisingly quick. She stayed ahead of him as he made his way along the side wall of the parking structure. Then he passed her and ran along the back walls of the buildings on the strip mall. There had been shots — loud, repeated shots — and the only way out now was to get into the car and be gone before the cops arrived.

He stepped up onto the pavement of the strip mall, ran for the human-sized gap in the chain-link fence and onto the big black-top parking lot. The car seemed to be incredibly far away, sitting in the midst of the small group of cars in the splash of light near the grocery store and the pharmacy.

Now that Jeff was on empty asphalt and had a light ahead of him, he ran harder. He held the canvas bag cradled on his fore-arm like a football, pumping his arms and running on his toes, his head up and his strides lengthening with his momentum. As he left Carrie farther and farther behind, he ran even faster. When he was forty feet from his car, he took his keys from his pocket and pressed the remote-control key button, saw the dome light go on and the lock buttons pop up.

He flung the door open, ducked inside, started the car, then drove back the way he had run. He flicked his headlights on as he moved up on Carrie, then reached across the seat to paw the door handle down, and stopped abruptly so the door swung open be-side her. She flopped onto the seat and he accelerated so her door slammed shut.

He glanced at her to be sure she wasn't hurt. She had her knees on the floor and her elbows on the seat, and she was shaking, laughing uncontrollably.

Jeff drove to the farthest exit on the other side of the lot, pulled out to the left against the red light, and drove hard to get around the curve on Laurel Canyon to the freeway entrance past Moor-park. He swung onto the freeway heading east and accelerated, then looked at her again. "What the fuck are you laughing at?"

"It was just so amazing!" She climbed up onto her seat and fastened the seat belt. "It was the best. Thank you so, so much for taking me with you."

"You are one crazy bitch. You could have got us both killed."

"Am I? Thank you so much. This is the best night of my whole life!" She paused. "Is it? I think it is. Yes, it is!"

"Jesus."

"My heart is still pounding like crazy and it won't stop, you know?"

"Yeah." He knew what she meant. He could feel his own pulse in his chest and his neck.

"And there's blood, like, pumping its way into every part of me at once. The lights are actually brighter. Let's go back to my house. I'll give you the best sex of your life. That's a promise."

Jeff knew that Lila was going to be home from work soon, and she would want to see him waiting there for her. But through the upper part of the windshield he could see bright stars in the black sky, and as he pulled off the freeway, he opened his window to listen for sirens. There was still silence and the night smelled sweet. "I can stop in for a little while."

to the first apartment building after the Christian Science church on Whitsett, trotted along the side to the back of the building to the Dumpster, opened a plastic trash bag, and was overpowered by the fishy smell of cat food. He put the guns inside, retied the bag, and ran.

He ran back across the bridge to Ventura Boulevard, but he'd gone only a few feet on Ventura before he realized why there had been no sirens. The street in front of the bank was full of police cruisers and other official vehicles, all of them flashing bright red and blue lights. They all must have converged on the place silently from side streets, the way cops did on burglary calls.

He approached cautiously. He could see the ambulance parked in the driveway of the parking structure. There were EMTs pushing a gurney with Guzman on it. They lifted it into the back and Corona tried to jump in after it, but a cop held on to him and kept him back.

Gaffney had thought both of them were hit, not just Guzman. Corona apparently had just decided to play dead. Part of Gaffney was angry at him. Maybe if the two of them had gone after the robbers, there would have been some chance of at least seeing their car.

Gaffney considered going up to the group, but then thought better of it. As it was, it looked as though they had been here, just the two of them, trying to make the nightly deposit, unarmed. The crazy robbers had shot at them and taken the money. If there were only two of them, then there would have been nobody to get rid of any guns.

He walked to the other side of the street and went the other way. He walked a couple of blocks west and dialed his phone.

After seven rings he heard his brother Jimmy's voice. "Yeah?"

"It's me. Jerry."

"What the fuck do you want? It's after three A.M., boy."

"We got robbed making the night deposit from Siren. Guzman got shot, but that son of a bitch Corona played dead, so I had to stand up alone, dodge the bullets, and go after them. Now the cops have my car, so I need a ride home."

"Where you at?" Jerry could hear the jingle of Jimmy's belt buckle, so he knew Jerry was pulling on his pants while he held the phone under his chin.

"Just about to Ventura and Coldwater. I'm going to head north on Coldwater, so I should be just about to Riverside by the time you get your dead ass in gear."

"Right. See you." He hung up.

Jerry Gaffney punched in Manco Kapak's cell phone number, but then decided not to complete the call. He dialed Kapak's home number, rang it, and heard Spence's voice. "Mr. Kapak's residence."

"Spence. It's Jerry Gaffney."

"What's up?"

"We got ambushed at the bank—me, Guzman, and Corona. Guzman took a round in the left leg. He's in an ambulance, and Corona's with the cops."

"How did you happen to be the one not shot or arrested? Just lucky?"

"Don't pull that on me. Guzman was down, Corona was playing dead, so I took all three guns and went after the bastards alone. After that the cops arrived. If they'd found guns on those two, they'd have been in trouble."

"What do you need—a ride home?"

"No, Jimmy's got that. I want you to tell Manco what happened."

"Too busy to call? Low phone battery?"

"Jesus, I called to ask you for a favor. If you won't do it, just tell me."

"No, just savoring the peculiarity of the situation. He's not home yet, but I'll tell him what happened. How many were there?"

"Two. I suppose the one must have been Joe Carver and the other was a girl."

"A girl."

"Yes, a girl. The guy wore a ski mask. He said to give him the money. I told him he had to be kidding. But the girl was behind us. She didn't wait for the rest of the discussion, just opened up. She was crazy, probably on drugs. She didn't even do a good job of cover, just shot Guzman and stood there in the open jerking the trigger, so shots went all over the place."

"That's enough to tell Kapak for now. I'll call him." Spence hung up.

Jerry kept walking along the dark street. Coldwater was all apartment buildings from Ventura to Moorpark. As he walked, he looked into the windows that were still lighted at 3:00 A.M., wishing he were behind one of them. Even at this hour, a few cars were out, and every time he heard an engine and saw the sidewalk ahead begin to glow and pick up his walking shadow, he felt tense. It could be his brother, Jimmy, coming to end his ordeal, or one of the cop cars that must be fanning out farther and farther by now, searching for the guy and the girl.

Jerry was beginning to have an uneasy feeling about Kapak. There were certain guys who had fate on their side, and others who didn't. He had always believed that Manco Kapak had it, but now he wasn't so sure.

There were lots of times when a leader lost his luck. When he did, everybody around him was in for a rough time. Everything they tried to do was five minutes late, one man short. He and Jimmy had been working with Calvin Sturgess in the hijacking business when the universe turned its back on him. They stopped a big semi late at night in North Carolina. There had been one guy who was supposed to jump into the cab of the truck and drive it another fourteen miles to a particular stretch of the woods where it could be unloaded. Instead of getting out to let him do it, the truck driver pulled out a gun and shot him in the chest, and then ran into the woods by the side of the road.

The truck driver was out there somewhere in the dark with a

gun. The truck was stalled on the side of the highway, and none of the three able-bodied crew had any idea how to move an eighteen-wheeler anywhere. They managed to get about thirty cases of single malt Scotch out of the truck and into their cars before they needed to leave. They left at least a hundred in the truck, wrecked the springs of two cars, and had to abandon one of them outside the next town after their own driver bled out in the back seat. That night was when the Gaffneys decided to make their new start in California. Later, he heard Sturgess and the others all got caught within a month.

Jerry heard the familiar engine of his brother's six-year-old Ford, turned, and saw it pulling up. He got in and Jimmy drove him away. "We'd better get you up to Kapak's house right away, don't you think?"

"No, I don't," said Jerry. "It's after three, half the people out are cops, and I'm tired. Why should I go see him?"

"Because he expects it, and he's paying us every week whether we do anything useful or not."

"I called Spence and he agreed to tell him what happened."

Jimmy looked at Jerry, concerned. "Spence is too fucking smart to trust. If he feels like it, he could really screw you."

"He has no reason to."

"There's a good argument. Now I feel better. Jerry, when you're guarding money and it doesn't get to the bank, it wouldn't be too much of a stretch to think you took it. Kapak might be thinking that already. If Spence nods his head—"

"Haven't you maybe begun to feel the wind change a little bit?"

"What are you talking about? Who pays attention to the wind in California?"

"Not the wind out there, the one in here." He pointed to his head. "First Kapak gets himself robbed of the day's take right in front of a bank on a major street. Then we all spend a month looking for the thief. When we finally find him, he batters the shit out of two Hummers with a crane and makes us glad to get out alive.

The guy then walks into Kapak's house for a visit, and the next day Kapak is having a doctor picking bits of glass out of his privates. I haven't heard there was any damage to Joe Carver. Now there's tonight. We were carrying over thirty-eight thousand in that bag, right into an ambush. We're in a crossfire between Carver and a crazy woman."

"So the wind has changed." Jimmy shivered involuntarily. He hoped his brother hadn't seen it. To prevent it happening again, he closed his window and fiddled with the car's air conditioning. The truth was that he held his brother at an uneasy distance, because Jerry was the one who had inherited their mother's gift—if it was a gift. Seeing flashes of the future had never revealed anything to her but more drudgery and disappointment, but she was unerringly accurate. Jimmy said, "All of those things are annoying, but I don't know if it's a big deal."

"If you had been there tonight watching that madwoman fire a gun into Guzman, I think it might seem bigger to you."

"I suppose I would, but that wouldn't mean it was. Seeing somebody shot gives most people the creeps."

"It's more than that. It's the sense of doom that builds up when a man's lost it. This is deeper than logic. Human beings have spent ten thousand years working to deny and ignore and get rid of their pure animal instincts and senses. But we still haven't entirely defeated ourselves, because we can't help sensing things about people."

Jimmy was feeling more and more uneasy. "Like what?"

"Things that mean danger. Look at Stacy Grenier. She's the most beautiful girl anybody has seen working in a strip club in a hundred years. Every inch of her isn't just perfect, it starts at perfect and extends beyond there to be something your poor imagination couldn't invent or wish for, so every time you look at her, you're amazed all over again."

"She's a goddess."

"But nobody wants to go out with her."

"I went out with her."

"You did? Why?"

"What you just said. She's beautiful. And she seemed to be nice. It didn't work out so well. I took her to a nice dinner at that restaurant down by the concert hall. Everybody was really dressed, the women were attractive, but nothing like her, of course. So afterward, we're standing outside waiting for the valet to bring my car around. She lights a cigarette, takes a couple of puffs, and then leans really close to me — and puts it out on my hand."

"There," said Jerry. "That's what I mean. People take one look at her — or maybe two — and they sense that something bad is going on behind the eyes."

"After the burn, she behaved normal for a while."

"So why isn't she my sister-in-law?"

"After we slept together, she got abnormal again. She told me she had AIDS and that she only had sex with men to get back at all of us for being such assholes. She wanted to kill all of us."

"Was it true?"

"Her having AIDS? No. The hating and killing? I think so."

"As anybody other than you can tell after a minute. But forget her. Manco Kapak is the one I'm thinking about. He's beginning to give off a bad vibe."

"You think so?"

Jerry nodded. "I do. In fact, I think you're right about going to his house to tell him everything in person. I think we better take a close look at him and see whether we ought to do something about what we see."

"We can't leave, or it would convince him you stole his money yourself. By the way, do you still have a gun?"

"No. I threw mine away with Guzman's and Corona's. You got one?"

"No. I was asleep, and you asked me for a ride. I don't sleep with a gun."

"Maybe you ought to start. Maybe we both ought to."

11

JORGE GUZMAN WAS in pain. He had endured nearly two hours of being wheeled from one place to another in the hospital—x-rays, a surgical area that seemed to be on the same floor as the emergency room where they doped him and cut and stitched, and then a regular patient room.

Corona had been with him for part of the time because the first doctor had the idea that Guzman couldn't speak English, but one of the nurses was Mexican and could tell Corona wasn't translating, just talking. She made Corona leave.

The cops had arrived while he was still lying in the little examining room bleeding. They asked him the same questions Corona told him he'd already answered. Then one of the cops took a picture of his face and another one of the tattoo on his neck, and left.

The final move was to bring him up here to the third floor. Now he had a real bed, not as hard or narrow as the thing he'd been on. But he felt his left shin all the time, throbbing with each heartbeat. He couldn't look at it because it was in a hard bandage like a cast, but it felt as though the bone was exposed. A nurse walked past his door and he shouted, "Hey!"

She took one step into the doorway. "Use the button. You'll wake everybody up."

"Hey, you know, I'm not some kind of gangster. I'm a victim."

She shrugged. "When one of you shoots, the other one is a victim. Next time you'll get to shoot, and he'll be a victim."

"I'm hurting bad."

"Sure. You got shot."

"Can't you get me something?"

She stepped in, looked at his chart, and allowed a bit of compassion to show in her eyes. "I'll get you something." She hurried out.

He wasn't sure if he had dozed off for a few seconds waiting for her or if she had shot him up, but he woke, and it wasn't as bad. But then the door filled with the shape of a man. Guzman said in Spanish, "Hey, my friend. Thanks for coming back."

An unfamiliar voice said in flat, toneless English, "I'm not your friend." He stepped close to Guzman's bed. "I'm Lieutenant Slosser, LAPD."

"Did you catch them?"

"Not yet, but we're looking. You and I need to talk a little."

"I talked to the cops a while ago, and so did my friend. I told them everything, just the way it happened."

"Yeah. You did fine. Nobody is saying you lied about it. But they didn't ask you about what happened to your guns, and where the keys are for the car you took to the bank."

"I don't own any guns."

"I see. And the car?"

"They must have took my keys after I went down. They were thieves."

"So there wasn't a third guy with you who took the guns and split so the police wouldn't find them?"

"No."

Slosser was tall, with square shoulders and thick arms, so his body looked younger than his face. One of his big hands touched Guzman's temple and Guzman reflexively pulled away and turned his head, so his tattoo was visible. Slosser nodded to himself. "You and Corona are the last of the Mohicans, huh?"

"Mohicans?"

"The last two from your gang. The Sombres."

"We are."

"I remember that. It must be what? Eighteen years? I was working up in Devonshire then, but that night they called every division for extra men. So I've seen a lot of tattoos like that one, but until tonight, not on anybody alive."

"I got shot, and I don't feel so good. Is there some reason why you want to talk about eighteen years ago?"

"Maybe. It explains what your doctor gave us for a preliminary report — that you have three other bullet scars."

"He didn't look hard enough. I got four."

"I'll correct the record in case we have to identify your body sometime." He stared into Guzman's eyes. "How long have you worked for Manco Kapak?"

"About five years."

"What's your job?"

"Security. We check IDs, protect the talent, bounce the guys that get crazy, take money to the bank, that kind of stuff."

"And you drove the car to the bank. That means Corona carried the money, right?"

"I'm finding it hard to remember. I think he had it this time and I drove, but that could have been last time. You should ask him. He didn't get shot or anything. He'll remember."

Slosser didn't move his eyes from Guzman. "When I found out who you are, it occurred to me that maybe I could talk to you. Of all the people involved in this, you and Corona have the best reason to know that getting into a war is a bad idea. If you know who did this to you tonight, I'd like you to tell me. I'll do my best to protect you and your friends from whatever is happening. It won't be you and a dozen friends against a hundred this time. It will be nine thousand cops against them."

"Why would you give a shit about Manco Kapak?"

"I don't care about him in particular. But I'm a cop, and I can't have people getting shot down on my streets. I don't want him dead or you dead, and I don't want either of you shooting anybody else. So if you know anything else about the robbery, I'd like to hear it."

"I told you everything I know. The thing happened so fast I was down before I saw anything much. It was a guy with a mask over his head and a gun. Then behind us there's this girl, and she opened up and hit me with her first round, and I was out of it—didn't see, didn't care. The pain just took me."

"Okay," Slosser said. "I'm leaving my card on the table. If something comes back, call me."

"Joe Carver."

"What?"

"Joe Carver," said Guzman.

"Who is he?"

"Just a name. There's a rumor that he was the one who robbed Manco. People say he's the one. I don't know if you can find him. But what happened tonight was almost the same, except for the girl. She's new."

Slosser patted Guzman's shoulder. "You did the right thing to tell me. I'll see what we've got on him, and what we can find out. You talked to me, so I'll talk to you. I'll let you know what I get. Don't be in a hurry to get out of the hospital for now. There's nothing out there that you'd like, and nothing you can do."

Slosser walked out of the room. After a few minutes, Guzman began to wonder whether he had imagined him. Guzman was so tired, so completely used up by this long, hard day, that he knew he was slipping in and out of consciousness. He remembered now that the nurse had returned and added something to his IV. Or maybe that was a dream too.

106

He floated in the bright morning sunlight to the chicken yard outside his little house in the village in Guatemala. He could feel the sun's warmth on his back and his neck as he squatted in the dust tossing feed to the chickens. Their copper bodies and emerald green tail feathers and bright scarlet combs glowed in the morning light. The world seemed so beautiful, and so safe.

12

JOE CARVER FELT good in Kapak's guesthouse, his sense of well-being dramatically improved by the fact that he was resting in comfort unseen within two hundred feet of his enemies. He wasn't completely sold on the style that Manco Kapak had chosen — or more likely, just paid a decorator for — to furnish his guesthouse. There was a heaviness to it. The sideboards, dressers, and night-stands all had a curvy line to them, so they were narrow at the top, then widened like bass fiddles, and then went inward again near the bottom to sprout legs. Carver couldn't name the style, but his prime suspects were the French. Being in a room with that furni-ture was like standing in a crowd of elderly, fat women dressed in pastels. But he liked the bones of the house — the solidity of the doors and placement of the windows.

The guesthouse had a very good shower in the bathroom, and the linen closets had a generous supply of soft, thick tow-els. If he had wanted to cook, the kitchen would have been more than adequate for a dinner party. The living room had a big set of bookcases, but Kapak's decorator had chosen to fill them with questionable Chinese pottery to play off the view of the bamboo through the windows on this side. Like all the pottery he'd seen in southern California, it was stuck in place by a gummy puttylike substance intended to hold it still in an earthquake.

Carver had studied everything closely. There was no dust on the pottery, no scent of unwanted moisture in the shower that might cause mildew. At some point during the week, the place must be visited by a serious cleaning service, so he wouldn't be able to really move in and live here. He would have to sleep somewhere safer. This could only be a forward observation post he could use to watch his enemies.

This evening, he had lain down in his clothes and dozed off on the big couch in the den. Now he was lying on the couch slowly returning to full consciousness. Suddenly, he was surprised by the sound of an engine. He opened the shutter to see a moving glow of headlights on the far side of the house. He watched two more sets shoot into the sky as the cars came up the driveway, then lower as they reached flat pavement.

He moved quietly through the living room and out to the yard. He assumed that Kapak came home late every night from his clubs. But something more must be going on tonight. He walked up toward the main house along the narrow path through the bamboo grove.

He emerged from the bamboo and stepped quietly through the tropical garden to the side of the house, trying to listen for voices but not hearing anything through the closed doors and windows. He kept moving until he was beyond the edge of the tropical garden, where he could see in the large back window.

Kapak walked across the room, his hair curly black and wild tonight. It looked as though he had been tearing at it. He went to the bar, poured himself three fingers of vodka, drank some too fast, coughed, and put the glass down on the bar. When he called, "Spence!" it was loud enough for Carver to hear through the glass.

The man who came in from another room was thin and seemed to be about three inches taller than Kapak, but still shorter than the big Russian, Voinovich, who arrived after him. Spence was wearing his sport coat open, so Carver could see the butt of a pistol protruding from the inner pocket. Kapak shouted, "Everybody get in here." Men began to walk into the room.

Carver started to move toward the next, unlit window. He hurried to the French doors outside the living room, used his knife to flip the latch upward, and opened it a half-inch so he could hear.

"All right," Kapak said. "So, Jerry. You got there and the guy in the ski mask asked for the bag. Did he seem to know who you were?"

"I couldn't tell. He just said to give him the bag. I said there were three of us and one of him. He said 'Look behind you,' and I did. It's this girl, and she opens up and hits Guzman. Corona goes down next. I toss the guy the bag, and the two of them run around their corner of the building. Nobody said names or anything."

Kapak said, "You know what was in that bag. I lost thirty-eight thousand to these two tonight. In two tries they got about sixty-one thousand just for waiting around the bank at three in the morning."

"You think this was the same guy—Joe Carver?"

The sound of his own name jolted Carver. What did they think he'd done? It sounded as though somebody had taken more of Kapak's money.

"It could be," said Kapak. "Or somebody else who just read in the paper that people are stupid enough to make deposits at three A.M. How do I know? But I'm going to put a stop to these night deposits beginning now. Each night we'll put all the cash in a safe until daytime. We'll leave that son of a bitch waiting at the night deposit forever."

Spence said, "I think you shouldn't stop sending people to the bank. You can stop sending money with them."

"There's an idea," said Kapak. "We've got one guy thinking, anyway. We've got to keep trying to get this robber, but we don't have to keep losing money."

"I'd like to be on that one," Jerry Gaffney said. "All we'd have to do is have a couple of guys in that parking structure before he gets there, and then send in the guys with the fake deposit."

"But you wouldn't want to be the one holding the bag again, would you?" Spence asked.

"No, I think it's your turn."

Kapak waved his hand in front of his face as though to clear away the irrelevant chatter. "Who was it in the first place who said Joe Carver was the one who robbed me?"

Jimmy Gaffney said, "We were all asking around for two, three weeks, and two different girls mentioned him. They said he had arrived in L.A. about a month before, didn't say much about where he came from, and he was in the habit of spending a lot of cash. They said he might be the one. Nobody said anybody else might be."

"Who are the girls?"

"Just regular girls we met. One is named Sandy Belknap, and we met her in a club. The other is Sonia Rivers. We found her in line waiting to get into a concert at the Roxy."

"So you don't really know either of them."

"No. We were just asking around, giving out cards. Jerry and I said we were private detectives working for the bank. We took their names and numbers."

"I can't believe you two sometimes," said Voinovich.

"You can find them again?"

"Sure," said Jerry Gaffney.

"Good. I want an update on Carver. Have they heard from him or seen him since the last time? Find out where he is and what he's doing. If you need it, take a thousand each from the jar on the bookcase and take them out to dinner and all that."

"We'll get on it."

"Tomorrow morning."

"Morning?"

"I meant when you wake up. Go get some sleep."

Jerry and Jimmy Gaffney stopped at the big urn on the shelf in the hallway. Jimmy reached in and brought his hand out with some money. He counted it as they walked outside and closed the door.

Voinovich said, "Do you think he robbed himself?"

Kapak shook his head. "I could believe he did it. But Guzman wouldn't let himself be shot in the leg for a third of thirty-eight grand. That's not even thirteen thousand bucks. The hospital bill just for tonight should top that."

"I guess that's right. So what do you want me to do?"

"Tonight we'll let the cops try to solve this for us. Corona is still hanging around the hospital to keep Guzman company. Give him a call tomorrow and we'll get him to tell us what he thinks happened in the robbery."

"Okay."

"Good. See you tomorrow."

Voinovich turned and went toward the door. As he passed out of the living room to the entry, he ducked his head to get through the doorway.

The only ones left now were Kapak and Spence. "Tomorrow you and I will make an arrangement with one of the armored car companies."

"Maybe they'll have some kind of deal to lease safes for Siren and Temptress that they open and close, so we're not responsible."

"I don't think so," said Kapak. "I don't want a bunch of strangers to have the combination. There's a pretty good safe in Siren. We can use that for now."

"Whatever you want to do about money, it shouldn't involve any of us carrying it around in cash. That's primitive."

"Cash is an opportunity, and it's a problem. We just have to handle it right. Do you have the videotapes from the clubs?"

"They're in the screening room. You want to see them now?"

"I'll take a look at them before I go to sleep. The bar receipts at Temptress looked a little light tonight. I want to see if the camera picked anything up." He walked to the small room off the same hall as the master bedroom, inserted the first tape labeled "Temptress," and then sat down on a big leather chair before he pressed the remote control and started the video. He pressed Fast Forward so the people on the big high-definition screen went back and forth in quick, jerky movements. At one point he slowed the action to normal speed and watched carefully. "Spence!"

When Spence came in, he was rewinding the tape. "See something?"

"Watch this." He started the tape again, and the camera showed the second assistant bartender, a man named Coulton. "He's making a drink. Gives it to the customer, takes the money. Rings it up. The register drawer opens. He makes change, hands it over. All okay so far. Now see the waitress? While he's still at the register, she comes in with the money from a round of drinks. He takes her money, gives her change, and she goes away. He never closed the register after the first sale, so hers didn't get rung up. He's still got it in his hand. He closes the register and his hand goes to his pocket. You only have to do that a couple of times a night, and you've got an extra hundred bucks."

"Is that all he does?"

"No. Near closing time, he's running tabs for some of the guys at the bar. When a couple of them get up and go, they leave a big bill to cover it. He picks up two or three at a time and rings up one. It's enough for me."

"You want me to have the manager do it?"

"No. We'll do it ourselves, Voinovich and me."

"Voinovich?"

"Yeah. When this guy goes, I don't want him thinking about talking to the cops about anything he saw, heard, or imagined, or to say something to the people who are still there. I want him to take a look at Voinovich and be really glad that he gets to leave at all."

"Want to look at more tapes?"

"No, I'm going to bed. Lock the doors and windows and turn on the alarm."

Joe Carver closed the door he had opened and moved onto the path through the secluded garden. He would have to drive to a motel he'd found a couple of miles from here to think before he slept. Now that he knew what his enemies were doing, it was time to work out how to get rid of them.

13

CARRIE SAT in the lotus position on the bed and Jeff lay across from her with the pile of money dumped on the sheet between them. The rules at the start were that one of them would pick out a hundred-dollar bill and say "A hundred," and the other would take a hundred-dollar bill and put it at his side. But now they had gone through most of the big bills, and they were down to saying "Twenty" or "Ten," or even "Ten ones."

Carrie yawned. "You know what?"

"What?"

"I'm really getting tired of this." She looked at the pile of money beside her, stood, and began stuffing it into a dresser drawer.

"What's going on?"

"I've got enough. You can have the rest."

He raised his eyebrows. "Are you sure?"

"Sure. I didn't come out tonight to make money. I wanted to have fun. More money than this doesn't make it more fun."

"All right." He stuffed the rest of the money back into the bag while she closed the dresser drawer and went into the bathroom. As soon as the door closed, he reached under the covers where he had been hiding bills since they had started, and stuffed those into the bag too.

She came out of the bathroom, crawled onto the bed, and kissed him. "It's really late."

"Yeah," he said. "I guess it is. Almost morning."

"This is the best date I ever had in my life. So much happened—we pulled a robbery and I shot some guys. We picked up some money, had sex about a million times."

"Really primo sex too."

"Yeah." She kissed him again. "I had a great night. It's time for you to go home. I put my cell phone number in your wallet, and I want you to call me. Don't send me flowers or call on the regular telephone, and don't just show up, ever."

"I get it," he said. He began dressing, then picked up the canvas bag. "Sure you don't want more money?"

"That's sweet, Jeff. But I'm sure you noticed I'm a chick. I hardly ever have to pay for things except clothes and gas. I sometimes do, but I don't have to. And this is what you do for a living. You were just nice enough to let me come along."

He tied his shoes and walked up the hall to the living room with Carrie following. When he reached the front door, he turned. "Good night, Carrie."

"Don't forget to call me." She smiled.

"I won't." He went down the steps and along the driveway to the garage, where he had hidden the Trans Am. The door opened in front of him, and he looked back and saw her face at the window. He started the Trans Am, let it coast down the driveway, and turned it down the steep incline toward the flatland. He turned twice before he switched on his headlights, and coasted the rest of the way down the hill onto Vineland. He made it across Ventura Boulevard on a green light, then accelerated along Vineland toward Lila's apartment.

10

JERRY GAFFNEY SNATCHED Guzman's gun from the ground and then yanked Corona's out of his open hand and ran after the man and woman. When he reached the back of the parking structure behind the bank, he was sure that what they'd done was slide down the embankment above the Los Angeles River, then take a run along the paved path above the concrete riverbed and come up at the Whitsett Avenue Bridge. From there they could disappear across the river into the tennis courts, or maybe just disappear into the neighborhood. Their car would be parked somewhere on that side.

He ran the quarter mile to the bridge without seeing another human being. He was far from the bank and carrying three guns. By now the cops and maybe an ambulance would be on the way. Soon he would hear the sirens.

Gaffney hated having to get rid of three perfectly good guns that hadn't even been fired, but there wasn't much choice. He ran

It took only eighteen minutes before Jeff pulled up at the apartment building and glided into the extra carport at the back. He was tempted to put the canvas bag under the seat or in the trunk of the car, but he thought better of it. He had known a pair of addicts for a while when he was just out of high school, and one night he had watched them going from car to car late at night outside some big apartment buildings. Jeff didn't think he could sleep if he lay there thinking about some junkies opening his car for the radio and finding all that cash.

He put his gun into the money bag, took it with him, and walked up the first-floor hall to Lila's apartment. He found his key, unlocked the door, opened it slowly and carefully, slipped inside, and closed it again.

He saw Eldon lift his head from the sagging couch in the living room and stare at him. Eldon seldom showed surprise. Jeff knew Eldon had heard and smelled him long before he reached the door. He suspected that Eldon's nose had told him all the essentials of his evening too, certainly the car, the gun, the paper money, the sex — especially that — and probably the fact that Jeff had felt about ten seconds of intense fear while Carrie was blasting away and bullets were bouncing all over the place. He felt a second of relief that Eldon couldn't talk. Eldon put his head down again.

Jeff stepped out of his shoes, walked slowly to Lila's bedroom door, and tested the knob. It was locked again. He moved toward the couch and saw Eldon was lying on a folded blanket and pillow from Lila's bed. The money bag fit easily and invisibly behind the couch.

He took off his jeans and his shirt, went to the end of the couch, and crawled in behind Eldon. Keeping Eldon on the outer side of the cushion made Jeff less likely to be the one who got pushed off. It took a moment or two for dog and man to adjust their positions to share the space. They both had their heads on the pillow together, and the blanket was draped mostly on Jeff's body. After a few minutes in which Jeff contemplated the nature of luck, opportunity, and the variety and sheer fullness of the world, he and Eldon dozed off.

He was awakened an astonishingly short time later when the sun, which belonged outside, fell on his upper body to light up his eyelids like lampshades and heat his face until it felt like cooked meat when he touched it. He sat up so he was out of the shaft of light. Then he seemed to recall that he had heard Eldon moving around in the kitchen, crunching food and lapping up water. He squinted and blinked, and saw Eldon waiting by the door of the apartment. Eldon gave a high-pitched whine, and Jeff swung his legs off the couch and stood.

He put on his pants, shirt, and shoes. He took Eldon's leash off the hook by the door, attached the end to Eldon's collar, checked his pocket to be sure he had his key, and then let Eldon lead him out.

They walked in the direction of the carports along the rear of the building, and Jeff made sure his car was all right while Eldon went from one clump of weeds to another, dousing each with urine, then moving on to sniff the breeze that reached him through the high chain-link fence. Jeff let Eldon lead him away from the building and around the block, then stop in the alley to defecate. Jeff had forgotten to take a plastic bag from Lila's supply by the door, but there was a McDonald's bag and an empty drink cup that worked well enough to clean up, and he tossed them into the first garbage can he passed.

As he walked up the alley behind Eldon, he reviewed the night's events. He opened his wallet and searched for a card or slip of paper with Carrie's number on it, but didn't find one. How could he have lost it? What if he had lost it inside the apartment?

He stopped, opened the wallet again, and looked through the card section and the currency section. He stuck his fingertips into every compartment, searching for something small enough to have been missed, but found nothing. He put his wallet away and thought about Carrie. She was absolutely crazy, and the first few things she had told him after he met her were lies. But he thought of her last night in bed and took out his wallet again. He took out the thin sheaf of bills he had left home with last night and began to leaf through it. He saw the one right away. He had not started the night with any one-dollar bills. She must have put this one in his wallet while he was in the bathroom or something. Written on the bill was "Melisande Carr" and an 818 telephone number. "Carr, Carrie," he whispered to himself. It wasn't a nickname. She had still been lying to him about her name when he'd left.

He wondered why a woman would be so completely open — bringing him into her house, having sex with him in every position he could think of for hours without showing a second's shyness or hesitation, let him see her shoot people in a robbery — and then be reluctant to let him know something as public as her name. And what kind of name was Melisande? She was one strange girl. He felt a little afraid of her, but he overwhelmed the feeling by flooding his brain with some recent views of her body stored in his short-term memory. Within a few seconds, he had forgotten his vulnerability and her nerve-racking unpredictability. There was only the attraction.

Jeff needed to forget about her entirely for the moment. She wasn't expecting to hear from him for many hours. It was barely dawn. He followed Eldon on his rounds of his neighborhood. He tied Eldon's leash to a table leg outside the Coffee Bean and Tea Leaf to buy two big cups of coffee. He was grateful to them for not making customers say "Tall" for small and "Grande" for medium. For years it had amazed him that nobody else seemed to see what fascist crap that was.

He put the cups in the little molded paper tray, went out to get Eldon, and followed him back to the apartment. At the apartment door, he set the tray on the floor, unlocked the door, and bent to scoop it inside, propping the door open for Eldon with his foot.

As he raised his head, he caught sight of Lila's bedroom door. It was open now and she was standing beside her bed, pulling the covers up. He looked and straightened, and his eyes focused on her. She was wearing the lingerie he had laid out on the bed before he left last night—the black thigh-high stockings, the bra, and nothing in between. She seemed to sense only now that he was back, and looking at her. She looked straight into Jeff's eyes.

In that instant the cold, half-lidded eyes conveyed everything—that she had come home from work at closing time, seen his little display of her underclothes made into an effigy and the money he was leaving her for their expenses. She had put on the outfit, thinking it was his cute way of seducing her. And then she had waited for him to arrive. She had probably explained his absence by thinking that he was out adding a surprise, that he would return shortly with champagne, flowers, things that were romantic because they were completely inappropriate for 2:00 A.M. Maybe because he had shown her he had some money she had thought of jewelry too—not a ring, which would be too premature to be anything but embarrassing, because she'd have to turn it down and then sleep with him anyway. But he could have been saving something nice, a pendant or bracelet to show that he had some kind of hope for a long-term relationship and the intention to let her know.

She stood still for another couple of seconds to permit him to see clearly that she had done her part, had put the wisps of nylon and silk on and waited for him in the bedroom. She had fallen asleep wearing them. Then she turned, walked into the bathroom, closed the door firmly, and clicked the lock.

He was sweating as he stepped to the door. "Good morning, baby," he called through the door. "Eldon and I brought you some coffee." He barely breathed. The toilet flushed. The shower handle squeaked and the water hissed. He turned away and walked back into the living room. This was bad. He had just arranged the clothes into an effigy of her for fun, without imagining that she would think it was a message, a request.

He had caught only a brief look at her standing still by the bed, but in her eyes were blame, rage, hurt, humiliation. He could actually feel them with her. He was horrified in another way by the blurred connection between playful intention and disastrous consequence.

He tried some different ways to explain. He could say, "I wasn't demanding anything of you. I wasn't thinking that way." No, that wasn't good. He could show her the money in the canvas bag and say, "I was out of money, so I had to drive to my bank to withdraw some cash. You have to do that in person. It's my bank in . . . where? Arizona? Five hours each way, driving through the night, over the speed limit each way. When I got here you had fallen asleep." He pushed the couch out a bit and snatched up the canvas bag.

The weight of it made him remember the gun was still inside. He took out the weapon and put it into the pocket of his suitcase in the closet, set the bag of money on the couch, and zipped it closed, then began to practice his story silently in front of the full-length mirror on the closet door.

He had trouble with his lines, because her afterimage was still floating in his vision. She was tall and long-legged, but her thighs and hips were slightly large for her body, so he'd always thought of them as imperfections. But just now she had been as appealing as anyone he had ever seen. He had the sense of an opportunity forever lost.

Lila came out of the bathroom wearing a big towel around her and another on her head. He studied her for any hint of eroticism, some slight, subtle, and maybe tentative signal. He took a step toward her and she recoiled, her eyes fixed on his arms and hands, not his face. He stepped back and she went to the closet for jeans and a top, to her dresser for everything else, and back to the bathroom and locked the door.

In a very short time, she came out dressed, with her long blond hair hanging in wet corkscrew curls. She said, "Are you waiting to say something to me?"

"I'm sorry I got home so late. I was —"

"It doesn't matter what you were doing."

"But it does matter."

"Not to me." She brushed past him and sat down at the kitchen table, her forearms folded and resting on the Formica surface. He lifted one of the cups of coffee out of the tray and set it in front of her, but it was invisible to her.

He sat across from her, lifted the other cup of coffee, and set her an example by sipping it. "It's still warm."

"It's time to talk."

"You're right. I was thinking this morning when I took Eldon out for his walk that we have to talk."

"You don't. I do."

He sat up straight in his chair, his shoulders held in a stiff cringe, nearly high enough to touch his ears.

"This relationship has gone on a few weeks now."

"Oh, shit."

"What?"

"When you say 'relationship' like that it sounds like you're thinking about breaking up with me."

Her head tilted a little and she looked at his face for a second, then away. "When we were in high school, we didn't even date. When you turned up again after all this time, I was interested — flattered, curious maybe. And maybe since high school, I'd seen such a pack of assholes that you seemed better than you used to, like something I'd overlooked at the time. But since you've been in the apartment, you've ended up on the couch more times than in the bed."

"I didn't want to."

"We just don't actually like each other enough for this."

"That's not true," he said. "We like each other a lot. We're still just getting used to each other, learning to communicate."

"I'm not going to let you tell me what my feelings are."

"This is about last night, isn't it? I had been feeling bad because you had been paying for everything all the time—rent, food, and so on."

"Thanks for leaving me the money. We can call it even."

He continued. "So I went to the bank to get some."

"I said thanks."

"Not that money. I needed to get more."

"At two A.M.?"

"Of course not. I left right after you went to work, and I expected to be back before you got off work."

"Jesus, Jeff. You expect me to buy that. What bank is open that late?"

"Bank of America. In Las Vegas. The banks are open later there, because they don't want to keep anybody from doing anything on impulse. I needed the money because I wanted to do something for you. I'd been traveling around a lot, and so that account was the only one I had left open."

"If you say so. What held you up?"

"Traffic. You wouldn't believe it, but there was this accident right as I was coming out of the low desert up into the high desert on Route 15. You should have seen it. A big rig jackknifed across the road and ruptured its tank, so the actual road was on fire. It was around a bend, so all these cars didn't see it at first, and there were five or six cars banged up, most of them before the fire started. I was stuck with everybody else just sitting still for hours. I sat there thinking about you, and feeling sorry that I hadn't brought my phone with me." He smiled with a vulnerability he had never shown her before. "I kept picturing you. You know, in those—"

"I'll bet," she interrupted. "I found your phone a few minutes after I got home. I called you and your duffel bag rang. Are you sure you didn't leave it here so I wouldn't ask you questions?"

"Of course I'm sure."

"You have any proof you were in Las Vegas?"

"I . . . Oh, I know." He got up, went to the closet, and pulled out the canvas bag. He held it in front of his chest and pointed at the words printed on it. "Bank. Of. America." He tipped it a bit so she could see a bit of the green currency.

"Great. I'm so glad you're not destitute. This makes me feel so much better."

Jeff smiled uncomfortably. He wasn't quite sure that he had succeeded in meeting all of her objections, and he was wondering whether making up with Lila was what he really wanted most, and why he was trying so hard. But then he remembered the sight of her when he had walked in this morning. "Feel better?"

"I do. I'd like you to get your stuff together and leave."

"Can I just say something?" He went on before she could answer. "I can see that my getting in that traffic jam in the desert last night was the most important moment of my life. All the time while I was sitting in my car, with the night lit up by those big gasoline flames, all dark orange with a blue ghost flickering around the edges, I was feeling desperate about getting home here to you. I was picturing you wearing what you actually were, with that beautiful, smooth white skin and golden hair and the face of an angel. And I realized right at that moment that I was seeing what I wanted most in the world. It was like that guy in the Bible, riding his donkey and he gets like a stroke, knocked right off his donkey onto the road. He gets up, and he's a new guy."

"Saul. When he gets up he changes his name to Paul."

"You sure?"

"Yes, I am. Didn't you go to Sunday School?"

"But that was just what happened to me. I got forced to sit still in the desert for a while and think about who I'd been and who I wanted to be. I realized that I may never be rich or famous or even an okay guy. But I would be happy forever if I only had you. After I sized up the situation, I had to turn off the radio to save the battery. I just stared into those flames and I saw you. It felt like a vision. I could see you in exactly the same clothes you had put on, waiting for me."

"That's not exactly magic. You laid them out for me."

"I got so concerned about you and what you must be feeling."

"What was I feeling?"

"At first I pictured you all ready and fresh and pretty, waiting for me, in a mood for romance." He saw her eyes and kept talking rapidly. "And then, I thought that you would know it wasn't like me to be thoughtless and leave you waiting, so you would get worried. I pictured you looking scared and sad, maybe calling the police and the hospitals. I actually got out of my car and walked up the line of cars that were blocked, asking people if I could use their phones. But it was dark and I was just this darker shadow coming out of the night. I might be a psycho or something. They all rolled up their windows. Some wouldn't even look at me. Finally one of the highway patrol cops that were keeping people away from the fire ran up and yelled at me to get back in my car."

"After they cleared the road, why didn't you stop at a pay phone and call?"

"When we finally moved, everybody needed gas, so they lined up at all the exits I passed for the next hour. I figured I'd be better off if I kept going until I found one that wasn't packed. Now that everybody's got a cell phone, there are hardly any pay phones, and I might have to wait forever. I knew you were probably feeling even worse by then, and a call from me telling you I was stuck in the desert wouldn't help. I had to talk to you in person."

"What did I feel then?"

"You were feeling taken for granted and humiliated. You felt that I had kind of talked you into doing something you were shy about to show me you really wanted me, and then wasn't even serious about it. That I got you to commit yourself, like saying out loud that you loved me, and then didn't say anything back. You felt betrayed."

She looked at him with new respect. "That's just about right."

Bull's-eye. He stood. He would come around the table to take her hand. He planned to touch it tenderly. Maybe he could even get her to start over and have the experience they'd missed. He was a little tired, but it was all right. They had a lot of hours before she had to go to work. He reached for her hand.

She snatched it back from the table, out of reach. "Don't."

"But doesn't what happened mean anything?"

"To you. Not to me. Get your stuff, put it in your car, and go."

"After all these years apart, and then finally coming together all the way out here in California, you want to dump me for being late coming home one night?"

"No, Jeff," she said. "I'm dumping you because you're not the one. That's what every single girl is on the lookout for—the one who was meant for her. You're not him. Having you here only wastes my time and diverts my attention."

"How can you know that?"

"I've known you since ninth grade, remember? I just let you live with me for over a month, with benefits. Believe me, if you were the one, I'd be aware of it by now. You're not the one for me, so don't let the door hit you in the ass on your way out."

"I won't argue," he said. "I suppose you've found another candidate for the audition."

She shook her head. "I don't have to tell you anything about my future except that you're not in it." She got up and he made a half-hearted grab for her, hoping to give her a hug that might soften her a little, but she was fast on her feet and strong from two years of carrying a tray of drinks through a crowd of drunken men.

She was in the closet, had all his clothes on hangers off the pole and hanging on the hook on the door, and then went back for more. She swept his underwear and socks off the closet shelf and into his open suitcase, tossed his shoes in on top, then went into the bathroom to scoop up his toothbrush, hairbrush, and deodorant, and tossed them into the mix.

"Wow," he said. "What's the hurry?"

"I asked you to go. I explained why. Then I listened politely to your full load of bullshit. I have no more patience."

126

He was angry now. He moved toward her and started to step over his suitcase so what he had to say would be said eye to eye.

"Eldon!" It was a tone Jeff hadn't heard before. "Him!"

A second transformation took place. Eldon was off the couch and standing five feet from him with his ears back and his inch-long fangs bared. His throat emitted a low growl that seemed to presage something awful.

"Whoa, Eldon," Jeff said quietly. "We're buddies." He reached out toward Eldon's head to pat it, but the dog snapped his jaws like an alligator and snarled as he took a step forward. Jeff was on one foot, lost his balance, and stepped in the center of his clothes in the open suitcase.

"Sit, Eldon." The dog sat, but now he looked to Jeff as though the idea of sinking his teeth into him had not entirely left his mind.

Jeff put the canvas money bag in his suitcase beside his right foot, stepped out of the suitcase away from Eldon, closed and latched it, and retreated toward the door. He was careful to keep the suitcase between him and the dog. "Okay."

"Take your cell phone. It's on the bookcase. But leave the key."

He picked the cell phone off the shelf, fiddled with his key chain to get the apartment key off, held it up between his thumb and forefinger, and set it on the bookcase. He opened the door, stepped into the empty space, and said, "A month from now, when you're sorry, just remember I tried to get you to listen." His hands were full, so he walked off and left the door open.

Lila stood perfectly still, heard the receding footsteps, and then the outer door open and close. She closed and locked her apartment door, but wasn't completely relaxed until she heard the big engine of the black Trans Am revving unnecessarily for a moment, then roaring off to propel Jefferson Davis Falkins into somebody else's life.

14

KAPAK WAS in his bathroom shaving when he saw Spence appear in the mirror. "Apparently someone has been using a company credit card to steal money."

Kapak's eyes widened, then narrowed again. "How much?"

"The bank said the balance was over the hundred thousand mark when they cut the credit line, but they don't know how much of the balance was legit. There was a cash advance of forty thousand, another twenty in American Express gift cards, some clothes, and a lot of jewelry—mostly diamond rings and watches and things."

"Why didn't they tell me before this?" He set his razor on the marble shelf above the sink and wiped the shaving cream off his face with a towel.

"They called the number they had, which was the house phone, throughout business hours and into the early evening. They also called your cell phone but couldn't get through. They said they left messages."

Kapak stepped past him into the bedroom, went to the table by his bed, picked up his phone, and looked at the display. The phone was turned off. He remembered turning it off when he went to the police station. But how could he have been carrying it around for the rest of the day without even looking at it? He pushed the power button and the screen lit up. "Twelve missed messages. How much of the hundred grand am I on the hook for?"

"Probably not much. There's a federal law that limits your liability to something like fifty bucks."

"Five zero? I only eat fifty bucks of this?"

"I'm pretty sure."

"Can you call them back and check?" He was taking the cards out of his wallet.

"No problem. First, could you look to see if you still have the credit card? That was the first thing they asked."

"I don't have it." He thought for a few seconds. "Joe Carver. He was here alone waiting for me when I came back from my shower in the guesthouse."

Spence nodded. "I'll use the phone in the kitchen to talk to the credit card people." A few minutes later he reappeared, and Kapak looked closely at him for the first time. His hair was still slightly wet, his face had a close shave. The white shirt he was wearing had just been unpackaged and his body heat had not quite erased the creases. He always seemed to be around, but he always seemed to be rested, showered, and shaved. No matter how hot it was, he was cool as a snake.

Kapak said, "I think we've got to look at a few things from a different angle."

"What things?"

"Let's start with Joe Carver. I think he's not just some defenseless guy we mistakenly blamed for robbing me. I think he's something much worse. When he came here yesterday morning, I was in the shower in the guesthouse. That's when he must have taken my credit card. But if you think about what he wanted, it gives you a better idea of who he is. He came here in person because he wanted to show me his face and prove to me that he hadn't robbed me. And it might have been true. The guy who robbed me wore a ski mask."

"So?"

"He knows what the world is like. It's a hard place with lots of spots to trip and get hurt. So he steals my credit card before he even talks to me. He knows that just showing me his face might not work. Maybe he's even smart enough to know it can't work, that I can't let it be noised around that I'm looking for him, and then let him go. And within minutes of leaving this house, he's already taking steps to get back at me."

"Steps? He seems to be attacking from every direction at once."

"Yeah. I'm getting to the point where I don't want to answer the phone. But now I'm starting to get the feel of this guy. I don't think he's just trying to rob me. I think I pissed him off. I think when he came here, part of what he was doing was warning me. I think now he's trying to ruin me, maybe even kill me."

"Maybe the Gaffneys will pick up something from the girls who accused him in the first place."

"If they do, I want you to be the one who gets it first. In the meantime, I'd like you to see what you can find out."

"When do you want me to start?"

"Now."

"All right." Spence turned and walked back to the rear of the house to the maid's room off the pantry. He kept extra clothes and a few other belongings there, and sometimes slept there.

Kapak watched him go and felt a bit better. He had come upon Spence a few years ago as a customer in Siren. He would come in a couple of nights a week, sit by himself, do some very slow drinking, and watch the dancers.

It went on for at least three weeks before one of the managers pointed him out to Kapak. He had assigned a waitress to keep an eye on him while she worked, and try to figure out whether he was from the liquor license board or the FBI or the local police. Kapak had to protect his clubs. Nearly every day there were couriers coming in with cash that needed to be deposited in bank accounts and then returned in the form of checks from the Kapak Enterprises Corporation. If there was a man coming in alone night after night who seemed to be intelligent and who never seemed to drink too much or let his eyes linger too long on the dancers, he had to be identified and cleared.

The waitress reported to the manager that the man said his name was Richard Cane. One of the other waitresses served him during the daylight lull and reported that he had a mild Southern accent. Kapak's English was nearly perfect after thirty years in the country, but he wasn't capable of placing regional accents unless they were extreme. And he doubted that the waitress could have heard Spence so clearly, even during the day, unless the music was turned off.

He kept coming, spoke politely, bought enough drinks to keep the waitresses happy, and drank few enough of them to keep the bouncers happy. The problem was that to the manager and to Kapak, he seemed to be the ideal cop.

A moment of clarity finally came, as Kapak had assumed it would. A man walked in the door while Spence was at his table. The way Ray the manager described it, Spence was like a hunting dog in point. He didn't make a move, just became abnormally still and looked at the man.

Once the new man stepped inside, his attention inevitably shifted away from the crowd around him to the girl working the brass pole on the nearest stage. He was drawn inward, walking closer to her until it happened. Spence came for him. One moment Spence was at his table, and the next he was about eight feet from the man and moving toward him. The man caught motion in the corner of his eye, looked, and saw him.

The new man was tall, and he was wearing a pair of cowboy boots that made him look taller. But the second his eyes focused on Spence's face, he began to shrink down to a crouch and back up. Neither man made any attempt to speak. There was no threat or explanation, just motion, as though the two had both known exactly what they would do if they ever met. Spence advanced, and the new man did his best to get out and away.

The man got out ahead of Spence and sprinted for a car parked at the far end of the lot. Ray made it outside with the two doormen, thinking he was about to see a fight. Instead he saw Spence step out, watch the man leap into his car and drive off, then get into his own car and drive after him.

There was nothing in the newspapers the next day that might be a mention of what had happened. There wasn't anything all week. It took about two weeks before the report appeared. A man's body had been found in a parked car in the hills above Tujunga. It had been driven about a hundred yards up a narrow, winding dirt road that led onto a parcel of undeveloped land rarely visited by a real estate agent working for the company that owned it. The agent who found the car could see that the victim had been shot once through the forehead.

Spence had not returned to Siren. But now Manco Kapak's curiosity had been stimulated. He and the manager studied the security tapes from the cameras mounted outside the building. Eventually he found a tape of Spence getting out of his car in the parking lot, brought it up to full magnification, and read the license number. Kapak went to the mini-mall where one of his minor businesses, Money Today, had its office. The company granted short-term loans that came due on the borrower's next payday. He asked his clerk to run a skip-trace based on the license number. After a half hour, he had the name Richard Spence and an address.

Kapak took both Gaffney brothers with him to Spence's apartment. He knocked on the door, and when Spence opened it, he asked if he could come in and talk. He made sure Spence saw the others before he and Spence went inside and closed the door. He told Spence that he knew he had killed the man in the abandoned car.

Spence didn't argue with him or seem concerned. He said simply, "I can put you down and get out of here before your men know what happened." He paused. "I also know that you've got bagmen coming into your clubs every day with money that you mix in with your receipts."

Kapak said, "You're smart and observant. I hope you're not going to leave town."

"I haven't decided."

"You want a job?"

"Not if it's killing people for you."

"No," Kapak said. "I've never wanted anybody killed and don't now. But if you work with me, you're my friend and brother. If an enemy comes for one of us, we do what's necessary."

That was the beginning of an understanding between them that had held for six years. Kapak had kept Spence close to him whenever he went to the clubs or other businesses. Spence was not a bodyguard, but a brother-in-arms, and sometimes a surrogate. Kapak trusted in Spence's strength and courage because he had killed at least one enemy. Half of their unspoken understanding was that Spence would be able to kill if the need arose. The other half was that Kapak would never ask him to do anything but choose Kapak's life over an enemy's when the time came.

Kapak sat in his living room and looked out the French doors into the tranquil, fern-shaded garden outside. Was this the time and the enemy? Having an understanding with Spence was like carrying a hand grenade. He had to be sure, because he wasn't going to get to use it twice.

15

JIMMY GAFFNEY HAD TO DRIVE in the morning traffic, because his brother, Jerry, still had not gone to pick up his car from the police impound lot. Jerry was anticipating a time-consuming and irritating interview before the police let him have his car.

Jerry stared out the window at the steep slopes to the right and left above the road. The thick foliage seemed to grow in the shadowy, cool canyon wherever it wasn't lopped off. It would have overrun the road in two weeks if it weren't for the twenty-four-hour traffic. Everything in southern California seemed to grow instantly when there was water and to turn brown in a day when there wasn't.

Jimmy steered the curves on Laurel Canyon like an unskilled race car driver. "This is bear country," he said.

"This?" said Jerry. "You're crazy."

"I'm not. It was in the paper that one of the very best places in the whole country to hunt grizzlies was Laurel Canyon."

"Could you be more full of shit? There isn't one grizzly bear in the whole state at this moment."

"I said 'was.' I don't mean now, you idiot. They said this was around 1860 or so. This canyon, right where we are, was full of bears. You can sort of feel where they must have been — right on those shady spots along the sides of the hills. Right up where you cross Mulholland there's a place where water just seeps out of the hillside and trickles across the road. That would probably be the spring that fed the stream in dry weather."

"Jesus, Jimmy. These are bears that got shot a hundred and fifty years ago."

"Places are what they are. Just because some people came and shot all the bears and changed the canyon into an unofficial freeway doesn't make it any less bear country."

They came out of the shade of the canyon into the bright glare of Sunset and headed west toward the clubs where they had met the two girls who knew Joe Carver. "Keep your eyes open," said Jerry. "We're getting into the part of town where Carver used to go — Carver country. We could easily stumble on the bastard and end this whole problem. He won't be wearing a mask today."

"We'd be better off if he was wearing one."

"What?"

"Well, neither of us has really seen Carver."

"I saw him from a distance the night he was chucking two-ton Hummers at us with a crane."

"You wouldn't recognize him, though."

"Yeah. So?"

"I was just thinking. A mask makes you stand out. So at the bank, Carver must have known everybody there would know it was him. The mask says, 'I'm Joe Carver and I'm robbing you.' So why wear a mask at all?"

"How the hell do I know what that deranged shitweasel might have been thinking when he went out to pull an armed robbery?

He was with this madwoman who opened fire on us. Maybe he didn't want her to see his face. Ever think of that?"

"Jerry, we've both met a lot of peculiar girls over the years. Did you ever meet any who would go anywhere with a man without ever seeing his face?"

"I don't know. There are girls who will talk to somebody online and then agree to meet him someplace without seeing him first. What about them?"

"Think he met her online and said, 'I love long walks by the beach, candlelit dinners, and discharging firearms at Jerry Gaffney's fat Irish ass'?"

"This isn't about me," Jerry said. "It's about Manco Kapak. Carver has it stuck in his head that Kapak is his enemy, and he's concentrating on getting him in every way possible."

"I don't know. It just seems to me that it doesn't make sense that this guy in the mask is Carver. He let Kapak see his face when he broke in, and that was to prove he wasn't the one who robbed him the first time. Why wear a mask now?"

"Jimmy, by now you must have guessed that I can't explain to you how this guy's fucked-up mind works. He just does what he does."

"That's your excuse for not wanting to look at things too closely."

"It doesn't matter if it is or it's something else. We've got a really simple thing here. We work for a guy, and he wants us to find out whether those girls know anything new about Carver. We find them and ask what they know. We're not getting paid to persuade our boss that what he asked for isn't what he wants. We're getting paid to do what he asked, even if it's pointless, like moving bricks from one pile to another and back."

"This isn't moving bricks. It's killing a guy. I think it would be smart to figure out if he's really the right guy. Otherwise, we take on a lot of risk and might have to go out all over again and kill somebody else."

Jerry shrugged. "That's what we do. And if we have to do it twice, he'll have to keep us on the payroll that much longer."

"There's the club up there. That's where we found her."

"I don't think she'll be there this time of day. It's not even noon. But pull over anyway, and I'll go check it out." Jimmy glided to the curb and Jerry jumped out and trotted to the front door of the club. Jimmy sat for a few minutes, staring at the club and reflecting on how bad a building painted black looked on a bright summer morning.

Jerry came out and got into the passenger seat. "Not there, of course. I know she works in a car place during the day. It's not far from here."

Jimmy pulled away from the curb into traffic. "What does she do in a car place?"

"Sells cars."

"Yeah? What kind?"

"Toyotas, mostly."

"She know a lot about cars?"

"I don't know. I suppose she probably has to know something. I mean, people ask questions before they shell out for anything as big as a car. If you don't know the answers, they'll go to another lot."

"So where are we going?"

"I'm checking it out." He fiddled with his iPhone, poking the screen with his finger, turning it and tweaking it to enlarge the display, and staring at it intently. "Got it on the map. Her Toyota place is down La Cienega not more than ten minutes south of here." He held the phone up to show Jimmy. "See that red dot?"

"Get that out of my face. I'm trying to drive." But he couldn't help glancing at it. "There are dozens of red dots on that map."

Jerry pulled it back and studied it. "But only one is her red dot. Turn and go west on Santa Monica Boulevard, left on La Cienega, and keep going until we're there."

They inched along in traffic for twenty minutes before they

freed themselves from the congestion. They were driving through the sudden range of strangely shaped hills south of the city that sprouted oil wells, and then in the flatlands that must have been swamp before the airport was put in. The businesses by the road were all big—plazas, carpet warehouses, car lots. Then they reached the Toyota dealership.

Jimmy swung his car into the entrance, found the visitors' parking lot, and parked. They got out and walked toward the showrooms. When they were only halfway there, a trim man in his thirties wearing the pants from a dark suit and a white shirt and red tie blocked their way. "Hello, gentlemen. What can I show you today?"

"Not sure," Jerry said. He glanced at his brother, then at the long aisles of shiny new automobiles in twenty shapes and sizes and a dozen colors. "You've got a lot of cars."

Jimmy said, "Is this the lot where Sandy Belknap works?"

"Sandy . . . Belknap?" He looked as though he were trying to make out the shape of a distant object in a dense fog. The Gaffney brothers silently agreed that the man was a terrible salesman, that Sandy Belknap did work there, but that he really wasn't interested in letting her get a sale he wanted.

Jerry stepped into the space in front of the man's eyes. "Yeah. You know. Twenty-five, about five feet five with long blond hair, the only woman car salesman on this lot, and probably one of three you've ever met?"

The man's body took a step backward without his volition, and his mouth began to smile, but not his eyes. "Oh, I know who you mean. Let me see if she's here this afternoon. Maybe she'll be free to help us find the right deal for you."

As soon as he had enough room, he turned and began to walk quickly toward the showroom.

Jimmy said, "I don't think you had to scare the shit out of him."

"He's going to get her. He isn't standing here wasting our time and making us crazy with his pitch for a car we don't want."

"I don't want to look like a pair of thugs. We should look like regular, sane people, and see if we can get to talk to Sandy."

"Look what he found." Jerry nodded in the direction of the showroom door.

Sandy wore a blue summer dress with straps that left her smooth, tanned shoulders bare, and as she came closer they could see a pair of blue stud earrings with small sapphires that made her eyes look bluer. She seemed to have recognized them through the big showroom window, so when she reached them she gave each of them a quick hug and an air-kiss. "Hi, guys." She looked at Jimmy. "It's Jeremy, right? And you're—"

"I'm Jimmy and he's Jerry."

"Close. How have you been?"

It was clear to the Gaffney brothers that their first meeting with her was not coming out of her prodigious memory as clearly as she wished. "We're fine," said Jimmy. He stepped closer to her, shouldering Jerry out of the way, and took her arm gently. "I'm a little nervous about maybe wasting your time, because I'm not sure whether a Toyota is what I want."

She looked up at him and gave her professional smile. "Don't worry, Jimmy. No pressure. I'm only here to show you what we have and answer questions. Of course, I think that once you see what we've got, you'll be tempted. I get a lot of sales from people who are just looking."

"At you?" Jerry said.

She expertly smothered a sarcastic retort that was in her head. "Thank you, Jerry, but I really do mean the cars." Jimmy was the one who had said he was shopping, so she never really diverted her attention from his eyes. "What sort of car are you thinking about?"

"I'm not really sure of a model. I want something that will be kind of cool, but not, you know, ridiculous."

"You're not an SUV guy, are you?"

"No. I hate driving those big-ass things."

She feigned a chill of delight. "I'm so glad we got that out of the way." She wasn't, because the profit margins were highest on SUVs. "So you really do mean cool. I know what you're after — something sleek and sexy. Come on and I'll show you something that ought to fit."

She led them to a low, streamlined, dark blue car with a front end that swept upward almost from the pavement back in a single curve over the roof and down to the road behind. Under the rear bumper were four chrome tailpipes, and a big silver *L* in a circle on the grille.

"What is this?"

"It's a Lexus IS F. It's got a five-liter, eight-cylinder engine that packs four hundred horsepower. See? Four doors, a very nice interior. It turns out only fifteen hundred RPMs at sixty."

He looked troubled. "I don't know."

Sandy put her arm around Jimmy. "Just tell me you think it's as beautiful as I do."

"I do," he said. "What's it like to drive?"

"Have you got a few minutes to find out?"

He gazed at the blue car and her blue eyes and said, "Yeah. I'll make time."

"I'll get the keys."

The brothers watched her walk back to the showroom. Jerry said, "I'd like to give *her* a test ride," loudly enough so Jimmy was afraid she might have heard. She disappeared into an office off the showroom floor for a couple of seconds and then reappeared. The brothers watched her all the way as though she were walking a tightrope. She handed Jimmy the keys and then opened the back door.

"No," Jimmy said. "Jerry will sit in the back. He makes me nervous."

They got into the car and Jimmy started the engine, then very tentatively pulled forward a few feet.

She said, "If you go out La Cienega toward the airport, you can get on the freeway." She watched him pull the car off the lot and accelerate.

Jimmy said, "You know, I've been meaning to talk to you."

"Yes. You know, I really appreciate that I only met you socially one time, and you remembered me when it was time to look for a car."

"Not that. It was about something else."

"Gee, I'm sorry, Jimmy, but I'm dating somebody pretty steadily right now."

"He can forget that if you can," Jerry said from disturbingly close to the back of her head.

She considered turning around in her seat to give him a glare, but she had begun to sense that there was something wrong with the Gaffney brothers, and it might not be to her advantage to make her discomfort overt.

"It wasn't that," Jimmy said. "Last time I saw you, we talked about a guy named Joe Carver. I wondered if you had seen him since then."

"Who was he, again?"

"I asked you if you or your friends had noticed any guy who was suddenly throwing around a lot of cash in the Hollywood clubs, probably somebody who hadn't been in town long. You said it was Joe Carver."

"Oh, yeah. We talked about other things too, but I remember."

"Have you seen him around since then?"

"You know, I saw him about three times right after that, but then he disappeared."

Jimmy turned up the entrance ramp to the freeway and accelerated so quickly that she was pinned in her seat for a moment. When the car's speed leveled off, she recovered her focus. "Feel that power?"

"Pretty good," said Jimmy. "I like the way it feels, the way it steers."

"It's like a sports car with guts, and it still has terrific comfort and a good ride. I can tell you that if you drive up in this, a woman is going to be persuaded from the beginning that you're somebody to pay attention to. And it costs less than a Jag sedan or a Mercedes. She won't know that, of course. Practically nobody has one of these yet."

Jerry reached over the seat. "I'd like you to take a look at this."

She looked warily at his hand. In it was a small black wallet that had a gold police badge and beside it a laminated ID card with Jerry's picture and the words "Detective Sergeant Allan Reid."

"I thought your name was Jerry."

Jimmy's irritated voice said to Jerry, "Is that necessary?"

"I think it is."

Sandy said, "I take it you're not really looking for a car."

"No, ma'am. We're looking for an armed robber. And anybody who might be helping him or concealing his whereabouts."

"It's a shame you wasted your time with me, then. I don't know anything about that. Can you take me back to the lot, please? I need to sell some cars."

"I'm afraid we need to talk with you about this today," said Jerry. "Since this apparently isn't a comfortable place for you to talk, we'll do this at the station." He said to Jimmy, "Detective Foley, can you aim this thing for the Parker Center?" He leaned back in his seat, and she could see a shoulder holster with a gun.

"Oh my God," Sandy said. "There's no reason to arrest me. I swear I haven't seen him since about four weeks ago at that club."

Jerry said, "This isn't an arrest—at least not yet. You're part of an important undercover investigation. We need to know where this man is, Miss Belknap. As of last night, it became a matter of life and death."

"Life and death?"

Jimmy became Detective Foley. His voice was deep and terse. "One of the victims was shot last night. The one who pulled the trigger wasn't Joe Carver. It was a companion."

"What kind of companion?" She thought she knew.

"A young woman," Jerry said. He stared at her, his eyes narrowing. "How tall are you?"

"I'm five-five." She looked as though she were in danger of fainting. "Why?"

"I was just trying to eliminate you."

"I'm not the one. I never robbed a bank. I never would. And besides, I was working yesterday from nine in the morning until well after the banks closed—around nine at night."

"Where did you go then?"

"Home to change, and then out to a club. It was Wash, in Hollywood."

"Anybody see you there?"

"I don't know. Sure. There were hundreds of people."

"Anybody who will remember?"

"I was with my boyfriend."

Jerry took a pen and a small address book from his pocket, and pretended to write. "Boyfriend. That's convenient. What's your boyfriend's name?"

"Paul Herrenberg."

"Address?"

"Nineteen eighty-five North Vermont, Apartment Three."

"What time did you get home last night?"

"I . . . uh, don't remember the exact hour. It was pretty late." There was a thin glow of sweat beginning to appear on her forehead and upper lip.

Jerry read her face. "Did you really go home, or did you go to his house?"

"His house," she said.

"Miss Belknap—"

"I was thinking it's the same thing, really. Either you're out or you're home, and we were home. It's like my home too, anyway."

"Why is that?"

She saw what was happening, but she couldn't stop being defensive. "I don't know. He's my boyfriend. We were in Hollywood.

143

It was easier to go right up Vermont instead of driving all the way down here."

"You sleep there often, don't you?"

"Well, we're practically engaged."

"When's the wedding?"

"We don't know yet."

"Has he asked you?"

"Not yet."

"So you're not almost engaged. You just go to this man's house to sleep with him."

"He's my boyfriend. It's not as if—"

"Was he your boyfriend when we interviewed you the first time?"

"Well, no. I guess not."

"That was less than a month ago."

"What? Is there a timetable for these things?"

"That's what I was wondering. Isn't there?"

"Why are you being mean to me?"

Jerry studied her with detachment. "I'm sorry if this makes you uncomfortable, Miss Belknap. But there are questions that need to be answered. If you'd like, when we get to the station we can have other detectives interview you."

"No," she said. "No. That's not necessary. I don't need to go there. I wasn't involved in a robbery and don't know anything about one. A month ago you asked me if anybody new was throwing cash around, and I gave you the name of one guy like that, and then forgot about the whole thing."

"You tipped us off to Joe Carver."

"I wasn't saying he was a robber. I don't know him, really, and I haven't laid eyes on him since. There might be ten thousand guys like him in L.A., and any one of them could be—"

"You named Joe Carver, and we've had it confirmed by other sources. Out of all those ten thousand guys, you picked the right one. Coincidence? Lucky guess?"

"Of course it is. Now please, take me back to the lot. My boss will be getting upset." She was very sorry she had told them to get on the freeway. They were moving along at seventy-five, and she had the sensation that they were taking her farther and farther from safety.

"Let's be honest and open with each other, Miss Belknap. We have a repeat armed robbery suspect who struck again last night, and left a victim shot. He's stepped over the line. From now on anybody who comes into contact with him is in immediate danger. He's got to be hunted down fast. You're our best link to him. If you were us, what would you be saying? What would you ask Sandy Belknap to do?"

"Oh, no," she said. "That's not fair."

"What isn't fair?"

"You can't expect me to be the bait for you to catch Joe Carver."

"There's an evil man out there who robs people. He's going to kill his next victim. And here you are, our best witness. Aren't you inclined to help?"

"I already did, and that's what got me here."

"When he kills somebody this week, how will you feel?"

"As though it's none of my business."

"It is your business, more than anybody else's."

"Didn't I say I can't do what you want? Wasn't that me?"

Jerry Gaffney sighed wearily and looked at Jimmy in the rearview mirror. "You want to tell her?"

Jimmy said, "I guess I should." He turned to Sandy. "The reason people decide to become a snitch or wear a wire is usually to get a lighter sentence themselves. Or sometimes if they give us somebody, they're not charged at all."

"A wire? Oh my God!"

"Don't worry. We're not asking you to do that."

"But you're implying that if I don't help you, I'll be charged with bank robbery."

"Well, not only that. It was the woman who actually shot the victim. And unfortunately banks are insured by the FDIC. There's no parole and no time off for good behavior with federal felonies. You'd be in prison until menopause is a dim memory."

Sandy Belknap was trying to manage her face, to keep it calm and at least minimally smooth, but it kept betraying her. Her lower lip was beginning to quiver, her forehead wrinkling badly before she noticed it, and then her eyes began to overflow with tears. "What do I have to do?"

"We need a way of putting our hands on Joe Carver," said Jimmy. "You need to devise a plan to do that. We'll protect you and help you carry out your plan, and then we'll take Carver away."

"I don't know how to do this." She had her face in her hands this time, crying.

Jerry rolled his eyes at Jimmy in the mirror. "I'll tell you where I'd start. First I'd tell everybody I know that I had a thing for Joe Carver—that I only met him a couple of times, but couldn't stop thinking about him. I'd be especially sure to tell your girlfriends who go to clubs. Make it a real story—that it's the craziest thing, but you've been dreaming about him and you really need to see him in real life, if only to get him out of your mind."

"But what if he doesn't remember me? Or if my wanting to see him isn't good enough?"

"Think of something else."

"But I don't know anything about him."

Jimmy looked sad. "I know you think my partner has been mean to you, and that he's a heartless jerk. The truth is that he's been the one to go to bat for you the most. He and I have a theory that you had nothing to do with this, but it's just a theory. Our boss, the lieutenant, thinks you suckered us the first time we met you, and that you're guilty. He sent us to arrest you. It was my partner who fought hardest to give you a chance."

She half-turned and reached up to the seat back to put her hand on Jimmy's forearm. "Thank you so much."

"I'm not eager to put another innocent woman in prison."

Her mind seemed to be dodging in different directions. "What about Paul?"

"Who's Paul?"

"My boyfriend. Can I tell him what's up, so when I say I have a crush on Joe Carver, he'll know I don't mean it?"

Jimmy said, "If anything goes wrong, if somebody blows the story and you don't attract Carver, then there are people who will say you had your chance to cooperate, but didn't. Then you've got to think about what happens if Carver—a killer in the making—shows up at your apartment and sees you've got a boyfriend with you. What does he do? Does he get jealous? Does he decide you must have been lying about being interested in him, so you must have set him up?"

"I don't know."

"Then maybe you ought to make sure your boyfriend's out of the way until this is over and Carver is locked up."

She nodded. "I'll just explain it to him."

"I'm afraid we'll have to ask you not to let anybody in on this. It's an undercover operation to get a shooter off the street. Telling anyone is a crime in itself. The lieutenant would put you away in a second and keep you locked up without bail until no officer could be put in jeopardy."

Jimmy said, "My brother—my brother officer will be the one to stick close to you until this is all over and we've got Carver."

"Oh, thank you," she said. "I just couldn't face this alone."

"It's the job. Let's get this car back to the lot," Jerry said. "I'd like to have you ask your boss for a few days off. You'll tell your boyfriend you've got to take a couple of weeks to think about your relationship and where it goes from here. You might mention the word 'commitment.' That will make him take a bit of time off himself. We'll want to start getting in touch with your girlfriends today and begin making arrangements for the party you're throwing for Joe Carver."

16

JEFFERSON DAVIS FALKINS SAT in his favorite seat in the diner and ate an early lunch while he used his cell phone to call Carrie's cell number. Each time he called he heard, "Your call has been transferred to the message center." He had plenty of time to think, but didn't want it. He had known Lila since they were in the ninth grade together at Louis Agassiz Central High School in Waldorf, Indiana. Or he had at least seen her and learned her name. It was true that they'd never had much use for each other at the time. She was chubby for a while, he seemed to remember, and then suddenly became tall and thin. He had pushed her into his peripheral vision for the four years of high school. She was over there to the left someplace doing something he didn't bother to quite see, or maybe she was a hundred feet down the hall beyond the girl he was actually looking at.

A few months ago, he had conceived the idea that it might be time to move to Los Angeles and called an acquaintance to find out whether he had any high school classmates living there. The person he called was Heather Fields. She had been in his home-room, the *F* through *H* room, and they had gotten to know each other fairly well. She had been one of those girls who acted as a kind of talent scout to direct boys' attention to appropriate girls. There had always been a hint of the traitor about her, an implication that she had, at least conditionally, decided to be on the boys' side. Being a girl, she knew other girls' secrets — what they had done, and with whom, and what they might be willing to do again. She would suggest a girl, and say far too much about her, in order to interest the right boy. She spoke plainly to boys and was a favorite for that reason. Heather had a great deal of power among the girls, because she was a kind of attention broker. It wasn't until years later that Jeff realized she was not a special person who was essentially sexless and therefore abnormally wise. She was just a girl who wanted that attention for herself, but never got it.

When Jeff called her, she told him that she'd heard Lila Porter was living in Los Angeles and she knew how to get her phone number. In return, Jeff gave her the phone number of his own apartment in Tucson, which he was about to vacate. He said he'd call with his new number when he got settled, but he never did.

He had called Lila, said he was going to be in Los Angeles, and wondered if she would have dinner with him. She accepted, and when he picked her up, his first surprise was that she was no longer a tall and gawky, ill-proportioned girl with a plain face and thick glasses. She had grown into her body and looked better at twenty-eight than she had at eighteen. The fine, corn-silk hair was thick and flowing now, not the thin stuff that had let her ears stick out. When she mentioned that she was working at a strip club called Siren, he was intrigued.

By the time the entrée was served, he realized that she must have secretly liked him in high school. Before dessert was over, she admitted it and laughed at herself, but kept touching her hair. He ordered them both after-dinner cognacs and waited for hers to take effect before he mentioned that he was having trouble finding a suitable apartment.

She said, "I have a small place and it's kind of crummy, but there's a secondhand couch I inherited from the last tenant. You could crash there for a couple of days, if you want."

He not only wanted to, but it had been his whole goal for the evening, until he'd actually seen the way she had grown up. At that point his list of wishes and desires expanded dramatically.

He should have tried harder to flatter her and make her feel appreciated. He should have talked about how beautiful she was. Having sex with her, while it implied attractiveness, apparently wasn't clear enough for women. He should have pretended to have a job. He should have pretended to think about her whenever she was gone, pretended to listen to her when she told him about her days and her thoughts and her memories. He simply had not thought things through. He should have planned, not just reacted. And he should have given her some money almost immediately after his first robbery.

All of Jeff's belongings were stuffed into the trunk of his black Trans Am out in the parking lot. He had an impulse to look in his address book and see if there was anyone else he knew around here, or anyone who might have connections, but his address book depressed him. It was a black notebook about five by eight inches that held many phone numbers, most of them crossed out. Many of the ones that were left were so old that they had to be obsolete. It was a record of people he'd offended.

Jeff finished his breakfast, drove to the movie theater where he and Lila had gone on a couple of occasions, then selected the movie with the longest running time. He bought a ticket, went to a seat to the far right along the aisle at the dark, empty back of the theater, and went to sleep. Last night he had gone almost without sleep, and now there was an opportunity to catch up.

He slept through the previews and the movie, and woke up when the lights came on again. Then he bought a ticket for another movie and fell asleep while he was waiting for the theater to fill up. This one was apparently no better than the first, because the seats nearly all remained empty. When the lights came on the second time, he felt rested and full of energy.

He stood, stepped into the lobby, and turned on his cell phone. The screen said "Eleven missed calls." He used his right thumb to show the whole list. Lila's number was not among them. All of the calls were from Carrie. He pressed Call and heard the ring.

"Hi," she said. "I wanted to tell you that I'm awake. Are you?"

"Yeah. I woke up a minute ago. I was wondering if you were a dream." He hadn't been. "You're too good to be real."

"So you're eager to take me out tonight?"

"Absolutely. What time do you want me to pick you up?"

"I think I'd rather meet you somewhere."

"The diner where we met last night?"

"No. I can't stand the idea of going to a diner so much that they remember us and say things like 'How you been?' If you tell them, then you're a regular. See? Sometime they'd say, 'Oh, her? She's one of our regulars.' Then I'd have to shoot myself."

"I can see the reasonableness of that. How about somewhere else?"

"I don't know. I was hoping this would be one of the times when you would surprise me and say something like, 'Even though I'm an outlaw now, I used to be one of the five best chefs in Shanghai. Why don't you come to my place and I'll cook for you?'"

"Sorry. I'm not a great chef, and I don't even have a place right now. But Chinese food does sound good. What's the best Chinese restaurant around here?"

"People in the know say you can get the best food outside of Asia right now in Monterey Park. Don't ask me why a bunch of great Chinese chefs would suddenly move to Monterey Park, but that's the story. I'll make a call or two and get us a reservation for eight."

"What time should I pick you up?"

"You don't know where Monterey Park is, do you?"

"Never heard of it. But I can read a map."

"Come to my place at seven and I'll drive."

"Can I come a bit earlier?"

"Why?"

"It you don't mind, I'd like to use your shower."

"That'll be fun. Come at five."

As the number on Melisande Carr's kitchen clock changed from 4:59 to 5:00, she heard the sound of the black Trans Am turning into the driveway. She looked out the window and pressed the remote control unit to open the garage door, then watched the black car glide into the unoccupied space beside her white Acura.

She watched Jeff Falkins swing his legs out of the black car, stand, and slam the door. He was wearing the same clothes he'd worn last night. He opened the trunk and took out a bundle of clean clothes, and then walked to the kitchen door. She opened it quickly and pulled him inside, then pressed the button to close the garage door and hide his car. "We have some talking to do."

"And some showering," he said.

She looked at him with narrowing eyes. "And some shaving. But first, the talk."

"What about?"

"Why do you suddenly not have a place anymore?"

"I don't really want to go into it right now."

"If you want to be with me, you have to."

He looked down at his bundle of clothes but held her in the corner of his eye as he said, "It's just temporary. It happened this morning, and I haven't had time to do anything about it yet."

"So it was unplanned. You just got here a month or two ago, right? So you must have been renting. I know you have enough money to pay the rent, because we stole it together last night. So it was a fight with a roommate, right?"

He wobbled his head from side to side. "Well, sort of. Don't worry about me. I'll find a nice place in a day or so and invite you over to see it." He held up the roll of clothes. "Is it all right if I take my shower now? I think we'd both like me better after I'm clean."

"Not yet," she said. "It was a girl roommate, wasn't it? Tell me the truth."

"Yes."

"And she figured out what you were doing last night and threw you out on the street."

He wobbled his head again. "Not exactly. Are you sure talking about this doesn't make you uncomfortable?"

"I'm positively enthralled."

"All right, then. She didn't figure out what I was doing last night. She and I didn't even talk about last night. She was asleep when I came in. I waited until she was up and awake, and then told her I was going to have to move out."

"You did?"

"Yeah," he said in a low, sad voice. "She's a nice person, and I realized that it wouldn't be fair to keep living there and giving her the impression that we might have some kind of future together. This isn't her fault."

"It's about me, isn't it?"

"It's about me. I know you've got some commitments of your own—a boyfriend and all that. It's just that if I could meet you by chance in a diner and feel the way I do about you after a couple of hours, then I have no business living with somebody else."

"Wow," Carrie said. "Wow." She reeled like a fighter after an unexpected punch. "I can't believe you're real. Where did you come from?"

"Indiana, originally."

"You're so sweet and dumb. Didn't it even occur to you that if you kept quiet you could have both of us?"

"I won't lie to you. Of course it did. But I went out for a walk this morning and thought about it. I decided I wouldn't want a woman to do the same to me."

"Amazing," she said. "He's reinvented karma, all by himself."

"My mother always called it the golden rule." He studied her expression, wondering if he had gone too far with that one. He saw that she was studying him too. Her eyes narrowed and her brow crinkled. Yes, he must have gone too far. She was going to throw him out too — the second one in a day.

"Oh my God," she whispered. "You're blushing." She placed both small, graceful hands on the sides of his face and lifted his head a little. "I can't remember seeing a man who blushed — and an outlaw like you too. A regular desperado." She kissed him. "Your face is so warm. Come on. Let's go get that shower now."

She took his hand and led him through the house to the master bathroom. She opened the shower door and reached in to turn on the faucets and adjust the temperature, then stepped back. She unbuttoned her blouse, took it off, and then the bra, and then seemed to notice that he was watching her. "Get undressed."

"Are you taking a shower too?"

"You just dumped your girlfriend for me. If I don't scrub your back, who's left to do it?"

"Look, Carrie. I didn't break up with her to make you feel guilty or something."

"Who's guilty? I don't do guilt. You just got me all turned on."

"Oh," he said. "That's good."

"You bet it's good. Hurry up. We've got a lot to do before we leave for the restaurant." She stepped into the shower and held the glass door open while he stepped out of his clothes and into the torrent of warm water.

They made love in the shower, and then again on the bed. In the lazy, comfortable minutes afterward, she sat up suddenly. "We've got to get ready."

"Yeah," he said. "I guess I'm getting hungry too."

"Did you happen to notice the way I was dressed when you arrived?"

"Yes."

"Like it?"

"Obviously."

"Then I'll wear those clothes. I only had them on for five minutes while I was waiting for you." She was up and scurrying around, stepping over him and leaning down to snatch up clothes she had left on towel racks and counters. She glanced at him. "Get moving, Bud. The razors and shaving cream are in this drawer." She opened it and stepped away. "Don't dawdle."

He stood and put on the clean clothes he had brought, and then shaved with a pink razor. While he was cleaning the sink, she reappeared with her makeup on and her hair brushed and her purse over her shoulder.

"You look amazing."

"Just so I don't look as though I just got laid. Toss your dirty clothes in the hamper in my dressing room. We'll wash them tomorrow."

"We will?"

"Can you really not know that I'd want you to stay here tonight?"

"I didn't ask because it seemed like assuming a lot."

"Get over it, and get going. Zip-zip-zip."

As he went into the dressing room and put his dirty clothes in the hamper, he marveled at the world. How could a woman as cynical, crazy, and alert be such a sucker? She was far too smart and too self-indulgent to get manipulated into taking him in like this. She should have seen him coming from two streets away. And there was the question of her appearance. A woman that beautiful must have been conned by older and more experienced men when she was about fifteen. By now she should have assumed that every man who spoke to her was a liar.

"Jeffrey!"

"I'm not a Jeffrey," he said. "I'm a Jefferson."

"Well, whoever you are, come on. Thousands of years of Chinese cooking and I have plans for tonight, and we're waiting for you." She snatched up a tissue from her vanity and whisked it across his cheek. "Missed a spot. Now you're beautiful."

She stepped past him to the dresser built into her walk-in

closet and pulled out her big .45 pistol. She checked the magazine, clicked it back in, and put it in her purse.

"They'll kill the chickens before we get there. You won't need a gun."

"Don't you have yours?"

"Not on me. It's in the trunk of my car with my stuff."

She stopped and folded her arms. "Go get it. I'll wait."

"I don't need it."

"Yes, you do."

He studied her. She stared back up at him, unmoving.

"You're weird about guns, aren't you?"

"I could remind you that we robbed some armed guys last night and shot one of them. I could say there are circumstances and reasons right now why your being armed will make me feel safer." She paused. "But yes. I'm weird about guns."

"You might want to put your therapist to work on that one."

She kept her head up and her eyes on him. "If you wanted me to wear a nurse's uniform or a French maid costume or a skirt with no panties or something, I'd do it. So I think you should wear a gun for me."

"Then so do I." He went out to his car, got the gun from the outer pocket of his suitcase, and put it in the inner pocket of his black summer-weight sport coat. Carrie seemed to be a woman who never lost an argument.

She came out and got into the driver's seat of her white car, and he got in beside her. He flashed the inside of his coat.

"There. Was that so hard to do?"

"Not so far. So where are we going?"

She backed out of the driveway, closed the garage door with the remote control, and headed down the hill. "I called some friends, and the word is that the Emerald Cloud Dragon is *la place du jour*. It's actually pretty new, but it's a version of a place the family owns in Taipei, which is a version of one they owned in Beijing until 1949. My friend said that about a month ago an important

156

politician-slash-gangster from Taiwan had a reception there. He flew everybody to L.A. and then home two days later."

"Your friends really know how to research a place. My friends would say 'Stay away from the egg roll.'"

"This isn't the kind of place where you stay away from things. It's the equivalent of a two-star place in France. Maybe even three."

"Am I dressed okay?"

"Have you got lots of other choices?"

"At the moment, no. I packed in kind of a hurry."

"Then we're just right."

It was a long drive on the freeway from the Valley to Monterey Park. The freeway traffic moved in surges, pushing forward at seventy or seventy-five for a few minutes and then slowing to a complete stop. Carrie drove with the feral alertness of a Los Angeles native. She was quick to make a lane change to get around a slow-moving truck, but if she was trapped for a time, she waited without any outward sign of her impatience.

The trip was a pleasant change for Jeff, because he had almost forgotten what it was like not to be the driver. He got to study buildings and streets that he had only seen in flashes as he drove past at high speed. And he got to look at Carrie while she drove.

Unexpectedly, he thought about Lila. He had made a foolish mistake. This morning, when he was trying to keep her fooled about him, he had shown her the canvas bag of money that he had stolen last night. He had even made a point of spelling out the Bank of America name printed on the bag. In his attempt to persuade her, he had momentarily forgotten that the three men he had robbed worked at the strip club where she worked. The only reason he had known enough to steal the night's receipts the first time was because Lila had worked at the club and he had seen her boss with a similar canvas money bag. Lila was not, by nature, a suspicious person, but she wasn't stupid either, and right now she was hurt and angry. She was probably thinking about him a lot today, finding fault with everything he had ever said or done. Could she fail to notice that the bag that had been stolen and the bag that he'd shown her were both from the Bank of America?

"Why are you so quiet?"

"I was wondering why things happen the way they do. You know, unexpectedly."

"I think I know part of it."

"Really?"

"Character is destiny, but not the way people think. Were you wondering how I turned up?"

"Yes. That's exactly it." He had noticed that she was one of those women who thought they knew what other people were thinking. She was almost always wrong, but letting her think she was right was a good way to control her mood.

"I saw you in the diner and thought you were cute. I was bored, so I came back to meet you. The reason I stayed was that you're the one I'm going to tell my grandchildren about." She shook her head. "No, maybe just one of them, my favorite granddaughter."

"Tell her what?"

"Everything, pretty much. That when I was still young and pretty, one of the things I did was have a passionate affair with an armed robber."

"You're going to tell her that's a great idea?"

She looked at him and smiled. "It depends. I don't know how this is going to work out yet."

Carrie parked her car on a side street, away from the shops and restaurants, and they walked to the Emerald Cloud Dragon. As they approached, Jeff could see through the big windows that the dining room was very large. He counted twenty-eight tables, all a blond wood that matched the floors, then stopped because he thought he must have counted a few twice. Carrie seemed to know exactly where she wanted to sit and pointed it out to the host.

When they were seated, Jeff said, "Sure you've never been here before?"

"No. But everyone I asked said this is the place."

"For what? What are we looking for?"

"Perfection," she said. "A perfect experience changes your life."

The waiter seated them and left them with menus.

Three waiters gave them tea and water and drinks from the bar while one stood sentinel over them to answer questions about the menu. When the proper interval had passed, Carrie held out her hand to the waiter and gave him a piece of paper with Chinese characters on it. He read it, bowed formally, and said, "Excellent!" before he left.

Jeff looked at her. "You know I'm going to ask."

"Of course. I asked too. I was told it means 'the Emerald Cloud Dragon's best dinner,' but not in those words."

"Who is your source for all this?"

"A friend of mine named Jenny Wang. Her parents are Chinese, and they take her to Monterey Park a lot."

The dinner was a spectacular succession of delicacies on little plates served with great care. To Jeff, it began to seem tragic that he could only eat so many pieces of wrapped meat or seasoned shellfish in one evening.

He and Carrie each tasted every dish set before them, trying a tidbit and then finding they couldn't resist another, then another. After two hours and forty-five minutes in the Emerald Cloud Dragon, Jeff paid the check in cash, and the two walked out into the night.

It was late and the street was quiet, and Jeff felt a sensation he remembered from summers when he was a teenager in Indiana. Other kids had rules about going home at some particular hour, so Jeff had often found himself out as the numbers dwindled and he was finally alone on a dark street. He had always stayed until the last one left, because for him, being with people meant being out.

He was the only child, and his mother was the only parent, and neither of them was good at the role. His mother had been seventeen when he was born, and the forty-year-old truck driver from

Alabama who had talked her into naming their baby Jefferson Davis had quit making his Indiana layovers in her town after about a year.

When Jeff was ten, his mother was twenty-seven and pretty. She dated the way avid outdoorsmen hunted. She took small game from the local area five or six nights a week throughout the year, and then occasionally went on month-long safaris in places far from Indiana. Jeff would be alone while she was in some warm place where rich older men spent their winters, and then again during the spring, when college students and people who could pass for that age partied. Her movements during the summer were unpredictable and varied. He would wake up late in the morning sometimes and find her bed still made and a message on the answering machine that she'd recorded for her male friends, not for him.

Whatever money she left for his use, he spent buying the best clothes for himself and small presents for the mothers of his friends, who invited him to family dinners. On holidays, if he received a gift from any of his mother's relatives, shamefaced because they had never done much to help her, he would exchange it for something that would make him look better.

As he and his mother grew up and got to know each other, they liked each other less and less. They argued loudly until he was about thirteen, and then avoided talking much during the rare times when they had to be together. Summer nights were freedom, a time for going out and staying out as long as the companionship and excitement could be made to last.

Carrie leaned on him as they walked. "I'm glad I found you." It was as though she had sensed what he was thinking and wanted to make him feel better.

Affection was an opening. "What's your name?"

"I haven't named myself yet."

"Your parents gave you the name Melisande?"

"Melisande Carroway Carr. If they had an excuse, they must have told me when I was too young to remember."

"When you wrote down your name and number for me, why did you use that one?"

"Balance."

"Balance because I told you my real name?"

"No. Because you already saw and touched everything about me, but didn't know anything."

As they approached her car, she took the keys out of her purse and handed them to Jeff. He looked to both sides, up and down the street, and back toward the alley behind the restaurant. "What are you doing?"

He said, "We just pulled out a lot of cash to pay in there. Sometimes it attracts attention."

She laughed. "From people like us."

He opened the car door for her and then went around to the driver's side, started the car, and drove toward the freeway entrance.

They were on the freeway for thirty seconds before she said, "I want to pull a robbery."

He felt a sudden tightness in his stomach. "I just finished eating the biggest meal I ever had in my life."

"It doesn't have to be right now. It's not even eleven o'clock. We can wait around until we feel less full."

"Don't we have enough money after last night?"

"If we do something tonight, we'll have even more money. And who's going to expect us to go out again two nights in a row?"

"But why take the risk?"

"That's why. The risk is what I love. You can have the money."

He glanced at her and brought back with him a picture of her beautiful face, the big brown eyes gleaming in excited anticipation. She looked absolutely crazy, but he could feel the beginning of an erection. He shifted in his seat. "I'll think about it."

"Not too long. If you don't want to, I'll have to drop you off and find someone else to go with me."

17

MANCO KAPAK WAS in Wash, his dance club on Hollywood Boulevard. He found the place much more alien than his two strip clubs in the Valley. He leaned on the wall behind the bar just to be out of the crowd for a bit and squinted his eyes to see through the dark and the flashes of light.

Wash looked as prosperous as he needed it to. The dance floor was full, and all the bodies merged into one mass compelled by the same sound, looking from his vantage point like the sea, with waves of movement sweeping across it and back. The tables on the far side of the big room were more than full, often with a girl sitting on a lap, or two of them sitting on one chair. The bartenders near him were pouring drinks as fast as they could.

The lights in Wash were throwing a reddish cast over everyone right now, and it gradually changed to yellow, then green, then blue. Laser beams swept across the room far above at the fourteen-foot level, thin green lines of light intersecting to make a moving web ceiling.

The whole spectacle was mesmerizing—the lights and music and the young men and women stepping, turning, gyrating to one beat. Kapak looked beyond the long bar at a group of girls dancing together in the crowd, and they reminded him of the girls in Budapest so long ago—faces with that fresh, smooth look, the long, shining hair, the bodies so perfect. He felt a sudden emptiness, a terrible longing to go back that was so strong that he could feel a film of moisture forming in his eyes. He blinked it away. The place he missed so much wasn't Budapest. It wasn't a place at all. It was being young.

He squared his shoulders, opened the hinged section of the bar, and began to walk. He made his way around the edge of the dance floor, patrolling the building, making sure every waitress, every bouncer, every busboy saw him. In all of these years in America, he had learned plenty of management secrets. One of them was showing up and displaying interest. All most employees needed to know was that the boss was paying attention. They could forgive the owner for being rich, because they could see for themselves that the price of getting rich was getting old. But if the boss didn't care about the business, he didn't care about them either. And they'd make him pay for it, punish him by stealing and being lazy.

Kapak made a second circuit around the cavernous club. Once he was sure everyone had seen him, he could go inside to the office where the music was shut out. He unlocked the thick, padded door in the back wall, went inside, and closed it. The anteroom he entered held a bank of television monitors above a control desk and an unoccupied table and chairs. At the control desk staring at the monitors was the club's security manager, a retired cop named Colby. He picked up a hand radio and said, "Bobby, take a walk over to the bar and get a look at the tall guy with the mustache and the wife-beater shirt. He looks like he's thinking of starting a fight." Then he set it down again.

Kapak said, "Hello, Colby."

Colby only nodded and said, "Mr. Kapak." His manner was

slightly cooler than it must have been when he had pulled speeders over in the old days. Kapak liked it, because it seemed to him to indicate a kind of integrity. Colby had spent twenty years watching people like Kapak very closely, and he hadn't liked them. Now that he was left with an inadequate pension and had to work for one of them, he didn't pretend he had changed his mind. He spoke to Kapak with the respectful formality that cops used to speak with people they considered enemies.

Kapak passed through the door at the other side of the room into the inner office, where Ruben Salinas, the manager of Wash, was expecting him. As soon as the door was closed, even the muffled beat of the music in the club was almost undetectable. Salinas stood up and came around his desk. He was young, and he dressed like his customers in tight designer jeans and a T-shirt, but he had the dead eyes of a fifty-year-old business executive. "Nice to see you, Mr. Kapak. Everything all right out there?"

Kapak was aware that it wasn't especially nice to see him, but said, "Nice to see you too, Ruben. Everything seems fine. I'm pleased."

"Thank you."

"Have we heard from our friend yet?"

"I just saw two of Rogoso's girls come in the front door on the monitor. It should only be a minute or two." He pointed at the monitor mounted on the wall where he could see it from behind the desk.

Kapak stepped up beside him and turned to look where he was pointing. There were two young women with long, straight black hair, short skirts, sandals, and tank tops like all of the two hundred other female customers. They both had big leather purses with the straps over their left shoulders and clutched under their left arms. Kapak was happy with them. If Salinas had not pointed them out, he would never have seen any difference between them and the others. He watched them make their way across the crowded dance floor, sidestepping or turning to avoid dancers as they came. Their movements had a graceful, playful quality, as though they were dancing their way through the crowd, half-unconsciously giving in to the rhythm, even though the world knew that there was nothing unconscious about the way twenty-year-old girls looked.

They reached the line for the ladies' room, stood watching the dancers and the lights and appraising the men who had noticed them and had not looked away. Kapak saw the other girl now, the blond who worked for Salinas. She moved in close to them, and he could see she had a purse that was identical to the purse one of Rogoso's girls carried. They leaned in close and talked for a few seconds, and then she turned and stepped away from them.

"Something's up," Salinas said.

"What?"

"She's supposed to switch purses with the taller one in the ladies' room, and bring the purse in here. She's coming in, but I didn't see a switch."

They waited, watching the monitor. The two girls waiting in line for the bathroom went in.

There was a knock on the office door, and Salinas stepped to open it and let the blond woman inside.

"What's wrong?" said Salinas.

But she looked at Kapak. "I'm sorry, Mr. Kapak. They want you to go with them to see Mr. Rogoso."

Salinas stood completely still and watched Kapak, but Kapak sighed. "Ruben, you'll need to count the take for the night and fill out the deposit slip. Don't put in a date. Leave that blank. Drive it up to Siren and give it to Voinovich, and he'll put it in the safe. I guess you'd better call the office at Temptress and tell them to do the same thing. I'd like all the money locked in the safe at Siren tonight."

"You're not actually going with those girls, are you?"

"Rogoso wants to talk to me. Maybe he'll tell me something I need to know." He turned to the blond woman. "Where do these two want to meet me?"

"In the back of the building by your car."

"All right."

Salinas frowned. "Aren't you a little . . . worried?"

"No," he said. "Just take care of the money, and things will be fine." He turned and went out through the security office and into the noise of the club. It was after midnight now, and the crowd was as big and active as it would be tonight.

He had lied about not being worried. Rogoso was a savage. He was a man without any sense of how a human being was supposed to behave. A couple of years ago, he'd had his first difference of opinion with him. Rogoso had sent a delivery of money to be mixed in with Kapak's nightly take, and when Kapak had opened the bag, he had found blood had soaked into the top thirty or forty bills in each stack and dried. Kapak had met with Rogoso and returned the stained bills to him.

Rogoso looked down at the pile of reddish-brown paper, some of the bills stuck together and some not. "It's just a little blood. You're supposed to be the money launderer, aren't you? Wash them."

Kapak sat quietly without moving for a few seconds. "There's no such thing anymore as just blood. It's *somebody's* blood. As soon as they do a couple of tests on it, they know who it belongs to. I'm assuming the cops already have the body this came from."

"Could be." Rogoso appeared bored and uninterested.

"I've already deposited all the bills that were clean in the bank, but not these. If this makes you short for the week, I can help you out. And I've already made out the check for the rest." He took it out of his coat pocket and held it out to Rogoso.

Rogoso reached out and took it, then tore it up. "Don't act like I'm some small-time guy. I can make my payrolls."

"Do I need to know whose money this was?"

"He was my brother-in-law."

Kapak had asked no more questions. He had simply passed over the topic and taken the first opportunity to go home.

Kapak knew he was being watched, so as he walked through

the club past the surging crowd, he looked up at Takito the DJ in his glass booth and waved, and Takito waved both his arms and grinned. Takito was an almost unnaturally skinny Japanese man of undeterminable age. Each night he took off his shirt to reveal his stringy muscles and the impression of bones, tied a headband around his forehead, and began to play a selection of music that the customers seemed to think could not be heard anywhere else, all the while dancing behind the glass and shouting down at the customers. Takito already had enough notoriety to get lots of other jobs at after-hours clubs and parties, so he probably would be moving on before too long. For this moment — these few seconds — he and Kapak were useful to each other. Takito looked good, and Kapak looked brave.

Kapak stepped out the front entrance into the line of young people waiting to be admitted and made his way around to the back. The two girls were leaning against the hood of his car, waiting and smoking cigarettes.

He pushed the remote control on his key chain, and the buttons popped up and the door locks opened. The two girls dropped their cigarettes on the asphalt, opened the rear doors, and got in, so Kapak had to sit alone in front like a chauffeur. "All right," he said. "Where are we going?"

The one over his left shoulder said, "We have to go the long way and make some turns to be sure your people aren't following us. Okay?"

"I guess it's all right, but I don't want to be out all night, because I have things to do. You tell me where to turn, and I'll do it."

"Left up at the light."

He glanced in the rearview mirror to find her. She was looking straight ahead, but the girl beside her was on her knees on the seat staring out the rear window, watching the traffic behind them. The taller girl had him make three turns in rapid succession, then told him to head west.

"Are my people following us, Maria?"

"My name is Ariana, not Maria."

"Well, hello, Ariana. People call me Manco."

"We know who you are, Manco," she said irritably. "We came to pick you up."

"Oh," he said. "That means you two like me, doesn't it? Do I make your hearts beat faster? Do you get butterflies in your stomachs when you see me?"

The two girls laughed, and then the other one said, "Stop making fun of us."

"Oh!" he said. "What voice is that? Ariana, aren't we alone?"

"You know we're not. That was Irena."

"Is Irena your imaginary friend? A lot of children have imaginary friends."

"No, I'm not her imaginary friend," Irena said. "I'm just as real as she is and more real than you are."

Kapak took his hands off the wheel, pretended to knock his right fist on his head, but made the loud rapping noise by tapping the dashboard with his left. "Hear that? It seemed real to me. How could you be more real than I am?"

"Nobody's taking me to see Rogoso. Pretty soon you could be a ghost."

"Irena!" said Ariana. "That's not funny."

"Are you both afraid of Rogoso?"

"Yes."

"None of the people who work for me are afraid."

"Why would you say that?"

"I'm just making conversation," said Kapak. "A lot of the time that means comparing one thing with another, or talking about the way things could be if they weren't the way they are. How far do we have to go to find Rogoso? Remember, I said I have some other things to do tonight."

"He's at the beach."

"What beach?"

"You know, the beach. Malibu."

"That's quite a drive."

"Irena! We weren't supposed to tell him that ahead of time."

"Oh, who cares?"

"What if he decides he doesn't want to drive out there? Rogoso will have Alvin and Chuy beat the shit out of us. At least."

"Oh my God. You have a gun. Nothing has to happen that you don't want," Irena said.

"It's not very smart to say that either."

"Well, it's true." Irena sat facing forward. "Manco. Drive west to PCH and go north. Ariana will tell you where to stop. Okay?"

Manco shrugged. "I guess it'll be okay. I hope you were kidding about me being a ghost, though. I don't think I'd like that much."

"She was kidding."

Kapak drove toward Santa Monica, and when he got there he took the exit down the incline onto Pacific Coast Highway. To his right was the high bluff and to the left was the ocean, shining black at this time of night. "See the moon?" he said.

He heard the two moving around to see it. "Beautiful," said Ariana. "I love to see it shining on the ocean like that." Almost immediately after she said it, the first of the houses cropped up on the left. After that, for a time the view consisted of a succession of garage doors and high gates, the houses shoulder to shoulder as though they were trying to hide the whole Pacific Ocean.

"Sometimes I don't think anybody ought to be able to own something like that — put something up so he can see the ocean, but nobody else can," said Irena.

"I wouldn't say that if I were you," said Ariana. "You know who owns a house here."

Irena sighed.

"Okay, Manco," said Ariana. "We're almost there. When we go by it, you've got to hang a U-turn and pull forward to stop in front of the garage. There's no other place for a car."

"Okay, but watch for cops."

"See the big white place up there, the one that's about three stories?"

"Yeah."

"That's it. Now go past. Turn around. There. Nice. Now pull up there."

Kapak stopped the car, looked into the rearview mirror to be sure nothing was coming in the right lane, and then got out and stood at the back of his car and watched the two girls get out. He studied their bodies closely while they weren't aware of it and decided there was no place for a gun on either of them except their purses. When they came closer, Ariana said, "He's waiting."

She went to the front door and opened it, and Kapak followed the girls inside. Rogoso came into the foyer from a brightly lighted living room. He was not as tall as Kapak. Although he was at least forty-five, he looked no more than thirty-five years old, with thick dark hair that seemed to sprout from halfway down his forehead, just above his bushy eyebrows. He wasn't smiling.

Kapak said, "Nice house, Rogoso. How are you?" and held out his hand.

Rogoso kept his hands at his sides. "I'm not happy, Kapak."

"Why not?"

"I've been hearing all kinds of stuff about what's going on with you."

"What?"

"This Joe Carver guy is robbing you blind and killing your men, and you're too scared to go to the bank to move money around, and there's a police lieutenant downtown making a full-time job out of watching you."

"Who told you that?"

"Everybody!" he shouted. "Every-fucking-body!" He spoke more softly. "The whole town knows all about it like they were all there at the time and saw you get robbed, and people are saying that you're too old to do this anymore. That you're weak."

Kapak laughed. "I don't feel weak. Do you want to arm-wrestle?"

"Don't be stupid."

"Well, none of my men has been killed. One of them got clipped by a ricochet off the sidewalk. It was a girl just firing wild all over the place, and she managed to get him a flesh wound down by his calf with like ten shots. He'll be fine. I got lots of other guys. And Joe Carver is nothing. There are guys like him all the time. Always have been. They come from some unknown place that they're goddamn glad to get out of, and they show up here and cause trouble for a little while, and then it gets too hot for them and they go away. I'm putting some pressure on him right now, and he'll either turn up or go someplace else. Don't worry. He can't hurt you. He doesn't even know about you."

"But he's got the cops watching you all the time."

"Not really. I just drove out here, and your girls can tell you that nobody followed us."

He looked at Ariana and Irena, standing a few feet to his right. Their dark, heavily mascaraed eyes watched Rogoso warily, waiting for him to turn to them.

"They're just a pair of drug mules. What the fuck do they know?"

"Probably more than we do. If they had ever let themselves be followed, they'd be dead or in jail."

"That's not proof of anything." He extended his arm and looked around him. "Take a look at this place. I just bought it a month ago. You know who owned it? Nick Criley."

"The singer?"

"The fucking legendary singer," he said. "It cost me eighteen million bones. Do you see what I'm saying, Manco?"

"You have an expensive house."

"That I'm building an empire. And let's talk straight here. I'm not a nightclub owner, and I don't have a few chicks pole-dancing and wiggling their asses to pay my bills. I've got over three hundred dealers on the street. If the cops get something on you, they'll fine you. At the worst, they'd take your liquor license so you'd have to retire. You know what happens if they get me?"

"I didn't find you and tell you to become a drug dealer. You were already doing everything you're doing now when I met you."

"You're missing the point, Manco. I'm not surprised, because your thinking is old-fashioned, like you were still dancing around a gypsy campfire in some part of Europe that God forgot a thousand years ago. I'm an important man, and that puts me in the center of the target. I can't have somebody who handles any of my money making this kind of spectacle of himself. You're attracting little small-time guys to come and steal from you, and that's a sign that they know you're weak. And when you try to fight back, you don't even win. All you do is attract the cops. Alvin, Chuy? Come in here."

Out of the living room came the two big bodyguards who went everywhere with Rogoso. As always when he'd seen them at night, they both wore lightly tinted shooting glasses to cut the glare from headlights and floodlights, and black sport coats that covered their weapons.

"Hello, Alvin. Chuy."

The two bodyguards nodded at him and waited in the doorway.

Rogoso said to Kapak, "I'm sorry I have to do this, but you and I can't do business anymore. You're too old and soft, and you're putting everybody in danger. Take him somewhere and get rid of him."

Kapak had been studying the two girls for the past minute — their exact positions, the clasps on their purses, even their breathing patterns. Kapak's left hand shot out and grasped Ariana's thin arm. He tugged her to him, reached around her into her purse, and pulled out her gun. He fired once into the center of Alvin's chest, twice into Chuy, and pushed Ariana away from him. He was already moving fast into the living room.

Rogoso was only about ten feet ahead of him, sprinting for the staircase. Kapak wasn't as fast, but he fired once, hitting him in the back. As Rogoso's dash became an uneven stagger, Kapak ran him down and shot him in the back of the head.

Kapak turned and moved to the wall of the living room, hurrying back toward the foyer. He reached the portal and stopped to listen, then spun around into the open marble space. He fired one round into Chuy's head and one into Alvin's. Then he took out his handkerchief and carefully wiped every surface of the gun.

The two girls were cowering in the corner of the room, their eyes wide and their mouths open. "Please don't," said Irena.

"I won't hurt you," he said. "I wouldn't have hurt them either. I just couldn't let them kill me." He stepped close to Irena so he could watch her expressions. "Is there anybody else in the house?"

"No. He thought he might decide to kill you, and he didn't want anybody but Chuy and Alvin to be around."

"Do you know where he kept his books?"

"Books?"

"The papers where he kept track of his business — the money that came in and the money he paid to other people."

"He would never let us see anything like that," Ariana said.

"All right. Do you two have a car?"

"No."

"Those two cars along the highway in front of mine. Whose are they?"

"Alvin's is the black BMW."

Kapak stepped to the spot where Alvin's body lay on its back, bent over, reached into the jeans pocket, and produced a set of keys. He tossed them to Irena. "I'll give you two ten minutes to get as far from here as you can. If you ever say anything about this to anyone, you'll have to die too."

"We know that," said Irena. She and Ariana backed their way to the door. As Irena opened it, she said, "And thank you."

"Thank you," he said. "For telling me about the gun."

They both went out, and a moment later he heard the sound of a car pulling away toward the city. Kapak looked at his watch. It was 12:36. He began to search the house, moving from room to room, but he could see that the task was hopeless. There were too many spots to hide something important, and too many reasons not to keep searching. He looked at his watch, and it was 12:45.

He found an office on the second floor, but he had seen nothing in it that might contain the records he wanted. He went to the desk, pulled the drawers out, and piled them up on the floor against the big wooden desk. He threw all the papers he could find around them. He opened the windows so the breeze from the ocean blew in and ruffled his hair. Then he moved on.

In the kitchen Kapak found the stairway down to the garage beneath the house. Two cars—a Maserati and a Bentley—were parked in the narrow space facing outward. He sighed. How could Rogoso have been foolish enough to buy such visible, obvious cars and drive them to this ridiculous house? Did he think the Internal Revenue Service wouldn't wonder where all the money was coming from? How could Kapak not have continued to check on him and found out about it? He was ashamed. He looked around the garage, found a can of paint thinner and a can of charcoal starter, and set them aside. He found a length of hemp rope, cut it into two twelve-foot lengths with a hedge clipper, then opened the two cars, popped the fuel doors, opened both gas caps, and stuffed the ends of both ropes into the tanks. Then he soaked the rest of the ropes with charcoal starter and left them trailing across the floor to meet near the steps.

He took the two cans with him as he climbed the stairs to the top floor. It was furnished as a recreation room, with a pool table, video games, a telescope on a tripod, an aquarium with three little spotted sharks gliding over lighted sand, and a full bar. He put a few bottles of liquor on the floor beneath the bar, poured some paint thinner over the wood, and opened the window. Then he lit a match to start the fire. When the flames went upward and began to lick the ceiling, he hurried out and descended the stairs into the office. He poured the rest of the paint thinner on the desk and empty drawers, lit another fire, and moved on. When he reached the bottom of the stairs to the garage, he splashed the last of the charcoal starter over the walls, lit the two ropes that led to the two cars, then tossed a match against the nearest wall. In a second there was a sheet of orange flame rolling up the wall. He turned and ran up the stairs, went out the front door, got into his car, and drove.

He kept listening for the two explosions that might occur when the fire reached the gas tanks, and he thought he heard a thud, but he was already a half mile away with the wind blowing and the car windows closed, and he thought it might be his imagination. As he drove back the way he had come, toward the start of the Santa Monica Freeway, he looked at his watch again. It was 1:10. He had given the girls plenty of time — much more than he had promised.

It wasn't until he was on the Santa Monica Freeway and moving into the right lane for his exit, climbing up on the elevated half-loop to swoop down again onto the northbound San Diego Freeway, that he felt the lightness in his head and the fullness in his lungs that he had known would come. In sixty-four years he had felt it many times. The fear-induced adrenaline that suddenly flooded the bloodstream eventually burned itself up with the exertion — the fighting and running — and then left him feeling weak and shaken.

He was an old fighter, a man who had arthritic knuckles because he'd fought with his fists, three long knife scars on his arm, chest, and back, and light-colored spots on his body where fire had turned skin into scar tissue, because this was not the first house he'd been in that was no more. Tonight had been a near thing, an unwarranted, unexpected attack that he had fought off, and he had known that his body, the animal self, would need to take these deep, sweet breaths to recover and reassure itself that no harm had been done to it. He opened the car windows a few inches and deeply inhaled the night air that rushed in.

But almost immediately his mind began to bring down his pulse, slow his breathing. He had not died. But the futility of this night's work, the stupid wastefulness of it, was impossible to forget.

The men he had outsmarted and killed weren't supposed to

175

be his enemies. They were allies. For years Rogoso had been paying him big commissions for moving his drug profits through the banks, to make it clean. Rogoso had been a regular, dependable source of money. And having an alliance with a man like Rogoso had probably been one of the things that had protected Kapak and his businesses.

That was gone now. Rogoso and his closest friends were dead. The big wooden beach house would be burning furiously now, would probably be dust and burned timbers in another half-hour. There wouldn't be much left to conceal any papers that referred to Kapak or laundering money. For all Kapak knew, he might also have burned millions of dollars in cash and drugs, but it didn't matter. What mattered was that Rogoso had decided he was weak and betrayed him.

He was heading toward his house, but then he changed his mind. He didn't want to go back and sit around in an empty house tonight. He needed to be out, to see people. He needed an alibi. If he hurried, he would be in one of his clubs in the Valley in fifteen minutes. He steered toward Temptress, which was a bit west of Siren, and closer to the 405 freeway. He took the exit at Sepulveda and drove along the straight, long road, timing the lights and keeping his eyes open for police cars.

When he arrived outside Temptress, he parked his car close to the building, locked it, and hurried inside. He looked at his watch again. It was only 1:24. That was a little bit early for him to pick up the cash for the evening, but perfect for him to establish an alibi. He needed to be seen. He made a casual circuit of the bar and the tables, nodding at his employees or calling them by name and asking them how things were going.

He took a seat just inside the bar and looked around him. The pounding beat of the music and the sight of the four girls who were on the small black stages across the big room didn't hold him in the present. He looked at the club and remembered the first time he'd seen it.

He had bought this building fifteen years ago, when he already had Siren and wanted to expand. The building had been a small factory and warehouse that made heavy packing cases for steel machine parts and screws and other devices that didn't travel well in cardboard cartons. It had served the aircraft plants in Burbank and Long Beach, electrical equipment manufacturers in Hawthorne. But one by one, the big places had shut down until there wasn't much to ship anymore.

Kapak had picked up the property cheap and remodeled the building quietly, using small crews one at a time. On opening day he had carpenters bring in the refinished bar from a failed German restaurant and install the four brass stripper poles. At 5:00 P.M., before the sunset, the sign that said TEMPTRESS in red neon script went up on the roof. The first girls had been hired as dancers for Siren.

Kapak watched the bar traffic for the final half-hour of the night. There were the usual number of young men who wanted to cheat the clock by ordering extra rounds of drinks at the end of the evening. He watched the waitresses scurrying from table to table to fill the last legal orders, scoop up their tips, and move on. He caught sight of Sherri Wynn across the room and thought about the payments on her Volvo. His gift to her hadn't slowed her down.

He got up and moved slowly through the crowded room past the girls working the poles. They seemed to have caught the same sense of urgency as the night ended, trying to attract the attention of the customers who were just breaking bills of large denomination they hadn't planned to spend and receiving cash back from the waitresses and bartenders. He saw a couple of men decide not to put the money back in their pockets, but tip one or two of the dancers.

The office was at the back of the building near the end of a corridor past the dressing rooms and the storerooms. Beyond it was only the kitchen, where he could see the cleanup was almost finished. The busboys and the kitchen floor man were mopping and wiping, and the dishwashers had the machines running hard. After closing, all that would be left were the last few racks of glasses from the late drinkers.

He opened the office door and stepped inside. Dave Skelley was on his feet, counting and banding the night's take and setting the bills in stacks. He said, "Salinas from Wash brought his night's take over here. He said you were busy tonight and asked him to do it."

"That's right. It turns out I'm not busy anymore. Somebody asked me to meet him, and then never showed up. Was Salinas worried about me?"

"No. The only reason he told me was that I asked him where you were."

"Wasting my time is the answer. I'll be back in a minute." Kapak stepped out of the office into the bare corridor, but just as he was taking out his cell phone, the four dancers came toward him on their way to their dressing room. "Hi, Mr. Kapak." "Hi, boss." "Long night." "So long." They carried bits of fabric that had been parts of their costumes they'd picked up from the stage area as they'd left.

He spoke in the direction of the whole group, his eyes at the level of their foreheads. There was an etiquette to talking to four naked women. "You're doing a nice job for the club, ladies. I hope the tips were good."

"Not good enough." It was the blond one whose name he kept forgetting. Mary Ann? Marian? Better not to guess and get it wrong.

Kapak snatched his wallet out of his coat pocket and extracted four hundred-dollar bills. "A tip from the house. Thanks for your effort." He handed each of them a bill and shrugged off two attempts to hug him. "Good night."

As soon as they disappeared into the dressing room, he used his cell phone to dial Salinas's. "Hey. It's me."

178

"Hi," said Salinas.

"Hey, pal. I wondered if Rogoso ever called the club tonight."

"No. I thought you went to see him."

"I went. They took me to a parking lot by the corner of Sepulveda and Roscoe where we'd met one time about a year ago, but Rogoso never showed up. I wondered if he had tried to reach me or anything."

"No, not that I know of."

"Well, okay. I didn't want to bother you while you're closing, but you know how it is."

"Yeah, sure. Anything else up?"

"No. Good night."

Salinas and Kapak both hung up. Kapak felt as though he was covered now. He walked back out into the club and spent some time talking with the waiters, bartenders, and kitchen workers. The security people cleared the club, trying to be firm but still keep the atmosphere cheerful and calm. After a time, he saw the last four dancers leaving through the swinging doors to the kitchen. With their makeup washed off and in their sweatshirts and blue jeans and boots and sneakers, they had transformed themselves from magical creatures to ordinary, plain, tired women. Two of the security guards went out the kitchen door with them and returned after they had driven away.

Kapak went back into the office, where Skelley the manager and Sherri Wynn had finished counting the money. Skelley said, "Twelve thousand seven hundred and seventeen in cash, nine thousand eight hundred and nine in credit and debit cards."

"The credit thing just keeps growing," Kapak said. "When I got into this business it was all cash. Nobody wanted to give his card and have his wife see the monthly bill."

Sherri smiled. "Would you?"

"I don't know."

"You don't?"

"I haven't been married in about thirty years. I just can't quite remember having a wife to catch me at things. What I'm wondering is if we ought to install an ATM machine in the back of each of the clubs by the telephones and see if we can get more cash. It might make more money for everybody who lives on tips."

Skelley shrugged. "I don't know. I can call a few banks to see what they think."

"Thanks."

"I'll get started tomorrow," Skelley said.

Skelley finished the deposit slip for the money and put the cash and the slip in the canvas bag. "Well, this is done. You don't want it driven to the bank anymore, right?"

"Right. Two robberies outside that bank were enough for me. We'll just keep everything in the safe at Siren and have a couple of guys stay with it all night. In a day or so we'll work out another system that's easier and less risky. Maybe we'll have an armored car service come around each night and pick it up. Right now what I want is to be sure we don't make it too easy for the bastards. We'll do things a little differently each night."

"Sounds good to me," Skelley said. He put the cash bag into a briefcase.

"Want anybody to go with you?"

"Nah," said Skelley. "I think it's safer alone. We've never done it this way, and so nobody expects it. Nobody notices one guy driving alone." He and Kapak walked through the club to the parking lot.

"No matter what, be careful," Kapak said. "I don't know what Carver is up to, or where he is at any moment, or how many people he has working with him. He could be out there somewhere in the dark, watching us right now and waiting for us to make a mistake. If it looks like somebody's following you, drive right to the police station. If you can't make it, toss the money out the window and let them chase it."

"I'll do that."

He got into his car and gave a little wave, then drove off into the night. Kapak watched his taillights disappear, then went back into Temptress, where everyone but the bouncers had left for home. As he made his way back to the office, he considered telling the last couple of security men to go home, and then sleeping the night on the leather couch here. He stepped in and closed the door, then turned and saw that Sherri Wynn was perched on the edge of the desk again. "What's up, Sherri?"

"I thought I'd wait for you."

"Something wrong?"

"Not with me. You just seemed kind of lost tonight, as though you didn't know what to do with yourself. Aimless, maybe."

He smiled, but his heart had stopped and then begun again. He had to persuade her that nothing was different.

"Maybe it was the way you looked when you said you hadn't been married in thirty years. Some nights a person just doesn't feel like being alone."

He looked down at his feet, then back up at her. She went on. "I thought maybe you'd like to come over for a while. I'm not sleepy, and I could make you a midnight snack."

"Gee, Sherri, I don't know. I'd like to go, but I wonder if it's a good idea."

She shrugged. "What are you worried about?"

"Is this because I gave you that bonus last night?"

"You mean do I feel like I have to be nice to you because you gave me money? No."

"I didn't give it to you because of something I wanted you to do. It was for things you'd already done. Good work, I mean. And being a cheerful person."

"It meant something to me to know you were paying attention to me. You noticed that I was working my ass off for the tips, and you knew that I had a few bills I was worried about, because I'd bought some things that I really couldn't afford unless everything went perfect. And it doesn't. It never fucking goes perfect for long. And I was in one of those bad times last night."

"So you're trying to pay me back."

"I'm not doing that. I realized that I had a friend, and it felt good. You looked down tonight, so I'm just trying to show that you have one too."

"Sherri, I'll tell you the truth. I'll admit it. I'm having one of those nights when I don't feel like being alone."

"I could see that. I know you're thinking about what you lose if you come over. Unless you've got a better-looking girl waiting in your car, you'll lose nothing. Nobody will know, and I won't remind you of it later. Just come over, and we'll talk and have a drink, and relax a little. No promises, no pressure."

"Thanks, Sherri. You want to ride with me?"

"No, thanks. I need my car tomorrow. You follow me. If you get lost, it's 3907 Willow Oak Avenue in Sherman Oaks. Can you find it?"

"Off Moorpark. Right?"

"That's it."

"3907."

She slid off the desktop and walked to the door. As she passed him, she looked at him out of the corner of her eye, but he wasn't sure how to interpret the glance. "See you in a few minutes."

"Right."

Kapak couldn't help watching her as she went out. In the tight waitress uniform with the long stockings, she still looked good enough to attract the wistful eyes of the young customers. He wondered whether he was just making a fool of himself. He turned off the lights, locked the door, and went out through the club. He stepped behind the bar, surveyed the shelves in front of the long mirror, and picked up a bottle of Hennessy's cognac. He looked at it, put it back, and then reached up to a higher shelf and took an unopened bottle of rare Armagnac that cost over three hundred dollars, took the bartender's pad, and wrote on it, "I took one bottle Armagnac. Kapak." He was careful to put a big diagonal line below the name, so nobody later could write in "and a case of

Dom Perignon" or something. He walked out with the last security man and watched him lock up before he got into his car.

Driving in the Valley at night was almost automatic for Kapak. He'd had various enterprises all over the more commercial parts of it, and he knew his way around. He arrived on Willow Oak just behind Sherri's Volvo. He watched her pull it in the driveway and into a garage, then close the garage and lock it.

He watched her walk up an exterior staircase to the upper floor on the left side of a double duplex, then switch on a light. Then he took his bottle and followed. He had been thinking about Sherri all the way here and wondering. He reached the top of the stairs and found the door open an inch, so he pushed it inward and stepped inside.

Just as he was closing the door, she entered the kitchen. "You didn't have to bring your own bottle. I have some things here to serve a guest."

He held his hands out to his sides in a helpless gesture. "After two A.M. it's hard to find fresh flowers."

She smiled and shook her head to herself, then stood on her toes and reached up to a cabinet and took down two small aperitif glasses. "I don't have snifters." He uncorked the bottle and poured an inch for each of them. She lifted hers to the light. "It's pretty, like amber."

He sniffed his. "Salud."

She sipped hers. "That's nice. Come sit down."

He brought the bottle and followed her into the small living room, set it on the coffee table, and sat beside her on the couch that faced the dark television screen.

"Thanks for inviting me over. Sometimes being the boss gets a little lonely. People get uncomfortable around you."

"I didn't think I'd get you to come. I've heard the women you went home with were much younger."

He brushed the thought away. "How old are you?"

"How old? Who tells men how old they are?"

"I'm sixty-three." He wasn't sure why he had shaved one year off.

She took a bigger sip of her drink. "Forty-one." She watched him with intense, furtive eyes like a small, distrustful animal.

"That wasn't so hard. You're twenty-two years younger than me, and you look terrific. You've got a sexy, healthy, woman's body and a beautiful face. Be happy about who you are."

"Men like younger women, like the dancers at the club."

"Everything looks different from different spots. From where I am you're young—in your prime right now. Most of the dancers could be my granddaughters. I look at the dancers sometimes, just to see how they're doing—are they pretty enough? Is what they're doing the right thing to keep the customers coming in the door? If it's yes, then I start watching the bartenders." He chuckled. "And the waitresses."

She nodded. "I've seen you do it."

"Too bad. I wasn't always so clumsy that women knew I was staring at them."

"That's part of being the boss. You lose your fear that people notice what you do." She pointed at the bottle on the coffee table. "That's magical stuff."

"Why? Does it make me look good to you?"

"No, it makes me look good to me again. I just noticed my reflection in the dark window, and I liked it." She turned to look at him. "You just look the way you are."

"How?"

"Strong."

"Are you divorced?"

"You don't see him here, do you?"

"And you've been happier since then?"

"I've lived alone in places like this and gone to work and come home again. After a year or so, I started to think it would have been better if I had pretended not to know about the girl, and not divorced him. By then I was serving alcohol in little costumes like this one. I had learned a lot that I didn't know about normal male behavior. It occurred to me that maybe he wasn't as bad as I'd thought he was. Fortunately it was too late to go back, so I saved my pride." She sipped. "How about you?"

"She came from Romania to Hungary like I did when we were students. Eventually we came here. We had two kids here, and I thought things were working out, but I got caught doing something foolish and went to jail for about a year. She went with somebody else." He gulped his drink and refilled his glass, then hers.

"That's sad."

"Pay your taxes. That's how they got me."

"I didn't mean that. I meant her."

"It was a long time ago." Kapak leaned close to Sherri and waited to see whether she would turn away and make it clear they were just having a drink together or if she would turn toward him to indicate she wanted him to kiss her.

She turned her face toward him, lowered her right shoulder to bring her the rest of the way around, and their lips touched in a gentle kiss. After a moment he was ready to let her pull back and end it, but she didn't. She put her arms around his neck and prolonged the kiss for a minute, and then pulled back only a few inches so she could see him. "You're sweet."

"I like you, so I'm nice." He shrugged.

"But I didn't think you would be that way."

"What did you think?"

"I thought . . . I don't know. I was afraid that you might be like, I had already invited you, given you permission."

"You haven't done that."

"No, but I thought maybe just making it personal and not business might make you think in a different way. You know, about me."

"Do you wish it had?"

"No. Not then. Maybe I do a little bit now, though. Just a little."

He kissed her again, and this time the atmosphere had changed.

At first the change was so slight and gradual she might have thought she had imagined it, but this time there was no pulling back to talk, no pause or hesitation. In a short time he was removing her blouse and then unzipping and pulling off the black uniform shorts, then peeling off the shiny pantyhose, and then she was naked. The kissing and touching went on for a long time, and as it went on, at some point he finished removing his clothes too.

After a few minutes he could tell she knew there was a problem. She waited and appeared to be expecting nothing more to happen, as though the problem would solve itself, but Kapak could feel that he was doomed. He said, "I'm sorry."

She sat up straight. "Just a second." She got off the couch and disappeared into the bathroom. She returned with a glass of water and a blue pill.

"What's that?"

"It's medicine. Take it and it will make things nicer. You won't be sorry."

"It's Viagra, isn't it? What if I have an erection that lasts four hours?"

"I don't think you have much to worry about." She smiled.

He took it and squinted at it suspiciously. "Where did you get it?"

"Someone I know bought it online. I can tell you it's real, and I know it works."

"On who?"

"None of your business."

He put the pill on his tongue and washed it down with the water, looking at her as he drank it. She took the glass, turned, and walked off. He followed her to the bathroom, where he found her running water into an oversized tub. She got in while it was filling, poured a little bubble bath in, and beckoned to him. "Get in with me."

He stepped into it, facing her. "This is a really big tub."

"It's one of the reasons I chose this apartment. I always thought I would bring a man in here. It never happened until now."

He sat in the water, and they found that they could both fit if he kept his legs straight, and she put hers over his. After a few minutes she straddled his thighs and leaned forward to kiss him. They stayed that way for a time, and then she said, "I think it's time to get out, don't you?"

"Yes." He looked down and cleared some of the suds from the surface of the water. "How long will this last?"

"Long enough. Don't talk now."

They dried off and went into the bedroom. In concentrating on Sherri, Kapak almost immediately forgot that it was the medicine that had changed everything, and not some return of his youth. Then he forgot everything but her. She seemed to him tonight to be a composite and holder of the best qualities of all the women he had slept with when he was young: his wife, Marija; Ava the thirty-year-old whore he had paid with stolen money when he was fifteen and visited on the way home from school every day; the college girls in Budapest. She seemed to him to be a gift—maybe the final gift—the universe letting him remember why its creatures fought so hard to be alive.

Afterward, Sherri lay with her head on his shoulder, closed her eyes, and slept. He lay there staring at the ceiling of the unfamiliar little bedroom. He didn't want to move because if he did, she might not come back to his shoulder. He lay still for a long time, and while he thought, he began to feel the sensation. It wasn't exactly pain, just an uneasy awareness that something inside his chest wasn't right. It was almost a sadness. This was happening too late, after he had gotten old.

It didn't go away. He started to feel short of breath. It was as though each breath he took was more difficult, and when he exhaled, a belt tightened on his chest so the next breath would be shallower. Then there was a feeling as though weights were being piled on his chest. "Sherri." He had to take two breaths before he could say it again, so he touched her foot with his and said it louder. "Sherri!"

"What?" She lifted her head and brought her face closer.

"Something's wrong. It's in my chest. I've got to go to a hospital."

She got up quickly. She found his clothes and tossed them on the bed beside him. "All right. I'm going to drive you to Valley Presbyterian. It's the closest, and it's big enough to have a lot of doctors on duty." She drew back the covers and crawled onto the bed beside him. "I'll help you put on your clothes. If something hurts, just tell me."

"It's like a tightness. Hard to breathe."

She dressed him efficiently, and then threw on jeans and a sweatshirt. They walked out into the living room. As he passed the couch where they had been sitting, everything looked different. The clear sides of the half-empty bottle of Armagnac had a film that looked sticky and nauseating. The uniform he had taken off Sherri was still lying crumpled on the floor. She snatched up her purse, led him to the top of the exterior staircase, and said, "Wait here."

He gripped the railing and stood still, watching her lock the door, then run down the stairs to pull her Volvo out of the garage, then run back up to him. "Feel any different?"

"No." But he did. Besides the tightness in his chest, or maybe because the tightness had gone on for a time and made his muscles tense, it hurt. And time was part of the discomfort. Everything seemed to take an eternity. He let her help him down the stairs and into the passenger seat of her Volvo. She ran around the car and drove.

She drove with care all the way to the emergency room of Valley Presbyterian Hospital. He sat in tense immobility on the end chair of four that were connected, while she talked to the receptionist, then the triage nurse, and then some kind of clerk who handled insurance matters. As soon as she had her back turned, people came and sat down beside him on the row of chairs. Every one of them sat by simply releasing the tension in their knees and letting their buttocks drop a foot or so onto the chair. Each time it happened, Kapak would be jolted suddenly, his muscles would contract, and the pain would increase.

Finally, to nobody in particular, he announced loudly, "I'm having a fucking heart attack." All conversation in the room stopped while everyone looked at him. It was still a wait before the nurse called him into an examining room off the hallway, let him lie on a gurney, took his vital signs, gave him two aspirin, and disappeared. By then he had lost his sense of time. Sometime later another nurse took blood for a test, and he fell asleep. A young woman doctor in a long white lab coat appeared after that and spoke to him.

"Well, Claudiu, how do you feel now?"

"Like a crap sandwich."

She hesitated. "Crab?"

"Never mind. It doesn't seem to hurt as much, but I feel this weird pressure on my chest. Did I have a heart attack?"

She looked uncomfortable. "We looked at the test, and it's inconclusive. There's an enzyme we test for. If you haven't had a heart attack, there's no enzyme in your blood. If you did, there is. You had a tiny amount, so we can't really be sure. A cramp in the esophagus feels exactly like a heart attack. If you had one it was small. It was like a warning."

"A warning?"

"Your age is a risk factor for heart disease. So is your weight, and the fact that you get no exercise, and probably the cholesterol, fat, and sodium in your diet."

"So what happens now?"

"I'm releasing you and recommending that you see your family doctor tomorrow. He may order more tests and help you work out a plan for a healthier lifestyle."

Sherri drove him back to her house and helped him go back to bed. He fell asleep immediately. He woke up after two hours and saw her lying beside him. He touched her bleached hair, her sleep-closed eyelids and soft cheek, her smooth shoulder and thin waist and the swell of her hip. He had so much to regret.

18

IT WAS AFTER 2:00 A.M. Jeff and Carrie sat in her white car down the street from Siren and watched the building from a distance. A dozen people walked out the side door in a small gaggle, talking to each other, and stepped onto the darkened parking lot. A couple of them waved, and all of them got into cars. In the headlights from one of the cars, Jeff picked out Lila from the cornsilk blond hair and her tall, thin silhouette. She got into the little red Honda and started it. Jeff watched her as she drove off the lot and disappeared down the road.

"I don't see any lights on," Carrie said.

"There aren't any windows. It's a strip club."

"Oh. Yeah. I suppose they don't want to give it away for free."

"They're closed for the night, so the neon light on the roof is off, and the floodlights for the parking lot."

"How did you think of this place?"

"It's the club where the money came from last night. Those

three guys who were outside the bank last night work for Manco Kapak, and the money was his profit. They were depositing it for him."

"I could see what they were doing with it. But don't we have all their money now?"

"No. That was just last night's take—last night's money. We want tonight's money." He looked at her closely. "Unless we don't. You were the one who said you wanted to do a robbery tonight."

"I didn't say I wanted to rob a strip joint."

"Fine. Let's go home."

"Not so fast. I'm thinking. Have you cased this place—gone inside so you know your way around in the dark?"

"I have. I know the layout fairly well."

"You're so pathetic. Coming out here and sitting in a dark bar with a couple hundred of your fellow losers to see one girl dance naked. Couldn't any of you get a date?"

"In the first place, it isn't one girl, it's like four or five at a time. Over an evening, it's a lot of them."

"Oh. Only fifty to one, then. No wonder you're an expert."

"I was checking the place out so I could rob it."

"Were all those tits and asses better than mine?"

"The ones I saw weren't. But I may have missed some, because I was looking to see where the doors are and the windows aren't, and so on. So far, you're the best-looking woman I've seen."

"I wish it were lighter in here so I could see your face."

"I'm not lying to you. It's true."

"What's your plan for this place?"

"It's almost the time when they show up at the bank every night. We can't go back to the bank. They'll be expecting us. They'll have armed guys hiding all over the neighborhood waiting. So I'm thinking we might be able to stop the bagman before he gets there—maybe force him off the road and rob him. He's probably going to be alone tonight, because they'll want everybody else out of sight."

She smiled. "That's such a good idea, baby. I love it that you're not as stupid as I thought. Let's do it."

"Okay. The regular employees are gone. We can just wait until the bagman goes out to his car and heads for the bank."

They sat quietly, now and then shifting in their seats to get a better view of the Siren parking lot. Jeff was glad that all the waitresses' cars were gone. The idea of meeting Lila in the middle of a robbery seemed to be the biggest worry, and it was gone. After a time Carrie said, "It's been an hour, and nobody's come out that door. What do you suppose is going on?"

"Nothing that I can see."

"So why isn't it? Did they take the money to the bank already?"

"I doubt it. We were here at, like, eight minutes after two. They couldn't have counted all the money and bagged it and filled out deposit slips in eight minutes. Could they?"

"I don't know. You're the bandito."

"Exactly. I can tell you this is not normal."

"Maybe they're sick of getting robbed, so they're doing things differently."

"That's got to be it," he said. "You have a talent for this."

"I do?"

"Yes. Maybe what they're doing is having an armored car come and pick it up, the way supermarkets do. But no armored car came after closing, so the pickup must be tomorrow morning."

"So what do we do about it?"

"I've got to think. I can't see waiting and trying to shoot it out with an armored car crew."

"Nothing to argue with there."

He was silent for a moment. "I think I've got it. They've always deposited the money at closing time. They didn't deposit the money tonight, and the armored car didn't come, so it must be coming in the morning. I'm sure of that much. Meanwhile, there will be somebody in there watching the money. Does that sound right?"

"Yes. It does. It would explain why there are two cars still parked by the building."

He craned his neck to see the cars, then nodded. "It probably takes two guys to watch money, because they're mostly watching each other. It has to be the dullest thing there is to do."

"Sounds true."

"Those doors are going to be locked and probably deadbolted, so we aren't going to get through them. The two guys have to come out and let us in."

"Okay." She waited.

"We have two choices, I think. One is to go to the side of the building, find the phone junction box, and cut it. That will get rid of the alarm. Then we find the main circuit-breaker panel and flip the switch to kill the power. One of them will come outside to see what's wrong. I hold my gun on him and tape him up with duct tape. When he doesn't come back inside or anything, the other one will come at least as far as the door. He'll call out to his friend — 'Where are you? What's going on?' At that moment you put your gun to his head. We tape him up too."

"Then what?"

"If there's a safe, we make them open it. If they can't, we put tape over their eyes and make them carry the safe to our car. It won't be a big safe, or they could just leave the money in it and go home."

"What if they're asleep? If they're asleep, they won't even know the power and the phone are turned off."

"Well, that's true, but these are guys who work for a nightclub company. They have to be used to staying up late. If they don't come out after ten or fifteen minutes, we can knock on the door and pretend to be cops who saw their cars and want to know who's in there at this hour."

Carrie sat absolutely still for a few seconds, then said, "All right. I'm in. Let's get at it. Should I park at the back of the place, behind the Dumpster?"

"Yes. That way when they look out they won't see it."

She drove her car up the street, turned into the parking lot, turned off her headlights, and circled the building from a distance. She saw the spot she wanted and coasted up to it, then got out.

Carrie took her big .45 pistol out of her purse, pulled back the slide to bring a round into the chamber, and put the purse back into the car under the seat. She hid the gun in the back of her pants against her spine and covered it with her sweater.

She moved to the brick wall and walked along it to the door. She stood with her back to the wall at the hinge side and nodded to Jeff.

He moved off around the building to find the phone junction box and the circuit-breaker panel.

A man's voice, disembodied and electronic, seemed to come from the sky above her head. "I'm sorry, ma'am. But we're closed for the night."

"What?"

"I said we're closed now. The bar can't serve anybody after two."

She located the speaker, a little square gray metal box with holes on the front in a circular pattern. But what was above it worried her much more. It was a video camera mounted under the eaves of the building. Its single shiny black lens was staring right at her.

She pushed off to move out from the wall, wavering a bit as though she had been standing with her back to the bricks to steady herself, and put on a drunk voice. "I don't want a drink, thankyou-verymuch. I had some drinks already, and I've got all I want in the car. I'm not here for that."

"Then what are you here for, miss?"

"I'm here to audition."

"Audition for what?"

"A job. Isn't this a strip place?" She began to dance to unheard music.

"That's what you want—to audition for a job as a dancer?"

She shouted, both to let Jeff know that she was talking to someone, and to keep the man's attention on her monitor rather than spotting Jeff on another one. "Not dancing, silly! I don't want to dance. I want to strip!"

"Look, miss?"

"What?"

"The manager already went home, and the talent coordinator is only in on Tuesdays and Wednesdays from noon to eight. We don't do auditions in the middle of the night. Please go home, sober up, and give the club a call around noon tomorrow. The manager and the talent coordinator will make an appointment for you. Okay?"

"Fuck, no! I'm not going to leave work to drive all the way over here to take my clothes off at noon. I'm not going to be in the mood then. I'm in the mood *now.*" She did a wriggling, suggestive dance, lifted the front of her sweater, and undulated her hips, careful not to turn her body to let the gun at the back of her waistband show.

The man in the speaker chuckled. "Please. I can't deny you're hot. I'm sure you can get a job here any time you want. But hiring people—that's not my job. On nights like tonight, I sometimes wish it was. But it isn't."

"But you can help me get a job. I'll show you my act, and you tell me honestly what you think, so I can fix it."

"I can tell you without seeing the best parts of your act that you're qualified. Isn't she qualified?" There was some muffled speech. "My friend says you're more than qualified."

"I didn't hear that."

"He agrees you're good to go. But as I said, this isn't how you get the job. If our boss thought I told you different, I'd be out there looking for a job with you."

"Can't you help me? I'm the one being brave. I'm a shy person who works in a bank. If I do my act now for two strangers—two, right?—then I'll be over the stage fright, and it'll be easier to really audition." She began to move her hips again in a silent dance.

There was a soft scraping sound as though a hand were muffling a microphone, and then the microphone cleared again. "As long as you understand that we got nothing to do with hiring. We're just, like, night watchmen. You got it?"

"Absolutely," she said. "It'll really help me. All you have to do is watch my act and give me whatever pointers you can."

She heard the sound of someone fiddling with the hardware on the inner side of the steel door. She shrieked "Yippee!" so Jeff couldn't not hear it, then spotted his shadow near the corner of the building.

The door swung open, and there was a smiling man. He was very tall and broad-shouldered, with thick, dark hair and green eyes. He wore the pants from a black suit like the ones the men wore last night at the bank, but without the coat. His white shirt had the sleeves rolled up and the collar open. "Hello," he said. "What's your name?"

"Penelope," she said.

He bowed. "I'm very pleased to meet you, Penny."

"Penelope," she said with drunken insistence.

He turned to call to someone inside. "Jimmy, this is Penelope."

The other man came to the door and said, "Hi." He stepped back a few feet. "Come on in."

She was sure now that there were only two of them. Now that she could see them both, she took a step, leaned drunkenly against the steel door to keep it wide open, and used the awkwardness of the move to cover the hitch of her shoulder to pull the pistol out of the back of her waistband. "Don't move," she said.

"Shit," said the tall man. He made a quick move toward her.

She fired the gun high, so the bullet passed over his shoulder, and he stopped. She looked at the man behind him and said, "If you reach for it, I'll kill you."

He raised his hands and looked at her. "Penelope, why don't

you put that away?" He saw Jeff slip in the door beside her. "Oh, boy." Jeff was wearing a ski mask, and he handed one to Carrie, who put it on while he held his gun on the men.

"All right," said Jeff. "Just shut up. We're going to do this quick and easy. Both of you go up to face that wall, legs spread, hands out wide, and lean."

The two men obeyed.

Jeff frisked the two men cautiously, keeping his gun on one of them every second. He found two pistols and tossed them out the open door.

"We're here because we're sworn peace officers," said Carrie. "But not like any cops you've ever seen. If we decide to kill you, no local cop is ever going to ask us why."

"Oh, feds," said the big man.

"What's your name?"

"Vassily Voinovich."

"And how about you?"

"Jimmy Gaffney."

"All right. You should know that if we find out either of those are false names, you're going to jail for a long time. If you interfere with what we're doing, same thing happens. If you make either of us think we're in danger, you won't make it to jail."

"What do you want?"

"We're doing an audit of the money coming into this business. You're going to get tonight's take for us. Our office is going to look for particular serial numbers, do some chemical testing. If we don't find anything, your boss will get it back. If we do, God help him."

"We can't get the money for you. It's in the safe."

"Show us the safe," Jeff said.

"It's in the next room," Voinovich said.

Carrie pushed her pistol against his temple. "He didn't say 'tell us.' He said 'show us.' Everybody comes along."

The room was a small, neat office, and Jeff could see this was where the two men had set up to spend the night. The security monitor where the two men had seen Carrie was mounted on the wall, and their coats were hung on the chairs. There were two hands of a gin game laid out on the desk face-down. It told Jeff that the big guy who had gone to the door probably had not known that the wily-looking redheaded Irishman would look at his cards. The safe was a small one — only about two and a half feet high, and two feet wide. There was an electronic keyboard with the numbers zero through nine on the keys.

Jeff said, "Okay. We'd like you to open the safe for us."

The two men looked at each other in a silent inquiry that Jeff hoped was "Should we?" and not "I don't know how, do you?"

"We can't."

Carrie said, "Do you mean you don't have the combination, or you're aware that if you don't, we'll kill you, and you're willing to be killed?"

"The first one," said the big man, Voinovich. "No combination."

Carrie said, "That's bad news." She aimed her gun at his chest and kept opening and closing her fingers on the rubber handgrips of her big .45 pistol, trying to get the best hold on it to take the recoil.

"Wait. Hold it," said Jimmy Gaffney. "We honestly don't have the combination to the safe. If you were Manco Kapak, and you had two guys guarding your safe, would you give them the combination?"

"Looking at you, maybe not," Carrie admitted. "So we'll move on. First thing is that you guys are going to take the monitoring system apart. I want the recorder. Get started now." She turned to Jeff. "If they seem to be near to trying something — even thinking about it, kill them."

She crawled under the table where the safe was and examined it, then tugged on it, trying to rock it. "It moves a little. It can't be bolted to anything serious. Watch them while I look."

She went out the office door and around to the other side of the wall. She was gone a couple of minutes and came back. She had four nuts in the palm of her hand. "It's four bolts through the wall, the nuts on them only hand-tight. There was a little cabinet in front of them."

Gaffney said, "Kapak wanted it that way so we could get it out in a fire. Nightclubs burn down all the time."

"If there's anything else we need to know, you ought to tell us," Carrie said. "It'll go easier on you at your trial if you cooperate."

"What do you want me to tell you?"

"Where's the recorder for the monitoring system?"

"It's over there in the cabinet."

"Get it."

Gaffney went to the cabinet and opened it, then pulled out a thin rectangular box. He unscrewed the video cables from the back of it and set the box on the desk. Carrie followed the cables along the ceiling back to the camera outside to be sure that was what the box was, then came back. "Okay."

Jeff said, "Take your cell phones out and set them on the desk." The two men complied.

"Now you've got one more thing to do for us, to get the safe out of here and into the trunk of the car."

The two men knelt beside the safe, but didn't seem to be able to do more than rock it a little. Jeff tried too, to be sure they weren't faking. "Why isn't this thing moving?"

"I don't know," said Gaffney.

"Who owns the Toyota Land Cruiser out there?"

"I do," said Voinovich. "And it's a Sequoia."

"Give me the keys."

"I don't want to."

Jeff said, "Look. You've had guns pointed at you for ten minutes. Has anybody harmed or abused you in any way? No. Did we come in here and start shooting your toes off? When you said you couldn't open the safe, did we shoot one of you and tell the other one to do it? No. We trusted you. Now it's your turn. Give me the keys."

"I still owe money on that car."

"Then you'll be glad to be the one I shoot."

Voinovich reached into his pocket and produced the keys.

"Toss them near my feet."

The keys landed between Jeff's feet. He picked them up, then said, "Don't take your eyes off either one of them."

"All right, guys," said Carrie. "Stand close together so I can see you both."

The two men stood there with Carrie holding her gun on them. Then Jeff returned, uncoiling a rope as he came. "Okay, everybody out of the office and out here with me." The others came out and stood with him near the steel door.

Jeff tied the rope around the safe and went to the door. "Everybody stand clear."

He stepped outside, got into the Toyota Sequoia, and started the engine. The others could hear the engine accelerate. At their feet, the loose coils of rope snaked around on the floor like a whip, then went taut, vibrating like a harp string. There was a loud engine sound, angry and dangerous, now mixed with the screech of wood straining to pull free of nails, then wood popping and cracking. Carrie and the two men looked at the wall, which was beginning to cant toward them, dragged out of position by Voinovich's big vehicle.

Carrie held her gun in both hands, using her left arm to steady it. She shifted her aim now and then from Voinovich, who was looking frantic about the fate of his Sequoia, to Jimmy Gaffney, whom she didn't trust because his eyes were filled with guile. She didn't like being in the room with them, and she didn't like the fact that the office wall was moving, bottom first, toward the door.

There was a higher squeal of nails, a last bang of wood breaking, a shredding noise, and the wall fell inward into the office.

The safe skittered across the concrete floor to the doorway, hit the slightly raised weather-strip, tipped, and bounced end over end into the parking lot.

Jeff returned. "Okay, guys. Here's the last bit of work we'll need from you. Come out here and lift the safe into the back of this thing so we can be on our way."

Voinovich said, "Don't take my SUV."

Jeff said, "What choice do I have? Nobody else has a car that can even hold it."

Voinovich turned to Gaffney. "Say something."

"Don't take his car. It'll break his heart."

Jeff said, "I'll leave it in perfect shape on the street somewhere and call the club to tell you where it is."

They walked out to the place where the safe lay, a few feet behind the SUV. Voinovich said to Gaffney, "If we had the combination, this wouldn't have happened."

"No shit," Gaffney said. "I would have taken the money myself and be halfway to Rio."

"You wouldn't fit in there. Everybody is brown. You'd look like a freak. Help me lift this. And get it onto the carpet so we don't scratch my bumper." They squatted, lifted, and strained. "Use your legs, not your back."

They lifted the safe onto the bed at the back of the SUV. Then they both sat on the bumper, breathing heavily and stretching their strained arm muscles. Gaffney looked at Jeff. "Jesus Christ. Getting robbed by you two is a lot of work."

Carrie walked up with the two pistols that belonged to Gaffney and Voinovich, handed one to Jeff, and kept the other.

"Okay, guys," Jeff said. "We've got to finish up and get out of here. Let's head inside."

"You're not going to kill us, are you?"

"Not if you do as we say," said Carrie.

They made their way past the fallen wall into the office. Jeff said, "Sit down on those chairs." The two men did, and he wrapped duct tape around their wrists to bind their hands behind them, then taped their ankles together, then ran tape around and around them to keep them on the seats. He went to the desk, removed the batteries from their cell phones, then took the recorder from the security system.

"Well, good night, guys."

They nodded sullenly. As Carrie was leaving, Gaffney said, "Would you really have killed us?"

"I'm still thinking about it."

"Oh."

Jeff and Carrie went outside, locked the steel door behind them, and stopped to look at each other for a moment. "What do you think?"

"I'm glad they don't let strip clubs operate near residential neighborhoods. If they did, you couldn't feel good about firing a gun. But here you could set off bombs." She smiled up at him. "Can I shoot them?"

"What? Why?"

"Because I never have, and this is such a great opportunity. I really, really want to."

"Get your car. I'll follow you home."

"How about just one, then?"

"We've got to go. The police come by these places regularly, just to check the doors."

He followed her back onto the freeway, onto the exit ramp at Vineland, and up the hill to her house. When they arrived, she opened the garage door and he drove in. She threw an old folded tarp on the floor and covered it with two sheets of plywood. They slid the safe out onto the plywood so it wouldn't chip the concrete garage floor.

She was beaming. "You know, tonight was even better than last night. Robbing a strip club. Holding hostages. Grand Theft Auto. And tomorrow, safecracking. I think I'm falling in love."

19

JERRY GAFFNEY WAS only half asleep, because his mind couldn't quite shut down. He was thinking about too many things, or rather, passing over each of them in a repetitive cycle. Words, phrases, images had to be revisited. He slowly rose toward consciousness. He was lying on the clean, crisp white sheet on the big California-king bed in an apartment in Manhattan Beach. He looked at the digital clock on his right side and it said 4:15 A.M. He looked to his left and in the dim light he saw the creamy back of Sandy Belknap.

It was a short, abruptly tapering back that started with lean but square shoulders that looked as though she did some kind of workout, and then narrowed quickly. The ridge of backbone near the top became a recess at mid-back until it flattened just above the dimple that announced the start of her perfect bottom.

Jerry felt reverence for the beauty he could see at this moment in the dim predawn light. He had no right to be with her, certainly no right to be naked with her in her bed. It was one of those sudden phenomena, rare and unexpected like hailstorms.

He had spent much of the day after his brother, Jimmy, left driving her around in a new sedan with dealer plates that she had borrowed from the car lot. They had gone from restaurant to bar to office building to apartment, talking to her friends. At each stop she'd introduced him as her cousin from St. Louis. Her girlfriends were all temptingly attractive.

But Sandy Belknap was not somebody who suffered from competition. She had been a cheerleader at the University of Missouri and had held some kind of national sorority office. She was not a genius, but she could speak fluently and confidently, and that probably was about as useful as high intelligence. She was beautiful in a blond, blue-eyed, Midwestern kind of way, but maybe not clever or single-minded enough to be what she so obviously must have wanted to be, an actress. All good-looking young women from other states wanted that, even if they didn't do anything to accomplish it except present themselves in Los Angeles.

He lay in the bed feeling the subtle circulation of cool air from the grate over the bed and back into the intake in the hall ceiling at the other end of the room. The day had been one of those Los Angeles high-pressure summer days when the sky was a perfectly unvarying light blue bowl of infinity. The heat was the sort that radiated upward from the pavement to mid-thigh while the sun scorched the shoulders and back. Movement in the city was toward the ocean, like a tide that only began to subside around dusk as people moved inland to cool, dark bars.

When Sandy had introduced him as her cousin from St. Louis, the girls she was talking to seemed to take it for granted that she was lying. He would find an excuse to leave them alone for a few minutes at each stop, and she would confide to the other girl that she had an uncontrollable crush on Joe Carver and wanted him to have her address and cell phone number. She was even planning a party so he could show up without bothering to call or ask for a date.

But something else happened during the day, a kind of slow current that was always working on them and changing their course just a bit. As they went from place to place in the searing heat, they would get thirsty. He would buy them a drink. Twice they got into traffic jams, sat motionless in the skin-cooling conditioned air blowing over them, and talked. The alcohol made them imagine they'd known each other longer than they had.

In the evening they stopped for dinner at the Water Grill because the name sounded cool, and the fact that only fish seemed light enough to eat. They were already in a state of habituation from mere proximity, so many stops, so much talk, so many times when they had brushed against each other, breathed each other's air. The dinner revived them, disguised the effect of all the alcohol, but it added to the talk and the familiarity.

They made it into three clubs afterward — Wash, Stable, and The Room. The experience began to blur into one long trek past turning faces in a long, dark tunnel with music so loud he could remember feeling it rather than hearing it. Lights sputtered, wavered, and swept, and the young faces appeared for a moment and then drifted away.

During the evening the talk that went on was between Sandy and her women friends in ladies' rooms. At 1:00 A.M., Sandy got tired and he drove her to her apartment in Manhattan Beach. She warned him that she hadn't been there in almost a week, and when they got there he had to help her carry a huge stack of unopened mail. A few letters slipped off her pile, and she bent to pick it up off the carpet and lost her balance. He steadied her, picked her up, carried her to her bed, and set her down gently. He assumed she would close her eyes and fall asleep instantly, but she didn't. Instead she popped up on the bed, pressed her lips against his, and put her arms around him.

He had the thought that he didn't belong there with her, but it was only a passing sensation and not the most powerful at the time. It was like the acknowledgment he had made a few times that this or that money didn't belong to him: it didn't affect his behavior. He had been wishing for this moment since he had met her, without allowing himself to think about it in specific terms, and now he knew that something similar must have been in her mind too. It was different for her because she had known, of course, that all she had to do was signify willingness and it would happen. Now it had.

It was 4:15. As he thought back on what they had done, he was pleased. To the extent that he could interpret her sounds and movements, he believed that she had fallen asleep happy and satisfied. But it had left him in a state of pleasant agitation, not capable of real sleep. She was a daylight creature, somebody who got up early in the morning and went to work. He had worked nights since the day after he had liberated himself from tenth grade fifteen years ago.

He could feel that the night was reaching its most silent, the bluish half-light that would allow him to sleep. He drifted off.

Ding-dong DONG dong. Dong-dong DING dong. There was a pause in the chime sequence, but it made the mind alert and disturbed, because it was waiting for the rest of the tune to complete itself.

Sandy sat up suddenly in the bed, her eyes wide. She leaned over him, her right breast brushing his shoulder as she squinted to see the clock on his side. She saw it, jumped off the bed, and had her feet on the floor. Jerry was startled by her athleticism. She'd had no more than an hour of sleep, and she must still be feeling the drinks, but she was moving fast.

She was at the window looking down at the doorstep just as the ring began again. She turned to Gaffney and spoke as though she were resuming an ongoing conversation. "It's Paul. He's here."

"Paul, your boyfriend?"

"Yes. Paul Herrenberg. I knew I should have told him I was helping you."

"Give me a second." Jerry Gaffney sat up, snatched the pile of his clothes beside the bed, and pulled them on at high speed. He was dressed just as the next dreadful ring began and the man out-side started to pound on the door. Gaffney stepped into his shoes, pinned the badge to his belt beside the buckle, and slipped the gun holster onto his belt where it would show. "Okay."

"Okay what?"

"You've got choices to make. If you want me to hide, I'll hide, and you can say you were too drunk to drive to his apartment. If you want me to tell him about the case, I'll do that. If you want me to throw him out, I'll do that."

"Get in the closet." She went to the dresser, plucked a folded flannel nightgown out of a drawer, and pulled it over her head while she walked toward the apartment door. She opened it and then went down two more steps across the tiny foyer to open the outer door.

Jerry Gaffney wasn't happy about being trapped in a closet, but there was little choice in the one-bedroom apartment. He slipped inside and closed the sliding door most of the way, leaving only a small space open at the end.

He could hear her in a stage whisper. "Paul! What in the world are you doing here at this hour? It's four-thirty."

"Where the hell have you been?" the man's voice said, much louder.

"Be quiet," she whispered. "People are asleep."

"You didn't answer me. Where were you tonight?"

"Here, mostly. I was exhausted. It was so hot yesterday."

"Bullshit!" he bellowed. "I called you over and over, like a dozen times. I left messages on your cell and on your regular phone. You obviously weren't around to hear them."

"When I go to sleep, I turn off my phones. That means I don't want to be bothered."

"That's great, Sandy. That's just fucking great. I wait most of the night for you to show up, and you don't even have the decency to call me."

"I never said I was going to your apartment last night. There was no reason to call to tell you I wasn't coming, because there was no reason to think I was."

"Look, Sandy." He spoke with a quiet fury, slowly and plainly. "I was worried, so I started calling your friends."

"You called my friends in the middle of the night?"

"People said they saw you in clubs at midnight, quarter to one, one-thirty. It sounded like everybody in town saw you at one club or another, so stop lying about it. You were out with a guy."

She laughed, but it was a difficult thing to do well. "If you only knew."

"I do. You told half the city his name. Joe Carver."

"That is just so completely wrong. I can't believe you called everybody and embarrassed me like that. I can't believe anybody told you anything, and that you got it all wrong and put the most sickening interpretation on it. I'm so shocked. Just go home."

From his closet, Jerry Gaffney heard her begin to close the door, but then there was a thump like the heel of a hand striking the door and the wood vibrating. "Don't you shut the door in my face. Too much has happened for that." As Paul talked, Jerry could hear that the voice was coming nearer, up the steps and into the apartment. When he spoke again, Paul was in the small living room just ten feet from the bedroom door. "Why didn't you invite me in, Sandy? What's different that you'd stand in the doorway to try to keep me out?"

"Nothing is different. I never would have wanted anybody to come banging on my door at this hour. I asked you to go, so do it."

"Not yet."

"I'm asking you to leave." Jerry Gaffney could tell from the way her voice sounded that she had stepped in his way, blocking his entry into the bedroom. Jerry could have told her that it was the wrong way to keep him out.

Paul Herrenberg's voice became a tortured bellow. "He's here, isn't he? You've got the guy in the bedroom with you. Carver!

Come on out! Joe Carver!" His footsteps were heavy as he brushed past Sandy.

"What do you think you're doing? You have no right to barge into my bedroom."

"I want to meet Joe Carver, the guy who's so much better than I am." Herrenberg was pacing around in the bedroom now. Jerry could hear him walk to the bathroom and look in.

Jerry Gaffney was not a man who was reluctant to deliver a cheap, surprise punch, which was one reason he was listening intently to Paul Herrenberg's location at every moment. But he had been in enough fights to know that he would be foolish to throw away any opportunity to avoid fighting, so he was listening even more intently for reassurance that Herrenberg wasn't about to open the closet. So what he heard next was both unwelcome and welcome at once. Paul Herrenberg had been staring at Sandy Belknap's sheets like a detective, and then he dropped to his hands and knees to look under the bed. If he was doing that, he would certainly get to Sandy's closet next, but meanwhile, he could hardly be more vulnerable.

Jerry Gaffney slid the closet door open, delivered a top-of-the-foot kick to Paul Herrenberg's face, belly-flopped onto his limp body, and dragged his arms behind him to close the handcuffs on his wrists.

"What the—"

"Don't talk," said Gaffney gruffly. Herrenberg was much bigger than Gaffney had anticipated, and he was already thinking that if the cuffs didn't close in time, he was going to have to go for the gun. "I'm a police officer, and I'm going to—"

"You son of a—"

Jerry dazed him with a punch to the side of his head. "I asked you not to interrupt. You're going to have two choices. You can cooperate completely, or you can act like an angry asshole. If you do that, you're going to jail, and the trip will not be easy or pleasant. There are enough charges already to hold you."

"You can't just hit me like that. I've got a witness."

"Yes, I can." Gaffney punched the other side of his head, then grabbed him by the hair and pulled his head up as though he might slam Herrenberg's face on the floor. He held it there for a long, tense moment, then released it. "Now. Do you want to get through this without anything turning ugly?"

Herrenberg seemed to think for a minute, then went limp. "Yes."

"You just pushed your way into a lady's apartment after she told you that you weren't going to be allowed inside. That's forcible entry. You pushed her aside to get in. That's battery at least, and maybe even assault. Given the hour and the fact that you saw she isn't wearing much, you might draw some class-one felony charges."

"So what are you doing in her apartment?"

He grasped Herrenberg's hair again and hissed into his ear, "I don't have to tell you anything." He released him. "But I will. I'm attempting to apprehend an armed robbery suspect named Joe Carver, who seems to be interested in Miss Belknap. That means that any single stupid thing you do or say is interfering with a felony investigation. It's also harassing and threatening a brave citizen who has agreed to place herself in danger to act as bait."

"Oh, shit," Paul mumbled. "I didn't mean to."

"Now I want you to listen carefully, because what you say and do next is going to pretty much determine what the rest of your life will be like. If you're going to be a hard guy, you might get off with ten years, which is only five served if you're lucky. But you don't strike me as lucky."

"What do I have to do?"

"First, apologize to the lady."

"I'm sorry, Sandy. I apologize."

"Now apologize to me for obstructing justice and making me compromise an ongoing investigation."

"I'm sorry."

"Sorry who?"

"I'm sorry, officer. Sir."

His voice sounded so obsequious, so fearful and weak, that Gaffney looked up and saw that Sandy's face held a look of distaste.

"Now I want you to get up. I will walk you to the door. Then I'll take the handcuffs off. If you go silently and voluntarily, get in your car, and go away, we'll forget about filing charges. If I, or some other officer, have to put the cuffs on you again, the charges come back, and we'll do things the hard way."

"Don't worry about me. I'll go."

Gaffney took his arm, helped him up, and guided him to the door. He half-turned. "Sandy, I'll call you later. Okay? Just to talk."

She frowned. "Uh, I don't think so, Paul. I don't want to talk. If I ever do, I'll call you."

"But—"

Gaffney tightened his grip on Herrenberg's arm to stop the circulation. "She's being pretty clear. Don't you think so?"

"Yes." He half-turned again. "You won't even talk to me?" There were tears forming in his eyes.

"No. I want you to go away."

The tension went out of Herrenberg's muscles. Gaffney unlocked the handcuffs and removed them, then put his hand on his gun, but Herrenberg didn't even look back to see the gesture. He stepped out the door, down the steps to the outer door, and kept going.

Gaffney closed and locked the door, and turned.

Sandy was standing in the doorway to the bedroom, looking at him with her arms folded. "Are you sleepy?"

"Not now."

"Me either." As she stepped backward into the bedroom, she pulled the nightgown up and off, then threw it aside.

20

SPENCE SAT on the roof of the Bank of America building on Ventura Boulevard and watched the sun lighten the sky beyond the gradual curve where Du-Par's and Trader Joe's were just visible. He could hear one of the local flocks of escaped parrots screeching in first flight, and the cars that went by on the street weren't late-night partygoers and insomniacs now. These were regular people on their way to work.

He knelt and reached down for the .308 Remington rifle he had lying on the blanket. He ejected the box magazine, opened the bolt to be sure there was no round in the chamber, and took the weapon apart, removing the barrel and trigger assembly from the stock. He wrapped the parts in the blanket and put it into his backpack. It was clear by now that Joe Carver wasn't planning to show up to ambush whoever came with the night's take from the clubs. He wasn't too surprised. It had seemed unlikely that Carver would strike two nights in a row, and that unlikeliness had been Spence's main reason for coming.

He slipped the straps over his shoulders and crossed the roof to the back of the building, then climbed down the steel rungs set into the wall. He stayed behind the bank building, then walked along the side of the parking structure to get to the sloping lawn above the Los Angeles River, followed the high metal fence that marked the concrete bank above the concrete channel, and turned where the bridge crossed over the river at Whitsett.

While he was still on Ventura, he passed two other men walking toward bus stops and wearing backpacks. Since the cost of gasoline had gotten ridiculous, more and more people in the eastern part of the Valley had stopped taking cars to work and begun riding the bus wearing backpacks. He passed the bus stop at Whitsett and crossed the bridge.

The night had not been completely wasted. It had given Spence time to think.

Kapak was not wrong about Joe Carver. He really did seem to want to blow Kapak's life apart. It seemed to Spence that Carver had taken up the work with enthusiasm, and he was actually making progress in ruining Kapak. But it didn't make Spence relish the idea of killing Carver.

Spence approached his car watchfully, then put the backpack in the trunk, got on the freeway at Laurel Canyon, and drove to Kapak's house. He left his car a hundred feet from the front gate and went through the pedestrian gate with his key. As he passed the garage, he looked in the window and noticed that Kapak's car was gone. He looked at the house. The windows were all still dark. He went inside, then walked through the building quickly, looking for signs that Kapak had been here.

When he reached the hallway to Kapak's master suite, he removed his shoes and walked slowly along the hardwood floor in his socks, opened the door, and saw that the bed had not been slept in. On the way back he stepped into his shoes and thumbed through the directory of his telephone. Voinovich's phone said, "The customer you dialed is out of the calling area," which probably meant the phone was off. He got the same recording for Jimmy

Gaffney and for Jerry Gaffney. He almost called Guzman, but remembered he was in the hospital recovering. He called Corona.

"Yeah?" The voice was sleepy.

"It's me. Spence. I just got to Kapak's house, and nobody's here. He hasn't been in his bed. Is something up?"

"Not that I heard."

"How's Guzman?"

"Not bad for a guy that was shot. They're giving him a lot of pills for pain."

"Tell him I'm sorry I haven't been to see him yet. There are probably a few people watching to see who shows up."

"I know the cops are, for sure. They're making a list. I'm on it, but you don't need to be. Guzman's sleeping half the time anyway."

"Just so he knows the rest of us haven't dumped him there."

"No problem. And I'll call you if I find out what's up with Kapak."

Spence went to the other end of the house to the room off the pantry where he liked to sleep when he was in Kapak's house. He sat at the table in the small room and looked closely at each of the sections on the security monitor screen until he was satisfied that no human activity was taking place.

He lay down on the narrow bed in the small room and placed his cell phone near his head so if it rang he would wake and get it quickly. He took his pistol out of his belt and put it under the pillow, then slept.

Joe Carver stepped out of his room at the motel and studied the morning for portents and omens. Yesterday it had been clear and hot, and today would be an exact repetition of the day. The weatherwoman on television — a person who had been so surgically altered that her body was like a child's drawing of a woman and her face had the wide unchanging stare and protruding mouth of a bass — had stood in front of a chart that displayed a row of seven calendar days that each held a perfect yellow ball of a sun and the number 102. Carver knew that the best time for moving around the city was now, before it was fully light out.

He found his car undisturbed in the motel's parking lot, held his breath while he started it, and then chuckled at himself for being nervous. There was no reason to imagine any of Kapak's men knew he had a car, and even if they had found it here, that any of them was capable of rigging it to explode. He drove toward the plaza in Encino where there was a restaurant that served customers breakfast in a shady, enclosed alcove down a flight of stairs below street level.

Now that his anger was fading, he was ready to decide exactly what he wanted to do next. He knew he wanted Kapak's men to leave him alone so he could restart his new life in Los Angeles. He wasn't sure how to accomplish that without destroying them, and he wasn't a murderer. At least, he had managed to keep from being one so far. The fact that he was here in Los Angeles at all had been because of a problem in Chicago that made the Kapak situation seem irritatingly familiar. He remembered the night it started.

It was late. His name was still Pete Rollins and he still smoked. He stepped outside the bar he owned and stood in the shadows under the awning, smoking a cigarette and watching a gentle snowfall building a feathery white layer over the sidewalk.

He saw a man drive up in a black Cadillac Escalade and stop in front of the building. Two men wearing long overcoats got out and headed into his bar. He snuffed out his cigarette in the sand-filled urn beside the door and went inside to make drinks for the newcomers.

He stepped into the warm, quiet room with the dark antique wood paneling and thick woodwork, and the glowing lights behind the bar that made the liquor bottles look like amber and emerald and diamond. He was proud of his establishment. As he walked in, he actually relished the sensation of surprise and pleasure his new customers must be feeling.

He came through the inner doorway just as the guns came out from under the long coats. They looked to Rollins like AK-47s with the wooden stocks cut off. The shorter man started firing into one of the customers at the bar while the other turned his body in a semicircle, sweeping the barrel of his rifle like the gun in a tank turret, ready to open up, but searching for a target. Rollins was astonished. The man who had been standing at the bar remained upright for a moment, and then collapsed into what looked like a pile of blood-soaked clothes on the floor.

Rollins ducked behind his bar, swung the short-barreled shotgun up over the wooden surface, and dropped the shooter. The second man opened fire at Rollins and backed outside into the cold night.

Rollins ran after him, stepped over the body on the floor, and realized he knew the two shooters. He had met the two men a year earlier at a poker game that was run by his liquor distributor. The men were two brothers named Storrono. He made it to the door in time to see the Escalade arrive outside the bar and the surviving shooter step in. Rollins remembered the bloody footprint where he had stood. As the SUV drove off, Rollins ran inside, snatched up the telephone behind the bar, called the police, and told them what had just happened and who had made it happen. The anger carried him through the crime-scene examination and the long police interviews that night.

He hadn't thought much about the danger he was in until he was ready to leave the police station the next morning. The police detective in charge of the case said that if he saw anything that worried him—any sign that somebody was unusually interested in him—he should request temporary protection.

Before the trial of the remaining Storrono brother, the case suddenly changed, or the police view of it did. The suspect talked. The murdered man was not an enemy of the Storronos. They had simply agreed to do a contract killing. The man they had killed was one of the targets of a federal investigation. The man who had

216

wanted him killed was another, much bigger, and more important organized crime figure. From that moment, the main concern of the authorities was keeping Storrono alive. Pete Rollins was still in danger, but he was no longer essential.

Federal officials took over the case, and shortly after that they told Rollins he was going to be relocated to South Carolina. His name would be Joseph Carver. They supplied him with a driver's license, birth certificate, Social Security card, high school diploma, and a job in a furniture factory outside Charleston.

It was hot work, operating machines with sharp steel blades spinning rapidly and sanders that filled the air with fine sawdust that stuck to his skin and found its way past his mask and goggles into his nose and eyes. After a few months, the government determined that he could never be Pete Rollins again and had intermediaries sell his bar and his house. They paid his mortgages and sent the remainder in two checks made out to Joe Carver. He decided to move to Los Angeles.

Carver arrived in Los Angeles with plenty of money and a notion that it was time to open a new business and start over. He spent some time at first just getting used to L.A. nightlife and meeting people. He spent a lot of money on drinks and dinners. He had overdone it, he knew now, and he regretted it. He had gotten to know a lot of women very quickly, but he had not made the right impression. Two of them thought he was probably an armed robber and had told Kapak's men.

Last night he had overheard the names of the two women — Sandy Belknap and Sonia Rivers. To his surprise, he actually remembered both women clearly. He had met Sandy Belknap in the Adder Club. She was a young blond who seemed fresh and enthusiastic, with a cute face and blue eyes. He had not had any serious intention of forming any kind of relationship with her, because she was too much engaged in being pretty. But he had learned over the years that the best way to attract the attention of women was to be seen with the best-looking ones. The others seemed to find that intriguing. Maybe they thought it meant he had been cleared of their worst suspicions — he couldn't be a dangerous creep. Since he wasn't as good-looking as the woman he was with, maybe he was rich or clever or funny. The first night he started talking to her, other women began to drift in his direction, and then to put themselves behind her, in his line of sight.

He had actually met Sandy Belknap five times in three different clubs. After the first time, she had always been the one to approach him. She'd found it most comfortable to make her entrance by coming up to a friendly acquaintance who bought her first drink and gave her a few minutes to study the crowd without being overwhelmed. It was possible that she subscribed to the same theory he did, that people were most attracted to the person already taken. When he and Sandy had legitimized each other for a few minutes, they had parted with an affectionate hug and found other partners.

Sonia Rivers had seemed to Carver to be more promising. She didn't have that protective wall of self-satisfaction that Sandy had. She was not at ease in bars trying to meet men. The first night he had met her, he had caught an expression now and then on her face that he interpreted as a kind of astonishment at finding herself in a club.

He had approached her in a quiet moment while a band was leaving and the DJ was getting set up, and asked if he could buy her a drink.

"Gee, I don't think so, thanks."

"Why not?"

"I don't want one."

"It's not really about wanting the actual drink. It can be a soft drink. No alcohol. It can be water, and you don't have to swallow any of it. A drink is symbolic."

"Of what?"

"That you're willing to hang out with me for a bit and talk and stuff."

"And stuff?"

"I'm not promising stuff. That's only if we like each other. Otherwise, just a friendly chat, and no stuff. If the issue is me and not the drink, you say, 'Get lost.' Now, would you like a drink?"

"I feel funny about it, to tell you the truth."

"Why?"

"I don't want to look like a woman who goes to bars to pick up men."

"Isn't that why you're here?"

"Not really." She considered. "But I guess that's one way to look at it."

"What's another way?"

"That I'm here to have fun."

"Great," he said. "Let's have some fun. Do you have any board games? A piñata?"

"I'm sort of starting to see your point. The fun I was thinking of does involve meeting a guy. So, okay, let's see about that fun. Do you dance?"

"Tonight I do."

They had fun that night. They danced for a while. Then he took her to the Pacific Dining Car for a late-night dinner, and then back out to the clubs. He had always favored champagne for late-night excursions because it was less debilitating than distilled liquor, and since he was buying champagne for a woman, it had to be good champagne. He had not wanted to leave a credit history in the name Joe Carver because of the Storronos, so he had to spend cash. So he supposed he had been guilty of flashing a lot of cash in front of her like a bank robber. That was certainly where those accusations had come from. She hadn't imagined it. But there was an incredible distance between spending a lot of cash and being a robber, and he wondered what he had done to make her take that leap.

That night while they were alone in the relative quiet of the all-night restaurant, she had asked him lots of questions and he had answered them more or less truthfully. He had mentioned that he had come to Los Angeles only a month earlier. So that had supplied the other half of the story. He was a man from elsewhere who had arrived a month ago and was around town spending lots of cash. But that was all.

He got into his car and drove. He was going to find Sonia Rivers and see what he could do to correct her first impression of him. Telling Kapak he hadn't robbed him hadn't worked. Maybe getting the two women who had implicated him to change their minds might add some credibility to his denials. If that didn't work, somebody was going to end up dying.

21

MANCO KAPAK AWOKE in Sherri Wynn's bedroom and then remembered the hospital. He'd had a heart attack—or maybe he hadn't, but he'd had something. He walked carefully into the bathroom to urinate. His prostate gland was enlarged—not unusually so for his age, his doctor said—and he was used to getting up from sleep like this. He moved slowly and silently to keep from waking Sherri. This time the darkness was already being replaced by half-light, so he could see some of the obstacles he had missed in the dark.

He stepped into the bathroom, and when he turned to close the door, he saw his naked reflection in the mirror on the medicine cabinet. It was a terrible reminder.

While he was with Sherri early in the evening, he had somehow fallen into imagining himself as he had been when he was young. How could he have forgotten what time had done to him? He had been, in his own mind, a fit and distinguished-looking man in middle age. He wasn't that anymore at all. He was an old animal that was limping toward death. In the dark, with the help of the Armagnac, he had simply forgotten. But his heart had remembered how old he was.

Kapak felt an overwhelming urge to get dressed, to cover himself. When they had made love it had been in the dark, so she had probably not really seen him. Maybe he didn't have to leave her with the memory of his body. He sneaked into the bedroom and began to gather his clothes from the floor.

Sherri stirred. "What are you doing?"

He faced away from her. "I'm sorry. I didn't mean to wake you up. I was just getting my clothes off the floor."

"Come back to bed. It's too early."

"I don't want my clothes to be wrinkled."

"You've just been through a big ordeal. You shouldn't be doing things like this." She got up out of bed, still naked. She picked up his shirt and his pants, walked to the closet, took down two hangers, and hung them. "There." She came up behind him, put her arms around him, and kissed the back of his neck. "Come lie down with me. There's nothing you have to do at this hour. We'll get some more sleep and I'll make you a nice breakfast."

She slipped around him and tugged the sport coat he was holding in front of him, but he didn't let go.

"I get it. You're shy."

"Don't be silly."

She pressed her body against the coat and spoke with her lips against his cheek. "I've seen everything there is to see, really close up, if you remember. And I think you look just fine. You're not twenty anymore. Neither am I. I've had my own problems with that over the years, but not last night. I feel comfortable with you, and I don't want to put clothes on now, and I don't want you to, either. Come on."

He let the coat drop and sat on the bed. In a moment they were lying on the bed together in a gentle embrace. "It would have hurt me if you sneaked away at dawn. Don't worry. I can keep a secret. Nobody ever has to know this happened."

He remembered what he had done at Rogoso's house, and that she was his alibi. "No," he said. "That's exactly what I don't want. If somebody asks who you were with last night, tell them."

"Really?"

"Yes. Only don't tell them I had a problem and had to go to the hospital. If you do, say I had an erection that lasted four hours."

"That doesn't sound like a very nice time to me."

"No? Then make up what does sound nice and say that."

"He made me feel happy and special. Afterward I was so sleepy that I slept better than I have in months."

"That's good? Sleepy?"

"If I tell other women that, they won't leave you alone."

"Then you don't have to tell them."

"I won't. Now close your eyes, relax, and lie still."

He took a few deep breaths and lay there with Sherri's smooth body touching his. He gave a tentative snore that woke him, and then she turned away from him and they lay together like spoons in a drawer. Then he was asleep.

Some time later the telephone rang. Sherri jumped up, grabbed the phone, and slipped into the bathroom with it. "Hello?" she said quietly.

Kapak was awake. The sun was bright in the places where it shone through the blinds. He could hear Sherri talking in a hushed voice beyond the closed door.

After a minute the door opened and she came out, looking concerned. "You're awake?"

"Yeah. The phone woke me."

"It's Skelley. He's calling from Temptress."

"What's he doing there already?"

"He wants to talk to you." She held out the phone.

Kapak took it. "Skelley. How did you find me?"

Skelley said, "Your phone was off, and Spence didn't know where you were. I was worried so I looked at the surveillance footage from last night to be sure nobody hit you over the head after I left. I saw you and Sherri in my office, so I took a guess."

"Very smart." He was beginning to feel optimistic. His alibi was getting stronger and involving more people. "Well, you've got me now. What's up?"

"We've got lots of trouble. Siren got robbed last night."

"Robbed? Where were Voinovich and Gaffney?"

"They were there. The day manager at Siren found them tied up with duct tape."

"Are they all right?"

"Yeah. They said it was a man and a woman, both young, just like at the bank the other night. They stole Voinovich's SUV and drove off with the safe. They pulled down the wall to the office to get the safe out."

"I just don't see how this happened. How did they even get in the building?"

"What can I say? They got suckered. Gaffney was kind of vague on what happened, but I got Voinovich alone and talking about his SUV, and he got pissed enough so he wasn't thinking about how he and Gaffney looked. The chick that Joe Carver brought with him pretended to be drunk, banging on the door and wanting to audition as a dancer."

"So Jimmy let her in."

"Yep. Apparently she's really hot."

"So why the hell is she doing armed robberies?"

"I can't imagine."

"I'm really starting to wonder why Joe Carver won't just give up and go away. He's already got me for what? A couple hundred thousand, probably. I met him once. Does he want me dead? He must be crazy." He sighed. "What time is it?"

"About six-thirty. Want me to call the police?"

"Is there anything around the building that we don't want anybody to see?"

"No. Gaffney and Voinovich had guns, but they don't now."

"Let me think for a second. No. Call them. Maybe the cops can find Carver. Let them try."

"Got it. I'd better call them right away, if I'm calling, or they'll wonder why I waited."

"Do it. And then call Spence and tell him what happened." Kapak pressed the End button and tossed the phone on the bed where Sherri could reach it. "I'll have to skip that breakfast," he said. "But thanks."

"Are you going?"

"Yeah. I'll go home and change my clothes and then see what they did to Siren. There was something about knocking down a wall to get to the safe."

She went to the closet and brought Kapak his clothes on hangers. "I'm sorry about the club."

"Things happen. You just have to do what you can to fix them."

"I'm going to forget about what happened to you last night — the hospital and all. I understand why you want to keep it quiet. But you should remember. You need to take it easy."

"I'll do that after I've done what I can to protect my clubs."

"I'm working again tonight."

"Yeah?"

"In case you feel like coming over again. You know when I get off."

He looked up as he buckled his belt. She shrugged, apparently unconscious of the fact that she was still naked. But her eyes were averted, looking at the wall, and he could see she was nervous about what he was going to say.

"You mean I'm invited?"

She turned and met his eyes. "Yes. Any time you want to come."

"I don't know what's going to happen today. The last couple of days have been kind of complicated." He watched her face turn down to look at the floor in disappointment. "But it's nice to know that at the end of it I'll be with you again."

She hugged him, then pulled away and went into the bathroom and came back with a thick white bathrobe, which she cinched tightly at the waist. "I'll walk you out."

22

KAPAK SHOWERED IN HIS master bathroom and dressed in fresh clothes. He wished he had time to shower in the guest-house, but he was in a hurry this morning. Just as Kapak finished brushing his teeth, he heard the doorbell. When he came out of his suite, Spence was already moving toward the door, but he waved him off. "I'll take care of this. Just stay out of sight."

When he opened the door, Lieutenant Slosser was standing in front of him, a bit too close, and looking down at him intently. Kapak was too old and had seen too much to allow himself a startle reflex. He kept his face empty. "Hello, Captain."

"I'm a lieutenant."

"Did you hear we got robbed again?"

"I heard that. It's getting to be an expensive habit."

"Expensive, yeah. It better not be a habit. Come on in."

Lieutenant Slosser stepped inside, and Kapak closed the door. Kapak followed Slosser's eyes and saw the tray with two cups and a pot of coffee. "I see you're just having coffee."

"You want some?"

"No, thanks. I already had enough today. I wasn't sure you'd be up. But since you are, would you like to go up to Siren with me? I'm going now to take a look around."

Kapak hesitated. This couldn't be anything but an attempt to entrap him. But he needed to know what Slosser knew and what he thought. "Maybe I'll take you up on that. Let me just get my wallet and keys."

Slosser stepped into the living room. His eyes never stopped moving, collecting details, making their way from one end of the room to the other, then through the French doors that led out to the garden of tropical plants among big stones that looked as though they'd come from far away, and on to the other windows. There seemed to be nobody here but Kapak, which Slosser judged was highly unlikely for a man who was under a barrage of attacks. He would have at least a bodyguard or two. And if Slosser had come with a warrant, he knew he would have been able to find plenty of weapons without much of a search.

Kapak returned, putting things in his coat pockets. He went to the front door and held it open for Slosser.

"I'm just curious," Slosser said. "Don't you have people with you?"

"Right now? No. I usually have a driver to take me places, and I sometimes have one or two club security people around at night if I've got reason to be worried. But everybody stays up late and sleeps late. I'm only up because of the robbery, and I don't think the bastard will kidnap me today. He's already got my money."

"He?"

"It's just a way of thinking. There's always a 'he.' He's the one who thought of the plan and told the others what to do. He's the one we have to outsmart."

In the driveway was the big, plain blue Ford that Kapak had expected. Slosser opened the passenger door, and Kapak ducked in. Both men were aware that Slosser had the habit of putting his hand on a prisoner's head to keep him from bumping it on the car door frame, and that Kapak was trying to slip in too fast for that.

Slosser drove in silence for a few minutes before Kapak said, "You might want to take the freeway to Sepulveda. That's how I go."

"Oh. I just need to make a quick stop before we head to the club. I figured you wouldn't mind."

Kapak shrugged. "The money's already stolen. It's not like we could stop it if we got there now. You got cops already at the club, right?"

"Sure. Detectives, fingerprint people, photographers, crime scene people, the whole crew."

"Then I can wait. They have to be out of there before I can clean up and put the pieces back together."

"You know where we're going?"

"How would I?"

"Sometimes people will make a lucky guess." Slosser stared at Kapak, but he couldn't quite tell whether Kapak was reacting or not. If so, he was good at hiding it. For days Slosser had been sure Kapak was in a war with somebody. Maybe what had happened last night in Malibu was Kapak's counterattack. "Sure you don't want to guess?"

"Pretty sure."

"The sheriff's people asked me to stop at another crime scene for a few minutes, and then we'll go up to yours."

"Another robbery?"

"No," said Slosser. They reached the Santa Monica Freeway, and Slosser headed west. He drove until the final exit, where the freeway ended in the incline onto the Pacific Coast Highway. "Wow. The ocean. You can feel it when you go down that incline. And all of a sudden you're in another, better world. The air is fresh and clean. The temperature goes down about ten degrees just on that ramp. Know anybody who lives along the ocean, like in Malibu?"

"I don't think so," Kapak said. "A house on the beach has got to cost quite a few million. I don't know anybody with that kind of spending money."

"I would have thought you could live there yourself. Maybe you could get a few of the girls at your clubs to chip in, and you could live down here with them, like a harem."

"The dancers?"

"Sure."

"Girls like that don't need to buy a beach house. They get invited."

"You said you don't know anybody living there."

"Not now. A few years ago there was a girl named Alisha Dolan. She danced under the name, what was it? Tiffany Rose. She got hired to be an extra in a movie, and she caught the eye of the director. She played him right and became his girlfriend. It lasted a long time. They lived in Malibu. I think he died, though."

Kapak could see the house coming up on the left. It didn't resemble a house now. The fire he had set had simply devoured the building. He kept himself from betraying any knowledge of the place by staring openly at it as Slosser drove past. "There must have been quite a fire there."

Slosser was uncertain. If Kapak had pretended not to notice the black pile of charcoal where a big beach house had once stood, he would have known. But Kapak had not.

"Yeah. They say it went up quick. The firefighters came right away, but all they could even try to do by then was run in to search for survivors and wet down the two houses on either side."

Kapak said nothing, even when Slosser turned across the two left lanes and came back toward the burned ruin.

Slosser glided to a stop behind another plain police car and a white vehicle that had LOS ANGELES COUNTY CORONER stenciled across the door. He got out and went to talk to the detective in the other car. He leaned on the car and spoke to him with his face turned away from Kapak for a few minutes, then turned around and came back to Kapak. "Come on. Let's look around."

Kapak got out of the car slowly. If he refused to look, Slosser would think he was feeling guilty about killing the three men and burning the building. He felt a small, hot spot of anger in his chest. When he was young he had felt bad if he had to harm someone, even if they had brought it on themselves. But he felt no guilt about Rogoso. He had been a betrayer, an enemy who had set up a trap and then spoken to him with contempt before sending him off to be killed. Kapak was proud of killing him. But he reminded himself that the pride was worse than the guilt, because the natural impulse was to hide guilt and flaunt pride.

Slosser walked close to the foundation of the building, which was now just a rectangular wall around a deep hole, mostly covered with fallen lengths of charred wood and dust, and below that, a glimpse of the blackened frames of Rogoso's Bentley and his Maserati in the garage under the house. The only remnants of the upper floors were a frame of steel I-beams that supported those levels, a few pipes, and the brick chimney.

Kapak followed Slosser as he walked along the side of the foundation away from the road. He could feel the concrete give way to gravel, then to loose, grassy soil, then to pure, fine, salt-white beach under his shoes. Once he could see past the ruin, the blue ocean dominated his vision. The destruction was an improvement.

"You see Rogoso's cars?"

"What?"

"The cars he had in the garage when it went up."

"Rogoso? Is that the name of the owner?"

"Yeah. Very fancy cars."

"Too bad. But I suppose they're insured."

Slosser went on, walking in the sand on the ocean side of the ruin, looking at everything as though it meant something to him. Kapak wasn't giving anything away, but Slosser knew he was guilty. The perfect detachment of his reaction was almost an admission. He pretended to know nothing, and he asked nothing.

Slosser could see the coroner's crew who had been working in the rubble now had something in a body bag, and together they lifted it onto their stretcher. The two men rose on a signal and stepped out of the wreckage carefully, their eyes on their feet. Slosser said, "I guess that must be the third one."

"The third what?"

"Body. The firefighters got the first two out right away when the fire hadn't reached them yet. But then the ceiling went, and this one wasn't reachable. He was a distance from the other ones on the stairs."

"Three killed, eh?" Kapak seemed to be showing only polite interest. "Too bad."

Slosser knew Kapak wasn't going to lower his guard. He had said nothing that would give Slosser an opening and made no slips. "That's all I needed to see," said Slosser. "Let's drive up and see your robbery."

They got into the car again and Slosser drove back toward Santa Monica along the Pacific Coast Highway. He tried again. "Did you ever hear of Manny Rogoso?"

"I don't think so," said Kapak. "Is he famous?"

"Why would you say that?"

"People who live in places like this have a lot of money."

"He was a drug dealer. Nothing special about him. He wasn't the biggest or the scariest. I would guess that if he hadn't gotten shot to death, his next big problem would be the bank foreclosing on that house. He paid fifteen million for it."

Kapak said nothing, but he thought about Rogoso. It was typical that he would exaggerate how much the new house had cost, when most people would have respected him more if he had paid less. "I suppose if he had been sensible, he wouldn't be a drug dealer, and he wouldn't be dead."

"Just out of curiosity, where were you last night from, say, midnight on?"

"Is that why you brought me all the way down here? You think I killed some drug dealer?"

"No need to get upset. You weren't at Siren last night. Where were you?"

"I was at Wash, my dance club on Hollywood Boulevard, until one or so, and then I went up to Temptress, my gentlemen's club in the west Valley. I don't get to every place I own every night."

"But I hear you sent the cash from all your clubs to Siren last night for the first time to put it in the safe."

"That's right, and I didn't think it would help to have me and everybody else show up there at closing time. It might draw attention to what was going on. I already had two security guys staying with the money."

Slosser said, "Well, you just have to excuse me for asking. When a company does things differently for just one night and there's a killing, I have to wonder if somebody's making himself an alibi."

"Is there some reason why I should let you drive me all over the county and ask me questions? Or are we going to stop and pick up my lawyer?"

"The lawyer I met? Gerald Ospinsky? Jesus, why would you bother?"

"To protect my rights."

"You had a business hit by armed robbers last night. You called the police. We didn't call you. How's this? While your club was being robbed last night, were you at home?"

"I don't know exactly when that happened yet. I know it was after two, because I had the managers of my clubs bring their cash to Siren after closing time. I was at Temptress watching the money count, said goodbye to Skelley, the manager, when he left to drive to Siren with the bank deposits. That makes it, like, two-thirty or so."

"What about the rest of the night?"

"I went home with a lady friend who works at Temptress."

"Dancer?"

"No. Waitress."

"Name?"

"Sherri Wynn. I was there until Skelley called me around six-thirty to tell me about the robbery."

Nick Slosser sat in silence as he drove, studying and memorizing the details of the story, comparing each part of it with what he knew about the club business, Kapak's habits, and human nature. The time of the fire in Malibu was pretty well established at 1:10, because neighbors heard the noise of a gas tank blowing up, saw the fire, and called 911. But that didn't mean that was the time of death for those three men. They might have been dead a bit earlier. He considered Kapak. He was a man in his mid-sixties, strong but not used to physical labor anymore. If he had killed those three, he almost certainly wouldn't have done it alone. Probably he would have sent people. He glanced at him. "It takes a lot of guts to sleep with your own waitresses."

"Only if they don't want to," said Kapak.

"You know—you're rich, they're not. They can file sexual harassment lawsuits, maybe a reprisal suit, and claim just about anything. It's safer to go down the street and date somebody else's employees."

Kapak shrugged. "I'm old. I can't live like I'm afraid all the time. She's a nice, respectable, grown-up woman."

"Been going together long?"

"No. But she's worked for me for six or seven years, so I know her pretty well."

They drove up the San Diego Freeway and then turned to the Ventura Freeway and got off in the northeastern industrial part of the Valley. It was full of warehouses of every description, auto wrecking yards, machine shops. They reached the parking lot of Siren, where there were more cops and technicians, white vans, and plain sedans. The building was set off by yellow crime-scene tape.

Slosser and Kapak got out and ducked under the tape, crossed the small stretch of parking lot that was taped off, and entered the building. "Shit," said Kapak. The office wall was lying on the floor in what used to be the rear loading area for deliveries. The place was a mess. There were white and blue insulated wires dangling from the ceiling where they used to meet the wall that had been torn out.

He saw his day manager, Kearns. "Kearns, this is Lieutenant Slosser from the police. He's been looking into all the robberies and things." Kearns nodded, and the two shook hands.

Slosser said, "I'm sure the other officers have gotten your story, but let me try to catch up. Do you have any idea who did this?"

"The guys said it was a man and a woman, both carrying guns. They got our two security guys to open the door, then took off with the safe in an SUV that belonged to one of our guys."

"Have you looked at the surveillance tapes yet?"

"No. They were smart. They disconnected the whole box and took it with them."

"We'll see just how smart," said Slosser. "If the box turns up for sale, then they were dumb." He walked outside to talk to the other cops for a few minutes, then came back in. "They're just about finished out there. They've got all they can from the scene. No fingerprints, but a couple of brass casings. You can probably clean the place up and open by happy hour."

Kearns said, more to Kapak than to Slosser, "I called a carpenter already. They should be here within an hour." He looked at his watch.

"Want to stick around here, or you want a ride home?" Slosser stepped toward the door.

"My guys can handle this," Kapak said. "I'll go with you."

"Okay."

The two men walked across the parking lot. The tape had already been taken down, and Kapak could see deep marks on the pavement that he supposed were gouges made by the heavy safe.

Slosser said, "Are you ready to tell me who's at war with you?"

"It's a guy. I don't know much about him, but his name is Joe Carver."

234

"I'll check that out," said Slosser. He'd had detectives looking into it since the shootout at the bank. The problem was that there were lots of Joe Carvers, all over the country. Given a year or two of solid work, it was possible to check on each one — even call them all on the phone and talk with them. And the detectives were doing that. But so far there was no clear connection between any of them and Manco Kapak, and no evidence that any of them had a history of bank deposit robberies.

23

CARRIE SAID, "What are you doing?"

"You'll see." Jeff knelt in front of the safe, held the flour in the palm of his hand, took in a slow, deep breath, and blew. The fine white cloud flew from his palm and covered the keypad of the locked safe. "See? Look closely."

She knelt beside him and leaned close to the keypad. "Oh my God. Fingerprints."

"Right," said Jeff. "There are prints on the one, the seven, the eight, and the four. No prints on any of the other keys. If you have ten digits, then there are a billion possible combinations. But if you have a ten-digit keypad with fingerprints on only four numbers, then the combination has to be an arrangement of those four numbers. That's, like, twenty-four possible combinations."

He took up the paper and pencil, wrote 1478, then pushed those keys. Nothing happened. He tried 1487, 1748, 1784, 1874, 1847. "Okay. Now we start with 4." He tried 4178, 4187, 4781, 4718, 4817, 4871. "Now eight." He punched in 8147.

"I'll go make some coffee." Carrie got up and stepped toward the back door.

"Got it."

"What?" She turned to see him swing the safe door open.

"It's 8147."

She moved closer to him as he looked inside. "Four bags this time. Does that mean what I think it means?"

He pulled the first bag out and handed it to her. She opened it and looked inside. "It's money, all right." She pulled out the deposit slip. "Twenty-six thousand from Temptress." She set the bag down and picked up the next. "Twenty-two from Siren. Only sixteen from Wash. This one doesn't say what it's from, but it's got over eighteen in it."

"I guess we paid for last night's dinner."

She put her arms around him and squeezed, rocking him from side to side. "I can't believe you. You're so dumb and so smart at the same time. You always surprise me."

"Then at some point you'll expect to be surprised, and so you won't be. Still want this safe?"

"I don't know. Should I?"

"There are pros and cons."

"What are the pros?"

"You and I don't have to haul the damned thing somewhere in a stolen SUV and dump it."

"What are the cons?"

"If you leave it in your house, somebody can always look at the serial number and trace it to the strip club. Or you sell the house and some future owner forgets the combination, so he writes to the company and asks for it."

"Not good," she said. "Let's get rid of it. I don't want to do it myself, though. We just stole, like, eighty grand. Can't we just find some neighborhood kids we can pay to drive the SUV away and ditch it?"

"I'd like to, but even if they didn't get caught doing it, they'd talk about it later, and eventually the cops would be asking us about it."

"I hadn't thought about it that way—that whoever dumps it could get caught. Maybe it will be a sort of adventure."

"An adventure?"

"Yes," she said. "You know I love that. It's the best." Her eyes were glowing.

Sometimes he felt as though he had managed to grab the mane of a running horse, but holding on took all his physical strength and presence of mind. And it could only end one way that he knew of.

He was trying to learn to think faster than he usually did, because she could never be stopped, only diverted onto another path that she'd gallop down at the same frenzied pace. "We'll do this. Let's take the Sequoia and leave the safe inside when we dump it. Do you have any Windex and paper towels?"

"Sure. I have some out here in the garage." She went to a cupboard on the side wall that held supplies. "What do you want cleaned?"

"The safe and the parts of the SUV we might have touched—door handles, windows, dashboard."

"I'd better do it," she said, and began to spray the door handles and wipe them off.

"What—men aren't good at cleaning things?"

"Not men. You." She sprayed the Windex in his direction, but he dodged it. She wiped every interior surface, then all of the door handles, and stood on the running board and wiped great swaths of the doors and roof. Then Jeff pulled the SUV out of the garage, hosed it off, wiped it with a chamois while Carrie went inside to get ready.

Carrie came out wearing a crisp summer dress and flat shoes that looked like ballet slippers. "I'll drive the big one," she said.

"Are you sure?"

"Yes, I'm sure."

He knew that she had made the determination that driving the stolen vehicle with the safe in it was more exciting than driving the getaway car, so he knew that there was no way to talk her out of it. And ordering her not to would make her start searching for greater risks. "Then wear a pair of gloves." He reached into the trunk of his Trans Am and handed her a pair of clear surgical gloves.

He watched her put them on. "We just want to get rid of it. That means park it someplace where the neighbors will put up with it for a day and then call the cops. Don't pick a place where there will be cameras. No shopping malls, airports, public buildings, parking structures. It should be along a curb in a residential neighborhood. We keep it absolutely simple. Okay?"

"Okay," she said. Her big, clear eyes were unblinking and the smile on her lips seemed almost innocent in its sincerity. "I know a good place. Just follow me." She put on the gloves, climbed in, and shut the door, and began to back the big vehicle down the driveway.

As Jeff stepped to his car, he began to think of other things he should have said before she left. She was driving a car stolen in an armed robbery. It would not be wise to drive it very far. She shouldn't speed or otherwise draw attention to herself.

When she finished her descent down the driveway, Jeff began his. He heard her step hard on the accelerator to start down the hill toward Ventura Boulevard. She reached Ventura Boulevard at around forty-five miles an hour, and bounced across the intersection. Jeff reached the intersection and found the traffic signal was red, so he had to make a right turn onto Ventura, a left into the parking lot for the big Ralph's Grocery Store on the corner, and come out the exit onto Vineland Avenue.

He could just see the Sequoia disappearing around the right turn far ahead at Riverside Drive. He accelerated and came within sight of her as she went up the freeway entrance ramp. He followed, heading east toward Glendale and Pasadena. As they drove, Jeff began to feel calmer. It wasn't wise to drive a stolen vehicle far on a major freeway, but there were no police cars in sight at the moment, and as long as she wasn't unlucky, she would probably be able to do this. They could be home by 9:00.

Carrie left the freeway at Colorado Boulevard and drove toward the quiet neighborhoods surrounding the Cal Tech campus. Jeff approved. There were always lots of unfamiliar faces around a university, most of them young. All she had to do was pick the right street, park the Sequoia, and leave. She made an abrupt left turn without having time to signal, and went down one of the streets fast.

Jeff looked in his rearview mirror, saw a police car, and understood. She must have seen the car, and seen one of the two cops doing something that she interpreted as showing interest in the big Toyota Sequoia. Jeff heard the sudden *blip-blip* of the police siren, and saw the red and blue lights come on. He quickly pulled into the left lane, trying to look like a dumb, confused driver who was blocking the left turn while he tried to get out of the way. The siren behind him *blip-blip*ped again, and then a cop switched the microphone to public address, and his amplified voice said, "Pull ahead to the right. Pull ahead and to the right." Jeff deliberately made a terrible mess of it, signaling for a lane change to the right, and looking over his right shoulder at the nonexistent traffic to his right, but not moving at all.

The police car's engine roared, and the car swung to Jeff's left, making a long diagonal in the oncoming lane before it made its left turn. All Jeff could think of was to follow. He drove after them, trying to hang back so the cops didn't realize what he was doing. There had to be some way to manage this, to rescue her before they caught her.

By now they would be on their radio describing the Sequoia, maybe reading the license number. They would be giving her location and direction, and in a couple of minutes she would start seeing cops who were ahead waiting for her, blocking the road or putting down spike strips to puncture her tires.

Ahead of him, he could see her turn south. What was that

street? Fair Oaks? As she sailed through the intersection, cars stopped and rocked forward against their brakes, and the ones behind veered into odd angles to keep from butting the ones in front. She picked up the first of the police reinforcements at Fair Oaks.

Jeff was already making a kind of peace with his doom. He would be in prison for the next twenty years. There was no way Carrie could elude the two police cars. At the next street another patrol car slid into the intersection and blocked her lane. Carrie slowed down, so the police officer would be in no doubt about which choice she was making, but then at the last moment she turned left and shot off behind him.

The two cars chasing her did the same, while the car in the intersection remained immobile. When Carrie and her two pursuers had passed, the third police car turned and joined the chase.

Jeff pulled out his cell phone and dialed her number.

"What?" she snapped.

"We need to end this fast. In a minute there will be choppers and a dozen cop cars."

"Agreed. How?"

"Do you know a place along here where there's an alley?"

"Sure. There's an alley behind Raymond."

"Drive in the alley, ditch the car, run through the back door of a restaurant and out the front, and get in my car."

"Once more around the block."

"I'll be on Raymond waiting."

Jeff drove north again, turned up Raymond, spotted a parking place that a car was just vacating, and pulled into it. He heard the sirens now as Carrie approached, a chorus of syncopated *blip-blips*. Louder and louder. When the sirens went silent, he pulled out.

Sooner than he had anticipated, Carrie dashed out the front of a Chinese restaurant. He stopped, she threw herself inside, crouching on the floor, and he drove off. He turned at the first corner, went to Del Mar and stayed on it, then swung onto the freeway entrance. He accelerated hard all the way to the split where the 210 and the 134 diverged. He chose the 210 west through La Canada toward San Fernando because its curve put him out of sight the soonest.

The seconds passed, and Jeff traded each one for another stretch of pavement, another small increment of speed. He kept glancing in his mirrors, searching for blinking emergency lights, but he saw none. He kept going as fast as he dared. Every time he passed a slower vehicle, he thought of it as a barrier he had placed between them and the police.

She was still kneeling on the floor with her elbows on the passenger seat. "If I get any more excited I'm going to faint or something."

"We haven't made it yet."

"Can I get up now?"

"Just give it another minute or two. How did you get from the car to the restaurant without getting chased down?"

"I wanted to get into the alley with as much time to spare as I could get. I knew right where I wanted to go, because I had passed it just a few minutes earlier. So as I was coming to it, I sped up, and so the cops behind me did too. At the last second I hung a right turn because I figured if I tried a left I'd probably roll over in that big-ass SUV. The first two cop cars went past because they were afraid if they stopped quick, the ones behind would run into them. Then I guess they backed up to get to the alley, but I didn't have a chance to see how that worked out, because I was down the alley looking at the backs of buildings. I saw the restaurant, with its door open to the kitchen, so I pulled in front of it, reversed, swung the SUV in a half-circle until the rear end hit the building across the alley, and left it crossways. That left the SUV blocking the alley, with my door facing away from the cops. I took the keys, jumped out, ran into the kitchen, through the dining room, and out, and there you were."

"I'm getting off the freeway." He coasted down the off-ramp onto a surface street and kept going. "You can get up now."

Carrie turned and sat in the passenger seat and buckled her seat belt. "Wow. That was the absolute best. Losing the cops in a car chase. I don't think there's much in the line of bad behavior that tops this."

He looked at her uneasily. "You know it was a fluke, right? We were lucky. If we tried it a hundred times, ninety-nine of them they'd either catch us or kill us."

She smiled. "I'm not going to do it even one more time. They don't get a do-over on the car chase. But I sure as hell did it this time. I beat them."

"You kicked their big blue asses for them."

"Yeah." She laughed. "I said I wanted an adventure, but I was just thinking of a little adventure, like dropping off that SUV and then having sex in a place where there was some small chance of getting caught."

"Oh?" he said.

"That's why I changed into this dress. See?" She lifted the skirt. "There's nothing under it but me."

"Oh my God."

"You know, like in a restaurant we both go to the restrooms at the same time, only it's the same one? Or we go into the changing room in a department store?"

"I get the picture. I just don't know what to say."

"Wow. A big, beautiful, dumb boyfriend who knows how to crack a safe and outrun the police. What's next?"

24

JOE CARVER PARKED a block away from Sonia Rivers's apartment building in North Hollywood. He had learned after he had caught the attention of Manco Kapak what a good idea it was to leave his car somewhere about the distance he could run at a dead sprint, but not close enough to be visible from his destination.

He walked to the apartment building, studying the area for places that might become dangerous later on — apartments that had no curtains or blinds, buildings with flat roofs that had ladders built into the wall, an empty lot with thick brush at the back. He arrived at the building and rang the bell for Apartment 6.

After a few seconds there was a female voice on the intercom speaker that he recognized as Sonia's. She sounded a bit startled and irritated. "Yes? Who is it?"

"Hi, Sonia. I hope you remember me. I'm Joe Carver. We met at a club about three weeks ago."

"I remember you. It's eight in the morning. I'm getting ready for work."

He tried to sound grave and yet respectful. "I'm sorry. I was afraid it might be an inconvenient time for you, but I really have to talk to you."

"It hasn't been three weeks. It's actually been almost four weeks. Is this the first time you ever thought of getting in touch? Eight A.M. on a workday? Don't you own a telephone?"

He had noticed that she hadn't refused to see him. She just wanted to make him listen to her indictment in its entirety before she let him in. He didn't let that knowledge make him complacent. "I'm sorry I couldn't call."

"Couldn't call, or didn't?"

"Couldn't. The reason I couldn't was that something you said to a third party has put me in danger, and I've been hiding for three weeks."

"Look, Joe. I remember you clearly. At the time, I thought you were funny, and you had a certain charm. And I know there are girls who find weird approaches and wacky pickup lines cute and irresistible. They'll swoon and hang your picture in their lockers at their high school. But I'm not one."

"I know this sounds like that, but it isn't. I'm not out here feeling clever and funny. I'm feeling scared, which is why I was wondering if you'd let me in while we talk."

There was a loud buzz and the door lock clicked, so he turned, opened the door, and stepped inside. He went to Apartment 6 and the door opened inward. Sonia had one hand on the doorknob and the other furiously brushing her long, dark hair. She stepped back to let him enter, but didn't stop brushing. "Now, please tell me that you really have something to say."

"Here's what happened, as I understand it. Soon after you and I met at Wash, one night you were in line for a concert somewhere in Hollywood. Two men came up to you and started a conversation. One of them had bright red hair, and the other had dark red hair. Do you remember them?"

She was frozen with the hairbrush in her hand, her eyes wider. "Go on."

245

"You talked with them for a while. There were other women in line, and they talked to a couple of them too. At some point one of them asked you if you happened to meet a guy who was new in town and who had been spending a lot of cash. You gave them my name."

She reddened. He watched the pink begin just below her collarbone, then move up her neck to her cheeks and forehead. "There were two red-haired guys. And I did mention your name. I . . . have no excuse at all. I wasn't trying to hurt you. What I was doing was flirting."

"With two guys?"

"I wasn't interested in two guys. I wasn't necessarily interested in either one. There were other guys in the line for the concert too, all kinds of people. I was out in public, and I wanted to seem nice, and I wanted to seem to be one of those people who goes to the right places and knows lots of people. They asked if I knew anybody like you, and I said yes. I really hope this hasn't harmed you. Can you please say it didn't, so I don't have to stand here waiting for some horrible thing to come up?"

Carver sighed. "Those two were Jerry and Jimmy Gaffney. They're a pair of thugs. They work for a man named Manco Kapak, who owns Wash, the club where we met, and a couple of strip clubs in the Valley, and a few other businesses. He's basically a gangster. About a month ago he got held up while he was making a night deposit at a bank. He and his people figured it was somebody too new in town to know who he was robbing and too dumb not to spend the cash. In other words, me."

"Oh. I'm so sorry. It didn't seem as though their reason for asking could be anything like that. They were so normal, like anybody."

"I know. That's probably why he sent them. He also has two guys with tattoos all over their necks and the backs of their shaved heads, and a Russian who looks about seven feet tall."

"And they're after you? Oh, Joe. I feel just terrible."

"All I can say is that I've never robbed anybody. And I like to think that if I were to start now, I'd be smart enough not to pick the kind of businessman who has leg-breakers on the payroll. The reason I was spending cash when you met me was that I had pretty much maxed out my credit cards moving here from South Carolina, but I had closed my bank accounts there and had taken a lot of it in cash."

She stared into his eyes with determination. "I'm going to do my best to undo this," she said. "I've got to make it right."

"I didn't come here to get you to do anything. In fact, if gangsters could be talked out of what they wanted to do, we wouldn't need police. I just wanted you to know why I hadn't called."

"I usually leave at eight-fifteen—ten minutes from now, but I don't care if I'm late for work. I'll call these people and tell them they're wrong."

"Staying home to do that isn't necessary. These guys are all-night people. You can't call them up at eight-fifteen A.M. and expect them to have a rational conversation. They don't get up before noon."

"Oh." She shrugged. "Of course. That makes sense."

"Please. Go to work. If you want to call later and plant some doubt in their heads about me, that would be all to the good. But I'm here because I didn't want to leave you under the impression that I was a robber."

"No," she said. "I never thought you were. I didn't think anybody was talking about robbers when I mentioned your name. All I can do now is try to fix it."

He moved to her door. "I'd better be going now. You need to go to work, and it's best if I do all my errands in the morning before those guys wake up." He grasped the doorknob and gave a little wave.

"Call me?" she said.

"I'll try."

As he walked out to the front door, he wondered whether he

had overdone it at the end. Playing on someone's guilt was a delicate thing. Just going a tiny bit too far would make her sympathy vanish. He should have sounded more eager to call her. She had harmed him, and any observation that proved he had deserved it would be a reason not to bother to make up for it. He hurried back to her door before it closed. "What I mean is, I'd absolutely like to see you the minute I'm sure that it won't put you in danger."

He felt better as he went out the main door at the foyer. Guilt only worked if it came from her own sense of responsibility. He walked back to his car studying the apartment complex. He searched for places where a man could watch Sonia Rivers's apartment without being noticed. He had checked the area from his car when he had arrived, just to be sure that one of Kapak's men had not anticipated that he might visit. But the view from the sidewalk was much closer and more complete. He could see the places where a man on foot could lurk. He noted the four most likely without changing his pace.

Carver got into his car and drove. The other girl the Gaffneys said had mentioned his name was Sandy Belknap. He didn't know her as well as Sonia, even though he'd seen her on more occasions. Their talk had always been breezy and superficial. He knew that she worked at a Toyota dealership on the way to the airport and lived somewhere in Manhattan Beach. He stopped at a gas station that had a pay phone. Her number was unlisted, but he found the right number for the Toyota lot and dialed.

"My name is Joe Carver. I'm trying to reach Sandy Belknap. Is she in this morning?"

"No, I'm afraid she's not coming in today."

"I wonder if you could possibly give me her number." He knew the receptionist would never do it, but he also knew that salespeople didn't want to miss calls.

"Please hold and I'll see if I can connect you to her personal number."

There was a series of clicks and dead seconds, and then he heard a ring signal. The phone was snatched up immediately.

248

"Hello? Joe?" It was Sandy Belknap's voice, but it sounded oddly distant and unclear.

"Hi," he said.

"This is a surprise," she said. "I haven't seen you around lately. What have you been up to?"

"Do you have me on the speaker?"

"I'm sorry. Most people don't notice, but it keeps my hands free. I was just getting dressed."

"Just give me a second to picture that."

She laughed. "It's okay, but only if you have me wearing a nun's habit or a space suit."

"That ruined the moment."

"It's supposed to. So what's up? We've missed you at the clubs."

"Who's the rest of 'we'?"

"The girls. Nobody's that fun lately. That's the consensus." There was a hum in the background, as though someone were whispering to her.

"Is somebody there?"

She didn't answer directly, but he heard a distinct irritation in her voice. "Just a sec. Let me turn the TV off." He heard a change in the sound as she turned off the speaker and picked up the phone. "Hi. Still with me?"

"Yes," he said. "Let me tell you the reason I called. Since the last time I ran into you, I've been having trouble. There's a powerful man named Manco Kapak. I don't know if you've heard of him."

"Manco Kapak? No. What an odd name."

"He owns Wash, on Hollywood Boulevard, and a couple of strip clubs in the Valley."

"That's who owns Wash?"

"Yep. What happened was that he was out late depositing money in his bank's night drop, and a guy robbed him at gunpoint. He got mad. He sent a few of his goons out to find the robber. So they asked a lot of people—mostly girls in clubs—if they knew somebody who had just moved here and was spending a lot of cash. I think you might have seen two of them. They're both tall, with red hair."

"Oh my God." It was quiet, just above a whisper.

"What?"

"Oh, nothing. Just what you're saying. It's so scary. They think you did it?"

"Yes. I've been trying to find out how they even heard I existed."

"I . . . can't imagine."

"It doesn't matter how, I guess. I just wanted to call you in case the rumor reached you. I've never robbed anyone in my life. It's true I was new in town when I met you, and I guess I was spending more cash than I usually would, so it might seem odd to people who didn't know me. I had just flown in and paid to have my furniture shipped, and put a lot of other charges on my credit cards. But I had cash from closing my bank accounts in the East."

"Look, Joe. We really should talk."

It was the kind of statement he had been waiting for to confirm his suspicion. Next she would say she wanted to meet him someplace at a particular time to discuss the past relationship they'd never had and the future that would never come. "That's really all I wanted to say. I'm on a pay phone and I'm out of change. If you hear any of those rumors, please tell people I'm not a thief, I'm a mass murderer. That way they won't want to get near me."

"Oh, I will. I promise."

It took Sonia Rivers three calls before she got the right number for Manco Kapak's house. It rang a few times, and then a man's voice came on. "Mr. Kapak's residence."

"May I speak to Mr. Kapak, please?"

"I'm sorry, miss, but Mr. Kapak isn't at home right now. Can I take a message?"

"My name is Sonia Rivers. I think there's been a misunderstanding, and I'd like to correct it as soon as I can."

"My name is Richard Spence. I'm Mr. Kapak's assistant. If you tell me, I'll be sure your message gets to him as soon as possible."

Sonia hesitated for a second or two, until she felt the awkwardness increasing. She had to talk or hang up. "A month ago, two men who work for Mr. Kapak began talking to me while I was waiting to get into a concert. One of them asked if I happened to know a man who was new in town and who had been in clubs spending a lot of cash. I thought—I don't know exactly what I thought—maybe this was somebody they knew and they were going to tell me something funny about him, or they had met a man like that but didn't know his name, or something. So I said the name of a man I'd met in a club a couple of days before. I just heard that Mr. Kapak was told I thought this was the man who had robbed him. I never thought that, and never meant it that way. It never even occurred to me."

"I understand," said Spence. "And just to make sure I get the story straight for Mr. Kapak, what is this innocent man's name?"

"Joe Carver."

"Joe . . . Carver," he said, pretending to be a man at a desk writing things down. "Do you have an address or anything for him?"

"No, I don't."

"Then, your name and address, just in case the police would like to talk to you?"

"Sonia Rivers." She recited her address and phone number. She marveled at herself for doing it, but this man seemed so bright and businesslike.

"Thank you, Miss Rivers. I have no idea whether this Mr. Carver was a serious suspect or not, but you can never be too careful with someone else's reputation."

"That's just how I feel," said Sonia. She detected in herself an unexpected curiosity about this man, and realized that she had been stalling to give him time to say something to reveal more about himself. "Well, goodbye."

"Goodbye."

She should have been in her cubicle at work, staring out the part of the window she could see from her desk. Today there was a thin copper-colored smear of smog hanging near the tops of the tall buildings of Los Angeles, all in a little clump in the center of the million low buildings that covered the basin. She decided the man she had spoken to was probably nothing as interesting as a criminal. Kapak owned several businesses. Of course he would have a few dull, serious people like Spence to run things for him. She wondered if she should go in to work late, but the moment had passed. She took off her gray suit and hung it up for tomorrow.

At Kapak's house, Spence moved from the kitchen to the small maid's quarters where he had been sleeping. He picked up the backpack that still held the disassembled .308 Remington, pulled his .45 pistol from under the pillow, and put it into the backpack too. He looked at the address he had written down, went out the back door and locked it behind him.

A half hour later, Spence had found Sonia Rivers's apartment. The only reason Sonia would have made the call to Kapak's house today was if her relationship with Joe Carver had improved since she'd talked to the Gaffney brothers a few weeks ago.

He studied the neighborhood and began to search. In another half-hour he had found a vacant apartment with a clear view of the windows along the side of Sonia Rivers's apartment building. He went in and used a lock pick to defeat the cheap doorknob lock, then stood at the window. From his second-floor window he could see down into her apartment. In the front was the living room, then the smoked glass of the bathroom, then the two bedroom windows near the back. As he went through the vacant apartment, he found an easy chair with torn upholstery in the living room, undoubtedly left by the last tenant. He moved it to the window and tried it, then looked around for a few more minutes before he decided to go out and buy a cup of coffee for the wait. On his way out, he unlocked the door to save time on his return.

25

AT 10:15 A.M. Lieutenant Slosser stopped his unmarked car in front of Kapak's long, low house. Kapak pushed his door open and slowly swung his feet to the curb as he had seen frail old men do, then stood. "Thanks for the ride."

"If you hear anything else that might be useful to us, give us a call," Slosser said.

"Joe Carver. If you can find Joe Carver, this will be over."

"Maybe," Slosser said. "But usually, in my experience, if somebody you never heard of makes a full-time job out of making your life miserable, usually he's working for somebody else—somebody you know."

"He's the one I'm sure of. I'll take my chances on people who might be telling him what to do."

"We'll see." Slosser's window closed and he drove off. Kapak turned and went up the walk to his house. He liked the lush plantings of palms and bananas, bamboo and eucalyptus, bougainvillea and ferns and orchids around the house. Now and then the gardeners would surprise him with a new planting of something colorful and exotic.

He caught sight of one of the gardeners across the front yard and waved his arm. They always tried to do their work unobtrusively, like stagehands in a theater, but now and then, on a rare day when he was awake in the morning, he would glimpse one or two of them from a distance. He seldom saw the cleaning crew either, but he noted that their van was parked at the curb this morning.

He went inside and listened. He could tell that the cleaning women were working in the kitchen end of the house, so he went the other way, to his bedroom suite. The room was finished, with everything in order, the floor polished, and the bed linens replaced. He turned on the television set and found the local news, and tuned his ears to listen for the words *Rogoso* and *Malibu.*

It was nearly eleven, and he was getting hungry. This was before he usually had his breakfast, but he'd been up most of the night and then was up again at 6:30, so his body wanted something. He knew it was ridiculous that he was intimidated by the thought of going into the kitchen and having to talk to the cleaning women while he made himself a sandwich.

He supposed they had a very specific idea of how he lived, and had opinions about it, but that only bothered him if he had to go in there and think of things to say to them.

He lay on his bed, closed his eyes, and listened to the 11:00 news. There was an Asian Pacific festival, a report from the USGS that a huge new fault had been found under the northern part of the city capable of generating massive earthquakes. There was always some kind of festival to celebrate some other country, always a series of threatening reports from scientists about what people ate or where they lived. There was a police shooting in one of the southside cities, where the police had mistaken a thirteen-year-old for an armed fugitive. Then he heard "A fire in the Malibu home of a local man with a record of narcotics trafficking," then the words "After this."

He sat up, propped a pillow behind him, and watched the commercials. They went on and on. There were cars, then a motorized wheelchair that the government could be called upon to pay for. There were more cars, a clothing store, and then a diet drink that melted off the pounds.

At last he saw the burned ruin he'd seen this morning, and the coroner's white van with the blue stripe and the words LAW AND SCIENCE SERVING THE COMMUNITY. The reporter was the middle-aged black woman they always sent when somebody died. She stood in front of the charred pile and the ocean beyond.

"Sheriff's deputies say that sometime after midnight last night, an intruder shot and killed three men in this Malibu beach house. He then set the house ablaze. By the time the fire trucks arrived, no more than ten minutes after the first call, the three-story house was fully involved. Firefighters managed to remove two of the victims from the building, but both were dead on arrival at County-USC Hospital. The third body was in a stairway that firefighters couldn't approach. He is believed to be the owner of the house, Manuel Rogoso, age forty-five. The other victims were reported to be employees of his. The house, which had recently been purchased for fifteen million dollars, was a total loss."

As she stepped back from the camera, it panned to survey the pile of blackened wood on the charred, cracked foundation. "The police have no theory as to the cause of the triple murder-arson. They ask that anyone with any information call the nearest police station."

Kapak aimed the remote control at the television set and the screen went black. He lay back and stared up at the ceiling. He had killed them in self-defense, but he knew that was a technicality. The killing had been the end of a disagreement among criminals engaged in a scheme to launder drug money. There were no innocent parties, only some dead criminals and a living one. Even if he could have argued that he'd had no choice, that argument vanished once he had burned the house.

Marija entered his mind. She would have glared at him and said, "See? That's the kind of man you are." No, but the idea of her would have, the Marija inhabiting his memory. The real woman would have denied to all bystanders that she'd ever known him, and then hurried away. She had wanted no part of the shame he brought her.

He was sure she had told his children things that had kept them from trying to see him. If they were people of ordinary curiosity they would have come to see who he was, at least. If they were like him and most of his relatives, they would have come looking for him to see if he had serious amounts of money.

He was sure that she had not even hinted at the truth. She had probably told them he had died when he was in jail. That way, when she had started going to bed with the periodontist who had lived next door, she wasn't a faithless whore, she was a pretty young widow who had found a reliable, respectable man to protect her children. Her children. They *were* her children, not his. He had not gone to claim them. When he got out of jail, he had been so angry that he wanted to imply to her that he no longer believed he had been the one to conceive them.

If he were to search for them now, he would have no clear path to them except through her, or if she was already dead, through the hated periodontist, Dr. Felder. He had no idea what city they'd been living in all this time, or if the children had kept his name or been given the name Felder. All he knew was that he had stayed in Los Angeles and kept the name Kapak. If they had ever wanted to see him, he would not have been hard to find.

Thinking about Marija and the children was like thinking about people in another century. It seemed to have taken several lifetimes for him to change from Marija's young, foolish husband to the man he was now. He thought about what he had done. He had obtained money. That was good, but not as good as he had thought it would be when he was young. And now the business itself was not the same. Last night, when he'd had to kill his most important and oldest ally, he had felt a change.

He had chosen nightclubs because so much of the money that came in was cash, and he could use that legal cash to hide a stream of illegal cash. Laundering money for drug dealers had made him a potent and dangerous man, someone with connections. But now he had killed the source of the illegal cash and the power. If he wasn't going to be laundering money anymore, what was he doing? Was he going to spend the final years of his life just running some honest bars? What for—to add a few more dollars to the bank accounts that would go unclaimed after his death?

He reminded himself that he was winning. The ally who had turned on him was dead and he was alive. There was still Joe Carver out there somewhere, but soon Carver would be dead too. There was no need for anybody to think too hard about who won and who lost. The winners were alive and the losers dead.

26

JERRY GAFFNEY AWOKE just after 11:00, his usual hour, but he didn't feel quite right. There was a distinct tightness in his right arm—more like a pain—and he wondered for a second whether he'd been stabbed. No, it wasn't as bad as that. He tried to roll to his back and realized what was wrong. His wrists were handcuffed behind him, and that was a feeling he'd felt before.

He drew in a breath in a gasp and sat up. He swung his legs, then realized that he was being restrained. A rope was tied around his ankles and then to the bed frame.

"Good morning." It was Sandy Belknap's voice.

The relief he felt was like a cool breeze touching his sweating forehead. She was still here. If this was serious, she'd have left him like this, gone somewhere else, and called the cops. He could still talk her out of this. "Good morning," he said. "This is an interesting development."

"Yeah. Interesting." He still couldn't see her, because she was somewhere behind him.

He said, "I assume these are my own handcuffs."

"Yes, they are. Nice girls don't have their own sets of hand-cuffs, I think. If they do, none of them ever told me about it."

"Well, this is a pretty cute trick."

"Yes," she said. "You're looking pretty cute over there, all bare-naked and trussed up. But I'm thinking that the joke has been on me all along."

"I don't follow."

"Well, there was a part of my conversation with Joe Carver this morning that you didn't hear. It wasn't on the speaker."

"What did I miss?"

"He knew that two men with red hair, one bright red—that would be you, the bright red—talked to me about a month ago at Wash, and that what we talked about was him."

"So why have I got handcuffs on?"

"I'm getting to that," she said. She walked around the bed and he could see she was dressed in blue jeans, running shoes, and a University of Missouri T-shirt. Her hair was pulled back in a tight ponytail. "The other thing he said was that these two men were brothers, a pair of thugs named Jerry and Jimmy Gaffney, who work for a gangster named Manco Kapak."

He looked at her in disappointment. "Well, of course, when we're investigating a series of class-one felonies we don't always go into crowds of unidentifiable people waving badges and using our real names."

"It's pretty amusing to watch you sitting there making all this stuff up, and I'll bet you could say more of it than I can listen to. But I've been up since that call, thinking."

"Good. Can you please unlock these handcuffs so we can have a real discussion about this?"

"Want to know what I thought?"

"Sure I do, but I'd like to have these handcuffs and ropes off first."

"Sorry. What I was thinking was that the way you and your partner treated me, and the way you treated my ex-boyfriend, well, it was kind of overbearing. The word Joe Carver used was 'thug.' I wouldn't have used that word, but I might have said 'bully.' And then I thought, 'Would a cop do that?' and 'Would a cop really sleep with me?'"

"Have you walked by a mirror lately? Ninety percent of cops wouldn't be able to help themselves. The others are straight women. As for your boyfriend, I was doing my duty. A police officer, even if he's just made what's technically an error in judgment, sleeping with a witness, can't let a contact with an angry civilian turn into a free-for-all, with everybody having an equal right to throw punches. We don't hold debates or try cases. We have to take charge and remain in control."

"Wow. Did you see that on TV?"

"It's part of standard police training."

"So is not getting citizens to sleep with you."

"I admitted I made a mistake. Rules are rules, but you're the strongest temptation I ever came across, by a mile. I know it was against regulations, but at that moment, I honestly didn't care. Right now I feel sorry that I failed, but I'd do it all over again."

"You've got the Oscar wrapped up, so don't overact."

"Why are you suddenly being so cynical?"

"While you were asleep I decided to do some checking. Your name is Detective Sergeant Allan Reid. That's what it says on your ID. But your driver's license, credit cards, and everything say Jerry Gaffney. Your badge says 'patrolman.'"

"My police ID is accurate. My badge is the one I got coming out of the academy, because the number belonged to my father. I still carry it because it makes me feel like he's looking over my shoulder."

"You tricked me, and you used me. But I had fun with you yesterday and last night. And without intending to, you forced me to take a look at what I was settling for as a boyfriend. It's something I needed. For those reasons, I'm not inclined to call the cops—the real ones—and have them come and haul you away like this. Instead, I'd like you to put on your clothes and skedaddle."

Jerry Gaffney looked at his feet, then into her eyes. "I guess I'd be stupid not to leave, huh?"

"I have the impression that impersonating a cop is a felony."

"It is. Want to unlock me?"

"You have to promise not to try anything."

"All right. I promise."

"I sure hope you're not under the foolish, mistaken impression that I won't have the heart to shoot you if you pull something. I'm a farm girl from Missouri. My dad is a gun nut. All the Belknaps are shooters."

She walked around to the front of him, pressed the magazine release on his gun and took out the magazine, then pulled back the slide to eject the round in the chamber, closed it, and tossed the gun on the bed. Then she reached into her nightstand and took out a .38 revolver. "If I have to shoot you, I'll use my own gun. I'm used to it."

He smiled. "Shoot lots of guys?"

She looked into his eyes for a couple of seconds, as though searching for some sign of intelligence. Then she tossed his clothes on the bed, walked around behind him, unlocked his handcuffs, and stepped back, her gun in her hand.

Jerry Gaffney dressed, not slowly, but not making any unexpected or quick moves. When he was ready, he said, "Sandy, I apologize for lying to you. I regret it more than you know." He stood and walked toward the side door.

"Wait."

He stopped and looked back at her.

"Oh, this is stupid," she said. "Never mind."

"What?"

"I said never mind."

He turned and went to the door, opened it, and stepped across the threshold.

"Wait."

He stopped.

"Are you really a thug working for a gangster?"

"I'm a security professional working for Manco Kapak. He's not a gangster. He owns Wash in Hollywood and a couple of clubs in the Valley. Once in a great while I've had to step in and physically prevent somebody from doing something foolish. I don't think that makes me a thug."

She sighed. "Better, but still not nearly enough. Don't you see? I'm a daylight person. I can't have a guy who's even a little bit of a thug once in a while—a night person. Even dating a cop was going to be a bit over the line, but I kind of tried you on, because I thought you got your scars protecting people from bad guys, and if it didn't work out, at least I gave a heroic guy a nice time. I could do that. But not somebody in a shady business, especially not somebody who's a bit of a con man. I can't be in a relationship with a guy and know there's no particular reason to believe anything he says. So that's that. You have to go. If I see you again, we'll have to do the police thing again, using real police. If you come in the wrong way at the wrong time, I'll have to shoot you."

"I understand." He stood there for a moment, then went out and closed the door. He walked slowly and deliberately to his car, got in, and drove. He put his Bluetooth earpiece in his ear and pressed his brother's number on his phone.

"Yeah?"

"Jimmy. It's me."

"Not only did my phone already tell me that, but since you're my brother, I might recognize your voice by now. Where you been?"

"Where you left me, using Sandy Belknap to get to Carver."

"Did you?"

"He called. The son of a bitch called and told her we work for Kapak."

"You didn't deny it?"

"Of course I did. She found some problems with my ID, so here I am."

"How did you leave it?"

"We left it that if she sees me again she'll call the police or shoot me."

262

"Sounds like the way you leave it with all your girlfriends. Did she mean it?"

"I've seen her cell phone, and I've seen her gun."

"Are we getting any closer to Joe Carver?"

"She and I noised his name around town for a while, and it got his attention. He called her once, and he'll call her again. She's wonderful."

"Can we put something on her phone to record it when he calls?"

"I'm planning to try, of course." He actually hadn't thought about his next move yet. His rejection still stung too much. "What about you? Have you just been sitting on your ass waiting for your big brother to get to Carver?"

"Last night, Kapak had me and Voinovich put all the money from Siren, Temptress, and Wash in the safe at Siren and sit with it. Carver and that girl you met at the bank the other night robbed us."

"You must be okay, since you're talking to me. Is Voinovich?"

"Nobody's hurt, but they hauled the safe away in that big-ass SUV Voinovich drives — that Sequoia. He's kind of sensitive about it."

"Jesus. Carver never sleeps. And that crazy girl, where did she come from? Did she fire any rounds?"

"She couldn't wait. Right inside the storage area in the back of Siren — *bam!* Right through the roof, to show us she wasn't shitting around. Every minute that woman was waving that big .45 around, I felt as likely to die as live. She gave me the impression that she actually wanted to kill us, but that Carver wouldn't let her."

"The whole thing gives me the creeps," said Jerry. "How did they even get into the building?"

"The police are looking into that," Jimmy said. "Look, I've got to get going on this other thing right now, so I'll talk to you later."

Jerry could tell that what Jimmy wasn't telling was that it was Jimmy's fault somehow. Jimmy had let them in, and it was probably something embarrassingly stupid. Jerry felt a wave of compassion for his brother. Having awakened naked and handcuffed, he understood, but compassion wasn't the kind of emotion that lasted. "What other thing?"

"I don't want to go into it on the phone. I'll talk to you later."

Jerry stared at his phone for a second, then put it in his pocket. He had a mission now. He drove to Sherman Oaks and stopped around the corner from the Eye Spy Shop, then walked the rest of the way. He knew that there must be cameras and things recording everything that went on at the store. If they had all that stuff, how could they resist using it?

Jerry stepped into the store, and he could see himself in the big monitor on the wall in high definition, stepping into the store. He surveyed the counters and shelves, which were full of gadgets that looked as though they were exhibits in a museum commemorating some repressive government that had fallen: buttonhole cameras that could peek out of a hat or coat or briefcase, microphones that could be inserted into telephones, others that could be plugged into electric outlets to transmit speech from rooms. There were video cameras disguised as clocks, radios, and audio speakers. There were lots of computer gear—keystroke counters, programs for collecting and reviewing instant messages.

He judged that the customers must be about evenly divided between parents who wanted to spy on their babysitters and nannies, and people who wanted to spy on their spouses. He found what he wanted right away. It was a radio transmitter hidden inside a surge suppressor. He had seen a power bar very much like it under the desk in Sandy Belknap's apartment from his hiding place behind the sliding door in her closet. It had several things plugged into it: a laptop computer, a phone charger, a printer.

He bought the proper receiver and recorder too. The transmitter had a range of only three miles, but he could listen to the recorder by telephone. He took his purchases back to Sandy's apartment building, and then drove in ever-widening circles until he found an apartment two blocks away. He found it in time to catch the building manager before he went off to work, and persuaded him to accept a deposit on the place and give him a key.

After another few minutes he called Sandy's apartment. There was no answer, so he drove by and studied the windows and looked for her car. He parked, walked to the front door, pretended to knock with his left hand while he slipped a credit card into the crack between the door and the jamb and opened it. He set his surge suppressor beside Sandy's and was pleased with the close resemblance as he plugged his into the outlet. He plugged her devices into his suppressor, making sure that they were in the same receptacles, took her surge suppressor with him, and left.

At his new apartment he set up his receiver and drove a few miles away to have lunch at a pancake house. In the lot he took out his telephone and called the receiver and listened. He heard a few sounds in her empty apartment, picked out the noise of a car going by outside, heard a siren. He hung up.

He had a late breakfast of pancakes with so much sweet syrup that it made his teeth feel as though they had a sticky film on them. It had been meant to be a consolation for losing Sandy, but it only accentuated the feeling that he had made another enormous mistake in a life that was full of them.

He went out to the car and called Voinovich's cell phone. "It's Jerry," he said. "I heard you and my brother had a bad night."

"They got my car, the safe, and maybe sixty thousand dollars in cash."

"Jimmy told me. Sorry about your car. Let's hope they'll leave it someplace without doing any damage."

"The cops got it back an hour ago, but they didn't get Carver or the girl. The cops want me to come in and get it, but I'm not sure Carver didn't leave our guns in it. I could go in and sign my name and have them push me into a cell. It happened to my cousin in Moscow years ago."

"This isn't Moscow. What I'd do is say they're Carver's guns."

"They could have our prints on them."

"Then think of a reason for that and have it ready in case you need it."

"It doesn't matter what you say if things are going against you. That's how I ended up here, so many thousands of miles from home. I had a job unloading ships in Odessa at night—foreign ships. The owners seemed to understand that by losing a little cargo, they were gaining a lot of goodwill. But then, my bosses started having setbacks. There was a police captain who needed to be paid off, and he wanted more than there was. So my bosses were going to leave. They sent all their money ahead of them to New York to put it into an American bank. Then they flew in. But when they were going through customs, the older one, Anatoly, fell down with a heart attack and died on the spot. He was carrying all the paperwork for the money transfer, and so the American police started asking questions. Andrei, the other one, got deported. The money couldn't be sent back with him."

"How did that get you stuck here?"

"I had come to New York ahead of time. I was supposed to make everything smooth. I rented apartments, leased a good car. I was waiting at the airport when I saw the ambulance come and take Anatoly away. The others had my name and address with the paperwork, so I couldn't ever go back to Odessa either. It was because Anatoly's luck changed."

"Do you think Kapak's luck has changed?"

"I don't know, but I'm watching. When it happens, it can take an hour. A minute. And who would take over if Kapak died?" asked Voinovich.

"That's a good question," Jerry said. "He hasn't made any arrangements that I've heard of."

"When a rich man dies, relatives show up," said Voinovich. "Then we'll see how our luck is."

Jerry said, "Maybe we should figure out how we want this to play out, and then make sure it happens the right way."

"Who would be in on it?"

"You, me, and my brother Jimmy."

27

SPENCE KNELT ON the bare floor in the apartment under the window and assembled the rifle. It was before noon, but there was no point in waiting to get ready. The girl, this Sonia, worked in an office, and that meant she left for work at eight in the morning and came home at six. Today she must have called in sick or left early, because she was home. But for Spence, it didn't matter what time it was.

He raised his head from his work and looked through his second-floor window down into the girl's apartment. She had changed into a pair of black sweatpants and a T-shirt that had been printed with the words "Mackinac Island." It wasn't a great sign. If she was expecting Carver to visit, then she should be dressed better than that.

But he wasn't going to assume Carver wouldn't show. He might arrive much later, when he would feel safe. She seemed to be fooling around in the kitchen, doing some kind of cooking, so maybe she was making a fancy dinner. And maybe he showed up here only at bedtime, when the sweatpants and T-shirt came off.

Spence was resigned to the fact that he might have to keep coming to this apartment and watching for weeks before Carver showed up. Spence moved back from the window to a dark spot on the floor where the sunlight didn't reach him and stared through the rifle sight at Sonia. He had the rifle's elevation sighted to a distance of a hundred yards, and this distance was under a hundred feet, so he would have to remember to adjust. She was turned to the side and staring down at whatever was on the stove. He sighted low on her temple, aware that the bullet would take her an inch above, but it would blow through her skull and embed itself in a wall. With the magnification he could see individual wisps of hair that had escaped from her ponytail and trailed near the delicate pink rim of her ear. He moved the crosshairs to the diamond stud in her earlobe. She turned toward him as though she had felt an unexpected chill, but her eyes were low, looking out her window at the empty lawn between the two buildings.

He didn't intend to shoot the girl, not even later. She was just bait. He lowered the rifle, released the empty box magazine, and set the rifle across the arms of his easy chair. He reached for the box of ammunition and opened it.

He heard a metallic *snick-chuck-snick* sound that made his breath catch—*shotgun!* He dove toward the side and rolled, trying to get closer to the corner of the wall where he could scramble out of the line of fire.

A voice said, "Stop, or I'll have to take your head off."

Spence already had the fingers of his right hand touching the handgrips of the pistol in his jacket pocket, but he knew he wouldn't have the time to get it out before the muzzle flash brought obliteration. "So why haven't you already?" He could see the man at the back of the room, standing and holding the short pump shotgun in his direction—not aiming, just carrying it with the muzzle at Spence's chest level so he could hardly miss. He knew that the man must have come in and sat in the bedroom or the bathroom waiting for him to arrive, then stood and watched him.

"Because I wanted to talk to you, Spence. That's why I brought you here."

"So this was for me—the girl and everything?"

"Yes."

"Why?"

"Because as I watched you and Kapak and his men, and listened to what you all said, it seemed to me that you were the solitary guy, the one that the others were afraid of and maybe didn't quite trust. So it had to be you."

"When did you get close enough to see that?"

"It doesn't get me anything to tell you how I do things. But this is the last time I try to talk to any of you. It's too risky to arrange meetings just to keep explaining over and over again."

"What do you have to explain?"

"I'm not the guy who robbed Kapak."

"Your girlfriend down there told me that."

"She's not my girlfriend. I met her just after I came to town, but when I heard that what she told the Gaffneys was what made Kapak think I was his robber, I realized she was the way to get to you. That's all."

"If you did or didn't rob Kapak, why did you stick around after you heard we were looking for you?"

"I figured if I hid out and waited awhile, then the real robber would turn up, rob somebody else, or even rob Kapak again. He'd get caught, and that would be the end of it. But when your friends started getting close to finding me, I knew I'd better go see Kapak. I talked to him and let him see my face, so he'd know I wasn't the one. I thought at first that he was persuaded, but when I was walking away, he took a shot at me."

"It hurt him more than you. He fired through a closed window and was up to his armpits in glass."

"It pissed me off."

"You have to understand him. He's been in a vulnerable position for thirty years. His clubs make a profit, but there are always people who are trying to rob him in one way or another. People want a piece of the profits, or they're selling protection, or a fee to keep the city council off his back, or a fee to prevent labor troubles. He tries to stay out of squabbles, but it isn't enough. He has to be somebody who doesn't put up with anything."

"It doesn't seem to justify killing me."

"When Kapak got robbed, it was right in the middle of Ventura Boulevard. The cops knew, so the newspapers knew, so everybody knew. Kapak had to make a serious effort to get whoever robbed him. It wasn't the twenty grand he lost that night. It was his reputation. Everybody who heard about it had to believe he wouldn't put up with that kind of thing or there would be a long line of people waiting to stick a gun in his face. When he sent guys out to investigate, the only name that turned up was yours, and it came up twice. Just because you said you weren't the one, it didn't mean you weren't."

"I showed him my face."

"The guy who does the robberies wears a mask."

"Kapak never said that."

"He was pissed off. Before you came to his house, you had already wrecked two Hummers with the crane."

"I scared a few of his guys and took some money. I could have done worse."

"You're reminding me that you can kill me."

"I can, but I don't plan to."

"Why not?"

"That's not what I want. Look, I've had to move around a bit over the past couple of years, and I didn't like it. I want to stay in Los Angeles, and I don't want to have to kill anyone to do it. But if I have to, I remember how."

"I can see you'd be fairly good at it."

"I'm looking for a different idea," Carver said. "Why don't you and I talk for a bit?"

"With a shotgun on me?"

"I told you I won't kill you."

"My rifle is on the chair over there, and you could see I hadn't loaded it yet."

Carver sighed. "There's a pistol in your jacket. That's fine if it makes you feel better. My shotgun means it doesn't matter. At this range I'd be able to see through the hole in you."

"I won't try for it. I'm not a killer either."

"Kapak acts as though you are."

"I killed a guy once, and Kapak found out. A girl I knew, a close friend of mine from school, got raped and murdered. The guy went to trial and got convicted. The verdict was overturned because of mishandled evidence. The only family this girl had was a mother and two little sisters, so it was up to me. I found out the killer was moving out to southern California, so I came and waited for him."

"And today you were waiting to get me."

"I'm starting not to be entirely happy about that. I think you didn't rob Kapak, which means we've been chasing you around for nothing."

"But you'll do it anyway?"

"No, I won't. I'm thinking you and I ought to try something different."

28

CARRIE ROLLED CLOSE to Jeff on the bed and propped her head on her hand. "You know what I think we need?"

He lay on his back feeling his breathing slowly returning to normal. He had a strong urge to keep his eyes closed, not answer, and doze off.

"You know what we need?" she repeated.

"I wasn't planning to guess. Maybe you could get it and surprise me."

"A machine gun."

"Why not an atomic bomb?"

"Because it's not practical."

"I'm not so sure. We could get one of those little ones that you can carry in a briefcase—the kind that only blows up the city and not the whole state. We could go up to somebody, hand it to him and say, 'Hold this for me.' Then we'd drive away, and when we got to the next state, blow them up. Next time we had a briefcase we'd get some respect."

"You're making a joke out of this."

"A machine gun *is* a joke. What would you do with it?"

"Say I walked into a bank with one. I could fire a burst into the ceiling, maybe ten or twelve rounds, and say, 'Give me the money.' I'll bet people would give me the money."

"Sounds like the 1920s."

"I don't mean one of those old-fashioned ones with the magazine that looks like a big disk. I mean the modern kind, the ones that soldiers carry in battle."

"Very good choice. You're a truly scary person and you've outdone yourself this time."

"Oh?"

"Yes. There's a big difference between sticking up an old man with a sack of cash in the street outside a bank in the middle of the night and going into the actual bank and holding it up during business hours. The first is relatively easy and not very dangerous. The second is the opposite: hard to do at all, and very risky. They have armed guards, surveillance cameras, silent alarms, bulletproof glass. If you succeed, they'll try to slip you a bag of money that blows up and covers you with indelible ink."

"See? That's why a machine gun is so useful. This is just taking a rational look at all of the bank's defenses and thinking of a single way of defeating them — fear."

"Then the nuclear bomb would be more like it. And if we had to use it, there wouldn't be any witnesses for miles."

"That again?"

"Every year, thousands of banks get robbed. And every year, thousands of bank robbers get caught. The failure rate is one of the things you have to look into when you want to commit a crime. You look at what your chances are of getting caught. For bank robbery it's like ninety-nine percent."

"Well, what's your idea of a better crime?"

"Let's see. White-collar stuff. They only catch, like, ten percent of tax evaders, maybe one percent of people who sell fake designer clothes. Even murderers-for-hire get caught only about sixty per-

273

cent of the time, and that's because their client is married to the victim."

"I don't think we're ready to do murders for hire."

"That's a relief. I like working for myself."

"I mean no murders at all. Look, baby. What you've been doing lately is like a childish prank—robbing one business over and over. We're going to have to grow up."

He opened one eye and looked at her. "In what sense?"

"Let me describe what you do. You pull a small robbery and get maybe twenty thousand dollars if you're lucky. Then you spend the next couple of months going out all night, drinking and picking up girls, and sleeping all day until the money is gone."

"I haven't picked up any girls since I met you."

"I'm describing nature. A giraffe is a giraffe, and it eats leaves, whether it's eating leaves right now or not."

"I see."

"Do you?"

"Sure."

"Do you also see what's wrong with it?"

"Eating leaves?"

"No."

"Picking up girls?"

"No again." With her free hand she swung her pillow in a rapid arc downward onto his head like a sack of disdain. "There's no progress. Every month or two, you start all over again with nothing."

He pushed the pillow off his face. "I've made great progress lately."

"You have?"

"Sure. Now when I go out all night and sleep all day, I've got you with me. That's a big improvement. And now, instead of twenty thousand, we've got, like, eighty thousand in cash. We could go on like this for a long time, since there's no need to flash a lot of big bills picking up girls. You *are* one already, and we only need one."

"It's just over a hundred and twenty thousand."

"The money?"

"Yes. You don't even count it, do you?"

"No. That's the whole point of being a bandito. You don't have to count your money."

"Are you challenged by arithmetic?"

"No, but I've thought about this."

"No, you haven't." She sat and glared at him for a few seconds. "What is it?"

"Limits. If I count the money and match it off against a certain number of days, then there are things I can't do, can't afford. If I don't, then I'm free. If I want something, I buy it. I know that when I need to, I can get more money. I give up knowing exactly how many dollars are in the bag at every moment in exchange for not having to know. It's a good deal."

She looked at him in alarm. "Oh my God. You're starting to sound smart, like a wandering Zen master or something. Let me get over that feeling. It'll take a minute."

"Take your time."

She sat motionless for a few seconds, then stood up. "I can't take my time. This brings me to another topic that's loosely related, and urgent."

"What is it?"

"I know you hate it when there's something you ought to know, but I don't tell you."

"No, I don't."

"This you would."

"Is it your boyfriend?"

She got up off the bed and looked down at him, her eyes wide with surprise. "Yes."

"What about him?"

"He's flying into LAX in just over — oops, just under — three hours. When he gets there, he's going to pick up his suitcase at the baggage claim, and he's going to want someplace to put it."

"Like your house."

"It's his house, technically."

"What's the technicality?"

"He bought it and paid for it, his name is on the deed, and he lived here before I met him."

"Three hours isn't a lot of time."

"No."

"So I assume you know what you're going to do."

"I've been avoiding thinking about it as long as I could."

"Are you going to choose between him and me?"

"Didn't you hear me just five minutes ago talking about our future?"

"That's not an answer."

"At first I was going to stay with him and see you on the side just for a treat once in a while, but then I asked myself why, if you can have the treat all the time, you wouldn't do it. I couldn't think of an answer, so I've decided you're the keeper."

"Is this guy violent?"

"Well, you know how guys are. Once they find out somebody else has been there too, if you know what I mean, it makes them all hormonal."

"You could kill me and tell him I'm a burglar."

"Keep trying."

"We could kill each other. He'd feel responsible."

"Please stop with the killing. It's making me upset."

"We could skip all the way back to Plan A, which is to pack up fast and run away."

"Shouldn't that have been the first thing you said? I mean, if it is Plan A."

"It's not a good idea to settle for the obvious right away, without exploring other options."

"Let's get the heck out of here," she said. She went to her dresser and began putting on clothes. As she opened a drawer and put on a garment, she would take all the others like it and set them in a pile on the bed. When she came to the closet, she took out a large suitcase, opened it, and began placing the piles of folded clothes inside.

When it looked as though the suitcase was completely full, she went into the next room and returned with a lot of bills, canceled checks, and papers. "Can't leave these papers here. I don't want him tracing us and turning up later."

"He would do that?"

"I'm out of space. Can you fit the bag of money in your suit-case?"

"I'll try to find room." He didn't like the way she changed the subject, but it told him the answer. He quickly got his suitcase out of the closet, tossed his clothes into it, and then unhooked the big laundry bag from the hook on the door, put it in on top, then closed and zipped the suitcase.

"Are you just about ready?"

"Yes," he said. "Want to take one last look around? I'd sure hate to have to come back while he's home and ask him for your great-grandma's cameo brooch."

"Don't worry. I already did my walk-through yesterday."

He picked up his suitcase, then hers, and walked to the door. As he set the suitcases down to open it, he turned to her and said, "But you didn't take anything that wasn't, strictly speaking, yours, right?"

The door swung open, hit the two suitcases and knocked them over onto the floor. Jeff had just enough time to leap backward before the man who had applied the force to the door came af-ter it. Jeff had time to see a shaved head, a patch of black beard, a wide mouth with bared teeth, as the charging man tripped over the suitcases and belly-flopped past him onto the kitchen floor.

Jeff said, "Hold on, now. We don't need to do this. We can talk like grownups," by which he meant "Don't hurt me."

The man rolled and his legs scissored at Jeff's calves to trip him to the floor.

Jeff jumped up and backward to avoid the legs, but he hit his back on the wall and dropped straight down onto the man's ankle.

"Yaaah!" the man howled. "You son of a bitch! I'll kill you!"

"No, Roger! He didn't do anything to you," Carrie said. Jeff felt in his heart that this wasn't exactly true, but said nothing.

The man snarled through clenched teeth, "In a minute you'll be wearing his balls for a necklace."

"Stop it, Roger. He didn't know you existed."

"But he'll remember me forever." With frightening agility, the big man rose to a crouch and sprang at Jeff, his arms wide to gather him in.

Jeff could see that he would not escape the span of stretched muscles and big, grasping hands. He reacted in a reflex to protect himself from the tackle. He lunged forward between the arms and lifted his right knee as he pounded both forearms into the back of the man's head, hammering the head downward to meet his knee with considerable force. He half-heard and half-felt the man's nose break.

The man's momentum expended itself, plowing both of them into the kitchen counter. Jeff toppled, and the man's arms closed on his waist in a powerful clamp. As Jeff hit the floor, Carrie shrieked, and he could already feel the man's hands clawing their way up his body toward his throat.

"Don't kill him!" Carrie shrieked.

He raised his left forearm to keep the man's clawlike grasp from closing on his throat. With his right fist he delivered a series of short, hard punches to the man's face and left ear.

The man released his grip and raised his arm to fend off Jeff's right hand and turned his face away. Jeff used the moment to give a great, wrenching turn to speed him in that direction, scrambled away, and got to his feet.

The man was still so unimpressed with Jeff that as he too rose, he barely looked in Jeff's direction. Instead, he glared at Carrie while he touched his bleeding nose tentatively, and then his battered left ear.

Jeff had no hope now of escaping the fight or ending it. All he could see was the inviting sight of the big man's momentary inattention. He advanced and delivered eight rapid punches, throwing each as he pushed from his back foot, so he battered the man backward with each one, until the man was pinned against the front of the stove.

Jeff felt the elation of battle, the hard, clean impact as his fists struck again and again in adrenaline-fueled fury. But slowly, he began to sense that something was not right. The exertion of pounding this man was making his arms tired. As he hit the man, he could see that the swollen eyes were open and watching him. There was a cold, reptilian quality to the way the eyes held him.

He hadn't seen it before, but there was no question of what it was. The big man was watching, waiting for him to wear himself out. In another few minutes, Jeff would barely be able to hold his arms up, barely be able to dance to avoid the thick arms. But when that moment came, the big man might be marked and bruised, but he would not be exhausted. He would still be able to fight. It would be his turn.

Jeff looked into the eyes, at the cold hatred behind them, and he knew that the man was keeping track, making his own personal calculation of his hurt. He was, in some perverse way, happy because he was soon going to exact a ferocious reprisal.

Carrie was suddenly at Jeff's elbow. "Roger, it doesn't matter what you do, I'm not going back with you, so I'm leaving now." She picked up her suitcase and started to drag it toward the door.

It occurred to Jeff that to an observer it would look as though he was not the one who needed help, but he was, and Carrie's announcement that she was leaving was not good news. He kept swinging, knowing his punches were hitting more and more sloppily. He had to keep punching, because he knew that if his punches stopped, Roger's would start.

When Carrie spoke, Roger seemed electrified. He straightened and stared at her with the sort of anger that he had been lavishing on Jeff. He ducked low so Jeff's next swing missed him, and lunged at Carrie.

When Roger moved, Jeff's eye settled on the iron skillet on the stove that had been hidden behind his body. He snatched it up and swung it in a single, desperate backhand motion. It hit the back of Roger's head and made a sound like a hammer hitting a coconut. Roger's lunge changed midway into a dive to the floor. He slid a couple of feet on the smooth kitchen floor, then lay still.

Jeff stood motionless for a moment, the skillet now hanging from his hand, trying to catch his breath while he watched Roger for signs that he might get up.

Carrie had the door open and she was tugging her suitcase out onto the steps. "What are you waiting for? Round two?"

Jeff set the skillet on the stove, clutched the handle of his suitcase, but felt too tired to lift it. He extended the handle, wheeled it to the doorway, and bumped it down the steps. He hurried to the car, wondering if he should have tied Roger up, or done something to prevent him from following.

Carrie was waiting, having put her suitcase in the back seat instead of waiting for him to open the trunk. He lifted his in too, got into the driver's seat, and turned to her. "Are you leaving your car here?"

"Technically, it's only my car because it's the one he let me use. Don't worry. I didn't leave him any keys." She gave him an appraising glance. "You want me to drive?"

"No, thanks." He started the car and backed down the driveway, feeling relieved when he got past the door without having Roger burst out into his path. He hit the button to lock the doors, pulled into the street, shifted, and headed to the turn that would take him down the hill.

"Jeez," she said. "I thought you were going to get us killed in there. Haven't you been in a fight before?"

"What do you mean? Roger is a very big, strong guy, and he didn't manage to hit me even once."

"He was getting ready to, and it would have been awful. You can't dance around like that and tap him. I could tell it was just pissing him off. That's why I decided to make him freak out like that — so you would have to come to your senses to save me."

"Come to my senses?"

"Yes. Before he killed you. We're both very lucky that the place he was coming from was the airport. Anyplace else and he'd have had a gun."

"Don't you ever date anybody who's not a criminal?"

She shrugged and smiled sweetly. "I guess all this time I've been searching for you."

29

IT WAS HOT. Lieutenant Slosser's office door was closed, and the three detectives were gathered in the room with their coats off, their shirtsleeves rolled up, and their ties loosened. Even Detective Louise Serra, who favored black suits with matador jackets, had hers off, so the gun in the small belt holster she wore was visible.

Slosser leaned back in his desk chair, masking the eagerness that he felt. "So who are they and where did you find them?"

"There are two of them," said Timmons. "Both of them young, and would you say 'attractive,' Louise?"

"Probably not, but you can. You say young and attractive goes with it. They're teenagers."

"Right. Their names are Ariana Rodriguez, and Irena Estrada. The surnames may be fake, because the IDs are. The first names are probably real, because a lot of people know them under those names. They were picked up in Sunland in a BMW that was registered to Alvin Tatum."

"The Alvin Tatum that got killed in the Malibu massacre?"

"The same. The car was parked on the street in Sunland near a corner where some coke dealers sell. At one, two A.M., this Beemer is not going to be noticed. At eight A.M., it kind of stands out. A patrol car comes by, the officer spots it, runs the tags, and it comes up stolen from a murder victim. They left it there and put it under surveillance for a couple of hours. Along come these two girls, Ariana and Irena, on foot. They unlock it with the remote on the key chain and get in. The chase cars roll in and block it, and they're in custody."

"What did they have on them?"

"The false IDs I mentioned. They each had a gun and a box of ammunition. If you unloaded the guns, the ammunition refilled the boxes. Both guns were new, probably never fired after the factory test firing. They both had the instruction booklets that came with them."

"What did they have to say?" Slosser asked.

"Not much. Ariana said they had borrowed the car from a friend because they didn't want to walk home in this heat."

"Was Alvin Tatum the friend?"

"No. They didn't know the friend's real name. He calls himself Gordo—Fats."

"So they claim to know nothing about anything."

"Right."

"How hard did you try?"

"Hard."

"Then it's my turn. How much time do I have?"

"They were brought in at ten. Nobody has asked for a lawyer or anything yet."

"Good. I'll see them in Room Three." He stood. "Tell me you've read them their rights."

"We read them their rights," Timmons said. "Here's the file on what we've got so far."

He took it. "Good. Serra, can you please bring them down? I'd like you there." Slosser walked out the door and down the hall to the interrogation room. He sat in a chair he selected for himself at the end of the bare table. When the door opened, Detective Serra held it open for the two girls. They stood at the other end of the table looking around at the uncomfortable room. He said, "Have you been given the chance to use the bathroom?"

They looked at each other, then looked at him. The taller one, Ariana, said, "I'd like to go now."

"Detective Serra, will you please take them there?"

"We know where it is," said the shorter one, who was Irena.

"I know."

While they were gone, he sat alone, thinking about his interrogation and studying the file. He knew where he wanted to go. It was only a question of getting them to take him there. His detectives would have kept them separated all this time, trying to keep them from concocting the same lies and to deprive each of the other's support.

As they came in the door, he looked at them. They were both thin, both Hispanic, with long, dark brown hair that had been straightened with a flat iron so it hung straight down as though it were heavy. They both wore tank tops, short skirts, and flip-flops. He watched them sit down near the end on opposite sides of the table, then turn to him, their dark eyes wary.

He said, "I'm Lieutenant Nicholas Slosser. I'm the boss of the detectives you spoke with earlier. This is going to be your best chance to make the rest of this experience smooth and easy by answering my questions and telling me the truth."

Their expressions didn't mask the fact that they'd heard it all so many times that the actual words fell to the ground before they reached them. It was always about the choice between cooperation and suffering. He decided to start with the taller one, Ariana. She had a naive, earnest look, not hard-eyed yet like the other. "Ariana. Your fake ID says you're twenty-two. How old are you?"

"Seventeen."

He examined the driver's license from the file. "It's a pretty good fake."

284

"Yes," she said.

"Why do you use it?"

"I like to go to clubs."

He turned to the other girl. "It's Irena, right?"

"Right."

"Same question to you. I assume you like clubs too. How old are you?"

"Twenty-one."

"Are you sure?"

"That's what it says on my license."

"It doesn't matter," said Slosser. "As long as you're over sixteen, it's all the same. You'll be charged as an adult."

"At Disneyland they charge you as an adult when you're ten."

"Really?"

"Yes. It's a lot too. Like a hundred bucks."

"Let's talk a little about why you're here. Last night, there was a murder in Malibu, at the house of Manuel Rogoso. He and two men who worked for him, Alvin Tatum and Chuy Sanchez, were shot to death. The house was set on fire. At noon today, Alvin Tatum's black BMW turned up in Sunland. Police officers watched the car, and then somebody came along, got in, and fired up the engine. You." He looked at Ariana. "Help me out."

Irena said, "Is there a question in there?"

"Tell me why I'm not supposed to think you two killed those three men, set the fire, and stole the car."

Ariana said, "Because we didn't do that. We never killed anybody or started any fires. We don't know anything about any fire or any murder."

"Then you're very unlucky. You're the only ones who can be positively placed at that beach house that night. The BMW was seen parked there before the killings, but wasn't there when the firefighters arrived and found the bodies."

"We have an alibi," Irena said. "We were at a party all evening."

"Where?"

"At my friend's house, in Echo Park."

"What's the friend's name?"

"Maria."

"Last name?"

"I don't know her last name. But she stays around there, near Echo Park."

"What time did it start?"

"Like eight o'clock."

"And it went until two," Irena said.

"Maybe later," Ariana said.

Lieutenant Slosser took a blank piece of paper from the folder and a pen from his pocket and set them down on the table. "Write down the names of some of the people at the party."

"Who, me?"

"Either of you. Both of you." He watched as the two whispered and added names. When they seemed to have run out of names, he pointed and said, "Who is this one to you?"

"A friend."

"This one?"

"My sister."

"This one?"

"A cousin."

Irena said, "Are you going to tell us that they don't count because they're friends and relatives?"

"No. That wouldn't be fair. But if you can please write down all the addresses and phone numbers you can remember, we'll be able to use them."

"What do you mean?"

"I'll have to have police officers go and pick them all up and bring them down here to prove your story before I can let you go."

"You can do that?"

"Sure. We just keep you in this room, and we'll put them in another and ask them where they were between eight and two last night."

Irena took the pen and began to write for a few seconds, then crumpled up the paper and held the ball in her hand. "All right. It wasn't a party. We just hung out together at Wash in Hollywood, but it got too crowded, so we left."

"Why did you lie to me?"

"Because we were afraid, and we wanted to be sure we didn't get arrested. We didn't kill anybody," Ariana said. "All we did was borrow a car, drive it to our neighborhood, park it, and go home."

"So you didn't steal the car from Alvin. You just borrowed it from him."

"Yes."

"You were at this house in Malibu and he just handed you the keys and said you could take it home?"

"No," said Irena. "We were at Wash. We were hot and tired and it was crowded, so we asked, and he gave us the keys."

"So you dropped him off at Rogoso's house in Malibu, and then drove straight home?"

"No. We didn't go to Malibu."

"Then how did he end up there?"

"I don't know. We were gone. Maybe he went there with a friend, or maybe he took a cab. Maybe anything. But he wasn't with us, and we didn't go near Malibu."

"Okay, so how did you know Alvin Tatum so well he would lend you his fifty-thousand-dollar car?"

"We met him at a club. It might have been Adder or the Room. I don't remember. Once in a while we'd see him again, and he would come over and talk to us. If it was late, he might ask if we needed a ride home."

"Do you know what he did for a living?"

"No."

"I do. I read his rap sheet. He started out selling cocaine on the street, but pretty early he learned that what he was really good at was taking care of the people who didn't pay or the ones who were trying to work the same neighborhoods, or people who weren't afraid enough of him or his boss, Rogoso. By the time he died, he had been a full-time bodyguard and killer for at least five years."

"We didn't know about any of that," said Irena.

"This is odd. I assumed that my detectives would have told you what we know about you already. We know that you've been working for Rogoso for a year or more, because your names have been mentioned by people we've talked to for that long. You carry drugs to the sellers and money back to Rogoso. You were in Malibu last night. Either you killed Rogoso and Alvin and Chuy, or you were there and know who did. Which is it?"

"Neither," said Irena. "We know nothing."

"I'd like you to think about things for a while. You could be convicting yourselves of three murders. Or you could be putting yourselves in front of a lot of guns. Whenever a guy like Rogoso dies, there are a lot of people who believe there must be a lot of money hidden someplace. You don't want them to think you've got it. There are also relatives of Rogoso who just lost a lifetime of living off him."

"Are you going to make sure they know about us?"

"My job is to try to keep people from dying, not get them killed. If you get charged with murder, though, there's no way it won't be in the papers."

Ariana was hugging herself and rocking back and forth, staring straight ahead. The sight of her seemed to weaken Irena. "How do we avoid that?"

"I'll tell you what I need from you. I need the name of the man who pulled the trigger. I don't know why you haven't told us yet. Maybe he paid you to set those three up, maybe you just happened to be there when it happened, and you owe him because he let you leave. I don't know. But if you tell me, I'll try to keep you from being charged as accomplices. If you don't, then the DA may decide to charge you with the shootings. One of the things that will strike him is that you both had brand-new guns in your purses. You must have thrown away the old ones on the same night. I'm going to give you a chance to think." He stood up, beckoned to Detective Serra. "We'll be back."

As soon as the door closed, the two girls moved closer, leaned together. "He means it," said Irena.

"I know. Shh!"

"He really does. You want to go to trial for murder? We don't have any money for good lawyers. They'll lock us up forever."

Ariana had tears in her eyes. "But we can't."

"Why not? We met the man once. We don't care about him."

"But we owe him," Ariana said.

"We do not. There wouldn't be any problem if it weren't for him."

"He didn't do anything. They were about to kill him. He didn't even bring a gun with him. All he did was fight back. He had to, and then he let us live. We were the only witnesses, and he knew we worked for Rogoso. If he had killed us there wouldn't be anybody left to tell on him. But he didn't. He even gave us the keys to the car so we could get away."

"They weren't his to give. And maybe he was smarter than we were and knew the car would turn out to be a curse. Maybe he set us up on purpose so we'd be blamed."

"You know that's not true. He even waited and gave us time to get far away before he set the fire."

"He's an old man, not a little boy. He knew what he was risking. Nobody made him do it."

Outside the room, in the smaller one that was marked "Cleaning supplies," Lieutenant Slosser and Detective Serra watched the television monitor and listened to the voices, amplified by the microphones all over the room. "Say it," he whispered. "Say the name."

Ariana said, "It was my fault more than yours. He took the gun out of my purse. I'll take the blame."

"I don't want either of us to take the blame. Why should we throw ourselves away, especially for a man we don't even know?

And he's a pig. He got rich by making women strip and then turn tricks in those private rooms."

"What are you talking about? A year ago that's what you wanted to do."

"I changed my mind."

"You got a better offer, more money just for carrying things."

"And I let you in on it too, didn't I?"

In the next room, Detective Serra said, "They're off the subject. Do you want me to go back in and remind them they have to come up with the name?"

"No, thanks, Louise," Slosser said. "This could take a while. I want them to get so used to the interrogation room and the predicament they're in that they forget we're out here listening. You can go back to your other work."

"Thanks." She went out the door and closed it.

Ariana said, "Why don't we make a story up? Why can't we say 'We met a man named Stanley in Wash, he drove us to Malibu, and argued with Mr. Rogoso.'"

"Then what?"

"Just what really happened. Make it all the same except the man's name. Mr. Rogoso told Chuy and Alvin to kill him, but he snatched the gun out of my purse. It was self-defense."

Slosser's face was close to the screen, his jaw working. "The name, honey. Time to say the name."

Ariana said, "I wish I could talk to him. I could explain why we have to do it."

"What would you say? Hello, Mr. Kapak. This is your good friend Ariana. I've got something to tell you that'll just kill you."

Slosser stood up. He left the tape running and walked back toward the big open office where the detectives had their desks. Nobody had told him anything to his face yet, but the big turn had occurred. He knew.

30

AT JUST AFTER NOON, Manco Kapak lay in his bed in a
troubled sleep. He dreamed he was in a field with golden stems
and fat seeds of grain. He knew he was young again, and back
in Hungary. He was with Marija. She was studying music in Budapest, but he was only posing as a student. He was the right
age—twenty-two—and he had acquired the bohemian look that
students had, the workman's clothes, a pair of round sunglasses
that he wore all the time, a modest beard.

He had told her and her friends that he was studying political science, because it seemed to be a subject that had no particular agreed-upon content, no specific books that everyone had to
read. It was also one of the dangerous subjects that implied mem-
bership in one of the opposition groups. But since he was on no
lists of students and never attended a lecture, he felt secure. He
and Marija were both Romanians—he from Bucharest and she
from a village not too far away where he had relatives—and he

suspected that much of what he had to offer was a cure for home-sickness, a chance to use her own language.

She sometimes asked him why he never spoke about his studies, and he answered that he learned more by listening than by talking. He said that at his age, all he would be doing was repeating the words of his professors anyway. He would speak and write his own opinions when he had learned enough to have a right to them. When the others in their set heard this, he gained a reputation for wisdom and humility.

But in his dream he didn't feel the contentment of those summers. He knew a great many things that none of the others knew, because he wasn't only Claudiu the student. He was also Manco Kapak at age sixty-four. Camping in the wheat fields was sure to disappear with the summer, and anyone would know that, but he knew that it would disappear forever. All of it—the smell of the plants that somehow clung to Marija's hair, the finger-touch of the gentle breeze, the steady sound of the chatter of their student friends, uncaring as the chatter of birds—was going to be obliterated. He knew that it was going to turn into a nightmare place. He tried to tell all of them that it was time to go, but his voice turned thick and slow, and he couldn't draw in enough breath to speak loud and strong. The others didn't seem to hear him. He had to save Marija, so he picked her up in his arms.

He knew the time was running out as he went along, holding her. He could not see the dips and rises in the earth, because the stalks of the plants hid them. He tripped and staggered and lost his balance many times. He made one long step and began to fall. He knew the hole was deeper than he had feared, and he began to turn as he fell, and gasped.

He awoke, lying there on top of the covers, trying to catch his breath. He looked past his feet at the tall, narrow windows copied in style from a French palace, turned and felt the smooth texture of the matching pillows and duvet on the bed. For an instant he saw it all with the twenty-two-year-old eyes of Claudiu the student. The old man he had become was richer and more secure than the most corrupt Communist bureaucrats he had met in those days. The thought brought him back fully to the present. He wasn't really old yet, because he could still move quickly. His muscles had strength, even if it was not the strength of the young. When he got bent over and could no longer walk without help, he would be old. The time was coming, and it no longer seemed so distant as to be only theoretical. He could already feel a taste of the pains that he would feel then, so he knew where they would be—his knees, his right hip, and his hands.

He lay there and his memory brought his trouble back to him. He was in jeopardy. He had killed Rogoso and his two body-guards. He sat up, swung his legs off the bed, yawned, and put on his shoes. He glanced at his watch. It was just after 12:00. He had slept late, and he felt anxious about being unconscious that long. There were forces waiting to take him down and destroy him. They were always there, and always had been, waiting like microbes for him to become too weak to fight them off.

He stood and held his place for a moment to be sure he had waited through the wave of dizziness from standing up too fast. He passed by the mirrored dresser and ran a brush through his hair to push it back down, and opened the door that led from the master suite to the hall.

He crossed the living room and looked, as he always did, to the left and right. To the left was the path through the tropical garden to the guesthouse, and beyond it, the bamboo forest at the back of the property. To the right was the formal front entrance with the two big carved teak doors that nobody ever used. It was protected from the street by a tight planting of trees. When the sunlight passed through all the greenery, it became soft and se-cret and the undersides of the leaves glowed.

Kapak walked down the far hallway past the pantry, the maid's quarters, into the kitchen. The women of the cleaning crew were all gone, and Spence was sitting at the kitchen table reading the *Los Angeles Times.* He always read it in a prescribed order — front section, California, Calendar, and finally Business and Sports — then refolded it and put each section back as though he'd never touched it.

Even after more than thirty years in the city, Kapak could hardly ever bring himself to read the paper. He supposed it was because most of the stories were about things that had no bearing on his life. He checked it only to be sure his ads had run, skimmed the headlines to be sure there were no stories about him or about live adult entertainment. He said to Spence, "Good morning. Only it's afternoon, right? You look relaxed."

"I am."

"How is that thing going? You know — the thing with Joe Carver. You got any leads yet?"

"I got him."

"You *got* him?"

"Last night. I'll show you something." He got up, left the newspaper spread on the kitchen table, went to the maid's room, and came back with a plastic zip-lock bag. He set it on the newspaper. "I thought this might make you feel good." He began to pull the bag open.

"Is that blood?"

"Yes."

Kapak looked down at it. "You don't need to open that. It's his shirt. I recognize the pattern. That's the one he was wearing the day he came here. We don't need to get any of his blood on anything."

"I just figured you'd like to see proof that it's over."

"Did you get the girl too — the crazy one who helped him with the robberies?"

"Sure. But I didn't bring back any souvenirs from her. Carver is the one we want to prove is dead."

"Thanks. And great work. I was beginning to think this was going to go on forever. You'll be getting some kind of bonus, when I think of something that would be big enough."

He retreated from the kitchen and walked back toward the living room. He stopped in front of a big leather couch and let his legs give way to deposit him in the middle of it. For comfort he stared out the window at the enormous translucent ferns above the stubby sago palms. Even though the tropical plants were out of proportion and came from a distant, alien place, they were natural and green, so they made him feel calmer.

Spence had surprised him. It shouldn't have been a surprise. He had been ranting for weeks that somebody should be able to find this Carver guy and get rid of him. But now Spence had done it. Kapak was beginning to feel a bit scared of Spence. He was like a genie. If you stated a desire in front of him, he would make it happen. But in the stories, the genie wasn't benevolent. He was cunning and dangerous, and asking him to use his power was a risk. If you didn't think carefully before you made the wish, there were terrible consequences.

Kapak tried to decide whether he had done the right thing. He was the one who had killed Carver and the girl, really. Spence's disinterested violence was a kind of innocence. Kapak was the one who made the decision and the one who received the benefit. He had committed murder. It was the first time in a long life of struggling and fighting that he had done that. He had killed a couple of men before last night's work at Malibu, but it had always had a fairness to it. Two men fight with grappling hooks on a moving boat, and one falls in. Maybe the propeller got him, maybe he drowned, and maybe he swam underwater to the far side of the boat, then ducked again to swim to the next boat. *Never seen again* wasn't the same as *dead.* Running another car off the road didn't mean he had killed the driver, or that the driver was even dead. If he was, he had certainly had a part in killing himself.

Joe Carver was the worst thing Kapak had ever done. He had ordered a man and his girlfriend killed merely for strategic reasons. It was what a king would have done. He had felt he had no other choice. He couldn't afford to let people all over town believe that he had allowed a solitary stranger to keep robbing him over and over in different ways. It would have made him a victim to anyone in the city who owned a gun. As it was, he had waited one day too long and tempted Rogoso to kill him for being weak.

Telling Spence to kill Carver had been a bad thing. There was no doubt about that. But that wasn't all there was to say about it. Life was more complicated than that. By having Spence kill Carver, he had put out a clear notice that anyone who attacked Manco Kapak was placing himself in terrible jeopardy. Kapak's men would search until they found him, even if it took a very long time.

Spreading that story was a good thing to do. It would not only protect Kapak, but also his enterprises and all of his people. He wasn't just thinking of the men like the Gaffneys, Spence, Guzman, Corona, and Voinovich, but also the bartenders, waiters, busboys, cooks, bouncers who worked in the clubs. If a bunch of men got up the nerve to pull a full-scale assault on one of the clubs, there would be shooting. In a crowded club, bullets could hit anybody, and they were far more likely to hit the people who had the least experience of gunfire. By making the decision to sacrifice Joe Carver, he may have saved ten or fifteen other people who depended on him for their livelihoods and their safety. He did not succeed in convincing himself.

He stood. The work was done. It wasn't as though he had a chance to undo it. Now what he needed was to keep the killing from being wasted. He went back to Spence in the kitchen. "Have you told anybody that Carver is dead?"

"Nobody but you."

"What did you do with the body?"

"I had rented a boat in Marina del Rey when I started looking for him. After I got him and the girl last night, I took the bodies about ten miles into the channel, almost midway to Catalina. I weighted them with chains and scrap iron I had collected and kept around for this kind of thing, and let them go. There's a chance they'll surface some time, but it won't be soon."

"All right. That's good, I guess. We don't want to get caught. But is there any way to let the word out that Carver has been found and killed?"

"There's his shirt and his wallet, with credit cards and license. We can leave all of it where it will get found, if you like."

"That ought to work," Kapak said. "We'll have to put some thought into where we want it found and who finds it."

There was a sudden, loud pounding on the front door. It startled Kapak so much that he gave a little jump, then felt embarrassed because Spence hadn't. He felt different about Spence today, and he'd only had a few minutes to sort it out.

Spence got up and looked at the monitor in the maid's room. "It's cops."

"What cops?"

"Take a look." He pressed the remote control and five of the small squares that shared the screen disappeared, so the view of the front steps took up the whole screen.

Kapak could see two men in sport coats and a woman in a pantsuit. "It's that Lieutenant Slosser who's been on my ass since the construction site thing. I just went for a ride with him this morning. You hide the shirt and stuff, and I'll go talk to him."

"Right." Spence snatched up the plastic bag, opened a cupboard, stuffed it into a covered pot, then closed the door.

Kapak hurried down the hall toward the living room. He took a deep breath, then opened the door. He smiled. "Hello again, Lieutenant. Did you find the people who robbed my club last night?"

"Not yet. I'm sorry to bother you again, but I'm afraid we have to go talk downtown."

"What about?"

"The deaths of Manuel Rogoso, Alvin Tatum, and Chuy Sanchez. We still have to clear some things up."

Kapak couldn't believe it. Here he was in his own house with the bloody shirt and the wallet of a murdered man, and here were three homicide detectives. But all they wanted from him was exactly what he wanted — to ride downtown a few miles from here to talk about something else. His luck must be returning already.

He smiled, almost laughed. "Of course. Just let me get my sport coat."

31

KAPAK SAT in the back seat of the car beside Lieutenant Slosser. The two detectives, Timmons and Serra, sat in the front. The male, Timmons, drove the car, and the female was beside him in the passenger seat. It seemed the same to him as riding in a car with his parents when he was very young. His father had bought an old East German Trabant when Claudiu was young. His father would spend every Friday night and Saturday trying in vain to tune it properly or making the repairs to keep it moving, Sunday morning washing the fiberglass exterior, and the afternoon driving it with the family all dressed up, sitting stiffly and listening to the engine, waiting for it to cough, stop spewing black smoke, and glide silently to the side of the road.

He could feel tension in the car now, emanating from the front seat. Maybe it was because these two were partners and they were driving their boss in their unmarked car. He sensed that they were uncomfortable sitting this way, with the man driving and the woman beside him, because they knew it suggested to the eye that they were a couple. That had to be forbidden. They never spoke, only listened for some comment from the back seat that would distract everyone from the way they looked.

He felt sorry for them for a few minutes, then reminded himself that he was the one being transported for interrogation. He turned to look at Slosser and found Slosser already staring at him. "Do I look different?"

"It's only been a couple of hours. But to me you look like a guy who's got himself in trouble."

"Getting older *is* trouble. Once you're over sixty, every day is a gift, but carrying your gift around wears you down. I don't know if young men would be such heroes if they knew that every bruise can turn into a pain that comes back later, and every twinge just might be the start of a heart attack."

"I've got old age figured out. When I can, I'm going to lie on a beach every day and have drinks with little umbrellas in them every night." He paused. "That's what you should have done."

"You may be right."

"I know I am," Slosser said. "But nobody quits while he's still okay and hasn't made a big mistake yet."

"People make mistakes because they're greedy," Kapak said. "They never have enough. That's not me. I just want to get through the rest of my life like I am."

Slosser said, "Will one of you please read Mr. Kapak his rights?" He turned to Kapak. "Since we're talking, I don't want to take advantage of you."

"Fine."

Detective Serra, the one Slosser clearly had meant, recited the Miranda warning, speaking slowly and clearly.

When she reached "Do you understand these rights?" Kapak said, "I understand," then turned to Slosser. "So now what did you want to ask me?"

"I think we can wait the last few minutes until we're in the station." He had sensed that Kapak was feeling too confident and comfortable, but now he had reminded him that their conversation would be recorded to be used at some future trial.

The car pulled into the driveway to the underground lot and stopped at the building entrance. Lieutenant Slosser and Detective Serra got out and escorted Kapak into the building.

The smell of floor wax and disinfectant filled Kapak's nostrils. It was the smell of governments, the smell of the physical power that dragged people in who were dirty or bleeding or vomiting and made them invisible in some cell or interrogation room, and then cleaned up the mess. It was a reminder that the government was big, its surfaces hard and enduring and polished, and that human beings were small, soft, dirty, and weak. Thousands of them could be herded through here and there would be no sign of it, not even a human smell.

They took an elevator upstairs to the corridor that Kapak remembered from his questioning after the fight at the construction site. They conducted Kapak up the hall toward the interrogation room. There were cops coming up and down the hallway, doors that were closed, others that were open. Kapak's mind tried to make sense of the place, his eyes scanning, passing over each sight. He could tell from Slosser's manner that he thought he knew something Kapak didn't. He knew that was not out of the question. The last time he was here, Slosser had known much more than Kapak about the fight at the construction site. He was determined not to underestimate Slosser.

His eyes turned to his right to glance into the next open doorway—the girls. Then he was past the doorway, with no way to turn and walk back to look again and be sure. He kept walking at the same pace as the others. In a moment he was inside the interrogation room, and he was sure. Both of them had been looking in his direction, and his eyes had met theirs for a second, he had seen them recognize him, and then he was looking at the plain dirty wall going by.

He sat at the table in one of the plain, hard chairs and considered the implications. There could be no weapon. He had taken it apart and spread the pieces where they would never be found. There could be no fingerprints, blood, fiber after a fire. He had seen the house and there was nothing left. His footprints and tire tracks were obliterated when the fire trucks arrived. There was nothing that could connect him with the actual killing except the two girls. What were their names?

Ariana. That was the tall one, with the sweet disposition. The other one's name was like it. Irena. There was something that he had seen and needed to think about. They had been surprised. If they had told what they had seen him do, why would they be surprised to see Kapak here?

Slosser watched Kapak sitting at the table, glaring at the wall. He caught Serra's eye and nodded slightly. She was behind Kapak, so she could risk a quick half-smile to acknowledge that, yes, Kapak had seen the two girls through the open office door, and the sight of them had eroded his confidence.

Slosser said, "Mr. Kapak. The reason I asked you down here was that I wanted to double-check some things from our earlier conversations and pursue a few others in case there's something you didn't mention the first time. All right?"

"Sure."

"A few minutes ago, Detective Serra read you your rights, including the right to refuse to answer questions and the right to have an attorney present. Would you like us to repeat anything or explain anything?"

"No. Are you arresting me?"

"No, we're not. We're just after information at the moment."

"Okay."

"Let's begin with Manuel Rogoso. Last time we spoke, you couldn't remember ever having heard of him. I wondered if you had placed the name since then."

"Why would I do that?"

"Any reason. Sometimes if a name makes the news and a witness sees a picture, he comes back to me and says, 'Oh, yeah. I remember him now.' Or 'I didn't know his full name. People just called him Manny,' or something. Anything like that happen to you?"

"No." He was becoming alarmed. The girls must have told Slosser he laundered money for their boss, Rogoso. That was a major crime, a federal crime. All he could do was hope there was no evidence left to prove what they'd said, and that maybe they hadn't told Slosser that Kapak had done the shooting.

"I've talked to a lot of people who used to see Rogoso. They say you knew him well. They say you took his drug money and mixed it with your take from the clubs. Then you would send a check to a fake company Rogoso controlled for some imaginary service — linen or advertising or something."

"They have the wrong man."

"They all say they have the right man, and that you had a business relationship with Rogoso for years."

"What people?" Of course it was the girls. There was nobody else who would know and tell. But maybe they'd had to give Slosser something but resisted giving him everything. Saying they'd been there and seen it would get them in trouble, maybe get them killed.

"Lots of people. Some worked for him, some didn't."

Kapak felt better. That's all it was. The two teenaged girls were all they had. Kapak could go into court and look pretty honest and substantial beside two teenaged drug mules in short skirts and tattoos. "Well, they're wrong. I never knew him."

"I think I know what must have happened. He was a mean, violent guy. Everybody agrees on that. He got upset because you got robbed a couple of times, and it made him feel unsafe. He called you in to see him, you argued, and he told his men to kill you. Isn't that right? And then you killed him in self-defense."

Kapak smiled and shook his head. "I did all of this last night?

I'm sixty-four years old. I don't go quick-drawing guns and shooting everyone in sight so I'll be a big hero. I don't own a gun, and I'm sure you must have checked my record to see if I ever did."

"I think you were at Rogoso's house, and that you shot the three men and burned the house to cover it."

"I didn't do any of those things. I wasn't there."

"Where were you last night between midnight and three o'clock?"

"We already talked about that this morning. I was at Wash, then at Temptress until two. I talked to my guys at Siren a few times."

"Anybody see you in any of those places?"

"A lot of people. Dozens of them," Kapak said. "I talked to them, and they talked to me. I stood around a long time watching bartenders to see how they were keeping up with the demand. I spent time talking to my manager at Wash, Ruben Salinas, and his assistant. I talked to waiters, busboys, even a few dancers, the security guys."

"Sounds like an awful lot of people. It seems almost as though you were trying to construct an alibi."

"It might seem that way, if I didn't do it every night. But I do—seven nights a week. You'll find out when you start talking to the people who work for me."

"I have no doubt your lawyers can bring in lots of people to swear you were in sight all evening, but it doesn't mean you were. I'll level with you. I've got really strong reasons to think you did this. I also know you did it in self-defense. If you'll just tell me exactly what happened, it will save us both a lot of time and effort, and you a lot of money. The law will also go a lot easier if you'll be honest about it. You and I both know what Rogoso was like. He was arrogant and vicious. He was trying to kill you right then. All you have to do now is agree with me."

They sat and stared at each other across the table for a long time. Finally Kapak said, "I'd like to call my attorney now."

32

JERRY GAFFNEY and Jimmy Gaffney and Vassily Voinovich were in the garage of Voinovich's house. Since he had come to Hollywood, Jimmy Gaffney had seen these little old houses with high-peaked roofs that made them look like witches or goblins lived there and wondered what sort of person really did. It turned out that the sort of person was Voinovich. Whatever it reminded him of in his Russian life, it seemed to make him calmer.

The garage was far too small for his SUV, and so it served as a workshop and storage space. Jimmy Gaffney pulled his body armor over his head, then blew out a breath of air. "Man, this is hot. I feel like I'm in some kind of press."

"It's not there to be comfy," Jerry said. "If you take a round in the chest, you'll be damned glad you're wearing that thing."

"Not always," Voinovich said. "I saw two bulletproof vests pierced in one fight when I was back home. It was a war between the security forces of a bank and a department store."

Jerry stared at him thoughtfully. "Well, probably nobody is going to be firing military ammo around here. If they do, at least now we'll know why we're dead."

Jerry put on his shirt over the armor and buttoned it. He had the same squared-off barrel torso that Voinovich had with his vest on. He put on a shoulder holster to hold his Glock pistol, then knelt to put a small ankle holster under his right pant leg to hold his .380 pistol. He put on a thin windbreaker over his gear and shrugged a few times to shift everything into the right places. He went to the workbench to pick up his ski mask and one of the three radio receivers.

Jimmy Gaffney began to pick up his gear and stow it in his pockets.

Voinovich stood fully armed and equipped, his head nearly to the lower rafters of his little garage. He tried pressing the Talk button on his radio and listened to the static sound as the channel came to life, then nodded to himself and put it in his jacket pocket. He said, "I'd like to talk about the plan some more before things start happening."

"All right," Jerry said. "We've got to stay loose. First we find out where he is. We take him in our car and drive away. Probably we keep moving. We call, or let him call, the club managers to arrange a ransom. All three managers have signature power for major accounts set up to run the clubs. None of them has the kind of history that would make me worry. They came up to where they are by making sure there are enough cocktail napkins and olives behind the bar. They're managers. So we give them something they know how to manage — getting us some cash. We pick it up, let Kapak go, and take off."

"Okay," Voinovich said. "We agree on the general outline. That's how it's done. It would be easier if he had a family, so we could deal with them and have them tell the managers what to do."

"Then there would be more money around," Jimmy said. "The kind you can put your hands on."

306

Jerry said, "Look, you've got to kidnap the guy you have, not make up some imaginary guy who would leave more cash lying around."

"It's all right," Voinovich said. "We've got to think about the details. We'll need plastic restraints for his hands and feet. We'll need a cloth sack to put over his head so he can't recognize any of us and doesn't know where he's been taken. That's important."

"We should try it on first," Jimmy said. "We want to be sure he can't see, but he can breathe."

"Not too well," Voinovich said. "If he can breathe easily, then he can yell too. We don't want that."

"No, we don't want that," Jerry said. "If we're quick and do this thing right, he won't have to wear it for long."

Jimmy looked at his brother. "What if everything doesn't go right?"

"What do you mean?"

"What I said. You're talking about everything going right. What if instead it all goes wrong? What if he doesn't come with us just because we point a gun at him? What if they can't come up with the money in one day? What if he does something stupid? Do we shoot him?"

"I guess we'd have to."

"Then what do we do with the body?"

"What?"

"You heard me. You're planning to go in with your guns drawn, and the whole thing depends on everybody saying yes and jumping to do what we say. If he doesn't, I guess you're saying we have to kill him. We can't just sit someplace with his body and hope it walks away on its own. We need to have a plan for getting rid of it."

"Well, if you're going to kidnap people, you have to be ready for bodies," Voinovich announced.

"Okay," said Jerry. "We'll just agree that if things go wrong we'll shoot him, and then hide the body. We'll put it in a Dumpster."

"What about the other people — say, people who work for him too, like Spence, or the waiters, or the bouncer?"

"We shoot them too, obviously, if it comes to that. We have to protect ourselves."

Voinovich thought for a moment. "Maybe the thing to do is just make him disappear. If we kill him we don't have to worry about him yelling or running away or getting his hands on somebody's gun. We just collect a ransom and give him back dead."

Jimmy Gaffney said, "When we started, we were just hanging out with him for a while. He might not even know he wasn't free to leave. Maybe we'd go to a bar or a restaurant. That's what you said, Jerry."

"I know. I did. And that's the way we all want it to be. We just breeze into his place like nothing's up. We tell him we want to take him somewhere and then go there, stop in the men's room to call the clubs for the ransom money. The other stuff is just in case it sours. Vassily feels more comfortable if he knows what to do in the worst case."

"Are you saying I'm a big coward?"

"No, Vassily," Jerry said. "I would never say that about you. Never." He turned to Jimmy. "He was just being prudent."

Jimmy was animated by frustration. "Being prudent isn't finding out that there's only a half-assed plan, and then going ahead with it. Prudence is stopping before it goes bad."

"There's a plan," Jerry snapped. "Don't go saying there's no plan. We just have to keep a few details undecided until we're on the scene and can assess the conditions. And we've got quite a few decisions worked out in advance so if certain things go wrong, we're not wasting time arguing about what to do. We all know and agreed ahead of time."

"You're both ready to shoot Kapak, who's been pretty good to us, ready to shoot anybody who stumbles in, and then put all their bodies in Dumpsters. Are we all supposed to agree on where the Dumpsters are?"

"Don't worry about any of that, Jimmy," said Jerry. "He's not going to be able to cause trouble or anything. We'll walk in, and nothing he does to stop us will work."

"Why is that?"

"For the same reason we have to do this in the first place. He's not the old Kapak. He's lost his luck. He's a magnet for trouble and ill fortune."

"You're really sure about that?" asked Jimmy.

"I'm so sure I can feel it and taste it and smell it."

Jimmy looked at Voinovich. He was at the workbench loading extra magazines for his gun, pointedly pantomiming that he considered this a private dispute between the brothers. It wasn't his business.

Jerry leaned close and spoke quietly. "You don't want to be the one who sticks with the old man after his luck is gone and the money has been taken, and all the others have bailed out."

Jimmy could see that their mother's expression of clairvoyance had appeared on Jerry's face—the wide-eyed expression of conviction and absolute confidence in his vision. It brought back the many times when their mother would lean close that way to impart her latest prophecy. Jimmy's spine chilled and he felt a little shiver. Jerry and their mother had been born with the terrible gift, but Jimmy hadn't. He had never felt a half-second of envy, but the sheer strangeness of it had created a distance with him on one side and his mother and only brother on the other. Maybe Jimmy's only gift was to feel the chill to warn him that his brother was in a state. "Okay, then," he said. "If you're so sure, then we'd better be going."

They walked out of the garage to the driveway and climbed into Voinovich's SUV. The big vehicle backed out into the street, and Jimmy heard Jerry cycle a round into the chamber of his gun. He hoped that didn't mean Jerry'd had another premonition.

33

KAPAK SPOKE into his cell phone. "I just spent nearly an hour talking to Lieutenant Slosser. I need you to come and pick me up at the Parker Center."

"I'll be there as soon as I can." Spence pressed the red phone symbol to end the call and put his phone away as he stood up. "He's at the police station downtown. That lieutenant is bugging him again."

"It's an opportunity. You know what you want him to feel," said Joe Carver. "So you say the things that will make him feel that way. If you run out of ideas, call. I'll be right here in the guesthouse."

"Just stay out of sight. I'll probably be bringing him back here." Spence went out the door of the guesthouse and made his way up the path through the tropical plants to the back of the house. He went right to the garage, got into the black Town Car, and backed it out of the driveway.

Spence drove downtown quickly. He had planned to pull up

near the Parker Center where he had waited for Kapak during his first police interview, but when he reached North Los Angeles Street, he could already see him. Kapak was standing on the sidewalk in front of the white stone with the weathered brass letters: DEDICATED TO WILLIAM H. PARKER, CHIEF OF POLICE. Spence stopped in front of the sign, leaned over, and pushed the door open, and Kapak climbed in looking irritated.

"See if the bastards follow us," he said.

Spence drove a couple of blocks, turned, and went back the other way, then made a U-turn and then a series of right turns until he was near a freeway entrance with a split ramp that sent cars on the 110 freeway or the 101. He went onto the freeway, stayed to the 110 side until the last second, then changed lanes to go onto the 101. "Nobody was following. What did they want you for?"

"Lieutenant Slosser got the idea that I killed Rogoso last night and burned his house in Malibu."

"Somebody did that?"

"Yeah. He had two men with him too — Alvin and Chuy. Slosser got the idea that it was me. I put up with the accusations as long as I could, until he got on my nerves. Then I said I wanted my lawyer, and he told me I could go."

"I guess you must have been incredibly shocked to hear about Rogoso to begin with."

"Not so much."

"You did it?"

"I wouldn't tell you, but since you did Joe Carver and didn't make any big thing of telling me, I have to. Yeah, I did it. He was a rotten, crazy, greedy son of a bitch, and he was getting worse every day. He decided I was drawing attention to myself by letting Joe Carver rob me over and over. I'm listening to a man who had just bought a fifteen-million-dollar house on the beach at Malibu telling me I'm drawing attention. What he really thought was that I must be too weak to fight him off. That he could take over my clubs and kill me."

"Jesus."

"Yeah. He told his two monsters, Alvin and Chuy, to take me out for a ride and kill me. There wasn't much choice."

"If they're dead and you're here, you must have done the right thing."

"That's what I think."

"And you killed everybody there and torched the house?"

"Well, there were a couple of girls — drug mules, no more than seventeen or eighteen, I think — who had come to take me to meet with Rogoso. I guess he used them because they didn't look scary. And maybe because nobody wants some guy frisking him for weapons, but a girl can get away with checking everywhere."

"Let me get this straight. What you did last night was kill Manuel Rogoso and Alvin and Chuy, and burn down the house. But there were also two witnesses, girls who worked for Rogoso."

"Yeah."

"Are they dead too?"

"No. I gave them the keys to Alvin's car and told them to get out of there. I gave them time before I lit the fires in the house."

"Holy shit. Where are they now?"

"I saw them a little while ago back at the police station."

"Oh my God."

"They're drug mules. They could be in the station for anything — possession and sales is what they do — or maybe they're out of work since Rogoso died, and they were caught turning tricks or boosting things from stores."

"The day after the killing?"

"Young kids don't know how to save money anymore."

"They had to be in the police station ratting you out."

"Could be," Kapak admitted.

"It's got to be," Spence said. "Talking to the police is probably their only shot at staying alive."

"Think so?"

"If Rogoso's people know the girls were in the house when you killed Rogoso, how can they not think the girls helped you?"

"I guess you're right. The police will protect them, maybe get them out of town."

"How are we going to get you out of here?"

"What do you mean?

"You can't stay in L.A."

"Wait a minute. I haven't decided anything like that. I mean, think about it. We've all had a rough week. It's all just part of the Joe Carver problem. He robbed me a month ago, but we didn't find him in all that time. That was what caused all this trouble for us. The worst thing it did was make that rat bastard Rogoso think he could kill me and take over. But you got Joe Carver, so he's not going to be a nuisance anymore. I got Rogoso last night, and so he's not a problem. There was a war going on for a few days, but it didn't bring us down. We won. Our enemies are dead. It's over."

Spence said, "If you killed three men last night and the police have two eyewitnesses, then your trouble is only beginning."

"Even if those two girls testified at a trial, the jury might not believe them."

"I don't see why they wouldn't."

"They're criminals."

"Do the girls know you did business with Rogoso?"

"They know something. They delivered Rogoso's money to me a few times."

"Think back. Can they say you were in business with Rogoso and how the business worked?"

"Sure, but who's going to believe them?"

"Mr. Kapak, I don't usually step out of line and give advice to my elders, or to the guy I'm working for. I shut up and learn. But you seem to be asking my opinion. Is that right?"

"I guess it is. Yeah," Kapak said.

"Okay then. Will a jury believe two girls who worked for Rogoso when they say they saw you kill him and Alvin and Chuy? Yes. They will. Unanimously."

"All I've got to do is pay one guy to hold out for innocent."

"If there's a hung jury, they don't have to let you go. They can have another trial."

"We can pay the next guy."

"Even if we do, the whole story will have been in the papers and on television everywhere, every day, because it's about a drug dealer with a house in Malibu and a strip club owner who's been running dirty money through his pussy palaces for years to help gangsters. You'd be in worse trouble. Everybody in Rogoso's organization, and all of his relatives, will know who got him. Getting off in court doesn't get you off with them. There will be bunches of them out for revenge. There will also be people who can't imagine anyone burning Rogoso's house without first backing a truck up to the place and filling it with money and drugs. They'll want to take you alive, but they'll settle for dead, because then they can search your house and the clubs."

Kapak let his frustration show. "I had no choice. What the hell am I supposed to do about any of that?"

"What I thought you must be doing already—getting out of town as fast as you can. Have the cops filed any charges yet?"

"No."

"How do you know?"

"I asked Slosser before I left."

"And he didn't say you can't leave the city?"

"No. And fuck him if he did."

"This is good. It's great. You're still free. We've got to keep you out of sight and away from them. They'll probably try to keep an eye on you so they can yank you in as soon as they've finished their investigation. They could even be running the case by the DA right now. Once they arrest you, you're stuck."

"But what about Rogoso's people?"

"I don't think they can know it was you yet. The girls would be crazy to tell anyone before they were under police protection, because Rogoso's people would also want to know why you let them go and how they got away." He sighed. "Of course, the minute you get arrested, it will be on the news. Then you worry about Rogoso's people."

Spence judged it was time to be silent and let Kapak think about his predicament. He drove the rest of the way to Kapak's house, waiting for Kapak to change his mind and name another destination. He pulled up in front of the house, and Kapak said, "I've got some things to do right now. I'll call you in an hour or two, so keep your phone on."

"Don't you want somebody around to watch your back?"

"No. This is stuff I have to do alone. And besides, the only ones who might come now are the police. If they do, I don't want you watching my back. I want you miles away. It doesn't do me any good to have both of us arrested."

34

AT 1:30 in the afternoon, Voinovich parked the big SUV on the street around the block from Kapak's vast backyard. There was a grove of bamboo trees in that quadrant. They were thirty feet tall, with trunks that were at least five inches thick at eye level and tapered to thin whip-tips at the ends. In the slight breeze the only sounds were the thousands of small leaves whispering, the creaking of the trunks, and the occasional clack when two flexible waving shafts touched.

The three men moved deep inside the shadowy grove so they couldn't be seen. Voinovich spoke in a whisper. "I've never been back here before. Why are we coming in this way?"

Jerry Gaffney said, "This is the way Joe Carver came to see him and then got away. You can't say that about any other way in."

Jimmy said, "I thought we were going to talk him into coming with us, not sneak in his backyard. What's he going to think?"

"We talked about this. Don't you remember?"

"No. Who talked about it?"

"We did. We'll tell him it's safer for him if he gets into the habit of doing things in less obvious ways."

"Why?"

"So if something goes wrong in there, then when the police ask questions, there won't be eight neighbors who say they saw Kapak leave with us."

"I mean, what do we tell Kapak the reason is?"

"Jesus, Jimmy. The man is under siege. There's Joe Carver robbing him once a day, with his crazy girlfriend yet. And didn't you hear the news about Rogoso on the radio? The evil son of a bitch got killed last night. If somebody got him, then Kapak could be next. He's the one who had Rogoso's money taking round trips. Kapak has a hundred reasons to lay low."

Jimmy thought for a moment, then nodded. "All right. He has reasons to be careful. I didn't know Rogoso was dead."

"You must have been in the bathroom or something when we talked about it. Anyway, we're here."

Jerry and Voinovich put on their ski masks and checked the loads in their guns. Jerry produced a small hand-held device.

"Is that a stun gun?" Jimmy said. "A stun gun? Are you crazy?"

Jerry slid a switch with his thumb, a small light went on, and the device crackled in his hand and gave a hum, then switched to a higher frequency, then off. "Yes."

"What's it for?"

"Don't worry. It's just a precaution."

"You zap a fat sixty-four-year-old with that and you'll be thumping his chest to restart his heart."

Voinovich was impatient. "Can you two talk about this later?"

"Yeah," said Jerry. "Let's go."

Jimmy breathed audibly through clenched teeth as he followed.

They emerged from the bamboo grove and walked into the sunlight, up the winding path toward the guesthouse. Voinovich stopped. He whispered, "Hold it. Stop."

The Gaffney brothers turned to look at him. He was motionless, his head cocked slightly to the side, his hands in front of him clutching his gun. "I heard something."

"What?"

"Leaves rustling. Somewhere up there." He gestured toward the guesthouse. "Like something moving into the underbrush."

"You serious?"

"Of course he's serious," said Jerry. "Kapak doesn't have a dog, right?"

There was a long moment of deep silence, when even the fluttering of the bamboo leaves was muted. In the middle of it there was a sound of metal sliding on metal. The three men turned toward the guesthouse.

There was the loud roar of a shotgun, and the dust of the path in front of Voinovich puffed upward in a cloud. Voinovich had been in firefights, and he knew enough to instantly calculate two values: the time it would take to find and kill the shooter, and the time it would take to get behind something. He dove, rolled, and was on his feet, running with his head down. He crashed into the grove between two tall bamboo stalks, his momentum carrying him through the narrow space and a few feet deeper, where the shooter could not see him.

The Gaffney brothers ran the other way, making a sprint for the guesthouse. The cover of a brick building seemed much better to them than bamboo. They reached the porch at the same time and hurled themselves against the wooden door, but it didn't budge. Jimmy turned the handle as Jerry threw his shoulder against it again, and it flew open and swung into the wall as he sprawled on the living room floor. He got to his feet to join Jimmy in his rush to the windows on the far side of the house. As he ran, Jimmy had a moment when the extremities of his body felt icy. The window he was running for was already open.

It was too late to change course now. He reached the low window, sliding along the last three feet of hardwood floor on his knees and then stopping hard, already scanning through the window to see the shooter. He saw nobody. The tall pines on the far side of the yard had no foliage near the ground to hide anyone, and nothing about the low, leafy plants in the tropical garden seemed to hold any menace. He leaned outward and craned his neck.

Blam! It was a roar so loud that it seemed to be a part of a larger reality, like an explosive charge going off. He did not duck back so much as allow the surprise of it to propel him onto his back on the floor. He said quietly, "What the fuck."

Jerry started firing his pistol out the other window, volleys of three shots each, an insistent staccato *pop-pop-pop!* Each time he paused, the three brass casings ejected to the right clattered on the hardwood floor.

"Where is he?" Jimmy cautiously peered out his window.

"Out there!" Jerry fired two more volleys, one to the right, and the next to the left.

"Did you even see him?"

"No, but he's there."

"Hold it. Stop firing."

Jerry held his fire, ducked back in to release the magazine of his pistol and slip in a new one, then pull the slide back to let the first round into the chamber. "Why stop? The bastard's shooting at us."

"Think, for Christ's sake. He must have been in here and we startled him, sneaking into the yard with ski masks over our heads. He doesn't recognize us."

"That was a shotgun. Know what you'll look like if he hits you with double-ought?"

"We don't want to kill him."

"Did I mention he's shooting at us?"

"I'm not talking about that. I mean he's not worth anything to us dead. He can't pay if he's dead. Nobody will pay if he's dead."

Kapak had heard the gunfire coming from the back of his property. He stood in the small room off the kitchen staring at the security monitor. He had been there since it started, trying to make out the shooters and figure out how to avoid them. He could see there were at least three men wearing masks and windbreakers intended to hide their faces and their gear. They charged into the guesthouse, and then he lost sight of them.

He had not expected Rogoso's friends to know enough to come after him this quickly, less than a full day after he'd killed Rogoso. He also wondered who was down there fighting them off with a shotgun. He hoped it wasn't one of the gardeners, some innocent who had simply been cornered and found the gun in the cabinet. He supposed it was possible Spence had not left after he had dropped Kapak off. Maybe he'd just gone down to the guesthouse to watch the rear of the property—to watch Kapak's back, as he had said. Spence was a real soldier.

Kapak was worried. After the second shotgun blast, he had heard a series of three-shot bursts, one after another, only one gun firing. Had they killed the defender? *Blam!* The shotgun. He was still alive.

Kapak squinted, trying to make out human shapes in the backyard foliage. Suddenly the guesthouse door flew open and two men dashed out, sprinting across the open lawn into the invisible dim spaces of the bamboo. The shotgun was silent, as though the defender felt he had done all he wanted by making them retreat. He apparently didn't want any bodies in the yard. That would be like Spence, and he was grateful once again to the man. Killing one of the invaders would have created a new problem.

There were already enough problems. Spence had to plant the bloody relics of Joe Carver to prove he was dead and imply to the people in the club scene that it was Kapak's people who had done it. There was also the continuing problem of the police. Lieutenant Slosser clearly knew he had killed Rogoso, and by now his detectives were talking to people who had been at the club last night, trying to break his alibi. They would also talk to Rogoso's people to establish that he had reason to kill Rogoso. When they had enough, they would arrest him.

He hurried to the other end of the house, picked up the pistol from the nightstand by his bed, put it into the inner pouch of his briefcase, threw on a summer-weight jacket, and looked around for anything else he might need to bring with him. He unexpectedly knew several things that he hadn't before. One was that he had never actually liked the big house, only the gardens that had attracted him to the property in the first place and the guesthouse that he had built. If he had seen clearly before, he would have put an office in the main house, stationed a couple of men there for protection, and lived in the back of the lot in the guesthouse.

Another thing that he now knew was that if today had happened to him when he was thirty, forty, or even fifty, it would have meant little to him. One place was the same as another. He had moved to one country and then another with a few briefer stops in between. Each move had involved a wrenching departure, a great deal of effort, a period of getting used to strangeness and language difficulties. But each, in the end, had left his life improved.

Now he was getting old and feeling reluctant to face the upheaval again. It wasn't the effort so much as the time. He couldn't help making rough estimates. Did he have five years to waste while he was getting settled again? He felt his mouth contract into a sad smile. There were already assassination squads sneaking around his house on a sunny summer afternoon. There was little choice.

He filled his briefcase with financial papers from the filing cabinets in his office, locked the door, and hurried to the garage. He got into his Mercedes and drove. As he reached the first turn, he looked in the rearview mirror, but not at his house. He was only looking to see if his death squad was following, or the police.

After he turned the corner, he heard a siren a few blocks away, and looked behind him once more. He saw nothing but clear pavement.

Voinovich made it through the bamboo to the street long before the others. He sat at the wheel of his Sequoia with the motor running, listening to the last sounds of gunfire with his eyes closed, picturing what must be going on by the guesthouse. It didn't sound good to him. He had confirmed the fatalism that was natural to his temperament through a lifetime of error and disappointment. Whenever he was on the edge of great fortune, he found that something unexpected made all efforts laughably inadequate. Some ideas, some places on the earth, some souls, were simply doomed.

When the gunfire stopped, he heard the sound of feet running down the narrow path through the bamboo grove. He calculated the relative likelihood that the footsteps were the Gaffney brothers and decided it was a one in five chance. Instead it was probably some new security men that Kapak had hired, or some of his regulars, possibly Spence and Corona.

If they had killed the Gaffneys, they'd be coming for him. He reassessed how much faith he had in the Gaffneys, then pulled the mask back over his face, chambered a round, and aimed his gun at the open end of the path.

To his amazement, it was the Gaffneys. He withdrew his gun from the window, tugged off the hot ski mask, and pressed the button to unlock the doors. The first Gaffney swung the back door open and dived onto the back seat. The second scrambled in, slammed the door, and shouted, "Go!"

Voinovich stomped on the gas pedal and accelerated away from the curb abruptly, so the two Gaffneys were pinned to their seats before they could get into a sitting position.

"Jesus," Jimmy muttered.

"Jesus, Mary, Joseph, and all the saints in California," said Jerry. "I've never been so shocked in my life. I thought the old man would just be sitting there alone in his kitchen having lunch or something. What the hell was that?"

"It was an ambush," said Voinovich.

"An ambush set up for whom—us?" said Jimmy. "How could Kapak know we were coming? We weren't even sure we were going to do it until an hour ago."

"I don't tell people things," said Voinovich.

"What are you looking at me for?" Jerry said. "I only talked to you two."

Voinovich shrugged. "All right. Then it was the old man."

"He told himself?"

"He's been around for a long time. When he was coming up, it was a different world. In the Balkans, where he lived, you couldn't close your eyes. People hated you for things your great-grandfather did. Anybody who lived must have gotten good at figuring out what other people were going to do before they did it."

"He figured out that we would come for him?"

Jimmy said, "How could he?"

"He knows us, he knows that his luck has been disappearing fast," said Voinovich. "Maybe he knew that the next thing was going to be that his own people would turn on him. He didn't have to know who it would be."

"Wait a minute," Jerry said. "We can't just assume something like that. We'd have to do something—leave the state, kill him—and we wouldn't even have any proof that he knew it was us."

"If he's smart enough to know what we were going to do before we knew, then how are we going to get him to admit he knows it was us?"

"I don't think we want to just show up at the front door right now."

"Call him."

"On the phone?"

"What else is there?"

Jerry reflected. "Maybe we should. If we do it now, we sound like we couldn't be the ones who just came to his backyard. And he doesn't have time to think things through and make a plan to trap us." He held out his iPhone. "Here. Call him."

Voinovich didn't look at it. "Did you notice I'm driving?"

Jerry held the phone out to his brother.

"Not me. You two were the ones who have this great plan to call him. Your second great plan of the day, by the way."

Jerry scowled, pressed an icon on his phone, and smiled. "Hey, boss. It's me, Jerry."

The others watched him for a moment while he listened. His facial muscles relaxed. He looked relieved, then actually smiled. "I'm out trying to find out what I can about the other girl who told us about Joe Carver. I'm pretty sure Carver will show up at her house sometime."

Jerry's eyes widened. "Wow. Scratch that, then. Anything else you want me to do now?"

"Tell him we're here too," said Voinovich. "It's not just you."

"I'm with my brother and the Russian," he said. "I felt sorry for the poor bastards, getting humiliated like that last night, so I'm taking them to lunch. You want to come?" The expression on Jerry Gaffney's face was vulpine. He was staring intently, his green eyes open and a toothy smile occupying his lips and baring his teeth. "Oh. Okay, I'll see you at the clubs tonight. Siren first? Okay."

He put the telephone away. "He doesn't know. He wasn't home. Can you believe it? He wasn't even at home when it happened. He knows nothing. Zip."

Jimmy said, "I can't believe you tried to get him to come with us even now."

"Why not? He doesn't know. We could have scooped him up and it would be like the regular plan we already had."

"But he didn't go for it, right?" said Voinovich.

"No. He's busy, running some errands today," Jerry said. "But we're okay. We're safe. He doesn't suspect anything."

"Thank God," Jimmy said.

Voinovich's head gave a sudden twitch. He looked in his left mirror, then the right. "Cops."

"Oh my God," Jimmy said. He whirled in his seat and stared out the back window. "I think he wants you to pull over."

"How can I? We have loaded guns and ski masks and body armor."

"You have to," Jimmy said. "You can't outrun a police car in this fat-assed mammoth-mobile."

Voinovich hit the gas pedal and the SUV's hood rose as though the vehicle were about to angle off into the sky. The back of Jimmy's head slapped the headrest and stayed there.

Jerry took out his gun, released the magazine, and seemed to count the rounds he had left.

Jimmy said, "No. You are not going to get in a gunfight with the police. This is still something we can live through, maybe even with nothing but fines and probation."

"Don't be stupid," said Jerry. "If they search this car, we don't want anything to be loaded or strapped to us. Unload yours and then Vassily's." He leaned forward with difficulty as Voinovich took a quick turn. "See if you can get us to a curve where we'll be out of their sight for a few seconds. We can toss the guns."

"Right." He handed his gun over the seat to Jerry, then turned his body to face ahead again. He drove faster. The police car's siren began to blip, and its lights flashed.

Jerry gathered the guns on his lap, stuffed two of them into his ski mask, the others into Jimmy's. He opened the window beside him. "I just figured out where to go," he said. "We can't make it up to Mulholland. Go along Ventura Boulevard to Carpenter and head for Laurel Canyon."

"By the elementary school?"

"Yes."

Voinovich sped along Ventura Place to the Boulevard, zigzagging in and out of the cars. He moved into the left-turn lane, then cut into the right and onto Carpenter. It was a narrow, quiet road where cars had to pull to the side to let each other pass, but he was going over fifty past the elementary school and through the stop sign at the intersection. Just past the school, the road turned and narrowed, and there was a high wooden fence to the right.

Just as the road curved to the right, Jerry hurled the first bundled pair of guns, then the second over the fence. He could see them fall, and then bounce down the hill twenty feet into a tree-lined chasm at the edge of a big estate, where a small, rocky stream bed meandered. He remembered the gun on his ankle, tore the

Velcro fasteners of the holster, and threw them both and looked back.

Two seconds later, the police car appeared again, and it was coming close to the back of the SUV.

"Better stop now," said Jerry. "He's getting ready to hit us to spin us around."

They made it around the last arc of the curve and saw there were already two police cars ahead, the officers sheltering at their sides, ready to shoot.

Voinovich stopped.

There was a swarm of angry policemen, dragging them out of three doors and onto their faces on the pavement. Cops knee-dropped onto their backs, twisted their arms behind them, and clicked handcuffs on their wrists.

"Lie still. You're under arrest."

"What for?"

"Stealing that SUV, for starters."

Voinovich, a few feet off, yelled, "I didn't steal it. It's mine."

"It was reported stolen early this morning, and the thieves are armed robbers. That got anything to do with you?"

"I reported it, and the Pasadena police found it and gave it back. I'm Vassily Voinovich."

Jimmy Gaffney lay on his belly in silent rage. The cop who had handcuffed him said, "You want to tell me why you're all wearing bulletproof vests?"

"Vassily and I were robbed last night. My brother was robbed two nights ago. It's not safe around here."

An older police officer who had not taken part in wrestling them to the pavement called, "All right. Get these guys ready for transport. Feldman, Gaithers, start back along the road on foot and see what they threw over the fence back there near the school."

Kapak drove to Siren, went into the manager's office, and asked if he could borrow his car.

He drove the manager's car, parked it across the street from

Sherri Wynn's duplex, and climbed the exterior wooden steps to her apartment. He knocked, rang the bell, and waited. He looked at his watch. It was nearly 2:00 in the afternoon. He had been pretty sure that Sherri would have caught up on her sleep by now, and be up.

He took out his wallet to look for a business card, then any piece of paper. He wrote his cell phone number on a credit card receipt. His name was already on it. Then he hurried to the car to drive to the Bank of America. He pulled into the covered parking lot in the back of the building, so the car was difficult to see. He walked to the side door and went inside.

He withdrew twenty thousand dollars in cash. He got four electronic transfers made out to the four entities he owed money to—the Alcohol Control Board to keep his liquor licenses current, his credit card company, the liquor supply company, and the accounting firm that handled his business accounts.

The next banks were all along Ventura Boulevard. He went to Wells Fargo, City National, Citibank, and United California Bank. At each he withdrew thousands of dollars in cash, then ordered wire transfers to a company called Claudius Enterprises. At the last bank he sat in a quiet private office to prepare instructions for his attorney, Gerald Ospinsky, then called him and told him to get to work on certain arrangements.

Finally, he called Spence. "It's me. I want you to get a clean rental car. Then I want you to drive it along Moorpark Street, past the public library. Park as close to the library as possible. Then walk to Ventura Boulevard, pick up Skelley's blue car in the municipal lot behind the Bank of America, and drive it to Siren. Do not carry a gun or anything that's illegal on you, because you might get stopped by the cops. My car is at Siren. When you go home, leave Skelley's car and take mine. Do you have all that?"

Spence said, "Sure. Is something wrong that I don't know about?"

That answered Kapak's question. The man with the shotgun in Kapak's backyard could not have been Spence. It must have been one of the gardeners. "I wouldn't do this if I didn't think I needed to. Don't go to my house today."

"Okay."

"If they do pull you in, just be careful and polite and don't get involved."

"All right. I'll try to have the car at the library in an hour."

"Good. Thanks."

He hung up and took his briefcase full of money, left Skelley's car on Ventura, and walked to the public library. He was glad to be in an air-conditioned building after the walk. He used a computer at the library to make some reservations for flights and hotels, e-mailed more instructions to his accountant and his lawyer, and then took a short afternoon catnap, resting his head on the briefcase full of money. When he awoke, it was 3:00, about an hour since he had talked to Spence.

He went into the men's room, combed his hair and splashed water on his face, and went outside. He walked the block to the corner and found the car. It was a new Acura with the rental company's perfect wax job on it. Kapak got in, reached behind the visor, and found the keys. He drove off down Moorpark, staring occasionally in the mirrors to see if he could spot a follower.

He made a series of quick turns in the maze of small residential blocks north of the library, then stopped in the middle of a row of cars in the lot beside the baseball field at Beeman Park, but nobody arrived to join him.

He turned the car north and drove up Fulton, feeling secure and anonymous behind the car's tinted glass. When he reached Sherri's duplex, he parked around the corner and came back on foot. He climbed the stairs, but before he got to the top, the door opened and Sherri stood waiting for him. She was wearing a T-shirt, a pair of jeans, and some sneakers. It occurred to him that before last night he had never seen her when she wasn't wearing her work clothes: high heels, stockings, the short black pants, and the white top. "Where have you been?" she asked. "I've been calling and calling."

He took out his phone. "Oh. I guess I turned my phone off while I was at the bank and forgot to turn it back on."

"How old are you again?"

"Not that old." Suddenly he felt as though that weren't true. What was he doing? How could he imagine this was the sensible thing to do?

She took his arm and tugged it so he would come inside. She closed the door and kissed his lips. "So what's going on?"

"I don't have much time to tell you that. I guess you would say I've been having a bad month, and now this week seems to be turning out worse. The only good thing that happened lately is you."

"What bullshit." He could tell she was pleased. He could also tell that no matter how smart she was, she couldn't be anticipating anything like what he was thinking.

He said, "I have to leave for good. Forever. I would like you to come with me. I'll understand if you won't. Here." He searched the inside of his briefcase. "It's an e-ticket."

She looked at it. "Paris?"

"Yes," he said. "I'm sorry. I've got to go now. If you want, meet me at the airport at the Delta terminal at around five-thirty. Don't call anybody before you leave, and don't leave anything here that you care about." He opened the door. "Do you even have a passport?"

"Yes, but —"

"I'm sorry, Sherri. I'll be there. If you aren't, I'll understand." And he was gone. He hurried to his car, already dialing Spence's cell phone.

"Yes?" Spence's voice sounded guarded.

"It's me. I have a lot to tell you fast, so you'll need to listen closely. I'm making some big changes in my life, and because of that your life will change, and so will everybody else's. First, you've got to call a meeting of all the people who work for me. Call Temptress and Wash, and have them call their people together just before the shift changes at four. Here's what you've got to tell them . . ."

35

SPENCE STOOD on the central stage at Siren. It was a wooden disk-shaped dais two steps up from floor level, with a brass pole in the middle of it. The white spotlights shone down on him. The nearby tables each had five or six chairs occupied by waiters, busboys, dishwashers, and young women with long hair. Most of the crowd was dressed in blue jeans, T-shirts, or sweatshirts. Two bouncers leaned against the door, listening for latecomers.

"First of all," said Spence, "I'd like to thank everybody for coming here today, especially the people who work at Temptress and Wash. We'll make this short, because I know you've all got to get to work soon. As of an hour ago, Mr. Kapak has retired from business. He asked me to thank all of you for your loyalty and apologize because he couldn't be here to say it in person. He said he's sending every employee of his companies a bonus check in the mail. Some of you may get yours as early as tomorrow."

There was a wave of applause, punctuated with a few whoops and whistles.

Spence waited until the noise died down. "I strongly advise you to deposit your check as soon as possible. Sometimes when businesses change hands there are legal problems and accounts get temporarily frozen." He paused. "The next thing is that everybody still has a job. For now we'll run everything pretty much as it has been." There was more applause. "And the last thing I want to do is introduce my business partner."

He beckoned to the back of the crowd and a man stood up. "His name is Peter Rollins. He's the partner who will be overseeing the day-to-day management of the three clubs. Come up here, Pete. He's got a lot of experience owning and operating bars in the East, so if you have problems or questions, ask him."

The man who came forward and stepped up onto the stage was not someone who seemed familiar, although a few in the audience had seen him before, in dim light from a distance. At that time his name had been Joe Carver. But the man they thought of when someone mentioned the name Joe Carver had always worn a ski mask, and this morning he was very far from Los Angeles.

Since he left Los Angeles, Jefferson Davis Falkins had been driving the black Trans Am with the window open and his left arm resting on the top of the door, so it was already acquiring a red-brown tan. The silky brown hair of Melisande Carr was blowing around her perfect ivory forehead, but that didn't seem to bother her at all. Her expression was beatific as she reloaded the magazine with .45 ACP rounds, inserted the magazine, and pushed it home with the heel of her hand.

The three-thousand-dollar sound system mounted under the dash, in the doors, and behind them cried high and hummed harmonically in the foreground, and thudded in the background so deeply that it vibrated their teeth.

Carrie pressed the button on her armrest to lower her window all the way. The wind inside the car grew stronger, so her hair lashed about violently. She took a look behind the car at the long, empty road, then held her right arm out, gripping the pistol. As the little white metal sign with the number sixty-five approached, it seemed to be moving faster and faster, but as it came, she steadied her arm until she could hold the sight on it. She pulled the trigger, the big gun jumped and roared, and in the last second she could see the blue sky shining through the hole she had punched in the sign as it flashed by the car into the past.

"Did you get it?" Jeff shouted over the music.

"What?"

He lowered the volume. "Did you hit it?"

"Drilled it. That's some dead signage."

"That's what — six in a row? You're really improving."

She put the safety on and slid the gun into her purse on the floor. "While you've got the radio off, we should talk about what we're going to do before we get there."

"Get where?"

"To the next place."

"Oh," he said. "I thought we'd check into a nice hotel for a few days, to get over the stress and strain of being on the road all this time without stopping. We'll eat some good food, drink some champagne, and hang around the pool. And we can catch up on all the sex we've missed."

"What a surprise. Then what?"

"While we're doing all that, we take a close look at the town and see what seems good to us."

"How long does this go on?"

"Until we see something we like or see that there isn't anything good and move on."

"If there is, then I suppose you want to plunder it and then move on?"

"That's the general outline of the idea. So what do you want to do?"

"That. Exactly that."

She leaned her head against his shoulder as he guided the car down the long, straight highway. Far ahead he saw a car moving along in the right lane, a bright red dot on the gray ribbon. He was going fast, so after a minute or two he was gaining on it visibly. He could see now that it was a Corvette, and there were two heads in it. He could see for miles ahead, and no car was coming toward them, so he pulled to the left to pass the Corvette. The driver of the Corvette kept his speed constant instead of trying to race with him, and that was a relief. As he accelerated past, Carrie leaned away from him and straightened. He glanced at her in time to see her raise her right arm to the window. He drew in a breath to shout, but there was the loud report of the pistol, her hand jerked upward, and something terrible happened inside the Corvette.

On the Corvette's windshield a hole had appeared in the center of a blossom of milky, pulverized glass. The driver's head jerked against the headrest but didn't come back. He slumped in his seat, and the Corvette wavered, then swerved, then bounced off into a field of alfalfa, grounded itself on some unseen obstacle, and stopped.

Jeff stood on the brakes of his Trans Am, guided it to a stop along the shoulder of the road, threw it into reverse, and backed up quickly. He swung open his door, pivoted out of the driver's seat, and ran. He sprinted across the field to the car, and as he came, he could see the disaster through the windshield. The driver had been a man about fifty years old with a balding head and a pair of aviator sunglasses, but there was a perfect round hole in the left side of his forehead. The passenger beside him was a blond woman, a bit younger than the driver. Her face, hair, and blouse were spattered with tiny droplets of blood, and she was rocking back and forth, crying. It was a special cry, her red-lipsticked mouth in a wide-open, unchanging "Aaaaah! Aaaaaah!"

Jeff went to her side of the car, opened the door, and tried to pull her out. "It's all right. You'll be okay," he said gently. His words made as little sense as her cry. It wasn't all right, and she wouldn't be okay. The man beside her, who seemed to be her husband, had just had his brains blown out onto the headrest. Jeff wasn't even sure why he wanted her to get out of the car. He looked past her and saw, through the driver's side window, Carrie walking up. She still had her .45 pistol in her hand. She leaned in and looked at the dead driver. Then she walked around the car to stand by Jeff.

"Look at this," he shouted. "Why did you do this?"

"Because it's exciting."

Jeff had no words.

"I told you I wanted to do it. I've been telling you for days. I guess you haven't been listening to me — not really listening." She shrugged. She looked at the woman, who had, at some point, lowered her scream to a quiet, sobbing moan. "I guess I'd better do this one too, huh?"

"No," said Jeff. "What's wrong with you? You can't just kill people."

She leaned close to the woman and spoke distinctly. "His name is Jefferson Davis Falkins, and I'm Melisande Carr." She straightened and turned to Jeff, smiling. Her face was beautiful and perfect, but watching him from somewhere behind the big, liquid eyes was something that terrified him. "Well, what do you think, Jeff? Can I kill her now?"

He stood in silence for a few seconds, then turned and began to walk back the way he had come, through the tall alfalfa that whipped against his knees. He heard her yell after him, "You didn't answer, Jeff. Can I?"

He kept walking, staring straight ahead at his car and at the immense empty landscape beyond it. He raised his head without looking back. "Yes!" In a moment, he heard the loud report of the gun again. A moment later he heard the whisper of Carrie's light, graceful footsteps as she trotted through the alfalfa to catch up with him.

They drove on, the black Trans Am moving across vast, flat plains divided into squares of green or brown or gold so enormous that they were best discerned from the window of an airliner passing miles above.

After a few minutes, she said, "Somewhere dead ahead is a town whose luck is about to change."

Jeff glanced at her, and she was holding the gun again, smiling. For the first time, he was really afraid of her. He could feel the hair on the back of his neck rising. He looked ahead at the road. She had him now. He was completely under her control. No matter what insane whim she had, she would find a way to make him go along with her, to say, "Yes, sure. It's okay with me." And one day, she was going to feel the urge to get rid of him too. Maybe she would decide she wanted to see a man die while he was having sex with her. Or she would decide he just wasn't any fun anymore and have a few more seconds of amusement pushing him off a high place and watching him fall. He turned his head to look at her again.

She was staring at him, watching his face closely, and he felt as though she were reading his mind. "What's the matter, Jeffy? Getting to be a bit of a pussy?"

"No," he said. He kept his eyes on the road for a few seconds, then gave in to the urge to look at her. She was still staring at him, and she was holding the big .45 pistol again.

"What are you doing?"

She raised the gun and aimed it at his face, then said, "*Pow.*"

"Cut it out. That could go off."

"*Pow.* Afraid?"

"Carrie, that's enough."

"*Pow.*"

He was overcome with a rage that was partly fear, partly shame at letting her bully him, and partly anger at her for murdering the couple in the Corvette. He swung his right arm to backhand her face. She bent down, both hands coming together over her bleeding nose. The gun was in her lap, and he snatched it. Part of him thought that all he was going to do with it was take it away from her, but part of him knew that wasn't going to be enough. He fired it into the side of her head.

Instantly the inside of the car was coated with a film of tiny blood droplets. He could barely see out the windshield. His hands, his arms, his face were speckled with back-spatter. Carrie's head lolled against the broken side window, and he could see the stream of blood already draining onto the upholstery and the rug. "Oh my God," he said. He tried to clear the windshield with his hand, but the blood only smeared.

She seemed bigger and more frightening dead than she had been alive. What was he going to do with her? He couldn't stop in the middle of this empty landscape and dig a grave. People would see him from ten miles away. And he had to get as far as he could from the two dead people in the Corvette before he did anything—a couple hundred miles, if he could. With his right arm he pushed her body so it was crammed onto the floor space in front of the passenger seat. He was in terrible trouble now. He would have to try to drive to a place where there was a ditch or a river, and dump her out. Then he would clean his car. He would have to strip off these clothes, wash himself, and put on clean ones.

Even looking innocent might not be enough. People had seen him with her. If she was found dead, the girlfriend she'd been with in the diner could describe him to the police. And Roger, the ex-boyfriend. He would just love to be able to show the cops all the places in his house where Jefferson Davis Falkins had left his fingerprints.

Jeff drove faster, staring out the clear space on the left side of the windshield. He would have to pass every car he saw before they could get a clear view of him and his car windows. If anybody saw blood, they'd call the police. It would have to be night before he stopped, and the right sort of place, where there was cover and there were no people.

He looked ahead and drove still faster. As long as he kept the car moving fast, he would still be alive.

36

KAPAK DROVE the rental car to the office of his lawyer, Gerald Ospinsky. When he opened the door, the receptionist looked up and said, "Good afternoon, Mr. Kapak. He's in the conference room waiting for you." It was as though nothing had happened, as though this were his thousandth time here and there would be two thousand more.

Kapak smiled. "Thank you." He walked through the big oak door into the back corridor, past the offices of the partners to the conference room.

Ospinsky saw him and stood, but remained a bit bent over, like a man who was expecting a blast of wind to blow his papers away, and he would have to slap them down and hold them. He looked, as always, pale and worried. "Hello, Mr. Kapak. Sit down."

He shut the conference room door and moved to sit down across from Kapak.

"Well, Gerald," said Kapak, "is everything ready?"

Ospinsky's eyes roamed the table. "Yes. I believe so. Yes." He pointed. "First, here are the checks for your signature. Your accountants made them out according to your instructions. A hundred thousand to each of your closest . . . assistants and the managers of each of your clubs. Fifty thousand for each of the assistant managers, talent bookers, chefs, et cetera. Twenty-five thousand to each of the waiters, dishwashers, busboys, bouncers, and dancers." Ospinsky paused. "I have to say, if what you're trying to do is buy their love, then—"

"I'm not that stupid. I'm trying to make it go where I want now so the government can't confiscate it later." Kapak picked up one of the pens on the table and began to sign the checks in the stack quickly, moving them to another pile as he went. "And a hundred thousand to you. I hope you saw it. Oh, here it is." He signed it and pushed it across the table to him.

"Yes. I thank you for that, but I don't think it would be appropriate for—"

"Yours isn't a present. It's a retainer so you'll still answer the phone on the first ring."

"Well, okay. I'll have to have you sign a standard agreement."

"Put it at the bottom of the pile, and I'll get to it in a minute."

Ospinsky said, "I should bring up another slight problem. Or maybe it's intentional. You're transferring ownership of these assets but ignoring a few major ones. For instance, there are three liquor licenses. The going rate for a license this month seems to begin just north of two hundred thousand dollars. You can sell yours at auction or through a broker, or—"

"They go with the clubs. Each club goes with everything that's attached to it—land, license, building, sound equipment, security systems, whatever."

"That said, I have the transfer papers all ready, as you requested. My assistant, Harriet, is a notary, and I can sign as witness." He went to the door and called, "Harriet? Would you mind helping us out for a while?"

338

The signing went on for forty minutes, with Kapak moving from one pile of papers to the next, and Harriet and Ospinsky following to notarize, countersign, and fold papers into envelopes.

At the end of an hour, Ospinsky smiled faintly, his eyes still terrified, as though he were in the presence of a dangerous madman. "That's it, I believe. As soon as these are mailed, you're a pauper."

"Homeless, but not quite a pauper," said Kapak.

"I certainly hope you've made the right decision."

"It's not as bad as that. I'll be carrying half a million in cash."

Ospinsky's eyes nearly shut as he made his pained grimace. "In legal terms, I believe these bonuses and transfers are your best bet for avoiding confiscation. There's never been a claim the money wasn't yours."

"Good. Now let's pack up the letters and I'll mail them on the way."

"You don't have to do that. I can have my staff do it later."

"I'd like to do it myself."

"All right." The three worked together to put all of the remaining papers into the correct envelopes and collect them in a cardboard box.

When they were finished, Kapak held up a set of keys. "If you don't mind giving me a ride, I'd like to leave my rental car here."

"Harriet will do that. The police may have identified my car and be watching for it. They won't know hers."

Harriet said, "I'll be happy to drive you."

"Good. Gerald, thank you for everything. I'll call you in a few days."

"I wish you the best of luck," Ospinsky said.

"No. Wish me the strength to go on without it."

"Then I wish you that."

They took the elevator down to the bottom of the parking garage, where Harriet's car was parked. It was a gray Prius. Kapak set the letters on the back seat and went to the rental car to get his suitcase and a carry-on valise.

Harriet was a fussy driver, taking each turn with mechanical precision. She went down Vermont Avenue to the post office, and waited at the curb while Kapak carried his box inside and pushed the letters through the slot. He crumpled and tore the box so it would fit in the trash can, went outside, and got into Harriet's car.

Harriet said, "What does it feel like?"

"Lighter," he said. "It feels like dropping a sack of weights so you can swim."

At the airport she pulled up ahead of a hotel shuttle bus in front of the Delta terminal. She jumped a little when Kapak leaned over suddenly and kissed her on the cheek. He said, "I wrote a check for you before I closed an account today. It's good. Take it." He unfolded a check, and she could see it was handwritten, not printed like the others. When she took it he said, "Don't tell Gerald or he'll give you a lot of advice about investing it. Have a good life."

He picked up his suitcase and valise and hurried into the terminal. He scanned the crowd but saw no face he'd ever seen before. He waited in the line to check his suitcase. The line wasn't too long, because most of the business flights to the East coast left in the morning. The evening was for the overnight flights to Europe. He took his boarding pass and carry-on bag, and walked to the security barrier, took off his shoes, and put them in the gray plastic bin to be x-rayed with his telephone, his watch, his sunglasses, and the change in his pockets. He stepped through the metal detector, scooped up his belongings at the end of the conveyer, and walked on.

He sat down on a seat in a row of four set aside for the shoeless and tied his shoes. He sat still for a moment. He had rushed all day, trying to get here past the metal detectors with a valid ticket in his pocket. Now he was a little afraid to see what awaited him at his departure gate. He took a deep breath and let it out, then stood up and began to walk.

The gate was far down the concourse. He watched people run

past him, and he walked past others who were looking in shop windows or stopped at the television monitors mounted above the concourse to list arrivals and departures. As he approached his gate, he saw the sight that he had been dreading since he left the police station. He stopped walking and looked at it for a moment, studying the elements of it.

There were only three of them, but they had known they wouldn't need more. They were the same three who had picked him up this morning—Timmons and Serra standing along the wall like a couple who had spent so much time together that they never talked anymore, just leaning on the wall and staring straight ahead while their boss, Lieutenant Slosser, talked. The woman, Detective Serra, even had a bulging shopping bag from the bookstore across from the waiting area.

Kapak walked directly to the small group, stopped, and stood still. Slosser became aware that someone was behind him, turned, and saw him. "Hello, Mr. Kapak."

"Hello," said Kapak.

"Let's talk." He put his hand on Kapak's elbow, took his valise and handed it to Timmons, and walked with him out of the waiting area to a spot beside the big window of the bookstore. There was nobody standing near them. Even the male and female detectives didn't follow, and travelers coming along the concourse instinctively passed far from them. The pair stood by his carry-on bag, making sure nobody stole it.

Slosser said quietly, "I was happy to see you decided to fly to Paris. You'll be there in the morning. I'll notice you're missing and report it to Interpol sometime tomorrow evening, so they'll be too late to stop you and turn you back at the airport. After the police find you, hire a good lawyer and tell him the truth about what happened in Malibu last night. France won't extradite anybody who might be eligible for the death penalty. They're trying to have a civilization."

"Why tell me this?"

"You're leaving, and you're not going to be able to come back. That means I don't have the problem I thought I did."

"I'm your problem?"

"Not exactly. The problem is that Rogoso hasn't been dead twenty-four hours yet, and already shooters who work for Rogoso's Mexican drug suppliers are on their way here to find the one who killed him. The feds have already recognized three two-man teams and stopped them at the border. Two of them were pairs of teenagers. The gangs down there recruit these kids to be killers by hanging advertisements on highway overpasses."

"So how does my leaving help?"

"When you're gone, so is the threat to public safety. If you're here in jail, Rogoso's friends will kill you. If you're out on bail they still will, but you'll have a chance to get some of them too. Even worse, if I try to bring you to trial, I have to produce my two eyewitnesses. If I do that, then Rogoso's friends will know about them and kill them."

"You care about that?"

"My job is to ensure public safety. What that means is to keep as many people alive as I can. I don't see how your trial would make my division any safer. Do you?"

"No."

"Then *bon voyage.*" He turned, walked back to the waiting area, and nodded to Serra and Timmons as he passed. They followed him at a distance, but neither of them appeared to have noticed Kapak.

He waited until they were out of sight, picked up the carry-on bag they'd been guarding, and then sat in one of the blue seats and stared out the window at the big airplane with the accordion tunnel attached to it. It occurred to him that close up, they didn't look like birds. They looked more like big fish. He let his eyes go unfocused, staring into the early evening light. When this day ended, so would his thirty-year sojourn in America.

A hand touched his shoulder, and he stood up. He stepped

around the row of seats, put his arms around Sherri, and held her. "You came."

"Of course I came," she said. "Who puts out on the first date and then turns down the second date?"

"This is serious, Sherri. I'm never going to be able to come back."

"There are worse places than Paris. I think I might have spent the last few years serving drinks in one of them."

He kissed her. She leaned her body into him and made the kiss go on just a tiny bit longer than he had intended it to. She had always found that when a woman showed she was more interested than the man and at his mercy, it was easier to manipulate him. She amplified her feeling of passion by reminding herself that the carry-on case he was carrying had to be full of money. She let the kiss end, but looked up at him for a few seconds with wide-open eyes and slightly parted lips. Finally she sat down on the nearest of the connected chairs in the waiting area, as though she were trying to control her feelings, and he sat down beside her. She lowered her eyes shyly and looked at the purse in her lap. Inside was a large prescription pill bottle with her name and her doctor's on it. Kapak had already had his first heart attack. Sherri had enough confidence in her skills to be sure that with the help of this much Viagra, she could make him have his last. She glanced at the valise again. An attractive woman alone in Europe could have a nice time with that much money, even if she was no longer an ingénue.

Slosser and Serra and Timmons walked along the concourse together. When they reached a restroom sign with the silhouette of a woman, Detective Serra went inside. The two men continued a few yards farther and went into the men's room. A few minutes later, the three reassembled and walked on. They went down the escalator, past the baggage area, and out onto the sidewalk. Detective Serra handed Lieutenant Slosser the shopping bag she had been carrying. "Paree isn't going to be quite as gay as he thought."

"Thanks, Louise. You two can go off-duty now."

"Good night, Nick," said Timmons.

"See you tomorrow," Serra said. They stepped onto the crosswalk and went into the parking structure across the circular drive, got into their unmarked car, and drove toward the airport exit.

Slosser glanced into the bag. It was neatly packed with banded stacks of hundred-dollar bills. He did a rough estimate, then closed it again and began to walk along the sidewalk in front of the terminal. When he came to the first taxi stand, he went out to the island and waited his turn to be put in a cab.

In a moment he was sliding into the back seat of a cab. "I'd like to go to Burbank," he said. "4394 Cambria Street."

The cab glided forward, picking up speed as it headed out toward the overhead sign for Sepulveda Boulevard. He hefted the shopping bag in his hand. It was a lot of money. It was just the thing for Nick and Rachel's first college tuition payments, and he had been promising both wives new cars for at least a year.